THE DISCOVERY OF MAGIC

THE INTRIGUE OF MAGIC BOOK ONE

L. J. EVIAS

SILVER AMULET PUBLISHING

ALSO BY L. J. EVIAS

THE INTRIGUE OF MAGIC

The Duty of Magic – Prequel Novelette

The Dicovery of Magic

(More to come)

Keep up-to-date at ljevias.com or subscribe for a free ebook.

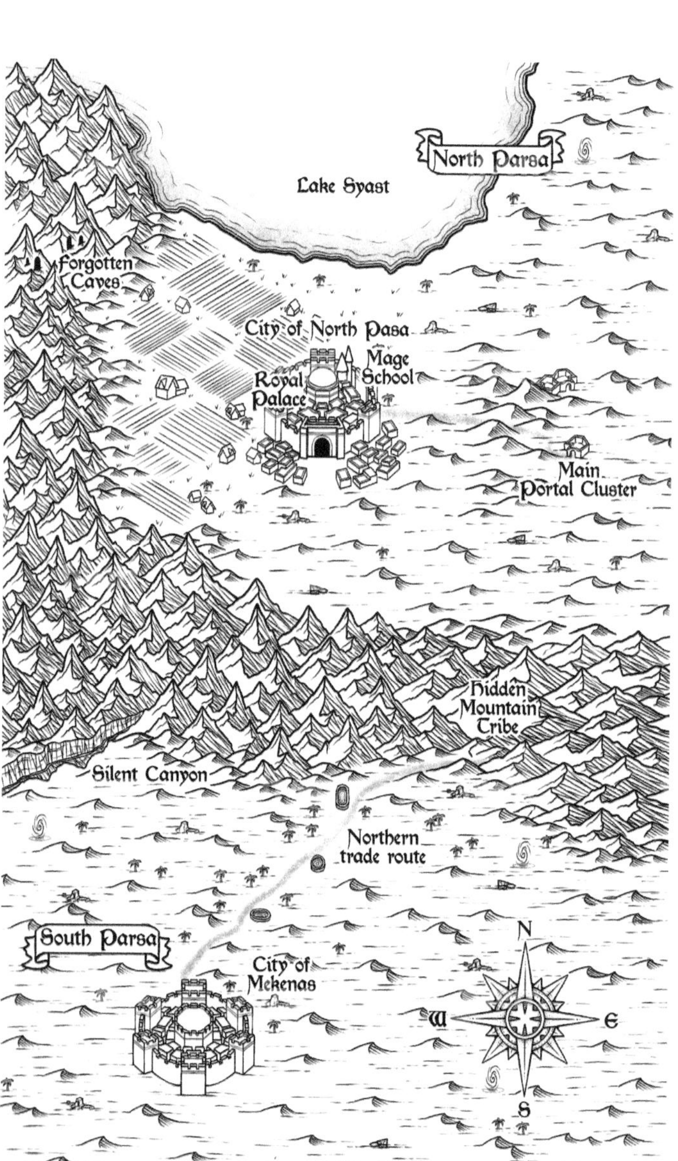

North Parsa
Lake Syast
Forgotten Caves
City of North Pasa
Mage School
Royal Palace
Main Portal Cluster
Hidden Mountain Tribe
Silent Canyon
Northern trade route
South Parsa
City of Mekenas
N
W
E
S

For the dreamers ...

PROLOGUE
South Parsa

Princess Safia carefully returned the priceless spellbook to the secret compartment. The knowledge inside couldn't help her. She had to find another way to secure the future of her kingdom. A marriage with a royal from the powerful north appeared to be her best option. But northerners could hardly be trusted.

"He's here." The messenger hovered by the wall, her lack of conversation betraying her uncertainty.

With a nod, Princess Safia dismissed her. All the palace was on edge. It always was whenever *he* visited, but she didn't need any more doubt today. This day had been coming for a long time.

Smoothing down her dress, Safia proceeded along the narrow corridor that led to the throne room, her breathing getting heavier with each step. For the first time in many years, her eyes were drawn to the portraits of her ancestors lining the wall, from the early conquerors and city builders to the wealthy rulers resplendent in scarlet and gold. They provided no comfort, nor advice.

How could they? No one so powerful had ever threatened their reigns.

For four years she'd ruled in this foreigner's shadow, with the support of her two brothers and an ever-diminishing council of elders. Despite having no ties to the south, on the death of Safia's mother, this man had declared himself protector over both Parsan kingdoms.

But with his protection came control. And that control benefitted the northern kingdom, not her people.

She could only resist so much. But she couldn't stand by and watch her kingdom lose its soul. She had to do better.

Few others were willing to challenge him. And those who were had a tendency to disappear. At the time of her coronation, the council had been thirteen strong, but now it stood at seven. It was true that times were changing, and more efficient policies required fewer councillors, but she couldn't help thinking that this was purely his doing.

The north had no council, nor elders, only a royal family. The kingdom was the poorer for it. Only in magic could it rival Safia's, but that might be all they needed to eradicate everything she stood for. It could be no coincidence that all this had started when *he* had arrived, but nothing could ever be traced back to him.

A cold breeze swept up the corridor, rattling the shutters and causing the light to flicker. Deep in the palace, this area was more sheltered from the blazing desert heat, but rarely had she felt cold.

Steeling her resolve, she strode ahead. She wouldn't be intimidated in her own palace.

Never before had the corridor felt so long, the walls so far away, and so unfamiliar. Near the end, she paused in front of her mother's portrait. A shadow of the true woman, dull brown eyes stared blankly at her from beneath a crown of ruby curls. As queen, Safia's mother had dealt with this man. She'd died in his kingdom. Yet she'd never been afraid of him.

How Safia longed to speak with her now. She would be able to put all Safia's doubts to rest.

Perhaps it had been a mistake to meet with him alone. Her brothers stood by her, but their responsibilities lay elsewhere. This was her decision and her future. Neither of them could save the kingdom. The future of South Parsa rested on her shoulders alone.

With a deep breath, she fixed her crown over her untameable ruby hair, and teleported to the throne room.

In the centre, a tall man waited quietly, his sleek blue-and-gold tunic at odds with the heavy stone columns. The Royal Mage.

Without their spells, his people would be considered fragile, but no sword could defeat magic, and rumours abounded that he'd defeated an entire army single-handedly.

Safia approached slowly, her footsteps echoing off the cold stone. The throne room had never been so quiet, yet many guards stood around the edges. They were little reassurance. They may as well have been string puppets for all they could do against this man. This man who could travel across the world in the blink of an eye, engulf the palace in flame with the sweep of a hand, or topple an army with a single spell.

The man's small, dark eyes and hard expression gave nothing away. They never did. But Safia's instincts wouldn't let the suspicion slip away. Everything he'd ever said to her had been true, but it was the things left unsaid that concerned her. The Royal Mage was hiding something. Her spies confirmed that, and they were the best.

She must be careful what she said to him. He was her only link to the powerful north, but he pursued his own agenda, and danger emanated from him in a cold wave that prickled her skin.

Plenty of people in the south possessed some magical ability, and she herself could cast fire, but few could compete with the mages of the north.

This was not why she feared him though.

Stories of the mages' insatiable appetite for power and reports of them interfering across many worlds were abundant, and always the common people suffered. She had to discover his intent for the south, without letting him know how much she knew. He could be a valuable ally, but as an enemy, he would destroy everything she held dear.

Her world was too small, and she had been protected too well. South Parsa was the same. In its small corner of the world, isolated by an expanse of desert and surrounded by mountains on three sides, it rarely had to face an outside threat. The worlds they traded with were the same, unchanged over centuries.

North Parsa faced invaders regularly. They had to adapt, build their armies, and develop their magic, just to survive. But now they were a threat to her kingdom. The disappearances could no longer be considered coincidences. She had to find out what the northerners wanted, but she couldn't do that here.

"I accept your proposal of an alliance," she finally said. "And I will marry a royal from North Parsa to solidify our arrangement. But first I will visit to gain a greater understanding of my new family."

The man's eyes twitched, a flicker of surprise so slight she might have imagined it. "You cannot accompany me. The journey north is arduous and dangerous. You have nothing to prove to anyone. Your reputation as a skilled and much-loved ruler is known across the north. Your groom will be happy to travel here for the wedding."

"The wedding will be here," she replied firmly, "but I wish to see your city with my own eyes. I have already proven my worth to my people and will be crowned queen when I marry, as our laws dictate."

"Very well," he agreed, before dipping into a rigid bow. Sweeping his gold starry cloak behind him, he retreated into his private chamber behind the throne room. Once a small meeting room, its current configuration lay unknown. The door shimmered with a blue shield, as impassable as hard rock, and no one had dared test their magic against his.

A flash of light announced his departure, as abruptly as he'd arrived. Her own journey would take much longer.

CHAPTER 1

EARTH

Alice hoisted herself up through the open window, determined not to let a few scrapes and scratches deter her from the prizes inside – the keys to her salvation and her freedom. There was no other way to get the money she needed in the short time left before her parents dragged her away from all she knew.

Despite the house being emptied weeks ago, Florin assured her there was a secret room, sure to be full of rare collectibles. "Hurry up!" he called.

Alice surged forward, leaving footprints in the dust. Following the sound of creaking floorboards, she entered a musty room, where the outlines of removed furniture marked the walls.

Florin stalked over to the corner, then turned to her with a grin, his fingers sliding against the wall. "This is where my buyer said it would be."

Something clicked, then the wall slid outward, revealing a small cupboard, the shelves stacked with books, carved idols and a treasure box.

Alice opened the bags and helped to stuff in the items. "How much do you think they're worth?"

Florin shrugged. "You don't need to worry about that. I'll make sure you get a finder's fee."

Alice froze, meeting his eyes. "I want my fair share."

"How about I buy you dinner?"

Alice scowled. "I want fifty percent."

Florin laughed. "For what? Helping me carry a bag? I only brought you along because I liked your smile."

The words struck harder than any blow, leaving Alice feeling hollow. After she'd found the gap in the hedge at the back of the house, after she'd made sure the neighbours weren't home to see, after she'd left her younger sister home alone, Alice deserved her fair share. But what could she do? The world was made for men like Florin.

Her eyes fell on a gold idol. That could cover her rent for a few months ...

Before she could reach it, Florin snatched it away. "Don't even think about stealing from me. You won't be able to find a buyer for any of this. Be happy that I'll treat you to dinner."

"You're stealing this! You can't accuse me of stealing from you."

With a snigger, Florin turned to retrieve the remaining items.

Quick as a flash, Alice scooped out a necklace and a book, and slid them into her jacket. They'd not fetch enough to allow her to move out on her own, but it was better than nothing. And her friend Emily would appreciate the book more than Florin.

With its peculiar markings, the book looked like a book of spells. A smile lifted her lips at the thought of magic. If only it were real, she'd have no problems at all. Florin wouldn't get away with this. She wouldn't even need to be here. She could make it so her parents would s tay.

She turned for the door. "If you're not going to share the earnings, then I'm leaving."

Florin's face fell. "Don't be like that. I'll take you anywhere you want to go. My treat."

Alice shook her head. "I'm late for something. I'm out of here."

Florin shrugged. "Suit yourself. But don't come complaining when you want something."

Alice blocked him out as she exited the building. She shouldn't have come. Not today. The archery competition was only an hour away and she still had to fetch her bow.

Now the competition was her only hope. If she won the scholarship, that might be enough to convince her parents that her future was here.

Alice gripped her bow tighter as she broke into a jog. All her training would be for nothing if she didn't make it to the competition on time. The field wasn't far away, but time was running out. If she hadn't met Florin she could have been there already.

The park offered a shortcut, but it brought back memories of happier times. Times where she had no responsibilities and no worries. Shrieks and the laughter of playing children soon filled the air. Once she'd been like that, never imagining she'd be separated from her friends, but now everything was changing. If she didn't do something, she might never see them again.

For the first time, Alice's fingers tingled with anticipation as she entered the archery range. Crowds peppered the field, all to watch the tournament, but that wasn't what set the competitors on edge. Not today.

First prize meant membership to the elite club, a scholarship, and a fast track to success. For Alice, it was the last chance to convince her parents that their future was here, not in some distant city she'd never heard of.

As she made her way down the field, the buzz of the crowd gave way to the chittering of birds in the nearby hedges. In the warm sun, it was almost peaceful. A great day to shoot, normally, but it did nothing to quell her nerves. The lack of wind would make it easier for everyone, which meant no room for error.

Ahead, competitors from other schools gathered, already stringing their bows, most newer or more expensive than hers. But none had trained as much as her. Finally, this was her opportunity, and she wouldn't waste it.

She spotted her group towards the end of the row, all clustered together for some reason. As she neared, and discovered the cause, her feet faltered.

Jaime had a new bow, and from the looks of it, it was top of the range. And he was almost as good as her without it. What if he won the scholarship and she didn't? How would she ever live it down?

Even worse, he'd kept it a secret. He was supposed to be her closest friend, aside from Emily. They'd seen each other only this morning.

Absorbed in the task of stringing his bow, Jaime didn't notice her staring. Nor the girls hovering around him, though Jaime never noticed things like that.

Before someone could catch her out, she put on her best smile.

As soon as she joined her classmates, one of the dark-haired older boys sauntered over, and put his arm around her, as if in consolation. "Tough luck, Alice," Marcus said. "Looks like Jaime's got the upper hand today."

Alice shrugged him off. "He'll need to practise with it first." Not that they would be officially competing against each other, but there was a healthy rivalry between both girls and boys in their group.

Looking sheepish, Jaime glanced up through overgrown sandy hair. "I've been practising all week. I wasn't going to bring it today, but then my parents insisted …"

With a smile, Alice moved closer. "It's much better than your old one. Why didn't you mention it?"

"It must have slipped my mind." Jaime ran an awkward hand through his hair. "Everything's been a bit hectic. You know how it is."

Alice forced a nod. Lately, Jaime couldn't seem to focus on anything. But that didn't excuse this omission. Jaime knew how important archery was to her.

Too annoyed to continue the conversation, she focused on stringing her own bow. The familiar movements chased away some of her impatience and banished her former doubt. Archery never failed to lift her spirits.

Jaime edged closer and held out an arrow. "You're up first."

Immediately, her heart quickened, but it was only a practice round. These scores didn't matter, not really.

With the smooth wood familiar in her fingers, she strode forwards and nocked her bow, a movement that took little thought by now. However, as a hush settled over the crowd, Alice's nerves prickled. Suddenly, she was questioning her position, her grip, and her aim.

Banishing the distractions from her mind, she drew her hand back towards her chin. As she did, a gentle breeze lifted her hair, carrying the barking of distant dogs and the laughter of children playing from the nearby park.

For a moment, she held her breath, relishing the peace, then with only the slightest movement of her fingers, she released the string.

The arrow shot forward, firmly planting itself in the outer gold circle. The next few shots only improved, until her confidence returned. Worrying about the competition would only distract her.

Only when she'd shot all her arrows did she glance around, satisfying herself that no one nearby matched her score.

But it was early yet. A few ends in and accuracy would become more difficult.

Not one to be fazed by a challenge, Jaime stepped up next. With his slender, toned physique and new bow, he looked quite the professional, even with his unruly hair. However, his arrow hit the outer red. His next two shots fared little better, missing the gold completely.

Alice frowned. He could do better. Even with an unfamiliar bow, he shouldn't have been that bad. He really was distracted.

By the end of the practice rounds, everyone was shooting well, though Jaime still worried her. If he kept shooting like this, he'd be the one missing out on the scholarship, and their days of shooting together would be over.

Concerned, she wandered over. "Did you bring your old bow?"

Jaime shook his head, his hazel eyes meeting hers. "The sight was off, but I've fixed it now." He glanced around at the few remaining people finishing their last shots. "The competition is strong today. Think you can win?" Normally, Jaime was quite shy, so the direct question took her by surprise. Though she did like this side to Jaime. Archery brought out the best in him.

She shrugged. "I'll try my best, as always."

"Today is a little different though ..."

Three blasts of the whistle interrupted their conversation, and they hastened forwards to retrieve their arrows. Once again, Alice's heart accelerated. No more practice shots.

This time it was easier to slip back into the familiar shooting rhythm, the soft thuds down the line as reassuring as a steady heartbeat. Jaime's scores improved dramatically, though the occasional shot went slightly astray, betraying his lapses in focus. Nevertheless, his overall score remained solid.

By the time they reached the final end, Alice was filled with the serenity that only came with shooting, and she finished off with a satisfying outer gold. All that was left was the agonising wait for the judges to collect the scores.

Also finished, Marcus approached with a grin. "Nice shooting."

"Thanks." Having given him little attention, Alice couldn't return the compliment. "I hate this part."

"You've got nothing to worry about." Marcus glanced sideways, watching Jaime's last arrow strike the gold. "It seems expensive equipment can't match your talent."

Alice frowned. "The scores haven't been counted yet."

"No one hit the gold that frequently. You've won for sure." He turned to Jaime as he approached. "What went wrong? Thought that new bow would make all the difference."

Jaime pushed his hair back out of his eyes. "It's not all about the bow. Next time though ..." Jaime grinned, unable to maintain his serious tone. "Hope they hurry up with the scores."

Alice nodded her agreement, but they could usually find a way to pass the time. "What are you doing this weekend?"

"I told Jordan I'd go LARPing with him."

"Again? Didn't you do that last weekend?" Sometimes, Alice didn't understand why Jaime and Jordan wasted so much of their time doing something so silly. Given that Jaime knew Alice's parents planned to drag her away, she thought he would have wanted to spend a little time with her in the short while they had left.

Jaime shrugged. "He's really into it, especially as football and basketball have finished. You should come, you'd enjoy it."

Alice screwed up her face. "I don't think so. I prefer to use real weapons." After all the years they'd known each other, she couldn't imagine why Jaime thought she would want to participate in LARPing. She thought she'd made her thoughts perfectly clear on that. Sure, she'd watched him fence, but that was in serious competitions.

Used to this attitude towards LARPing, Jaime took no offence, instead turning his focus to destringing his bow.

Alice frowned at his rush to be packed away. "Aren't you supposed to be helping your brother fix up his motorbike?" In all the times she'd visited Jaime, most often he was to be found in a garage tinkering over some engineering project with one of his three brothers.

"I prefer to spend my time with Jordan. He needs me more than my brothers and they've got each other if they need free labour." He glanced at her bow resting in its stand. "What are you up to?"

She hesitated before she replied. Unsure whether to say anything about Jordan's situation, she admired Jaime for sticking by his friend. "I could do something with Emily. It would be good for her to get out of the house."

"Bring her LARPing," Jaime said, despite knowing full well there was no chance of getting Emily doing anything so physical.

Alice laughed. "We'll figure something out. We might go watch the eclipse, or maybe we'll come and watch you pretend to hit each other with fake swords." She smiled sweetly at him, but that only made him frown more.

"They may be pretend, but there's real technique involved!" Jaime argued, pulling an obviously fake pained expression. "It's not that different to fencing."

She couldn't resist putting an arm around his shoulders, only half in jest, while they waited to collect their arrows.

It wasn't long before the whistle blew, announcing the end of shooting. As they made their way to their targets, Alice spotted several golds across the field.

Disappointment flooded through her. Everyone was shooting well today. Perhaps she hadn't done enough to secure the scholarship.

As she pulled an arrow free, it cracked in her hand. Another worry if she didn't win the scholarship. She didn't have that many spare.

Jaime frowned. "Someone must have nicked it. Here." Ignoring her stare of protest, he pulled out her last arrows and handed them to her. "Are you really considering bringing Emily to watch us on Saturday?"

"Sure, why not? You said it would be fun."

"Fun to do, not to watch!"

"We can bring a picnic. It'll be better than watching Emily read."

As everyone vacated the target area, Jaime grabbed her arm. "There's something else I've been meaning to tell you."

Her heart leapt into her throat. What could be so bad that Jaime needed to pull her aside?

He rubbed his sleeve. "I should have mentioned this earlier." He shifted awkwardly. "I've, er … I've joined the elite club. I would keep shooting in the school class, but their under-eighteens class is at the same time. I thought it might not matter since, you know, you're not going to be sticking around for much longer."

Alice's heart clenched. "You can afford the membership fee?"

"Uh, yeah. My parents can."

Her chest tightened, and her lungs forgot how to breathe. Jaime was abandoning her, and he'd waited until now to tell her. Never had the scholarship been so important.

She forced a smile. "That's great. Maybe with the extra tuition, you'll have a chance at winning."

"Yeah, maybe. You're not upset? I could blow it off for a few weeks …"

"Don't be silly. It's a great opportunity. And I might be joining you soon." She grabbed his hand and pulled him forwards. "They must be nearly done with the scores."

Most of the competitors had already gathered to hear the results, so they made their way over to join them, Alice contemplating what it would be like to shoot without Jaime. Archery probably wouldn't be the same.

"Bad news," Marcus said. "The twins have been at it again."

"At what?" Jaime glanced at the boys a few targets to their right, both wearing identical smug grins. Alice vaguely recognised them, but she had no idea what Marcus was referring to.

"Switching arrows. Have you never noticed that one of them always does really well and the other quite poorly? And the next competition they swap?"

Alice frowned. "You should tell someone."

"Who would believe me? You didn't notice."

"I was shooting." She bit her lip. No one would cheat that much. "They have different coloured arrows. They'd never get away with it."

Marcus shrugged, but on seeing them staring, one of the twins sauntered their way. "Something interesting?" the boy said.

"Are you colour-blind?" Marcus asked.

The boy grinned. "Something you want to say, Marcus?"

"We saw you cheating," Marcus said. "Turn yourself in and there won't be a problem."

The boy shook his head. "Making up stories won't help you win." He glanced at Marcus's target. "Did you even shoot?"

With a scowl, Marcus strode over to the nearest judge.

Alice took a step after him before realising there was nothing she could do. The judge would either believe him or he wouldn't.

"Nice bow," the boy said to Jaime, then strolled back to his brother, unbothered by Marcus's action.

Finally, one of the judges called for silence and congratulated all the competitors. A boy in their group achieved third place alongside a freckled girl from a school with only two competitors. Second place went to a girl who had been shooting near the other end of their field.

Alice's chest tightened. Had their school fallen so far behind?

Then ... "Jaime Carter, congratulations on achieving second place."

Marcus grinned and clapped Jaime on the back. "Not bad."

"First place, I'm proud to announce, goes to a regular competitor in the male competition. Alan Webster, please step forward." The judge gestured for one of the twins to join him to receive his prize. "As you all know, first prize comes with a full scholarship to the university and membership to their club."

All the breath left Alice's body. That could have been Jaime. That *should* have been Jaime.

"Guess they didn't believe me," Marcus muttered.

"I should have gone with you," Alice whispered.

"They wouldn't have believed you either."

"I guess not," Alice said, but the experience left a bitter taste in her mouth. She hadn't even tried.

"Don't worry about it," Jaime said. "It's not like I need a scholarship."

"And for the ladies, I'm pleased to award first place to a long-standing competitor. I personally saw her shoot one of the best ends we've seen here in a long time. I look forward to seeing what she will do with a scholarship."

Alice's heart sank. None of the judges had been anywhere near their end. At least not that she'd seen.

"Alice Harper, please join me."

She froze. Had she imagined that?

In slow motion, her group surged towards her, grinning widely. It was true. She'd won. The scholarship was hers.

Hands pushed her forward, and the crowd made way. Blood rushed to her cheeks at the attention, but that didn't matter. Her parents couldn't make her move now. Her future was here.

CHAPTER 2

EARTH

Jaime stared at the blueprint, trying to remember how he'd designed the remote-control car. That had been weeks ago, and he'd barely looked at it since. The project was due in a couple of weeks and all he had to show for his efforts was a pile of 3D printed components and a motor. He hadn't even sourced the radio parts yet, so he had no way to control it. Why had he picked something so complicated?

With a sigh, he began to sort through the pieces. With a little time and effort, everything would sort itself out.

As he clicked the suspension into place, his phone buzzed. Jordan. He couldn't ignore him. Not after everything he'd been through. Too many of Jordan's friends had abandoned him since he'd withdrawn from school, but Jaime couldn't blame him for struggling after his mother's death. He wouldn't abandon him too.

A little break wouldn't hurt, and he *would* need to eat at some point. After one final check that everything was stored safely away, he threw on a jacket and hurried outside.

He walked briskly, his mind preoccupied with the awkward conversation with Alice. What could he possibly say that wouldn't make things worse?

Any time the topic of her moving came up, she became sullen and moody, and it was impossible not to upset her. How was he supposed to fix something that wasn't his doing? He certainly couldn't reveal that he didn't think a scholarship would change her parents' minds. But at least she now had no reason to resent him leaving the school archery club.

Approaching Jordan's house, he picked up his stride, eager for an easier conversation. The sound of a ball bouncing against concrete revealed Jordan was shooting hoops in his yard.

Hopping onto the bin and leaping over the gate, rather than letting the squeak announce his presence, Jaime sneaked up behind Jordan, then lunged for the ball.

Though he was lightning quick, and had the element of surprise, Jaime missed. Jordan must have spotted him out of the corner of his eye, and expertly twisted the ball away from him. He bounced it twice and launched it through the hoop with a smug grin.

"Nice try," Jordan said, clapping Jaime on the shoulder.

"I'll get you next time," Jaime replied.

They played for the next thirty minutes, Jaime not quite adhering to the rules to ensure he could score a few baskets, until the house door swung open and an older man, overweight, bearing a few days' stubble and wearing an angry expression stormed out.

"I'm going out," Jordan's father grumbled. "Don't make a mess."

Jordan turned, his arms dropping to his side. "Okay, Dad, do you want me to buy any food for tomorrow?"

With no further words, Mr Smith threw his son one more disappointed glance, slammed the gate, and disappeared.

Having grown accustomed to this behaviour since Jordan's mother had died, Jaime said nothing. In an attempt to defuse the situation, he picked up the ball and attempted a rather ambitious trick shot, but Jordan was too distracted to stop him.

"Shall we find something to eat?" Jordan asked.

Jaime's stomach growled. "Yeah, I could eat."

Following Jordan into the kitchen, Jaime made no comment on the empty bottles cluttering the otherwise immaculate room, which was no doubt thanks to Jordan. Jordan never wanted any pity.

His expression sour, Jordan pulled his head out of the fridge. "Nothing. Unless you want on onion omelette?"

"Let's order pizza. I'm starved after archery."

Jordan raised an eyebrow. "If standing around pulling a string wears you out, you have no chance at LARPing on Saturday."

Jaime frowned. "I'm not tired, I'm hungry. Do you want pizza or not?"

With a grin, Jordan pulled his phone out. "You're far too easy to wind up."

Jaime shook his head and strode into the living room, the threadbare carpet hard under his feet. Empty vases and the disappearance of many photos gave the room a strange empty feeling, despite the well-populated media shelves.

Jaime cast his eyes over the new arrivals, dominated by the bold blues and greys of sci-fi. "Want to play video games or watch a film?"

"You're not fed up with losing to me yet?"

Jaime gave his friend a playful shove. "You may beat me at basketball, but you're going to be the one fed up with losing."

The evening passed quickly, both boys engrossed in video games and gorging themselves on pizza.

"I better head home before my parents wonder where I am," Jaime said, glancing at the clock.

"Take some pizza with you." Lounging more horizontal than vertical, Jordan gestured lazily at the box. "I can't eat any more. I can hardly move as it is. Still on for Saturday?"

"Yeah. I invited Alice along too."

"Alice is coming?" Jordan sat up straight.

Jaime blinked at his sudden reaction, but it *was* odd Alice had agreed to come. He still wasn't sure why.

"Yeah, and she might bring Emily."

Jordan's scrunched-up face echoed Jaime's own confusion now. "Emily with all the weird books, Emily? To LARPing?"

"Only to watch. I can't convince them to participate. Unfortunately, Alice doesn't appreciate the fine swordsmanship involved." He paused, expecting a response. "Is that okay?"

Jordan looked rather thoughtful, then his eyes lit up as if he was pleased at the revelation. "Yeah, I was thinking Saturday might be a good chance to ask out Alice."

"What?" choked Jaime. "You like Alice?"

"Yeah, what's not to like? She's gorgeous, and she kicks your ass at archery." Jordan shifted forward. "Unless you like her?"

Jaime struggled to process this new information. Since when was being able to beat him at archery an attractive quality, and why had Jordan never given any indication of his interest in Alice before?

"Er no, we're just friends. This is just a surprise. And she does not kick my ass, she's only a few points ahead this year."

"Okay then, you can talk me up before Saturday." Jordan looked expectantly at him, his dark eyes still sparkling.

"Um, I guess." Should he say how weird this felt? Perhaps Jordan was messing with him, and he'd forget about it by Saturday. Jordan wouldn't be the first to tease him about Alice, but his best friend wasn't normally like that. "You know she's moving away soon?"

Jordan shrugged. "Maybe I'll follow her. I'm sick of this place."

Jaime grimaced. Jordan had to be joking. He couldn't lose his two best friends. "Okay, now I really am going. See you at school."

"Catch you later."

As Jaime walked home, the thought of his two best friends getting together started to unsettle him, but did that mean he liked Alice?

Sure, she was attractive, and they got on remarkably well, but that didn't mean there was anything romantic between them.

He'd never thought about her that way, but thinking about her with Jordan made his heart race and stomach churn.

CHAPTER 3

EARTH

Jaime dodged sideways, almost too late, as a sword slashed at him from his right. It wasn't like him to be this distracted in a fight, but with his escalating schoolwork, his brothers' nagging and now Jordan's revelation, it was a wonder he could pay attention at all.

Fortunately, the large boy who had swiped at him stumbled before regaining his footing, allowing Jaime an easy victory. Others wouldn't be that cumbersome, yet Jaime's thoughts returned to Jordan and Alice.

A small hope remained that the girls wouldn't turn up, but that was currently being devoured by a monster that had recently taken up residence inside him, writhing in his stomach and filling him with anxiety.

Perhaps he could distract Alice or Jordan and delay the situation until he'd figured out what to do. Or maybe he could introduce Jordan to someone else. Then Jaime would have plenty of time to figure out whether he really did have feelings for Alice.

Up the hill, blonde hair blowing in the breeze caught his attention. Alice and Emily, with Eliot running ahead. This was no time to be putting all his hope into wishful thinking. He'd just have to tell Jordan he didn't like the idea.

His mind made up, he threw himself back into the melee, finding a new opponent, more skilled and more eager than the last. He lunged, then dodged, spun around his opponent, then lunged again, his sword slashing. Back again, dodging out of reach, then thrusting forwards until the other boy's tiredness began to show. Enthused, Jaime delivered the final blow, the clang of his sword ringing out above the din of the other combatants.

As his adversary yielded, two more rushed Jaime, one from each side, making him regret taking his time with his previous opponent. He couldn't afford to tire himself out yet, not while several people still fought.

Sucking in a quick breath, he swiftly sidestepped, swung his sword around above his head, and cut across the first rival before they could do anything to stop him.

At the same time, the other lunged, but he was not quick enough for Jaime. Darting behind the felled boy, Jaime brought his blade round to strike, and with a few well-timed blows, had the second boy on his knees, capitulating.

With the rush of victory surging through him, he glanced around for his next opponent.

Only Jordan remained, surveying him with a smirk. The expression unsettled Jaime. Although Jordan was more committed to LARPing, Jaime's fencing skill gave him a strong advantage, and Jordan knew it. Whatever Jordan had planned, he would not be easy to beat.

Approaching slowly and purposefully, Jordan let his gaze drift towards Alice. Both girls were watching intently. Even Eliot was quiet and still beside them.

Suddenly, Jordan's smile vanished, and he locked his eyes on Jaime, his intent to impress Alice written all over him.

Adrenaline coursed through Jaime, reawakening his tired muscles. The previous fighting had been just for fun, but this was his chance. He could stop Jordan. Beat him for his own good. He'd never ask out Alice then.

Jaime darted forward, then sidestepped Jordan's lunge. Jaime struck again, and this time they locked swords, the loud clangs blocking out all other noise. Faster, and ever more furious, they slashed at one other, each attempting to breach the other's defences.

Jaime had the advantage when it came to speed, but Jordan was stronger, and every blow that connected knocked Jaime back a step, tearing his breath from him.

Unable to dodge every strike, his arm throbbed. His sword became a dead weight, and he began to regret his earlier showmanship. He could *not* let Jordan beat him. Not in front of Alice.

Seeing an opening, Jordan attacked from above, using his height as an advantage.

With his arm too sluggish to parry, Jaime twisted away, but this time Jordan was too quick for him. Jordan's sword crashed into his left shoulder, numbing his entire arm.

As he staggered back out of range, defeat charged towards him.

This couldn't be over.

Panic shot through him, and the monster within lashed out. He recoiled, but he couldn't distance himself from that fear. He had to do something.

He stumbled and fell to the ground, his muscles coiled in anticipation.

As expected, Jordan seized the opportunity and raised his sword above his head to deliver the final blow, leaving himself exposed.

With a surge of jubilation, Jaime thrust upwards with his blade, right at Jordan's belly. If the sword had been real, it would have torn right through his friend's stomach and caused a rather unpleasant death.

Furious, Jordan flung down his sabre and glowered at Jaime. It took all Jaime's effort not to grin, but he couldn't help sneaking a glance at Alice.

Her smile set his heart racing again, but was she impressed or simply being friendly?

All Jaime's muscles stiffened. He had to get his emotions under control. He hadn't done this for her favour. Nor to humiliate Jordan.

Returning his attention to his friend, he shook hands and congratulated him on his performance.

Jordan shook his head in exasperation. "I was sure I was going to win that time."

"For a few seconds, I thought so too, but then my survival instinct kicked in." Jaime rubbed his shoulder. "That last blow is going to hurt though."

Jordan shrugged. "That's what you get for dancing around like an idiot." He glanced at the girls and lowered his voice. "You could have let me win this time. You know I'm planning on asking Alice out today. A good friend would have done that."

Shock jolted Jaime's core. Losing in front of her hadn't dissuaded him? What would? Despite the turmoil inside him, Jaime tried to keep his expression neutral. "Maybe, but do you want to be dishonest or do you want to be yourself?"

"We would have had something in common if I'd beaten you too." For that remark, Jordan earned a shove.

After changing back into their regular clothes, they joined the girls, where Emily predictably had her head in a book and Alice was absorbed by her phone.

Dressed in a long billowing skirt with a matching top, Emily looked like she belonged at the event, whereas Alice was dressed in her usual jeans and a geometric-print top. They seemed to have become her preference lately.

Before Jordan got any ideas, Jaime struck up a conversation, trying to sound nonchalant. "Hey, Alice. Were you watching the fight?"

"Yeah, I saw. Never knew you had it in you." Her eyes sparkled. Or was that just the sun? "It looked like Jordan was going to defeat you though, until that last moment."

His heart soared. She had been paying attention.

Beaming despite his defeat, Jordan shoved in front of Jaime. "You saw that, huh? He got lucky. I rely on strength and skill rather than trickery. If he hadn't cheated, I would have won."

Incredulity replaced Jaime's scowl. "Using an opponent's weakness against them is skill!"

Emily glanced up from her book, but didn't say anything. She gave Alice a disapproving frown, sighed, and returned to her page.

Jaime flushed. Could Emily tell what was going on? Jordan didn't seem to have noticed.

Sticking his hands in his pockets, Jaime edged closer to Alice. "So, what's so fascinating in your phone?"

With a cheeky grin, Alice looked up. "Photos of you two."

"Anything good?" Jordan asked.

"There's an excellent one of you knocking Jaime over."

The words lashed him sharper than a whip. "He didn't knock me over. That was me tricking him to let down his guard!" His own defensiveness surprised him. Losing to Alice in archery and being teased about it wasn't unusual, but this felt completely different.

Jordan stared blankly at him. "Is he this moody when he loses at archery?"

"I just defeated you!" Jaime exclaimed.

"I wish I could have seen you beating him at archery," Jordan said.

Fuming at Jordan's attempt at using him to get closer to Alice, Jaime slumped down beside Emily.

Alice laughed, missing Jordan's change of tone entirely. "Beating someone at archery isn't quite the same as knocking someone to the ground."

"I guess not. Are you hungry? Do you want to get some food?"

"No need. I've got a picnic right here. Will you help carry it?"

Relief washed over Jaime as Alice ignored Jordan's attempts to steal her away. Perhaps he didn't need to worry after all. This might sort itself out.

Jordan's shoulders dropped. "Sure, I'll help."

"I'll help too." Jaime bounded forward, determined not to give Jordan any more attempts at hitting on Alice, even if she was oblivious.

Alice handed Jordan the bag. "No need. You don't want to strain your shoulder more, do you?"

Jaime froze, only now noticing he was still rubbing his shoulder. Abruptly, he dropped his hand to his side, feeling rather emasculated and not at all like he had just won a melee.

"You can carry this bag," Emily announced, still with a book in her hand.

"Sure thing." Glad to be of some use, Jaime jumped to her side. He ignored the twitch of Emily's mouth. "Where are we going?"

"Down to the lake." Emily glanced around, her eyes widening. "Where's Eliot? Eliot!"

Alice exhaled loudly and gestured at the equipment tent. "I bet he'll be exactly where he's been told he can't go."

Thrusting her book at Jaime, Emily started running, though everyone else quickly overtook her, despite the bags they were carrying.

By the time they reached the tent, Jaime and Jordan were in a full race, and almost collided with each other at the entrance. With a challenging grin, Jordan shoved past and entered first.

Sure enough, they found Eliot right at the back, practising with a sword on a training dummy. Relieved, Jaime paused to catch his breath, only now noticing how Jordan still appeared fresh, despite the extra weight he carried. For the first time, Jordan's fitness irritated him. But then Jordan spent little time sat at a desk.

By the time Emily caught up, her face was bright red, yet despite gasping for air, she still managed to yell. "Eliot, you can't wander off like that! What if you'd got lost or hurt and no one could find you?"

"I'm sorry." Eliot squirmed, looking down at the floor.

Emily grabbed Eliot and hugged him close. "You really worried me. Please don't do that again."

"Okay," Eliot agreed, pushing her away.

"Here," Jordan said, holding out his sabre. "You can take care of my sword for me while we have our picnic. How does that sound?"

"Okay, let's go." Grabbing the sword, Eliot beamed at Jordan and skipped out of the tent.

More relaxed now, the group meandered down to the lake, where many people were already enjoying the picturesque setting, boating on the water, or playing Frisbee on the grass.

Almost predictably, Eliot veered towards the caves, before they had even selected a spot. "Can we go in there?" he asked.

"After lunch and the eclipse," Emily said firmly. "The eclipse will be in an hour, so you can sit down and have something to eat." Turning to Jordan, her voice softened. "Thanks for giving Eliot your sword."

"No problem. I wish I had a brother. Or a sister. Being an only child sucks."

A pang of sadness shot through Jaime. He had been trying his best to keep Jordan company. Whilst Jordan was distracted, he retrieved the picnic blanket and laid it out for them to sit on.

"It's a lot of work sometimes. Perhaps you could borrow him," Emily said, taking a seat. "Do you know anything about bugs or rocks?"

"Erm ... nope. Just sports." Jordan plonked himself besides Emily and grabbed a dish of potato salad, leaving Jaime and Alice to serve out the rest.

Ignoring Emily's request, Eliot proceeded to duel an invisible opponent under her watchful gaze. Occasionally, Jordan offered pointers, but these became ever less frequent as he became engrossed in his conversation with Emily.

Finally with Alice to himself, Jaime found he had nothing to say. Dazzled by her brilliant blue eyes, captivated by the way her golden hair fell seductively across her face, and entranced by her soft red lips, his mind had gone completely blank.

Why had he not noticed any of this before? What did they even talk about?

Tearing his eyes away, he reached for a bottle of water, but only succeeded in tipping it all down himself, making Alice laugh. He should have felt stupid, but the joyous sound made his heart skip a beat, confusing him further.

"Are you okay?" she asked.

Thinking of the first excuse that came to mind, he spluttered, "My shoulder."

Alice's brow knitted in concern. "Is it that bad?"

His mind still blank, he managed a nod. All he could think was how stupid he must look. How could she not notice him staring at her like this? He had to think of something quickly.

"Here, let me help." Leaning in with a napkin, she dabbed the water around his collar.

He froze, focusing on controlling his breathing. How could she not hear his heart thumping so loudly with her head so close?

As she moved away, relief and disappointment flooded him. He had to get a grip. Quickly. They were perfectly fine as friends. Nothing needed to change.

"Thanks," he replied, taking a deep breath. Glancing away, he sought a distraction. Anything to break the tension. But Jordan and Emily were still immersed in their conversation. Except ... "Where's Eliot?"

Emily's head snapped up. "Not again!"

"Don't worry, he'll be in the caves," Jaime guessed, glad for the distraction. "I'll go search for him. You wait here and enjoy the eclipse."

"I'll go with you," Alice said, sending fresh waves of panic through him. He needed to figure out what was going on with him, not wander round dark caves with a girl he'd recently realised he found attractive.

"No, I'll go," Jordan said, jumping to his feet. "You girls stay here."

Thankful for the change of plans, Jaime followed Jordan to the cave mouth, a slither of darkness in the rocky hillside towards the bottom of the slope. Hopefully, Eliot hadn't strayed far, though the darkness probably wouldn't have put him off.

The cave system itself stretched out far into the hillside, but it contained few interesting rock formations. A couple of large stalagmites stood proudly in the entrance and a few columns dotted the passageways, but it was not enough to attract tourists. Mostly, people used the caves to shelter from the rain, and people rarely ventured past the vast entrance cavern.

"So, Alice didn't take the bait," Jordan said, pulling out his phone to use as a light.

"What?" All Jaime's muscles tensed. Now would be the perfect time to confess things didn't feel right about what Jordan intended, but would Jordan ridicule him? Jordan was so confident, he could simply state his feelings and not be embarrassed. Jaime couldn't even be certain what his feelings were.

"I asked Alice to join me for lunch, but she didn't seem to realise I was asking her to go with me alone. Should I be more direct?"

"Oh, er, maybe." Caught off guard, Jaime tugged at his sleeves to give his hands something to do. "Or you could get to know her better, so you know how to ask." Annoyed at Jordan's persistence, Jaime called out to Eliot. He couldn't have gone far.

Only his voice echoed back, so he ducked into the winding corridor on the right.

Jordan bounded after him, his feet sending stones scattering across the floor. "That's what I've got you for, bud. You can give me the inside info, so I don't get rejected."

"Right ..." Jaime shrugged. "I'm not sure I know that side of her well enough. Emily would know better. You were talking to her, right?"

What could he say for Jordan to take the hint? His unrelenting eagerness was starting to become annoying.

"Yeah, but we weren't talking about Alice. We were talking about family and sports and bugs."

Tripping over a rock, Jaime lurched towards the wall. He threw his arm out to stop himself from falling, gaining a damp sleeve in the process. Cursing his bad luck, he rubbed his sleeve on his trousers. "Bugs?"

"Yeah, her brother is into bugs, so she kinda is, too. Did you know there are bugs that glow? We could use some of them now. My phone is running out of battery."

"I'll use mine." Darkness prevailed until Jaime raised his, but out of the corner of his eye, an odd flickering behind a cluster of boulders attracted his attention. He frowned, lowering his phone. "What's that light over there?"

He called out for Eliot again, in case he was the source of the illumination, but still no one responded.

"Where? I can't see anything." Jordan peered around Jaime, and, in his eagerness, stumbled over some rocks.

A jolt of satisfaction shot through Jaime, swiftly replaced by guilt, before he pulled Jordan upright. "Right there." Jaime pointed, but it had disappeared. "Huh. It's gone now. It mustn't have been anything."

"No, I see it now," Jordan said, squinting.

Jaime stepped back to Jordan and the faint white light reappeared, shimmering on a patch of limestone.

"Weird. You stay here and tell me when I'm close to it." Jordan climbed over a couple of boulders and slid behind an outcrop towards the light's origin. "Is it still there?"

Jaime focused his gaze onto the shadowy cavern. Jordan was standing right next to the faint oval of flickering light. "You're about two steps to the right of it. You really can't see it?"

"No, nothing." Jordan strode two paces to the left and disappeared. Jaime blinked. "Jordan?"

There were no rocks between them. Jordan couldn't be out of sight, yet the light failed to illuminate him. "Jordan! This isn't funny."

He waited a few moments, then scrambled over.

As he approached Jordan's last position, his foot caught on a jagged outcrop and he stumbled forward, flinging his arms out to stop him crashing into the rock face. His hands met nothing.

Bright white light blinded him, and a deafening roar filled his ears. Instinctively, he flailed his arms, searching for something to grip on to, but reality had abandoned him.

The world lurched away, and he couldn't fathom the air whizzing past his ears, the shift in gravity or the reason his stomach was now in his chest. Confusion took over as he kept falling, the cave floor failing to stop him.

Soon, a force began to buffet around him, and blobs of blue, green and brown flashed by. He thrashed, attempting to control his speed, but there was nothing to push against. He tried to spin around, to find Jordan, but there was only the bright white light.

And the deafening sound pulsing with his racing heart.

Nothing made sense.

Panic took over.

CHAPTER 4

EARTH

Once again, Emily glanced down the hill towards the caves. It must have been half an hour since the boys had gone in after Eliot, but no one had reemerged. It was always like Eliot to do something like this, but what would he do if for once she didn't go after him?

Shadow fell across them as a cloud obscured the sun. Typical. Now the eclipse would be ruined too.

"So, Jordan seemed pretty into you," Alice said, out of the blue.

Emily raised an eyebrow. "Only as much as Jaime was into you."

"Actually, Jaime wasn't saying a lot. He was being quite weird. I don't think it was just his shoulder either."

Emily resisted a smirk, quite sure Jordan's sudden interest in Alice had brought out Jaime's competitive behaviour, but Alice wouldn't want to hear that. She consistently refused to acknowledge that Jaime and her were anything more than friends.

But that didn't seem to be true anymore. At least on Jaime's side. Poor Jaime. It had been quite painful to watch.

Perhaps Alice would figure it out on her own, with a little help. Eventually. "Jaime's always been introverted."

Alice started to pack away their picnic. "Not with me, he's not. Anyway, don't change the subject. Jaime and I have been friends for ages. You've only just met Jordan and you couldn't stop talking."

"He seems to be a naturally loquacious person." She frowned. Her conversation with Jordan had been unusually absorbing, but everything had been about Eliot. "I thought he was more interested in you."

Alice dropped the plates she was packing away. "Me? No, he barely said anything. We were only teasing Jaime." A wrinkle formed on her brow. "I wonder if that was why Jaime was quiet."

"Jaime's not usually *that* sensitive."

With her lips pursed, Alice turned to watch the combatants spreading out around the field. Some strolled down to the lake, but others set out picnics on the gently sloping grassy hill. On this warm sunny day, no one lingered near the caves.

"He was quite skilled, though, wasn't he?" Alice said.

"They both were. Quite entertaining," Emily agreed. Her eyes followed Alice's and settled on the cave.

"Just don't tell them I said that."

"Never!" Of course she wouldn't tell Jaime that a day didn't go by where Alice didn't mention him. Nor would she point out how her eyes lit up whenever he was around. "One thing they are not capable of, though, is locating my brother. How can they not have found him yet?"

Alice stretched her legs. "I'll go find them." Alice knew Emily hated the caves, but Alice didn't mind them at all.

"You'll miss the eclipse."

"I won't. I've still got half an hour. If I can't find them by then, I'll come back to watch it and then we can both look for them."

Emily assented, already pulling out a book.

Ten minutes later, Emily glanced at the cave entrance for at least the tenth time. There was no way she could enjoy this book now, despite the fascinating Babylonian history. Putting it aside with a sigh, she clambered to her feet and set off after the others.

Dark and dank, the caves were not at all appealing. Just the sort of place that would attract her brother.

Avoiding the mud at the opening, she pulled out her phone and shone the light inside. This wasn't her first visit, but it was not an experience she liked to repeat. Although not particularly hazardous, loose rocks increased the chance of tripping, and outcrops jutted out at all heights.

Gingerly treading through the entrance cavern, she inhaled the musty air with distaste. With little hope anyone would be nearby, she called out.

Her words echoed back, distorted, followed by silence. No chance of avoiding the deeper, narrower chambers then.

With her phone held out in one hand and the other on the damp wall, she carefully proceeded down the long and winding passageway into a cluster of smallish cavities, smattered with graffiti.

Empty chambers yawned at her, so she carried on further, cursing her brother under her breath. Soon she would face a dilemma, because the cave system split into multiple directions, and she had no way of knowing which route anyone had taken.

She checked her phone, but there was no chance of a signal this far in.

They should all have gone in together and searched a path each. It could take hours to search them all.

Releasing her clenched jaw, she shouted for Eliot again, receiving only garbled words as a response.

When she reached the place where the cave split, she checked her phone again, desperate for guidance. Only three minutes to the eclipse. She was going to miss it!

"Eliot! Alice! Jaime! Jordan!" she shouted, before turning around to kick a rock.

Shimmering light at the back of the cave caught her attention. Slowly growing into a silver disc, as if reflected by a pool of water, it appeared to be cast from a vertical doorway, side on to Emily's viewing angle.

That was odd.

Against her better judgement, she clambered over the rocks to the source of the light, so bright it obscured everything else. It was as if an elliptical doorway had opened, and someone was shining a bright light through. Though the light was disconcerting, shimmering and twisting unnaturally.

She backed away and returned to the other side of the cavern, trying not to stumble. Which passage would Eliot choose?

"Eliot!" she shouted, her frustration straining her voice.

"Emily, is that you?" Alice's voice called back, distant and garbled. So Eliot wasn't down that path then. Perhaps she ought to see where the lit path led. Alice would soon catch up.

"I'm over here!" she shouted, then made her way back to the light.

Except now it was gone. There was nothing but rock.

Puzzled, she edged forwards. With the strange light's sudden absence, it was difficult to see. Her eyes had yet to adjust to the low light of her phone. But the rock was just ahead …

She reached out to guide herself, but her hand passed straight through the rock, knocking her off balance. Her phone clattered to the ground as she threw her other hand out to catch herself.

Bright light engulfed her, and instead of crashing into rock, a force pulled her sideways. She was tumbling through nothingness, the ground completely gone. Instead of echoing back to her, her shriek of surprise was swallowed up.

Terrified, she squeezed her eyes shut. She must have hit her head. Everything would be alright in a few minutes.

When she opened her eyes, the world had returned to normal. Someone must have carried her out of the cave because blue sky gleamed above. That would explain the sensation of being pulled along.

Still disorientated, she clambered to her feet, only to find a middle-aged man approaching her, uttering strange words. He was dressed in an unusual navy uniform, not one that matched those she'd seen earlier. The tall stone walls surrounding them only confused her further. Where had they taken her?

The man spoke again, and it took a moment for her to realise he spoke a peculiar dialect of Farsi, though she could only make out a couple of words. "… money … understand me?"

That was odd. Though not as odd as what she'd just experienced. Nor the shimmering light shining on the ochre stone ground beneath her feet. Still breathless from her experience, she spun around.

Just like the one she had seen in the caves, an oval of bright light hovered there. With a shaking hand, she reached out. She felt no sensation as her fingers touched the light, but as soon as her hand crossed the threshold, a strong current pushed her back.

Her heart raced as she realised the truth. She'd fallen through that doorway and there was no way back. But where had the doorway taken her? Had she ended up in the Middle East somehow?

The man coughed, clearly wanting something from her. With his arms crossed, he glanced towards a gathering of other uniformed men outside a small wooden building nestled in the corner of the walls. "Do you have the ..." She couldn't make out the last two words, but from his insistent tone she guessed he was asking for money.

Her heart sank as she realised her bag with all her belongings and money remained by the lake. Though her cash might not mean anything here, anyway. What would he do if she confessed that she had none? He didn't look too friendly. Especially with that sword at his side.

A ripple spread across the portal and out stumbled a woman clinging to a young child with each hand. The man reached out to steady her, but recoiled as she said something sharp.

The two adults exchanged words too quickly for Emily to catch, but the woman handed over a few coins, confirming Emily's suspicions. Clearly the woman expected to arrive here, so the portal couldn't be so unusual for them. Wherever they were, it was off any known map.

Another soldier marched up, from what looked to be an entrance, or exit, at the far end of the walled enclosure, and addressed the man before her. Although in the same general uniform, this man's buttons and belt gleamed with gold. All Emily could determine was that he was looking for something or someone, before he turned his soft brown eyes on her.

"Who is this?" the more decorated soldier asked in their language.

The other man shrugged and turned to her. "Do you have any money? Do you understand?"

She shook her head and replied in their language, "No money."

The soldier gestured at the hut in the corner, where the woman was already heading with her two children. The woman hadn't seemed afraid, and not wanting to be questioned further by these men, Emily quickly followed.

Inside the shelter, several people loitered, women in simple dresses and men in tunics. None wore uniforms or gold embellishments.

The woman she'd followed said something to her, but she spoke so quickly it was impossible to understand.

"I'm sorry," Emily said. "I speak a little Farsi."

A man in worn leather clothes ambled close, too close for comfort, though he paused in front of her. "I help," he said, then reached out to her forehead.

Emily backed away, crashing into whoever stood behind her. Before she could apologise, the man had grabbed her temples and was uttering strange words.

With a shriek, Emily grabbed his wrists to push him off, but he was already stepping back. "Can you understand us now?" he said.

Emily blinked. That was English. Though it sounded strange with the intonations on the wrong parts of the words. "Where are we?"

The man grinned. "The kingdom of North Parsa. Isn't that where you intended to be?"

"North Parsa?" She'd never heard of it. "Is it in Europe?"

The man tilted his head to one side. "I've never heard of Europe. Is that the world you come from?"

World? That had to be a translation error. "Asia?"

The man shook his head. "I never thought I'd meet anyone who'd not heard of Parsa. You're incredibly lucky to arrive here by accident."

"She has no money," the woman said.

The man shrugged. "That doesn't matter. No one goes hungry in North Parsa. There is work for all in the city." He glanced over the woman's two children. "What brings you here?"

The woman smiled proudly at her son. "My boy's going to be a mage. He can cast magic already."

"Magic?" Emily asked.

"Yes, show us," the man said eagerly.

"Luca," the woman called. "Show the people your gift."

Luca waved his hand and colourful sparks shot across the room. Emily staggered back. There was no end to the strangeness of this place.

The man laughed. "I take it they don't have magic on your world?"

Emily shook her head. What had she got herself into? Or, more accurately, what had Eliot got her into?

But why wasn't he here? "Has a brown-haired boy a few years older than Luca arrived?"

The man shook his head. "I've been here since this morning. All today's arrivals are here."

"They wouldn't have taken him anywhere else?"

"Not unless he could afford his own transportation. Or he could teleport." He grinned. "I can almost teleport, but why waste the effort when there'll be a carriage organised?" He shrugged off his leather coat. "Gets hot here though."

Emily peered out of the door but there was no sign of Eliot or any other travellers. Nothing had changed, except the well-decorated man had taken up patrolling in front of the portal. With a sigh, she dropped down onto one of the benches.

What was she going to do? Her parents would be furious when they found out she'd lost Eliot. She'd never be trusted again. And she wouldn't blame them.

The man sat beside her. "Cheer up. There are plenty of opportunities in the city. Even for those without magic. You'll have to work off the portal tax and your transportation fee, but the people here are fair. You'll get food and lodgings with your employment. What more can you ask for?"

Biting back her despair, Emily looked into his eyes. "How do I get home?"

He glanced away. "A trip to Parsa is usually one way. There are other portals, but ..."

"... they probably don't go to your world, dear," the woman finished.

Emily swallowed the lump in her throat and hugged her arms around herself. She was stuck here, and Eliot was missing.

All she had to look forward to was a trip to the city and work to pay off her debt.

But if there were other portals, perhaps Eliot had arrived through one of these. Maybe Jordan and Jaime had too ...

CHAPTER 5
North Parsa

Losing her patience, Alice glared at the man. Why wouldn't he speak English? In his peculiar uniform, he must be part of some historical reenactment, but he didn't have to be so unhelpful.

Shielding her eyes from the bright sun, she sought out someone else, only then noticing the wall surrounding them. And the ochre sand scattered across the hard ground.

What was going on?

In the corner of the enclosure, a wooden building appeared to be sheltering people from the heat, but a number of men dressed as soldiers stood guard along the walls. All wore double-breasted navy tunics with gold buttons, but none possessed the decorations of the man in front of her. He must be in charge. But of what?

The man, in his mid-twenties, and with chocolate brown hair, said something unfathomable yet again.

With a sigh, she pulled out her phone to text the others, but there was no signal.

Her skin crawled. This was very wrong.

Cold spread through her limbs as she turned to face the doorway, not a gap in the rock as she'd presumed, but an oval of shimmering light, standing proud of the wall. She gulped. *That* was not normal.

Swallowing her fear, she pushed against it, but a force prevented her passing.

There was no way back.

The man touched her elbow and gestured to a narrow gap at the end of the enclosure. He spoke more urgently now and looked at her phone with suspicion. Finally, in English, he said, "Come with me."

Alice almost laughed with relief. "Where am I?"

The pressure on her elbow increased and he gestured forwards with his other hand.

Alice shook her head. "Tell me where I am first."

The man barked an order in that unfathomable language, and soldiers rushed forward, eager to obey. In the narrow gap, a carriage appeared, with oversized wheels and a golden lion on the side.

The commander gestured forwards again. Could he not understand her?

"What is going on? Where are you taking me?"

He stared at her for a moment, contemplating her words, then said, "To the palace, to the king."

Alice's stomach knotted. There was no palace near her home.

Facing the rising dread, she skulked to the exit and stared upon the impossible scene. Desert dunes spread out each side of a stone path, and in the distance, a city poked into the sky, like nothing she'd ever seen. Everything looked to be made of stone, though two towers glinted peculiarly in the sun.

Beside the carriage, the officer held out an arm and looked at her expectantly.

With no way back and no answers here, a palace started to sound appealing. They might have people who could speak her language and explain what had happened.

With one last glance around, she stepped inside the carriage.

Alice exited the carriage in front of huge wooden gates engraved with the outline of a golden lion, separating the palace from the rest of the city. Massive stone walls stretched out in either direction, disappearing behind large, flat-topped buildings. Soldiers patrolled the walls above, all wearing identical blue tunics and dark trousers, their swords gleaming in the bright sun.

Beyond the gates, two towers soared high into the sky, far higher than stone should have allowed, dwarfing the walls' corner towers.

Craning her neck, she gaped at the gravity-defying peaks decorated in an obscene display of wealth. The eastern tower glittered with topaz stones and sapphires, while the western tower shimmered enchantingly, as if the surface itself were made of liquid gold.

A low growl attracted her attention through a human-sized door in the gate, and to her horror she discovered a pride of lions scattered on the other side, observing her with hungry eyes. At least, they looked like lions. But they were so tall their heads reached her shoulders, their tails were unusually bushy and their colouring peculiar. Some were dark brown, some black, and others had patches of the different shades.

Noticing her shrink back, the officer smiled and, taking her arm, led her inside.

When two lions approached, Alice halted, all her muscles stiffening, but her guide remained calm. He uttered something in a soothing voice, and the lions drifted away as quickly as they'd come. The voice did nothing to calm Alice's nerves.

Huge ochre stone arches adorned the path they walked, leading the way to the building's oversized golden-engraved entrance, which featured an intricate pattern of geometric shapes.

Utterly out of place in this dry environment, a tropical garden flourished in the centre of the spacious courtyard, complete with a dozen fountains. The flora was unrecognisable, the colours so bright they barely seemed real. A dragonfly the size of a dinner plate flitted past, weaving its way through the plants.

Alice could hardly believe her eyes. This place belonged to the history books, but everything was just a little bit odd and a little bit excessive.

Emily might have been able to explain the location, but deep down, Alice knew this place couldn't be real. She glanced around for her friend, in case she had found her way here, but she recognised no one.

Not Jaime. Not Jordan. Not Eliot.

Could they still be wandering the caves? What would they do when they couldn't find her? They could hardly imagine looking for her in a place that shouldn't exist.

And what would they tell her parents? She'd be grounded for a month if she didn't return when she'd promised.

Not that it would matter for much longer. Moving to a new town would be just as bad.

Before they reached the main entrance, the officer steered Alice to the left, and they entered through a smaller, less ornate door, leading to an empty room dimly lit by oil lamps. A minor disappointment compared to the display outside, it was evidently not designed to impress.

The man turned to her and, gesturing with his hands, he simply said, "Wait." Then he left the room, leaving her all alone to contemplate her extraordinary situation.

She hadn't even got his name.

The sudden absence of people and activity filled her with a sense of foreboding, and her earlier panic started to return. Should she stay in a place she knew nothing about, or should she try the city?

These people hadn't given her any reason to fear them, but this place was so peculiar, she didn't know what to expect. Or what they wanted from her.

But she'd never find out if she left now.

With her eyes adjusting to the poor light, she discerned a sprawling golden family tree glinting on the wall. In each generation, a name was crowned and another was marked with a star. She edged closer for a better look, but soon sensed someone behind her.

Expecting to see the officer again, she spun around, only to be stunned by the young man before her. Immaculately dressed and extraordinarily handsome, this young man looked extremely out of place in this room. His expensive silky tunic and the prevalence of gold suggested a position of supreme importance, but it was his presence that stunned. With his shoulder length midnight hair and eyes of deep liquid cocoa, he was difficult not to stare at.

Noticing what she was doing, she glanced away, a moment later realising he still stared at her. He couldn't be much older than her, yet he strode forward with perfect confidence and, with a casual flick of the wrist, shot a ball of fire into the air.

Caught off guard, Alice stumbled back. The fire just hung there, burning and flickering with nothing to support it. No embers fell, but she had no doubt it was real. Its heat warmed her face.

"Hello?" the man said, more of a question than a greeting. "Do you understand me?"

Words abandoned her, so she nodded. What was going on? She had seriously underestimated this place and the danger she faced.

"What's your name?"

Still paralysed, she blinked at him.

"I'm Darien. Would you like some food?" He paused. "Or perhaps you'd like to rest? You must have had a long journey." Apparently noticing her shock, he pulled a sweet from his robes. "Here. This is one of our best."

Instinctively, she reached out to receive the sweet and realised she could move again. Taking deep breaths, she sucked in the scents of ember and parchment, both emanating from this young man.

Above them, the ball of fire continued to hover, casting them in a warm glow, but weaving ominous shadows around them. It showed no signs of burning out or falling, though it seemed to bob around with a life of its own.

Not trusting anything yet, she pocketed the sweet and rallied her courage. He seemed friendly, despite his ability to summon fire, and at least he could speak English.

"Are ... are you the king?"

Reflecting the flickering light, his eyes danced. "No, I'm just a prince."

Alice flushed, feeling foolish. He wasn't old enough to be the king. Now that she looked closer, past his fine attire and confident bearing, his youth became apparent. He was her age, eighteen at most.

"I'm here to look after you. It must be quite a surprise finding us on the other end of the portal."

"Portal?"

"Yes, you came through one of our less-travelled portals. Officer Gul thought it best to bring you to the palace." He watched her carefully, his expression relaxed and friendly. "Have you never travelled through a portal before?"

She shook her head.

Now she was recovering from her shock, her ability to think started to return, and with that, her curiosity. "Where *is* here?"

"This is the Royal Palace of the north. You couldn't be in a safer place. The world you're on is called Parsa, and it's a little rough outside the palace. You're lucky my officer found you."

Alice's eyes widened. "World? I'm on a different *world*?"

"Yes. Do you trust me?" He held out his hand, waiting expectantly.

Something about his charm and confidence drew Alice in and she found herself compelled to reach out and place her hand in his. After all, she wouldn't get any answers if she didn't show any willingness to trust.

The instant their hands joined, the world jolted away and they no longer stood in a darkened anti-chamber, but a spacious room, its most distinctive feature a grandiose map on the wall. Sunlight caressed her skin instead of warm flame and an elaborate window revealed blue sky.

She whipped her hand away. "What just happened?"

"I brought you to the map room," he answered, as if teleportation was the most normal thing in the world.

Alice swallowed the lump in her throat. How much magic could he perform?

The prince gestured at the map. "Look. These are the known worlds and the permanent portals that link them. The fluctuating portals are shown in gold. This is the one you came through." His hand moved to point at a gold portal separate from a nearby cluster of blue portals, not too far from the city. Most of the gold portals stood apart from the others, though towards the south of the map many red portals spread out across what looked to be desert.

"All those portals lead to other worlds?"

Darien nodded. "Many of these portals lead to many worlds."

Horror gripped her. What if Eliot had found his way to a different world? That would explain why she hadn't seen him. And Jaime and Jordan too. "Could the portal I came through lead elsewhere?"

"It is unlikely. Why do you ask?"

"I think my friends might have found the portal too. Do you know where they might have ended up?"

Darien's brow wrinkled. "The current is very strong at that portal. It is doubtful they found their way out to a different world. Are you sure they entered the portal?"

"No. But what do you mean about the current?"

"Look," he said again, pointing to the map. "What do you see between the portals?"

"A river?"

"Exactly," he replied with his dazzling smile.

Despite herself, she blushed, before annoyance flickered through her. Just because he was outrageously handsome, she didn't need to lose her head.

"But there was no water," she protested. That was one thing she did remember from her journey.

"True, but in many ways, the portal realm most resembles a river. There is a current and a flow that will take you between portals. Sometimes that flow is weak enough to move against, but most of the time, you can only travel downstream. So, most portals are one way, or at least won't take you back to the place you started. Parsa is unusual with its numerous portals permitting travel between many different worlds, often in both directions. But that one is definitely one way. You'd have more luck swimming up a waterfall."

Alice nodded, though the information overwhelmed and confused. "But ... couldn't you just teleport to a different world?"

"You're rather inquisitive, aren't you?" Darien smiled and leaned against the wall as he contemplated his response. "No one can teleport through the portal realm. Those few that have tried have never been seen again. It takes a skilled mage to teleport even to the other side of the palace."

Alice's heart sank. "How will I get home then?"

"You needn't worry. Tomorrow, I'll take you to see the Royal Mage. He's the best person to track down a portal. In the meantime, let me do the honour of treating you to some royal Parsan hospitality."

She frowned. Was he not royal and a mage? "Who's the Royal Mage?"

"He's the highest mage of all the North Parsans, with the strongest magic. He has a position equal to the king, but he deals mostly with magical issues rather than everyday diplomacy."

Alice bit her lip. "I should go back to the portal to wait for any of my friends to come through."

"There really is no need. My officer will bring them to the palace. You needn't worry about that."

Alice consented with a nod. Who was she to turn down the help of the most accomplished mage they had? If all went well, she could be back home tomorrow.

It might take a bit of explaining when she did return, but when did her parents really care where she'd been? They might even start to believe that she wasn't going with them when she failed to turn up.

While here, it wouldn't hurt to find out a little more about this place. These people seemed willing to help, but that itself was suspicious. Why was a prince helping her at all?

CHAPTER 6
NORTH PARSA

The sun was low in the sky by the time the soldiers led the travellers out of the shelter. Eliot still hadn't appeared, and with each passing moment, Emily's thoughts became more preoccupied with his location. Eliot would surely investigate a shimmering doorway, so he must have gone through. The only question was, where had he ended up?

More apprehensive about their destination, Emily lurked near the back of the group. Despite her fellow travellers' reassurances, she wasn't looking forward to visiting a city that needed to be patrolled this heavily, nor where people could cast magic. These people might be seeking a better life, but their simple clothes and lack of belongings suggested they hadn't had much to lose.

Soldiers still stood guard along the wall, though now a peculiar man in blue robes stood between the exit and the portal. He didn't appear to be a traveller and he didn't interact with anyone. He just stood stiffly, watching proceedings with his hawkish eyes. With no sword, he probably wasn't a soldier, so his presence stood out as yet another oddity.

As Emily passed the newcomer, a shiver ran down her spine, though she had no idea what caused it. This man didn't appear any more threatening than the others she'd encountered. Picking up her pace, she pressed closer to her group.

A wooden carriage with a cloth cover waited for them at the entrance to the walled enclosure, barely big enough to fit everyone inside. A pair of gigantic donkeys, their colour matching the sand on either side of the cobbled path, shuffled restlessly at its front.

Lamenting the heat, Emily clambered inside. Hopefully there would be plenty of shade in the city. Given the talk in the shelter, it had a lot to live up to, but she didn't need much. Just news of Eliot and a way back home.

With everyone crammed aboard, the cart lurched into motion, forcing Emily to grab onto the edge to steady herself. After so much time spent waiting, it was a relief to be moving, but each time the wheels hit a divot or crack, the hard wood jolted her bones, until she thought she'd be shaken apart.

Several gasps tempted her to peek out from under the cover as the cart veered over a hill. Towering above the sand, even from this distance, huge ochre walls stretched across the horizon, much larger than those of the enclosure they'd departed. A jumble of stone buildings jutted out in front, far more disorderly than she would have expected, given everything she'd seen so far.

Some of the travellers hugged each other, relief written on their faces, and one even reached out to squeeze Emily's hand. She couldn't imagine what they had been through to get here, nor what terror these walls needed to keep at bay. If buildings could exist outside the walls, they probably weren't to protect from sandstorms, but if people came here willingly, there couldn't be too many dangers.

Beyond the walls, two enormous towers reached into the sky, beautiful in their architecture, and Emily couldn't help thinking she'd stepped into one of her books. Not that any could have described this place. The towers were so tall they defied gravity, and it was a wonder they stood at all.

She stared, taking in every fine detail, captivated by the golden tips and shimmering whirls. A show of wealth or a beacon to lure in unsuspecting travellers?

A shadow fell over the cart as they passed through a pointed arch, and Emily shivered, pulling her thin cardigan closed. Hooves clip-clopped upon cobble, sharper now that they entered a broad street, alive with throngs of people despite the low sun.

Before they reached the city walls, the donkeys veered to the left and the cart trundled into a bustling square where people still traded their wares. As their transport came to a stop, Emily's heart leapt into her throat. To avoid being arrested she had to find someone to pay off her debt, but who?

City folk surged forward, offering lodgings, but none mentioned work. Whilst the cart emptied of her fellow travellers, she found her legs would no longer move.

All she wanted was to go home, sink into a comfortable chair and drink hot cocoa with her mother. Normally, by now they'd be settling down for the evening, but today everything would be different for both of them. It was probably worse for her mother not knowing anything, but Emily couldn't guess what awaited her either. And she still knew nothing about what had happened to Eliot.

Another man who had no money made his way out into the square, under the watchful eyes of their escorts. There would be no running away from these guards.

Luca and his sister ran towards a man, shouting "Father", leaving their exhausted mother to follow more slowly. The sight jolted Emily into action. Now was no time for self-pity. There was a square full of people who might know her brother's whereabouts.

After half falling out of the cart, she stretched her stiff limbs and ventured towards a grocer with a good view of the square. If anyone else had arrived, he ought to have seen.

A jumble of powerful scents assaulted her senses, too numerous to identify any one, though an array of colourful powders in a nearby stall suggested spices were common here. It was a surprise they could grow so much in a desert. Unless they used the portals for trade ... That would explain why the road had led here.

An older woman in a plain blue dress cut in front of Emily and thrust a basket of purple fruit into the grocer's chest. He threw up his hands, refusing to take the basket, and the fruit tumbled out and scattered across the courtyard.

Emily darted forwards to scoop them up before they caused an accident. The woman continued to shout and rant, now directing her attention to an older man behind the stand.

The younger man hurried her way and held out the basket, letting Emily drop the escaped fruit in before it tumbled from her arms. "Thank you," he said with a smile. "At least someone appreciates my fruit."

Emily smiled back at him. "They look fine to me. Why didn't she want them?"

"They're probably too rich for her delicate tongue." Smirking, he held out a fruit. "For your trouble."

"Thank you." She ran her fingers over the rough surface, contemplating how it would taste. Regardless, the gift lifted her spirits. This world wasn't all taxes and debt. "Have you seen any other travellers arrive here today?"

"A few. This is the main arrival point from the portals."

"Have you seen—"

"You overcharge me, then give away fruit for free?" The shouty woman confronted the grocer again, her eyes on the fruit in Emily's hand.

The grocer's mouth dropped open. "You told me it was not ripe."

The woman's mouth twitched as she turned her attention to Emily. "Are you seeking work?"

Emily bit her lip. She couldn't expect to survive here on handouts, no matter how generous the population. And she still had her portal tax to pay. Since she'd arrived, the soldiers hadn't taken their eyes off he r.

This woman wasn't exactly what she had in mind for her salvation, but she couldn't know how many offers she might get. Reluctantly, she nodded.

"Negotiate with this man to pay three coins and I shall pay off your debt and allow you to work for me." Before Emily could answer, she strode off to another trader.

Bewildered, Emily turned back to the man. "Are three coins enough for this fruit?"

He laughed. "It is an insult, but I can hardly let such a kind-hearted girl be taken by the soldiers for outstanding debt, can I?" He held out the basket. "Promise me you'll visit me to buy all your fruit."

Emily glanced around the courtyard, looking for other options, but few people seemed interested in the travellers.

"Don't be put off by Madame Olsta's temper. She's a shrewd woman, always looking to pay less, but she's fair to her workers. You'll have food and lodging for as long as you need and you'll pay off your debt in no time. That's all the soldiers are looking for. Vagrancy is not something that is tolerated in this city."

Forcing a smile, Emily nodded. Hopefully, she wouldn't be here long enough to have to worry about finding something better. With her food and lodgings taken care of, she could worry about more important things.

"Have you seen a young boy with brown curly hair arrive today?"

A wrinkle formed on his brow. "Can't say that I have. Were you separated on the journey?"

"He didn't come through the same portal. I hoped he might have been brought here."

The grocer shook his head. "Not today."

Her heart sank. "Is there anywhere else he might have been taken?"

"You could try the main city, but it will cost you to get through the gates. Doubt he will have ended up there though."

She thanked the man and took the basket, before hurrying to catch up with the woman. Someone must have seen Eliot. She just had to find them.

Madame Olsta led her through a narrow, winding alleyway to a small, terraced house butting up to a tall stone wall. Clearly proud of the position of the house, so close to the central town, she beamed as she opened the door. To Emily, it looked cramped and run down.

Most of the buildings were the same, and each seemed to house a large number of people, though the people appeared happy enough, and many carried large pots of groceries inside. The pleasant aroma of cooking emanated from others.

Eliot could be in any and it would take her days to search.

Madame Olsta turned to her with a warm smile. "You'll find your feet in no time. Jena will show you your duties. If you work hard, you'll start earning money in a couple of weeks. For now, there are some old clothes in the wardrobe you can use."

Her throat dry, Emily bobbed her head. She'd need that money to get inside the city. Or back to the portal. Her time here was not going to be easy.

CHAPTER 7

DEEP IN THE DESERT

Jordan stumbled forward, determined to reach the portal, but it was no easy task. Every step he took, his feet sank deep into the sand, and his trainers refilled over and over, dragging him down. He half shuffled, half fell along the dune, seeking out that elusive doorway.

It had to be here somewhere.

A shimmer in the air caught his eye, and with determined optimism, he scattered sand across the aberration.

The grains dropped back down, unhindered, revealing nothing.

"It's no use," Jaime called from behind. "It's gone."

Jordan dropped his hands to his side. Jaime might be right. He'd seen for himself how far it had moved in the short time between his arrival and Jaime's. But with desert all around, trying to find the portal had been their best option.

Jaime's face twisted with horror, and he spun back in the direction they'd come. "Eliot! What if he found the portal too?"

Guilt tightened Jordan's chest. Why hadn't they kept a better eye on Eliot? He'd promised Emily he'd find him, and he had no way of fulfilling that promise now, unless Eliot had suffered the same fate.

There had been no sign of him in the caves, but that didn't mean he'd found his way here. He shook his head. "We'd have seen him."

Jaime clenched his fists. "He could have been behind a dune. We have to go back and check."

Jordan's earlier enthusiasm started to wane. At first, he'd been thrilled at their discovery. A portal that led across the world! They could have been famous. But what use was a portal to the middle of a desert? Especially if they couldn't find a way back. "We'll never find the portal if we head back that way," Jordan said begrudgingly.

"We tried. At least back that way heads towards mountains. It's our best chance to find water."

"They're days away! We'll never survive that long."

Jaime's voice softened. "What do you think we should do then?"

Jordan glanced around at the endless sands, only broken by their shadows. Nothing else was alive and nothing offered help. They had to hope they could make it to the mountains. Or stumble on another portal.

Where there was one there could be more …

"Alright," Jordan said. "Let's go that way. We'll check for Eliot, then head for the mountains."

Jaime stood frozen, staring in the direction they thought the portal had taken. "You don't think Alice and Emily will come looking for us?"

Jordan sighed. "It wouldn't have taken them that long to find us. We'd definitely have seen them falling out of the sky."

"Right." Jaime nodded. "Unless the portal moved further than we thought …"

Jordan shook his head. Why did Jaime always have to think the worst? "They're fine," he said resolutely. He grabbed Jaime and turned him around, causing yet more sand to fall out of his slightly too-long-to-be-practical hair. "Let's go."

As they trudged on, the endless sands gave no clue to the distance travelled, nor did the mountains seem any closer. No vegetation, nor anything else broke the scenery, and the dry air seeped into their lungs.

After an unbearable amount of silence, Jordan cleared his throat. "What are we going to do if we can't find water?"

"We can survive for a few days without water," Jaime replied unconvincingly, his voice as raspy as Jordan's.

"Not walking like this."

Reluctantly, Jaime nodded his agreement. They needed to find water soon, but how?

Already, Jordan's legs were stiff, so he suggested they take a short break, and they both flopped to the sand where they stood.

"If the girls did follow us and they found the portal ..." Jaime began.

"... they might not be in the desert." Jordan finished. "They could be in the mountains by a nice cool river waiting for us."

"Do you think they would head for the mountains too?"

"Yeah, Emily's really smart. She'd know exactly what to do," Jordan said with confidence. Though now, as well as lack of water and being stranded in an unknown desert, he had to worry about looking for his friends. The more Jaime mentioned it, the more he started to believe they would follow. But what had happened to Eliot?

"Alice is smart too, and capable," Jaime said.

A pang of guilt shot through Jordan's chest. Why had he said Emily's name, not Alice's?

Sure, Emily was obviously clever – she carried books around with her all the time – but Alice was too, wasn't she? "That's what I meant, they're both intelligent."

His cheeks burning, he sought a distraction. "Look, the sun's about to set."

Jaime followed his gaze. "We should get a better view from up on that high dune and at least enjoy the spectacle."

Jordan heaved himself up and half dragged Jaime to the top. The heat must have taken a greater toll than Jaime was letting on. Or he'd worn himself out fighting in the tournament. All to beat Jordan.

At the top, Jordan slumped down into the sand. It was Jaime's own fault for being so competitive. But why did he care that much? Jaime could be so odd sometimes.

Taking a deep breath, Jordan leaned back. Not a soul could be seen, nor another living creature. If they weren't lost, without water, it would have been beautiful.

They watched in silence as the sun dipped into the parched expanse and the sky blazed orange with its passing. Pink brushed the bottoms of the few fluffy clouds as they mourned its loss, and shadows crept into the dunes.

"What's that?" Jaime asked, pointing to a patch of disturbed sand behind a smaller dune.

Following his direction, Jordan observed other patches of disturbance between the dunes, weaving along the flat. "It's a track!"

Jaime's face lit up. "We should follow it!"

"But it'll be dark soon. How will we see it?" Already convinced they should try, Jordan clambered to his feet.

"We'll use our phones for light for as long as the batteries hold out."

With renewed vigour, Jordan bounded down the sandy hill, keen to follow the track as far as possible before the sunlight faded away completely.

Firmer than the dunes, the track wound its way along flatter ground, adding to Jordan's newfound hope and enthusiasm, which kept alive even as shadows stretched across their path and consumed the landscape.

Many hours later, under the silvery glow of the waxing moon, Jordan's limbs screamed, and his vision blurred. He shuffled forward, one heavy step after another.

They'd have to rest soon.

His foot caught against something, and he lurched forward, almost losing his balance.

A wooden arch was sticking out of the sand.

Leaning down, he traced the smooth arch with his fingers and discovered a length of fraying rope tied to it with a loop at the other end. Other bits of old rope were scattered across the ground. "What's this doing here?"

"It must be a hitching post. You know, for animals."

Sure enough, further evidence of animals emerged in the dung left behind. At the first signs of civilisation, fresh energy surged through them, and they split up to reconnoitre the vicinity.

Jordan veered off perpendicular to the track, away from the taller dunes. After a dozen or so paces, he stumbled onto solid, rocky ground. A little more exploration and he hit the jackpot. "A well! Jaime, come here. I've found a well!"

Under the light of the moon, Jordan grasped at the manhole-sized wooden cover, and with Jaime's eager help lowered the bucket into the scarcely protruding stone well. He held his breath as they wheeled it down, impatiently listening out for the sound of the bucket hitting water.

Further and further it went, and with it Jordan's hopes of finding water, until finally the rope jerked and went slack. The bucket had reached the bottom, but nothing revealed whether it had reached water or merely the rocky bottom of the shaft.

Hauling the vessel back up, Jordan peered down in silence, hoping they hadn't expended all this effort heaving up a disappointing dirt payload. Then, the sound of sloshing, and he grinned at his friend – their most desperate plea had been answered.

When the bucket emerged, they both grasped at it greedily, almost tipping the water over themselves. Seeing their error, Jordan helped Jaime gulp down a few mouthfuls before taking his share.

The cool, clear liquid hit his parched throat like a gentle caress, revitalising and rejuvenating his body and spirit. When he could drink no more, he splashed the water on his face, washing away the stress of their ordeal.

With his thirst satiated, he lay out on the sand to relax. They had plenty of problems still to face, but they had solved the most important one and were now most in need of a good sleep.

Jaime stretched out beside him. "Have you got anything to carry water with?"

"No, nothing at all, but we can't stay here. I bet there'll be more wells along the path though."

"Hopefully. Perhaps we can find an abandoned bottle in the morning."

"Or some camels," Jordan joked, his optimism in full swing now.

"Yeah, maybe. But now we should rest." Jaime flattened the sand beneath him to make himself more comfortable and Jordan copied.

"The sky is so beautiful. I've never seen so many stars," Jordan said.

"It's because there's no light pollution here. Though I can't find the Plough or Orion and I can usually recognise those."

Jordan searched the sky for familiar constellations, but it all looked so foreign above the dunes.

They must be far from home.

His thoughts wandered back home to his father. Would he realise Jordan was missing? Jaime's family would be out looking for him, worried sick, but it would be a while until Jordan was missed. Normally, that didn't bother him, giving him more freedom than his friends, but right now, he felt more alone than ever.

He peered over at Jaime, glad they were together, but he would have given anything for someone to miss him.

Alice and Emily's parents would be even more worried, especially if Eliot was here, too. Jordan couldn't imagine what the girls might be thinking if they were lost here. However, he could imagine them searching the caves, finding Eliot, and puzzling over their disappearance.

How long would they search for them? They probably wouldn't be that bothered about him, but Alice would search for Jaime. They got on so well that hardly a day went by without them talking.

Jordan rolled onto his side, facing away from Jaime. Jaime didn't know how lucky he was.

CHAPTER 8

North Parsa

Back on the ground floor of the palace, Darien led Alice through a wide corridor with a colourful mosaic floor. Numerous doors lined the outer walls, opening into a variety of small chambers with comfortable furniture, half hidden by an inner row of arches. Fire lamps formed of delicate golden lattices threatened to spill their flame on the polished tiles, though she felt no heat from these.

Oddly, she hadn't seen another person, despite the numerous reception rooms suggesting gatherings were an important part of palace life. Their emptiness exaggerated the unfamiliar and made her feel more awkward about her present company, but the prince behaved perfectly relaxed and not at all like he needed to be elsewhere. Two parts mysterious and one part danger, he was an intriguing guide.

Eventually, they reached the dining hall, and Alice's breath was stolen away. At least four times the size of her school hall, the grandeur of the architecture stood out the most. Huge, gilded columns lined the walls, interspersed with brightly coloured tapestries of all manner of patterns. Not a single one would fit on any wall in her house, but the designs were beautifully ornate and devoid of any person or animal, matching her own style perfectly.

Stained glass doors twice her height filled one wall, flooding the room with a kaleidoscope of natural light. Billowing blue curtains embroidered with gold framed each of the doors, hinting at the pleasant breeze that flowed through the room. Amidst the dry desert air, a faint hint of incense lingered.

Several huge tables dominated the room, all set out ready for banquet. All that was missing was the food and the people. Everything glittered gold, and it rendered her speechless once again.

Amidst the extravagance, loitered a beautiful girl with long ebony hair, and a blue-and-gold gown even more ostentatious than Darien's attire. As soon as she spotted them, her face lit up, and she glided over to join them, her silky dress flowing behind her.

"Good evening, Yasmin," Darien said. "What brings you here so early?"

A wrinkle formed on Yasmin's brow. "You know why I'm here. Why haven't you introduced your new friend?"

Darien grinned mischievously. "Alice, this is my sister, Princess Yasmin. Yasmin, Alice is from a world without magic."

Yasmin's eyebrows rose in surprise. A couple of years older than her brother and a similar height, she had softer, rounder features, but her eyes sparkled where his seemed depthless. "Hello, Alice. It is lovely to meet a friend of my brother. Will you sit next to me this evening?"

"Sure," Alice replied, a little taken aback by Yasmin's eagerness. Were all their people this friendly? Perhaps she had no reason to be suspicious of Darien.

"Forgive her," Darien interjected. "She doesn't get to meet many people her own age, so she can be a little forward." He smiled apologetically, then scowled at his sister.

"You'll need something to wear," Yasmin exclaimed, returning his scowl. "Why didn't you take her to the dressmaker?"

"And spoil your fun?" Darien turned to Alice. "Yasmin is the Royal Mage-in-Waiting, but she adores making extraordinary outfits. She'll make you a beautiful dress in no time."

Alice looked at Yasmin with new respect but had no idea what the title meant. It must be important if a princess held it, but Darien seemed to have the upper hand in this conversation.

"Come with me," Yasmin ordered, gleefully taking Alice by the arm.

Expecting to be teleported again, Alice held her breath, but Darien interrupted. "Where's Father?"

Yasmin's expression turned serious for a moment. "He's in his study working on the treaty." More firmly, she said, "He doesn't want to be disturbed."

Yasmin practically dragged Alice into a nearby cloakroom, though it was about ten times bigger than any cloakroom she'd ever seen, and the walls were draped in a rainbow of shiny fabrics.

Drawers and cupboards all sprang open as Yasmin glanced at them, and fine blue cloth and silks lifted themselves out, swirling about her.

Alice jumped back and stared in wonder, unsure whether it was safe to move from their spot in the centre of the silk tornado.

"What's your family symbol?"

"My what?"

"The sign of your family," Yasmin repeated. "These are mine." She pointed at the various embellishments on her dress. "This one is for the royal family of North Parsa," she explained, pointing at a fierce bushy lion. "And this one is the symbol of the Royal Mage," she continued, indicating a five-point star which shimmered in response to the attention.

Alice admired the designs for a moment, before her face fell. "I don't have one of those."

Taking in her current outfit, Yasmin smiled back at her. "Never mind, I'll make you a dazzling geometric design."

With a few intricate hand movements and some strange, soft rhythmic words, sapphire-coloured cloth wove itself into a full-length gown with a golden belt and golden lace sleeves. The detail of the geometric design above the belt and on the hem of the skirt was exquisite, looking as if it had been hand sewn, with quality that would last a lifetime.

Whilst Yasmin finished off the dress, she kept up a constant monologue on the various insignias of different houses, giving Alice little chance to interrupt. Though difficult to follow, it put Alice's mind at ease.

Still beaming, Yasmin beckoned to a changing screen at the corner of the room. "Go and put it on."

Alice obliged, and it fitted perfectly. "How do I look?"

"Perfect. It compliments your blue eyes and your golden hair. Just one more thing." Yasmin waved her hand once more, and blue ribbons wrapped themselves through Alice's hair in an intricate pattern matching the golden thread in Yasmin's.

Yasmin stood back to admire her work and with a satisfied nod, declared, "Now we're ready for dinner."

As they walked back to the Grand Hall, voices ahead spoke in that mysterious language, raising more questions.

"Yasmin, why is it I can understand you, but I couldn't understand the officer that found me?"

"Oh, that's because he's a commoner. He only knows a few words of the many worlds we encounter. We, of royal blood, can comprehend and speak all languages. All it takes is a small spell." She then uttered something completely incomprehensible and so peculiar it didn't sound like words.

Alice raised her eyebrows. "Was that the spell?"

"Yes, simple, wasn't it?" With a smile, Yasmin, flicked back her hair.

"Totally. So, commoners can't use magic?" She felt herself relax at the revelation. If only the royals had magic, perhaps this entire world wasn't *that* dangerous.

"Of course not, that's what makes them common! Only the royal bloodline and the mages have magic."

Alice grimaced at her prejudice, which seemed so naïve and innocent the way she said it. Should she point out that she didn't possess magic, so was – by her standards – a commoner? Yasmin probably didn't treat the commoners of her world this way.

Deciding to keep her thoughts to herself, she tried to return Yasmin's friendliness.

"How does the officer know my language?"

"We teach all the portal police some basic phrases in every language so they can communicate with travellers from all the known worlds."

"Does that mean other people from my world have travelled here before then?"

"It must do," said Yasmin, smiling. Without any warning, she looped her arm through Alice's and pulled her forward.

Much less apprehensive now, Alice marvelled at Yasmin's infectious joy. And if others had made it here, perhaps the portal wasn't that rare, and it wouldn't be too difficult to make it back home.

Outside the Grand Hall, the voices became distinctive. One she recognised as Darien, but the other was much older. Both seemed to be speaking in English, though the rhythm was slightly off, as if they struggled with the fluency. But Darien had spoken perfectly before. The result must be the effect of Yasmin's spell.

"Don't get distracted," the older voice said.

"I'm not distracted. This is the key to finding the portal," Darien replied.

As soon as they entered the room, the argument stopped. Both men stood near to the door, Darien with his arms crossed and his brows knitted, and the older man with a disapproving look she recognised all too well.

Both their gazes darted to her for a moment, then the broader man turned to Yasmin, whose arm was still linked in Alice's. Darien's eyes rested on Alice for a moment longer, his expression pensive, before he too turned to Yasmin.

What thoughts were swirling behind those eyes? Alice shifted uncomfortably and fidgeted with her new dress. Hopefully, she hadn't been the cause of the argument. She hadn't meant to take up so much of Darien's time.

"Yasmin, my dear. How beautiful you look as always," said the older man, much friendlier now. His scowl evaporated, and his eyes smiled with genuine delight. In his deep-blue tunic, embroidered with golden lions, he looked perfectly at home in the palace, but it was the crown on his head that gave away his position.

The king shared many physical similarities with his children, with the same dark eyes and dark hair, even if it was receding. He was not as tall as Alice imagined a king would be, though he had excellent posture and an air of authority about him.

"This must be your friend Alice. What a splendid gown." He dipped his head to Alice, put an arm around his daughter, and led the way to the high table.

Alice smiled at their close bond, her fears about a formal royal dinner evaporating. Though ... his ability to switch from stern to charming made her wonder if Darien possessed the same ability.

The oversized doors on the far wall were now noticeably ajar, flooding the room with a cool evening breeze, making the fire lamps periodically flicker and dance. Orange streaked across the sky, announcing the setting of the sun and raising a dull buzzing that reminded her of cicadas.

Other official-looking people filed into the room at this point, including Officer Gul, and soon the vast space filled with more than a hundred people, so many in blue, but no more with lions on their clothes.

Seizing her opportunity, Alice sped across the hall, weaving between the incoming guests. Hopefully, Yasmin's spell would now let the officer understand her.

He halted in surprise at her approach, his eyes darting back to the royal group as if questioning whether someone should retrieve her.

"It's Officer Gul, isn't it?" Alice asked.

The man dipped his head. "How may I be of assistance?"

The warm rush of satisfaction coursed through her. Finally, she could have a conversation with him. "Has anyone else from my world come through the portal?"

"None. Are you expecting someone?"

Her heart sank. They couldn't still be searching the caves. They would have found the portal by now. If they hadn't come through here, either they were somewhere else, or they had never found the portal. There was no way that it could exist permanently and there not be regular reports of disappearances. And Darien had said it was a temporary portal.

"Do you know where else they might have ended up?"

"I know a great deal about the portal realm, but the worlds upstream of that portal are difficult to reach. You could find out more about them from the people here."

Alice glanced around at the guests. She couldn't question over a hundred people herself. They probably didn't even know who had arrived on their worlds today.

Darien approached and dipped his head to the officer, who bowed in return. "Navid will send people to search these worlds for your friends," Darien said. "If they are there, they will be found."

Alice stared at him, puzzled. "Navid?"

Darien grinned. "My apologies. Sometimes I forget the company I keep. In formal situations, we address officers and soldiers by their surnames." He nodded to Officer Navid Gul. "I'll have an artist draw their likenesses to share. No one will resist a reward from North Parsa."

Relieved, Alice expressed her thanks and let Darien accompany her back to the royal table. Though it was a little odd that he'd spare people to search worlds for her missing friends and offer a reward. She hadn't even been able to convince her parents to let her stay with her aunt for a couple of years. Was this world that different?

Dinner proceeded promptly with a wonderful display of exotic food, like nothing Alice had ever seen before. Clearly being in a desert restricted neither their appetites, nor their ability to source a wide variety of food. Fish, meat, and vegetables, seasoned to every taste, soon filled the tables, and between them, stacks of fruit arranged in colourful patterns.

All the food was brought out at once, rather than in courses, and diners merely helped themselves to whatever they wanted. No one needed to worry about taking the last of a dish, either. As soon as one emptied, a server replaced it with a full dish almost instantly.

Alice had experienced nothing like it. With so many people on her table alone, she didn't know where to look or listen, finding herself mesmerised by the different people dressed in their finest clothes. So many resembled Yasmin and Darien, but there were others of different races with all styles of hair, though blond seemed to be a rarity.

Not knowing where to start, Alice followed Yasmin's example, taking a small amount from the same dishes as her. Before long, she'd tried a dish resembling orange broccoli that tasted sweet, a cake with seven different coloured layers, and things that looked and tasted like chicken wings – though they were twice as large. When a dish was out of reach, Yasmin would magic one over to her.

"Alice, do you always wear such strange clothes?" Yasmin said.

Alice contemplated what Yasmin would consider strange. All the women in the room wore dresses, so she supposed her tightly fitting jeans would have seemed peculiar. "I suppose so, but they're quite common on my world."

Darien's attention flicked back to her. "How do you make such material? I've seen nothing like it before."

"Er, I don't make my own clothes. Does everyone do that here?"

Darien laughed. "Only Yasmin does that. The rest of us go to the tailor. Is it the same on your world?"

Alice shook her head. "People only go to tailors for formal clothes. Most clothes are machine-made nowadays."

Yasmin narrowed her eyes at Darien, making Alice question whether they knew about machines. There were few signs of technology, but they didn't need it with magic.

Darien leaned forwards to address Alice more directly. "Does your world use machines to make many things? Officer Gul said you had a strange device with you."

Alice nodded. "I was trying to use it to contact my friends, but it won't work here."

"Darien, stop bothering Alice with all these boring questions." Yasmin scowled at him, then turned to Alice. "Tell us about your family and your home."

A wave of guilt washed over Alice. Her parents must have noticed her disappearance by now, but there would be no trace of her. Emily's mother would be worrying even more if Eliot had disappeared, too.

Helping herself to more food before she answered, Alice spent the rest of the meal telling Yasmin about Earth. Darien listened attentively, occasionally interrupting to ask for more detail.

After dinner, keen to continue being a good host, Darien escorted her to grand guest chambers with a view over the courtyard. "If you need anything, pull this cord. My personal server will be happy to find you anything you need."

He paused, looking at her more seriously. "Those clothes really do suit you. Princes from every realm would be fighting for your hand if they saw you."

"Erm, thanks." Her cheeks warming, she couldn't help wondering what the prince of this realm thought of her. Why had he invited her to their formal dinner?

As a final goodbye, he bowed, kissed her hand, and wished her goodnight. Before she could say anything, he disappeared from the room.

With his absence, the emptiness of the vast space yawned at her, the deep-blue walls seeming to absorb all the light. Only the swirling gold border at the top of the tall walls glinted ominously in the firelight.

Suddenly feeling very alone and out of place, she wondered what was wrong with her. Adventure had always called to her, but this was beyond her wildest imagination. Darien was as exotic and mysterious as she could hope for, with an abundance of charm, and both he and his sister were so friendly and energising to be around.

But why had he spent so much time with her, risking the disapproval of his father?

Her mind buzzing, Alice explored her chambers. Beyond the comfortable seating area, she found a room with a huge welcoming bed in the centre, an elaborately carved dressing screen and an ancient-looking bookshelf. With the four posts and silky curtains, the bed was fit for a princess.

Exhausted and overwhelmed, she curled up in the linen sheets. Tomorrow she would find answers, but for now she needed rest. Hopefully, this Royal Mage would shed some light on Darien's enthusiasm to help, as well as locating her friends and a way back home.

CHAPTER 9

DEEP IN THE DESERT

Jordan awoke stiff and cold as the darkness began to abate. Rousing himself from his slumber, he sought an isolated dune to relieve himself, then lowered the bucket down the well to fetch more water. The sun had not yet risen, but a glimmer on the horizon suggested it soon would.

After sipping some water and splashing more on his face, he climbed to the top of a nearby dune to view the spectacle. Slowly, a pale glow streaked across the desert, and a giant silver orb traversed into the sky.

This was no sunrise. Nor could it be moonrise. This was far too big, and the moon still hovered over the other horizon. Jordan stared opened mouthed as the orb became full and a second, smaller, globe joined it.

Electric tingling coursed through his body, and he couldn't help shouting to Jaime.

"What?!" Jaime sat up abruptly, still half asleep. "What's wrong?"

Jordan simply pointed at the second and third moons.

"Oh. We're not on Earth anymore, are we?"

"Guess not." A grin lifted Jordan's lips. This changed everything. "This is awesome!"

"It is?"

"Think about how famous we will be after we tell everyone we've discovered another world!"

"If we find a way back," Jaime said. "And if there is anything to this planet other than desert."

Trust Jaime to bring him back down to Earth, or rather, the planet they now found themselves on. "There are mountains," Jordan argued, but he began to see Jaime's point. His stomach tightened as the reality of their situation set in. If this was a different world, would there be anyone to help them? Would there be any digestible food?

Jaime moved closer. "We found evidence of domesticated animals, so there will be civilisation somewhere. We just have to find it. Come on, let's get back to the track."

"What if they are aliens and they try to eat us?"

"Then we eat them first." With a grin, Jaime pulled Jordan forwards. "Come on."

Jordan nodded. Death by aliens was probably better than starving to death. Half expecting a spaceship to fly overhead, he scanned the horizon for any signs of advanced life, but only a sea of sand stretched out from the distant rocky peaks.

Having rehydrated themselves and discovered a discarded waterskin by the well, they resumed their march through the desert, though nothing would settle Jordan's stomach.

"How are we going to rescue the others?" he asked.

"First, we need to find civilisation," Jaime replied. "So we can figure out where we are and where the others might be. Perhaps we can barter for some camels to search for them."

"Barter with what? All I have with me are the clothes on my back."

"We can offer to do work," Jaime suggested.

"How about you work and I'll go rescue them." That thought cheered him up. Alice would have to go out with him if he rescued her. And if he rescued Eliot, he'd be everyone's hero.

After a few hours of walking, the sun finally rose, distracting Jordan from his thoughts. The nights must be very long on this planet, though he had no idea how long they'd been asleep.

Realising he'd been ignoring Jaime, he started the conversation again. "So, you were gonna tell me about Alice. How do you think she'd like to be rescued?"

"Er, what?" Jaime replied, suddenly finding his sleeves immensely fascinating.

"You know, should I be heroic and self-sacrificing, or should I be super sensitive and be a shoulder to cry on after her terrible ordeal?"

"Er, I dunno. Just be yourself?"

At Jaime's failure to make eye contact, Jordan frowned. "Come on, you're her friend. You should know how I should seduce her. This might be the shot I'm waiting for."

"You've been waiting for us to get lost in a desert on an alien world?"

Jaime was really starting to get annoying, like he was being unhelpful on purpose. Jordan nudged him with his shoulder. "Come on, Jaime, help me out here. Give me a clue."

"I dunno. Alice is my friend. I'd rather not think about her that way." He stopped and turned to Jordan, his eyes pleading.

"But you're my friend, too. Don't you want your two best friends to be happy together?"

"Yeah, of course, but I'm not sure you're right for each other."

Anger and shame heated Jordan's face. Jaime may as well have punched him in the stomach. Especially after he'd already confided in him. "What do you mean, we're not right for each other? You mean I'm not good enough for her, don't you?"

"That's not what I said. You're just … very different people."

"What, because I don't have a perfect family and don't practise archery, I'm too different? I don't have that in common with you either, but you're still my friend. At least I thought you were."

"Of course I'm your friend. You're my best bud. I love hanging out with you and messing around playing video games, LARPing or just chilling in front of the TV."

"Then why won't you help me out?"

"Just drop it, please?"

Fuming now, Jordan continued the trek in silence. With their water long since finished, dehydration and hunger added to his rage. Jaime's words echoed in his head until they twisted into more familiar voices, his father loudest of all. *You're not good enough. You'll never be good enough.*

He tried to reason with the voices. Jaime was his best friend, always there for him. He'd never cared that his dad drank too much and couldn't hold a job, or that there was never any food in the house when he visited. He always watched his matches, joined him LARPing or hung out whenever Jordan needed a distraction.

The only time Jaime wasn't around was when he was fencing or doing archery. Archery. With Alice. It all clicked into place. "You *like* Alice." Even though he'd denied it, it must be the reason.

"No, it's not that," Jaime said, stumbling over his words, his face turning pink.

"Then what?" He had given Jaime a chance to declare his feelings, and Jaime had said nothing, leaving Jordan to make a fool out of himself. He would not let Jaime do it again.

"Well … I'm not sure, okay?" Jaime's eyes darted away.

Rage swelled within him. "What do you mean, you're not sure? You either like someone or you don't."

"Well, I never thought about it before, but after you said you liked her, I sort of started to notice her."

Jordan resisted the urge to shove Jaime into the sand. "You make no sense. You like her because I like her. You're just jealous."

"Maybe that's it," Jaime replied, looking pensive. "But it doesn't matter now. What is important is that we find her and the others and get back home. Then you can ask her how she feels and I'll keep out of it. Okay?"

"Okay," Jordan agreed, not entirely convinced of Jaime's intentions.

Although less angry, they proceeded in silence, though he couldn't help but sneak suspicious glances at Jaime until they came across the next well.

Jaime's oddly timed confession irked him, but didn't dissuade him. Jaime had had years to say something to Alice, if that's how he truly felt, but now was Jordan's turn for some happiness.

The next well was a little larger than the last and was accompanied by some rustic wooden shelters off to one side, easily big enough to house several people. Simple in construction and a little worn, the shelter's promise of shade was a welcome gift. More tracks led off in other directions, suggesting this was a resting stop for different routes.

Desperate for water, they drew up a bucket and patiently shared its contents, though the tension was palpable and the silence between them was deafening, made even more so by the isolating expanse.

After they had their fill of water, they split up to explore the site. There was no sign of any food, but they did find a campfire with spare wood stacked nearby and a few cooking dishes in one of the shelters. Wooden traps stashed in a corner looked like they would catch small animals, but they were unfamiliar in design and there was nothing to bait them with.

"Jordan, I think I've found something," Jaime called from another shelter.

Reluctantly, Jordan went to see what he had discovered.

In the corner of the shelter he'd been searching, Jaime pulled jars out of a cupboard, filled with a clear, gloopy liquid. "Do you think these might be edible?"

Unlabelled and unmarked, they didn't appear to be intended as food, but the boys hadn't eaten in over a day.

"Try it," Jordan said.

Jaime sniffed the jar. "What if it's poisonous?"

"The container would probably be marked if it were poisonous." Jordan reached out for the jar. "Give it here then if you don't want to try it."

"No, I'll test it." Jaime did appear quite sorry as he dipped his finger into the goo. After staring at it for a few moments, he put it in his mouth, then spat it out instantly, disgust written all over his face. "Eugh, that's *revolting*. It's so sticky and sweet, but it tastes horrible. I don't think we can eat that."

Jordan scrutinised him for signs of poisoning. "Do you feel ill?"

"No, it's just an awful taste. I wonder what it's for."

"Perhaps the aliens like it. Let's try it." Jordan dipped his finger into the jar, and without hesitation, sucked the gooey promise. Sickly sweet and with a metallic tang, it tasted far worse than Jaime had indicated. Jordan scrunched up his face and wiped the remainder of the sticky abomination on his sleeve. "Yeah, that's not for people. Now what?"

The sun's scorching rays were impossible to ignore, and he loathed the idea of carrying on in this heat. Without nourishment, he didn't know how much further he would be able to walk.

"Let's rest here in the shelters until it's cooler," Jaime suggested.

"We should keep going until we find food," Jordan argued, though that was the last thing he wanted to do.

"We should rest. There are lots of tracks here, so someone will probably find us and they'll have food with them."

Jordan frowned his annoyance. He should have thought of that. "Yeah, okay. I'll fetch some more water."

Making themselves comfortable in one of the empty shelters, they fell into a restless sleep. The heat disturbed them, making rest difficult, but they didn't have the energy to do anything about it, so they just lay there thinking about how hungry they were.

Hopefully, people would come soon. And they'd be friendly.

CHAPTER 10

NORTH PARSA

Clanking and the scrape of metal upon metal woke Alice the next day. Surprised, she jerked upright. Were they under attack?

Darkness still prevailed, but she felt like she had been asleep for a very long time. Though if they were on a different world, perhaps the nights were longer here.

Curious at the noise, she swiftly pulled on Persian-style baggy trousers and a matching corseted top, both blue and gold – the only choice available in her wardrobe – then darted out onto the balcony.

Below in the courtyard garden, lit by fiery torchlight, two men in full armour fought vigorously with swords. Long shadows flickered around them, making a true spectacle of the scene. The image reminded her of Jaime and Jordan the previous day, though these two men were more different in height and duelled seriously rather than showing off.

They continued for quite some time, parrying back and forth until the larger struck the winning blow. Expecting the fighting to stop, Alice was surprised when they started over again.

As the sun made its appearance, other men soon joined them, filling the courtyard with the deafening clanking of duelling warriors.

Suspecting that Darien might be among them, she headed out into the corridor to make her way down the tower. No sooner had she stepped outside her room than Yasmin appeared before her, resplendent in an elegant deep-blue floor-length dress with a golden embroidered criss-cross pattern. Looking immaculate, she wore her hair in a long ponytail secured with a thick golden band. "Did you sleep well?" she asked.

"Yes, thank you. How did you know I was here?" Already comforted by her friendly face and positive energy, Alice's spirits lifted.

Yasmin smiled back. "Oh, I set a spell on your door. It's easy magic." Entwining her arm in Alice's, she continued. "This way I get to spend some time with you before Darien steals you away."

"Is he one of the men fighting outside? I was just on my way to watch."

"They're only fighting with swords. You don't need to watch that. Come with me."

Alice had no chance to protest before Yasmin teleported her to a new room with no view of the courtyard. Much less official than the dining hall, it had more of the feel of a tearoom, with a few small round tables covered in blue flowery cloths and porcelain plates instead of gold. The walls were fairly plain, painted in ochre, with no tapestries in sight, and small cacti decorated the surfaces.

Disorientated, Alice clutched a chair to steady herself. "Where are we?"

"On the ground floor. Darien might join us when he's finished training. Though sometimes he spends ages fighting in the morning. At least when he doesn't venture off-world."

"He does that a lot?"

Yasmin nodded and pulled Alice into a seat. Immediately, a man arrived to pour them tea, and provided a basket of freshly baked bread and pastries, suspicious in colour and shape. Brightly coloured fruit oozed out of the delicate lattices and twisted creations in a spectacle far too extravagant for breakfast.

Still warm and pleasantly doughy, the bread tasted delicious, but Alice couldn't help but be a little impatient.

"Darien promised to take me to see the Royal Mage today. Do you think he's forgotten?"

A wrinkle formed on Yasmin's brow. "You've only just arrived. You can't want to go home already. We have so much left to talk about."

"I have to know where my friends might be. Eliot is so young. He can't take care of himself."

"The Royal Mage will help you find them," Yasmin said confidently. "He's the most talented mage on all of Parsa and probably in all the worlds. You're so lucky you came here."

Alice's chest tightened. If this mage was so powerful, would he even want to see her? Then again, he couldn't be that much more important than royalty. But why did they have so much free time on their hands? Royalty should have important duties.

"What will you be doing today?" Alice asked.

"I'll be studying, as usual. Magic takes a lot of learning, especially to reach the standard of the Royal Mage."

With little appetite, Alice picked at her pastry. She was about to ask whether Yasmin would take her to the Royal Mage when Darien walked in with another man who looked strikingly similar, though perhaps three or four years older and without any of the natural presence Darien exuded.

"Who's that other man?" she whispered to Yasmin.

"That's our cousin, Prince Javed. He spends even more time training than Darien." Yasmin didn't sound impressed, and quickly returned her focus to her blue pastry topped with orange heart-shaped fruit.

"Good morning, girls," Darien said, joining their table.

At once, more servers appeared to pour tea and deliver fresh pastries.

"I hope you slept well," he continued, looking directly at Alice.

"Yes, fine thank you," she replied, though caught in Darien's gaze, her cheeks flushed even more. Why must he stare at her so intently?

Despite being desperate to ask about the Royal Mage, she supposed she ought to ask about his day first. "How was your training?"

"Ah, I hope we didn't wake you, but we like to start early. There's lots to do today and we need to take you to see the Royal Mage. He's an extremely busy man, but he'll be keen to meet you."

Alice contemplated Darien more carefully this morning as he tucked into his generously proportioned breakfast. Nothing like the boys back home, he was so polite and courteous, going out of his way to help her, yet asking for nothing in return. Even so, there was still an air of mystery about him, but perhaps that was what made him captivating.

Throughout the conversation, Javed quietly observed Alice, but she paid him little attention. He was almost invisible next to his cousin, despite their physical similarities.

"Here, let me pour you some more tea." Filling Yasmin's too, Darien forgot about Javed, who quite happily continued munching through the basket of bread.

"Have you any news of Alice's friends?" Yasmin asked.

Alice smiled at Yasmin, comforted that she cared enough about her concerns despite her not wanting her to leave.

"Nothing yet, but their likenesses have been distributed. If anyone has seen them, we'll soon know. Tell me more about the portal on your world. Has anything changed that might have revealed it?"

Alice shook her head. "The caves were the same as I've always remembered them. There was nothing to explain the appearance of a portal."

Darien glanced at Javed. "It must be a temporary portal, one of the most fleeting. Some follow predictable patterns, but others seem to appear and disappear with no explanation."

Alice frowned. "That doesn't explain why my friends aren't here. They weren't in the caves, so they must have gone through the portal."

Darien surveyed her for a moment, his head tipped to the side, but it was Javed who responded. "They could have ended up in the south."

"A portal that leads to both the north and the south? That's unheard of," Darien said. "Though the portals in the south are not properly monitored. No one can know for sure." He sighed. "It's only a matter of time before trouble finds its way through a portal and we all suffer."

"That's why the treaty is so important," Javed said. "Once I marry their princess and become king of South Parsa, I'll have the power to properly regulate the portals and stop any potential trouble." Javed sat up tall as he spoke, enjoying the responsibility.

Alice's thoughts turned to the walls around the portal and around the city. They must have been built to protect the people from something. "When you say trouble, do you mean invading armies?"

"Potentially. But there are all sorts of people who make use of portals for nefarious purposes. Thieves, corrupt traders, and tax evaders all use portals for their own gain and are all rife in the south." Javed spoke confidently, as if these weren't a problem in the north.

"You will be the best thing that has ever happened to the south," Darien told him.

Alice expected Javed to be pleased by the praise, but he just nodded solemnly.

They talked more about the south as they finished their breakfast, but it sounded terrifying and uncivilised. She could only hope her friends hadn't ended up there. But wherever they may be, she was lucky to have arrived here, in a position to help them.

Darien brushed the crumbs off his hands onto the empty plate. "Would you like time to freshen up or would you like to see the Royal Mage right away?"

"Straight away." The sooner she found her friends, the sooner she could stop worrying.

"Alright. I'm afraid we'll have to walk most of the way up this tower. The Mage Tower is protected against teleportation."

They made their way through the same long hallway lined with arches and numerous doors before they reached another spiral staircase, this one with golden walls that seemed to shift and slide under her gaze. A shiver ran through her as they started climbing, setting her nerves on edge. Unlike the other tower, this one was the opposite of welcoming.

Around and around they climbed, surrounded by an optical illusion that wouldn't stay still. Eventually, she had to reach out to steady herself, and was surprised to find the wall solid under her hand. What was wrong with this tower?

With each step, her annoyance grew, forcing her to contemplate the nature of the man that required his visitors to make this journey just to speak with him. Was he a recluse that never left the tower, relying on his followers to carry out his commands, or was his magic strong enough that he wasn't restrained by the enchantments other mages were?

After what seemed like hours, Darien stopped and knocked on a shimmering golden door with an engraved double-edged star. Before entering, he turned to her and lowered his voice. "The Royal Mage can be a little odd, but as long as you do as he asks, you'll be fine."

Alice's chest tightened again. What was he was leading her into?

A young man dressed in long blue robes greeted them from behind a desk and asked them to wait on a hard wooden bench until the Royal Mage was ready for them. He swiftly returned his attention to the book in front of him as soon as they had seated themselves, focusing so intently he may have forgotten them.

Although his robes reminded her of various fictional wizards, she had expected him to be dressed more ornately, perhaps in a tunic like Darien or many of the guests she had seen at the previous evening's dinner. Despite being near the top of the tower, his robes were relatively plain, only decorated with three golden stars and a simple golden rope belt.

The rest of the room was quite grand, the walls lined with towering bookcases, spilling out books at all angles. Emily would have loved it here.

Beautifully patterned rugs filled the floor, each of them big enough to fill a normal sized room but seeming tiny in this space. In the centre stood a giant gold tree with tiny silver stars hovering above. Nothing appeared to be holding the stars in place, and Alice grinned at this charming use of magic. She could get used to this.

"It's a reminder of the past," Darien said, noting her appraisal. "There used to be two magical cultures, one represented by the gold tree and one by the silver five-pointed star. A long time ago they united and became the gold star that signifies magic in North Parsa today."

Alice resisted the urge to stand up and explore. Even though she wouldn't be able to read the words, she was still fascinated at what might be inside these magical texts. Instead, she tried to find out more from Darien, but he only smiled and told her they could talk about it all later.

Disappointed, she turned her attention back to the mage behind the desk. Sitting here was like waiting to see the headmaster, something she'd had the misfortune to suffer a couple of times. The waiting was all part of the show of power, letting her know what kind of man he was.

Sighing, she stretched her legs. She wasn't going to like this man, but she couldn't let that show, not when she needed his help. She glanced at Darien again, sitting with a serious face and a tight jaw. Surely, as a prince, he had nothing to worry about. Did he?

With her stomach tightening, she wished they'd hurry up.

After what felt like an inordinately long time, the mage stood, and announced the Royal Mage was ready for them, though there was nothing to suggest how he suddenly knew. He escorted the pair up more stairs into a small, comfortably decorated receiving chamber.

The chairs in here were cushioned, a welcome change to the hard bench. However, the room was empty, so she didn't know whether to sit or not. To her side, Darien waited stiffly, his eyes fixed on a curtained archway at the other side of the room.

A few seconds later, an extremely well-dressed man appeared in the archway, towering over everyone. He swept into the room, his dazzling gold-starred cloak billowing behind him, every step radiating power and confidence. Coal-black hair framed his angular jaw, but somehow his eyes were darker, abyssal black staring right through her.

She shuddered and hugged her arms to her chest.

As he glided towards them, the Royal Mage threw a sideways glance at Darien that Alice couldn't decipher. "Welcome, my dear," he said, bending to kiss her hand. "No one told me how beautiful you were."

Although this type of behaviour was flattering from Darien, it was a little creepy coming from this much older, imposing man. However, she was here to get his help, so – resisting another shudder – she pretended to be pleased.

"Come this way. We'll find you a way home in no time."

As Darien started to follow them, the Royal Mage turned back to him with a stern expression. "Don't worry, I'll take good care of her. You can return to your royal business." His mouth twitched. "Unless you would like to stay for a lesson?"

Darien's face fell and, looking as disappointed as Alice felt, he turned around and left without the slightest argument.

Resisting the urge to request him to stay, Alice forced shut her gaping mouth. Why would he accompany her all this way, then just leave?

The Royal Mage smiled at her. "Prince Darien is such a charming boy. It's a shame he isn't so dedicated to his studies."

Alice's cheeks heated. She didn't want to be responsible for Darien neglecting his studies, or getting into trouble because of it. But alone with this man, the words to defend the prince escaped her.

Her tension escalated as she followed the striking man into the next room, a long thin chamber decorated with an array of strange objects perched on a long wooden table. On the wall, a map of the known portals was displayed, though a greater number populated this version. As she moved closer to scrutinise the masterpiece more closely, one of the gold portals disappeared.

Noting her surprise, the Royal Mage moved uncomfortably close. "You've probably seen the basic portal map in the map room of the Royal Tower."

She nodded.

"This one is a little more special and tracks the temporary portals as they appear and disappear. Several mages are tasked with keeping an eye on these portals and reporting back. They are the only ones who can seek out these rarer and often hidden portals before they disappear again."

They both watched the illustration as he spoke, but no more portals appeared or disappeared. He stared at the masterpiece far more intently than Alice, but she supposed each portal was more than a mark on a map to him. She couldn't begin to guess at the worlds they might lead to.

"Can you track the portal I came through?"

Not taking his eyes off the map, he answered, "That's an easy one. You came through this fluctuating portal here." A long thin finger jabbed at one of the gold ovals. "Unfortunately, no one has mapped your world yet. Tell me about your journey. Was the current weak or strong?" He turned his cold, dark eyes on her, fixing her with an intense, disconcerting stare.

Confused at the question, and awkward under his attention, Alice could hardly remember how she had got here.

He turned back to the wall, releasing her from his gaze, and a little breath escaped her. "Reports are you arrived at high speed, so that suggests a strong current. Do you remember how long you were in the portal realm?"

Alice struggled to remember, but it was all just a blur now. "Erm, I'm not sure. It was really disorientating. I felt like I was falling and then I was in this world."

Continuing to contemplate the map, he scrunched up his face. "It sounds as though your world is only slightly upstream from the North Parsan portal then, but that the river is exceptionally turbulent there. It is surprising your friends could have fought against the current and exited somewhere else. The current that leads to this portal can't be fought against. Anyone who tries to venture out from it always ends up being pushed back. Unless there is a fork in the river between our worlds ..."

His eyes gleaming, he sought out a pile of journals, and started rifling through them. After many long minutes, Alice glanced around awkwardly. Did all mages have this ability to concentrate so hard on books they forgot everyone else in the room?

Whilst she waited, she occupied herself by trying to guess the purpose of the curious items on the desk. Made of wood, metal, and crystal, many consisted of complicated moving parts with intricate forms, whilst others comprised numerous dials with exquisite detail etched into their surfaces. No doubt they possessed some magical purpose, but she couldn't guess what any of them were for.

Jaime probably would be able to figure them out, even without any knowledge of magic. He was always building things like this with his brothers. Hollowness crept into her chest. What might he be thinking? He'd always followed her everywhere, but not this time. This time, she had to find her own way back.

She glanced at the Royal Mage, who was completely absorbed in his books, and slumped into a seat. There was nothing she could do but wait. This man had royalty at his beck and call. She might as well be a dust mite in one of his books.

As the minutes dragged on, her eyelids started to droop in the soft, warm glow of the firelight. She saw Emily again, clambering through the caves. Where was she now?

CHAPTER II
NORTH PARSA

With a start, Alice jerked awake, forgetting her location for a moment. The assortment of bizarre contraptions reminded her she was still in the Royal Mage's chambers, but she had no idea how long she had slept.

The Royal Mage still hunched over his books, oblivious to her presence, so she stood to stretch her legs and re-examined the desk. A bowl of purple crystals at the end of the table caught her eye, some as big as her fist, both smooth and jagged.

Contemplating the beautiful jewellery they would make, she picked up a couple of the mid-sized gems. In her hand, they started to glow, and she couldn't help but gasp in surprise.

The Royal Mage snapped his head up, his face contorted in shock.

Alice froze.

"I'm so sorry," he said. "I've been ignoring you for so long. You can't possibly know this, but I think you may have provided proof that the portal river forks somewhere upstream. That would go a long way to explaining why people of common ancestry populated both the north and south of Parsa long before the route through the desert was found."

His eyes moved to the crystals in her hands. "We shall have to visit the portal to be sure, and I'll journey south to confirm if your friends are there, but this could be the beginning of a new era." He paused for a moment, staring intently at Alice. "Now, tell me about your friends."

Alice described them all in as much detail as she could, repeating what she had told Darien, though she couldn't imagine what else he could do if Darien had spread their likenesses to all their neighbours.

His face hardened. "Many people with similar appearances to your friends travel to Parsa through the portals, but I shall find them if they are here."

Alice tried to think what might be different about them compared to the people she had seen. "Emily has green eyes."

He nodded. "That might help."

"What makes you think they could be in the south?"

"A surprising number of portals reach our world. If they are not here and no one we trade with has noticed them, the next logical place to search would be the southern kingdom. Strangers are often reported there."

"Can we go now?"

He shook his head, his eyes still fixed on the glowing crystals in her hand. She hastily returned them to the bowl. "No, I have something I must do first. We can depart tomorrow morning."

Alice gritted her teeth. That would mean she'd be missing another two days. Even she had to feel guilty about that. And her poor sister would have to walk herself home from school. That was something she was truly sorry about, but Natalie would be thrilled to hear about this place. She was just as adventurous as Alice, perhaps even more so.

"Might there be a route back to my world in the south?" she asked.

"Perhaps. There are many routes between different worlds, but I shall know more when I have interrogated the portal. In the meantime, you may stay in the palace."

The thought of that dizzying walk back down the tower, especially alone, had Alice tensing, but she didn't dare argue with the Royal Mage. Her stomach already felt hollow after her light breakfast, so she would just have to brave the journey.

The Royal Mage softened his gaze and spoke in what he must have thought was a kindly tone. "You should call in on Yasmin on your way down. Tell her I have some books for her to collect after dinner." His attention returned to the book in his hand, and Alice smiled as she contemplated how much Emily would love it here.

"Yasmin is in this tower?"

"Yes, as the Royal Mage-in-Waiting, she occupies rooms directly below. The door is unmistakable since it is the only one that bears the royal lion and the mage star."

Relief mixed with disappointment. She'd rested her hopes on this meeting, but for every answer, she had more questions. Hopefully, Yasmin would be more forthcoming with explanations. Ready to leave, she turned.

"Alice?"

She turned back. "Yes?"

"You're vulnerable here without magic. My advice is to stay in the palace. Yasmin will look out for you when I am away."

Not wanting to overstay her welcome in this man's chambers, she exited quickly. In the room where she had waited so long, the mage still read, as if he hadn't moved at all. He just about managed to glance up as she swept past him, then returned immediately to his book.

It didn't take her long to find Yasmin's room, but she paused to admire the decoration before knocking. Below the lion and the double-edged star, three smaller stars gleamed.

After only a few seconds, Yasmin answered, her face instantly brightening when she saw Alice. "Where have you been all day? You can't have been up here that long."

"Yes I have, and I'm starving." Despite Yasmin's normally infectious positivity, Alice remained glum.

Yasmin's face fell as she pulled Alice into the room. "You poor thing. I'll have to scold Darien for leaving you up here all day with no food. I've got some fruit you can have, since dinner won't be for a little while."

Alice gladly helped herself to a pink speckled fruit from the basket, which she already knew tasted a bit like an orange, but without the trouble of having to peel it.

Apart from the table and the chairs, there wasn't much else in the room. Just a bookstand with an open text and a small bookshelf with plenty of space for more volumes. It was the complete opposite to Emily's room, despite the overwhelming presence of books, but Alice supposed furniture would only get in the way of practising magic.

"Shouldn't we head downstairs now, since it will take us so long?"

Yasmin shook her head and leaned close. "Promise you won't say anything, but I found a way around the anti-teleportation spell on this tower."

Alice opened her mouth to promise, but Yasmin was already continuing. "I can only teleport to my chambers in the Royal Tower, and it takes most of my crystals, but it's worth it to save walking up here all the time." A slight scowl shadowed her face. "Actually, it was Darien who told me how. Somehow, he learns all sorts of secrets no one else seems to know. He must know some accomplished mages on some distant world no one visits."

Was that a trace of jealousy in Yasmin's voice? Yasmin quickly moved on. "So ... Did you find a way home?"

"Not yet. It sounds complicated, but the Royal Mage is going to interrogate the portal for answers tomorrow. Then we'll go to the south to see if my friends have turned up there."

Yasmin laughed. "You can't go with him. He'll be teleporting."

Alice's cheeks heated. "He can't teleport me like Darien did?"

"Not that far! It would sap all his magic." She shook her head. "I forget you don't know anything about spells." She took Alice's hand and gave it a squeeze. "It'll be faster and safer for him to go alone. The people there respect him."

Alice nodded, though it sounded odd that he would go to such trouble for her. About as odd as Darien offering a reward for finding her friends. They couldn't be doing this out of charity. There had to be another reason.

Alice searched Yasmin's eyes for answers, but they held only kindness. Tentatively, she asked, "Will the Royal Mage come to my world?"

"Not if it doesn't have magic. But he'll send others. Our worlds can become friends." Yasmin beamed at her. "Perhaps I can visit."

Alice forced a smile. Yasmin would be welcome, but their soldiers less so. And what if their magic did work on Earth? Maybe every claim of sorcery, of witchcraft, of voodoo on Earth was real, they just didn't know the spells these people knew. There had to be a reason Darien and the Royal Mage wanted to find Earth.

"What did the Royal Mage mean about interrogating the portal?" Alice asked.

"There are spells that can predict where portals will lead. The Royal Mage has been to many, so he might recognise the portal to your world. Then he'll be able to find another."

"Can you perform those spells?"

Yasmin wrinkled her nose. "I know the spells. But I haven't been to many worlds. I can only recognise those that link to our kingdom."

Reluctantly, Alice nodded. Her fate was in the hands of this Royal Mage. And perhaps the fate of Earth too. Yet she didn't know anything about these people or whether they could be trusted. For all she knew, they were planning an invasion.

Her curiosity returning to the palace, a question popped into her head. "Yasmin, why is there only a teleportation barrier on this tower and not the whole palace?"

Yasmin gave Alice a pitying look. "Because then everyone would have to walk everywhere and everything would take ages. I can cast the same barrier on my room if I don't want to be disturbed, but it's the anti-spy spell that's most impressive. It washes away all magical disguises and protects our magical knowledge, our most important treasure."

They continued to talk for a while about the differences between their two worlds and palace life, Alice covertly trying to determine their intentions, before Yasmin announced it was time to prepare for dinner. Alice found herself looking forward to the event, keen to understand more of their interactions with other worlds. And Darien might reveal something more.

"We'll change in my royal chambers," Yasmin said. "I've got plenty of material there to make a new dress."

She laid out a selection of purple crystals in a circle, stepped into the middle, then gestured for Alice to join her.

With a small lurch, they disappeared and reappeared in the opposite tower, in a room far more lavish. Still holding Alice's hand, Yasmin led her straight to her dressing room, which comprised at least a dozen wardrobes to fit her extensive selection of clothes. In addition, some partially complete outfits were displayed on several mannequins.

It was only then that Alice understood Yasmin's enthusiasm for fashion. "Don't you have any other colours than blue or gold?" Alice asked, having to glance away from the dazzling mass.

Yasmin's face contorted. "But they're the royal colours. Why would you want to wear others?"

Alice couldn't see an argument against that logic, so tried a different approach. "What if I want to wear a floral design with the actual colours of flowers, or if I wanted to wear an animal print?"

The princess turned her nose up at the sound of animal print, but considered flowers acceptable, and conjured a bouquet for inspiration. "The yellow ones are very pretty, especially if they were to sparkle."

Alice rolled her eyes. "I like the purple ones. Purple is a royal colour on my world."

"Really? I've heard red is considered royal in the south." She picked out a purple flower and twiddled it in her hand. "But you don't want to offend anyone by wearing red. They might mistake you for a southerner. Perhaps some purple would be acceptable since it's obvious you're from a different world."

With her lips pursed, Yasmin concentrated hard on one of the empty mannequins. Silks swept across the room and wrapped themselves around it. A gold bodice emerged, with gold stitching formed into floral patterns.

A blue skirt attached itself to the bodice, then turned deeper and deeper blue until it became a vibrant violet shade. Gold lace sleeves attached themselves to the top and a purple ribbon scooped up a flower from the bouquet and settled around the neck of the mannequin.

"What pattern would you like for the skirt?"

"That's perfect as it is. Why must every dinner be such a formal affair?"

Yasmin stared blankly, as if she'd said they should go to dinner in only their underwear.

Accepting this was the best she was going to get, Alice slipped on the new outfit, which somehow fitted her perfectly again.

"You'll need some shoes, too. Try these." Yasmin indicated some delicate golden sandals with a little purple flower on each.

Without Alice noticing, Yasmin had also changed her outfit into one inspired by her new friend. Although sticking with the traditional blue, the top was a much lighter shade, embroidered with golden flowers, and the skirt was a much deeper blue and as plain as Alice's.

She finished the outfit with a gold ribbon holding a blue flower around her neck and gold shoes with blue flowers to match. After fixing a flower in her own hair and then Alice's, she declared them both ready for dinner and looped her arm through Alice's.

A moment later, they stood outside the Grand Hall in a spacious entry chamber with more doors than walls. A second internal wall made almost entirely of pointed archways obscured the view of all but the nearest doors, giving the room a more private feel. Incense mixed with burning oil emanating from the fire lamps, completing the relaxing atmosphere.

In the dimming evening light, the flickering fire danced across the coloured tiles in a mesmerising pattern, almost as beautiful as the man slipping between the shadows. Pacing slowly, Darien waited for them, his brow furrowed and his eyes vacant, as if lost in thought.

His face brightened as soon as they appeared, and he approached with a spring in his step. "Alice, are you alright? I didn't know he'd keep you there all day."

"She's fine, no thanks to you," Yasmin intervened with a scowl. "She was starving after you left her there."

Darien frowned. "You know what Uncle is like. There's no arguing with him when he tells you to leave. I'm sorry." He flashed Alice an apologetic smile and Alice smiled back, before his words sank in.

The Royal Mage was their uncle? He looked little like the king, so he must have been their mother's brother.

"You should be nicer to him," Yasmin continued. "He's always kind to me."

"That's because you're his precious protégée."

"If you studied more, he'd think the same of you."

Even though Yasmin was defending her, Alice sympathised with Darien. Yasmin seemed to spend all her time studying, and she couldn't blame Darien for wanting to do other things with his time. After all, he could teleport and conjure fire. What more did he need to do?

"If you say so." Darien sighed. "Come on, dinner is waiting for us."

Yasmin crossed her arms. "You've been off-world again. Admit it."

Darien flashed a grin. "Only for a short while. I had to check a few worlds for Alice's friends, didn't I?"

"Did you find them?" Alice asked.

"Sadly not, but many are now looking out for them. It won't be long before they are found."

Her heart sank as they made their way across the hall. But at least some worlds had been ruled out.

Again, the table seated many official-looking people, but this didn't stop Yasmin and Darien arguing. It reminded Alice of her own squabbles with her sister. Apparently, being royal didn't change that.

"You know you stopped studying as soon as you earned your third star," Yasmin accused.

"Third star?" Alice echoed. "Is that something to do with the three stars on your door?"

"Yes, that's right," Darien said. "We're both three-star level mages, but Yasmin is studying for her fourth and will earn her fifth when she becomes the Royal Mage."

Yasmin glared at him. "You could easily earn your fourth if you studied more. You're just lazy."

"I'm not lazy. I have more important things to do. Besides, I don't think the examining board were too happy with the spells I used in my last examination."

"That's because you're supposed to learn the spells you're taught, not invent new ones," Yasmin snapped.

So involved in their debate, the siblings hadn't touched the food in front of them and Alice had to reach for dishes, rather than have Yasmin summon them for her. She hadn't a hope of getting a word in to ask Darien about his other activities.

As she observed his interactions with Yasmin, Alice's previous concerns about Darien started to evaporate. Despite their magic, they were still a normal family. Maybe more normal than her family had become lately. If only her sister was here, she might feel more at home. But she might even enjoy getting to know this family better while she was stuck here, and knowing more about them and this place could only help understand their intentions for herself and Earth.

Darien sighed his exasperation. "I didn't invent them. I just had a broader learning experience. Anyway, three stars are good enough for me. Father only has three."

Curious why she hadn't noticed before, Alice looked over at the king as he conversed emphatically with Javed, but he didn't display any stars either. Evidently, magic wasn't equally important to everyone, and perhaps explained why Darien had a slightly different attitude from Yasmin.

Javed met her gaze, and she felt a little guilty for staring, until he smiled. His attention turning to Yasmin and Darien, he shook his head and rolled his eyes, as if this was a common occurrence.

Reassured, Alice reached out for a dish containing some intriguing purple vegetables. She couldn't quite reach, but the dish floated towards her outstretched hand. She turned back to Javed to thank him, but his attention had already returned to his conversation with the king.

"But Father doesn't have our magical heritage," Yasmin went on. "Mother had four stars and could have earned her fifth if she hadn't died so young."

Keen to get a word in, Alice quickly spoke. "What do you mean, your magical heritage?"

Yasmin glanced at the Royal Mage, before turning to Alice. "Our uncle possesses extremely strong magic in his blood, much stronger than the typical North Parsan. Our mother had it too, so we both should have it." She stared pointedly at Darien.

Darien too looked at the Royal Mage, then said flatly, "Only the Royal Mage ever earns five stars."

"She could have earned five stars," Yasmin replied defiantly, ending the argument.

Alice frowned. It was clear from Darien's tone that there was only ever one Royal Mage and that was synonymous with achieving five stars, but Yasmin didn't seem to want to hear that. Perhaps their mother could have chosen to be the Royal Mage instead of queen. Or perhaps that's what Yasmin had wanted her to choose, just like her.

Dinner proceeded with more competitive conversation, so Alice joined in with Javed's discussion instead. They were talking about a recent battle Javed had been leading.

"So, the world is prepared to submit to North Parsan rule?" the Royal Mage enquired, fixing Javed in his intense gaze.

Unfazed, Javed replied confidently, looking him straight in the eye. "Yes, they have ceased all hostilities and pledged their support to North Parsa."

Not imagining Javed was old enough to lead an army or be this relaxed around the man who clearly made Darien nervous, Alice found new respect for Javed, but she worried about the type of place she had ended up. Were they a race of conquerors?

Concerned, she leaned forward. "Was there a lot of fighting?"

Javed shook his head. "Don't worry about us North Parsans. We can handle ourselves in a battle." He straightened, and his voice gained enthusiasm. "Besides, as soon as they saw our disciplined army, they were much more open to peace talks. I succeeded in negotiating terms beneficial to both our worlds. They won't be attacking our trade convoys anymore."

Alice nodded, relieved to hear they only attacked in self-defence.

"Good work, Prince Javed," the Royal Mage praised. His eyes hovered on Alice for a moment, so she quickly looked away before he asked her about battles on her own world.

CHAPTER 12

North Parsa

After dinner, before she could even stand, Darien appeared beside her, a gleam in his eye. "Alice, would you care to join us for a more intimate gathering?"

Yasmin wrinkled her nose. "Alice doesn't want to spend her evening listening to boring diplomats."

Alice opened her mouth to object, but Darien was already replying. "Not all our guests are boring, and Alice might enjoy hearing a little of worlds new to her."

"I would," Alice interjected, and Yasmin pouted. This might be the perfect opportunity to hear what other worlds thought of the North Parsans and whether they could be trusted.

Beaming his delight, Darien held out his arm. "Allow me to escort you." With a hint of impatience, he said to Yasmin, "Father would be pleased if you joined us, Yasmin."

Yasmin's pout turned into a scowl. "No mages ever attend these things, but if Alice wants to go, I will accompany you." Ignoring

Darien holding out his other arm, she strode ahead, scattering people out of her path in their haste to make way.

Darien shook his head. "I hope all princesses aren't like this."

Alice couldn't help grinning as he guided her into the corridor, then through one of the archways to a nearby chamber.

Much smaller than the Grand Hall, this room had few seats, but elegant tables with leaf-engraved legs were scattered around the room, allowing people to gather whilst standing. Soft satin drapes hung from the ceiling, intermingled with pale green vines sporting a vibrant mix of purple, red and yellow flowers. Only the walls remained sapphire, with the occasional splash of cerulean mixed in with the white floor tiles.

Still wearing a scowl, Yasmin stood beside one of the nearer tables, ignoring all others in the room. Most knew well enough to leave her alone, not even sparing her a glance, but Officer Gul looked like he might be summoning the courage to attempt to talk to her.

"Excuse me," Darien muttered before leaving Alice with Yasmin. He made his way over to Officer Gul, probably to stop him doing something he might regret.

"I might be wrong," Alice said, "but I think the point of these gatherings might be to talk to people."

"There's no one here worth talking to." Not bothering to hide her frustration, Yasmin cast her gaze around the room. "Those two are traders, trying to get a better deal whilst our head trader is away." She turned her nose up at the two men dressed in smart yellow tunics chatting at the back of the room. "It won't work. All those" – she swept her gaze across one side of the room – "seek my father's favour or assistance. Either in gold, magic, or soldiers, for some pointless pursuit." Her scowl deepened as her gaze settled on several well-dressed men and women talking beside the window. "Don't even go near those. They are here to find an advantageous marriage. None of them have a drop of magic."

Alice nodded, mostly to humour Yasmin, though the traders looked like they might bring interesting news. Unfortunately, they probably wouldn't talk so freely with Yasmin around. "What about Officer Gul? Where does he fit in?"

"He works for my father. Sometimes he has news." She sighed. "Darien enjoys talking to him."

Apparently not for very long, since Darien was already on his way back, with something in his hand.

"Not another gift," Yasmin exclaimed as Darien handed it to her. "What does that commoner think he's going to achieve?"

Darien glanced at Alice, but to her relief he didn't point out the obvious. "You don't know the power of your beauty. You should go and talk to him. He could tell you wonderful tales of all the worlds he's visited. You're always asking me about my travels and complaining about being stuck in the palace."

"I'm not going to talk to a commoner without an ounce of magic." Yasmin huffed.

Disappointed in missing out, and in Yasmin, Alice frowned. Why was Yasmin so accepting of her, when she clearly had no magic? Did Yasmin secretly think less of her? If she did, why had she joined them tonight?

"Not even one who can secure you a blue crystal?" Darien unwrapped a cloth to reveal the gift, a smooth oval gem, the perfect size for a pendant.

A gasp escaped Yasmin's lips, despite her attitude, mystifying Alice. Was there something special about the colour? They did prefer blue, but surely a princess could obtain all the crystals she wanted.

"Magic isn't everything, Yasmin. There's so much more the worlds have to offer."

"It doesn't matter. I can only marry someone of my class," she argued in her haughty tone, though she still stared entranced at the blue crystal.

Curious why Yasmin would jump to such a conclusion, Alice glanced at Darien, but he didn't seem that surprised. North Parsan society was going to take a little getting used to.

"I didn't ask you to marry him, only to talk to him. Besides, who could match your class?" Not at all bothered by Alice's lack of magic, he winked at her. The two siblings couldn't have been more different.

Yasmin crossed her arms. "I'm not going to talk to him and you can tell him that he can't buy my affection with gifts, no matter their value."

"I'm not going to do that. You'll have to tell him that yourself. He at least deserves that."

Confused, Alice edged closer to Yasmin. "You have so many crystals already. Why is that one so valuable?"

"Not blue ones. They're so rare and so powerful. They can enhance and hold a spell indefinitely." Unable to give it up, Yasmin turned the crystal in her hands, evoking a cool glow. Until her father ventured over with a foreign diplomat, and she hid it within her dress.

With a warm smile, the king dipped his head to Alice. "I hope you don't mind if I borrow Yasmin for a little while. Darien, why don't you introduce Alice to some of our other guests?"

"I'd be delighted." A slight smirk flickered across Darien's face at Yasmin's misfortune as their father whisked her away. "Who would you like to meet?"

"Actually, I'd rather ask you something about Yasmin."

"Just one thing?" Darien smiled. "There are so many things *I* want to ask about Yasmin."

Instantly at ease, Alice leaned one arm on the table and viewed the room. Yasmin was right about mages not joining them. Those who remained were mostly the senior portal police, soldiers, and foreigners.

"If Yasmin is curious about other worlds, why does she spend all her time in the palace refusing to talk to commoners?"

Darien chuckled. "You noticed that already? Yasmin has a very close relationship with our uncle and thinks the best way to become the next Royal Mage is to spend all her time studying and obeying all the rules. Royals aren't supposed to go wandering off without escorts and mages rarely talk to commoners."

Alice frowned. "But don't you do that?"

"Part of being royal means talking to everyone, regardless of whether they are a mage or not. As for wandering off, I guess I'm naturally rebellious and don't mind getting into trouble so much. There's so much to see and learn on other worlds and the people are so fascinating."

Shuffling closer, he lowered his voice. "None as fascinating as you, though, Alice. I am so lucky that you fell through the portal and Officer Gul brought you to the palace."

Alice blushed. He couldn't mean that. He was just being polite. But it was hard not to be captivated by what he might have seen. "You must have met so many people with all the portals here. I can't be that interesting."

"I have. But none have settled in so well, nor gained Yasmin's confidence. You don't seem to be impressed by Officer Gul's gift, though. Do you have many such crystals on your world?"

Alice shook her head. "We have gems and crystals. They're rare and expensive, but that's nothing compared to magic."

Darien nodded. "It seems likely that magic doesn't work on your world, but whatever suppresses it doesn't alter crystals permanently. They could be magic without you realising it."

The thought of magic hidden just beneath the surface was nice, but just a little too hard to believe. Parsa was a world with its own rules. Back home, crystals no more possessed magic than people could cast fire.

"If only you could remember how you got here, how many portals you passed on your route."

"I'm sorry. It was all a blur."

"Never mind. We'll find you a way back. Until then, you'll receive the best hospitality you'll find anywhere."

A middle-aged man in a smart blue tunic with four stars sauntered up behind Darien, his most striking feature an odd red scar that resembled vines running up his neck and onto his cheek. "That is a generous offer indeed." He dipped into a low bow. "Your highness. My lady, I don't believe we've been introduced."

"Ahmad, this is Alice, my guest in the palace. Alice, this is Ahmad, the head of the magic school."

Dipping awkwardly into a curtsey, Alice returned the greeting. "It's a pleasure to meet you, sir. There's a magic school?"

Ahmad's eyes flashed with amusement. "Of course. Where do you think we learn all our magic?" His eyes darted to Yasmin, still talking with her father and the foreign diplomat across the room. "We don't all benefit from direct lessons from the Royal Mage."

Alice's cheeks heated. "I'm sorry. I didn't mean–"

"No offence taken. You should visit sometime. I'm sure Prince Darien would be happy to escort you."

Darien's brow contracted. "I don't think the magic school is the best place to tour."

"Nonsense. You are welcome anywhere in the kingdom, and your guests will be treated with the utmost respect."

"Not all mages are as welcoming as you, Ahmad. And the Royal Mage wouldn't approve of our magic becoming an attraction."

Ahmad edged closer, peering at her intently. "So it *is* true. You don't possess magic?"

Resisting the urge to shrink back from this peculiar man, Alice replied confidently, "No one on my world does."

"How strange." Ahmad's brow wrinkled. "I could have sworn I detected a flicker of magic in you. Never mind. Magic isn't everything. And this one ..." He beamed at Darien. "He can show you more than enough. Though" – he lowered his voice – "the Royal Mage doesn't run the magic school. It wouldn't be the first time you've defied him."

Darien stiffened. "You should be the last person to encourage that."

Ahmad rubbed the marks on his neck. "Don't let this dissuade you. I fully deserved this punishment."

Alice swallowed heavily. It would be interesting to visit a magic school, but she didn't want to make things difficult for Darien. And if that's what the Royal Mage was capable of, she didn't want to invoke his temper.

She shook her head. "I really don't need to visit the magic school. All I want to do is find my friends and a way home."

"No doubt the prince and the Royal Mage have that in hand. No others have better knowledge of the portal realm."

Alice nodded. "The Royal Mage has agreed to search in the south for them." Though it didn't appear that he was making any arrangements.

Ahmad raised an eyebrow and glanced at Darien. "The south? How could that be?"

Darien shrugged. "We don't know enough of the portal realm. It could be possible."

"Fascinating. Well, if they are in the south, the Royal Mage is the man to find them. You may as well enjoy yourself whilst you wait. And you couldn't be in better company." Curiosity in his eyes, Ahmad edged closer and lowered his voice again. "What did you think of him, our Royal Mage?"

Caught off guard by the question, Alice tensed. "I don't have much to compare him to. I'd never met a mage until yesterday." Sucking in a quick breath, she straightened. "Princess Yasmin has full faith in him. I'm sure he'll be able to find a way to my world."

"Well said." Ahmad agreed with a nod. "Only here two days and yet you fit right in. You've even coaxed Princess Yasmin away from the solitude of her studies. A rare thing indeed."

Heat rushed to Alice's cheeks. She didn't have an answer for that. "I haven't spent that much time with her. I'm sure she spent most of the day studying in solitude."

"Oh, you misunderstand me. It's good to see the princess away from her books and her uncle. There's more to life than studying. Which reminds me ..." He held out a hand and a bottle appeared in it, filled with pale yellow liquid. A moment later, three glasses appeared on the table. His eyes sparkling, he began to pour. "This is one of my most recent concoctions."

Before he could pour the second glass, Darien blocked his hand. "She's not a mage."

Ahmad hesitated before withdrawing the bottle. "You're right of course. But surely you would like a taste, your highness?"

"Not tonight. Perhaps another time."

Ahmad dropped into a low bow. "As always, if there is anything I can do—"

"I know where to find you."

With the sweep of his cloak, Ahmad backed away and joined another group, all looking delighted to speak with him.

Darien grinned sheepishly at her. "Sorry about him. He means well, but he is accustomed to mages."

"He seemed nice enough. What was in the bottle?"

Darien shook his head. "You can never truly know what Ahmad mixes in his concoctions. Best to save them for special occasions." With a casual gesture, he waved over a server, who poured them two glasses of clear liquid. "This is perfectly safe and perfectly agreeable."

Alice sipped at the cool liquid, pleasantly surprised by the subtle citrus flavours and the tingling of her lips. Unlike anything she'd tried before, every sip changed, one moment bursting with blueberries, then another a milder passionfruit.

For a short while, she forgot her worries, then curiosity about Ahmad resurfaced. "What did he do to receive that scar?"

Darien's expression turned serious. "He's had it many years. Since around the time of the death of my mother. But no one knows what he did to offend my uncle. He had it before the battle."

A lump formed in Alice's throat. "I'm sorry about your mother. Was she killed in the battle?"

Darien nodded. "Enemy mages sneaked into the palace and killed Javed's parents, but my mother decided to fight. Not even my uncle could stop her being killed."

"I'm sorry," Alice said quietly. The shadows seemed to stretch out to her, an echo of the horrors that had previously infiltrated this place. "What happened to the enemy?"

Darien shrugged. "No one knows. All the survivors vanished. No one saw which portal they used. It's what they do. Every now and again they return and try to take the city, but they've never succeeded." Darien's expression hardened. "One day we'll find them."

"What if they come back first?" Alice said softly. She didn't want to be involved in a war.

"We're ready for them." He glanced up to find Ahmad waiting patiently a few steps away.

Ahmad dropped into a low bow. "Your father would like to speak with you, my prince."

Darien nodded. "I'll be back as soon as I can."

Ahmad smiled at her. "How are you finding our gathering?"

"Darien was just telling me about an enemy that attacked the palace."

"The Iybryrians? Yes, they are quite persistent. I hope they don't pay us a visit during your stay."

Alice's eyes widened. "Could that happen?"

"They haven't attacked in many years. Kavir decimated their army last time they tried. That's enough to dissuade anyone for a while."

"Kavir?"

"Our Royal Mage. He keeps us all safe." Ahmad inhaled deeply. "Though I fear even he won't stop them forever."

"But how can they have disappeared without a trace?"

"Most likely a portal hidden in the desert. Perhaps a temporary one. Sadly no one has calculated a pattern between their visits."

Alice repressed a shudder. At any time, these people could return, and no one could keep them out. She'd be totally helpless if they made it inside the palace.

A wrinkle formed on Ahmad's brow. "I hope I haven't scared you. With any luck, you'll never have to see them."

She shook her head. "I'm sure I'll be gone long before they return. If you don't mind, I'd like to talk with those traders before they leave."

"As you wish. It has been a pleasure, Alice."

Glad for the opportunity, she headed straight over to the pair who were still deep in conversation. However, on Alice's approach, the older woman glanced up. "Alice, isn't it? How may we be of service?"

Alice frowned. That wasn't the response she was expecting. "Are you from a different world?"

The woman dipped her head. "It would take two days and three portals to reach our world. Are you interested in visiting?"

"Do you receive visitors often? I'm looking for some missing people."

The man ran a finger along his chin. "We are aware. There's quite an award offered for them. You must be from an interesting world."

"There's nothing interesting about my world," Alice replied. "It doesn't even have magic. Why would you say that?"

The man shrugged. "Princes don't offer rewards for all lost people." He edged closer. "Unless *you* are the interesting one."

Her throat tightened. "Why would the prince be interested in me? There's nothing special about me."

The woman lowered her voice. "There must be. Can you think of nothing these people want from you?"

Alice shook her head. "They haven't asked for anything." She stepped closer. "Does North Parsa run your world too?"

The woman laughed. "Of course not. They may think they are at the centre of the universe, but they have no say in our world."

"They're not South Parsans," the man said coldly. "They're the ones you want to worry about invading your world. If there's something valuable there, you'd do well to form an alliance with the northerners."

"Can they be trusted?"

The man glanced around the room. "That depends on what you have to trade. If you've no magic, your world will probably be ignored. Unless there's something else interesting about it ..."

Alice gulped. Tomorrow, the Royal Mage might know the location of her world. And then she'd find out for sure what these people were after.

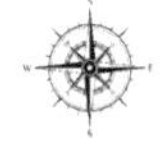

CHAPTER 13

North Parsa

By her third day in this desert world, Emily was allowed to leave the house to fetch water and groceries, though these were bought on credit since she was never trusted with money. However, now she could leave the house, she had much more freedom to explore and search for Eliot when her mistress was out.

Focusing on Eliot also kept her distracted from her situation. Although she had food and shelter, the house was far from home, and the inhabitants far from family. She could only imagine how much her parents were worrying, but that only drove her on. There was no going back without Eliot.

None of her neighbours had seen or heard about her brother, so she resorted to asking anyone she met. The marketplace was always a hive of activity, though she had no good news yet.

"How are you settling in?" the grocer enquired.

"Fine," Emily replied. "Everyone is friendly."

He smiled at her and lifted up a basket of brightly coloured fruits. "These are yours for six coins if you tell me your name."

Emily smiled back. It was a good offer, but she wasn't here to flirt. "I'll give you seven coins for them if you can tell me where someone might be taken after arriving through a portal." As she realised she had no coins of her own, she bit her lip. Hopefully the grocer wouldn't itemise her expenses.

"All newcomers are brought to the market square." He glanced around before moving closer. "Unless they are interesting enough to be taken to the palace. You don't want to worry about those though. They're only trouble."

Emily's heart leapt at the first good news in days, but as his words sank in, her stomach tightened. "What do you mean? Please tell me more."

"It's best to forget about them," he said, moving away.

She followed him along the row of haphazardly displayed groceries. "Please, I need to know more. It's important."

The grocer's voice softened. "Have you lost someone?"

"My brother. He's not trouble. He's only little."

The man scratched his jaw. "That is odd. There is a rumour about a newcomer at the palace, but I must confess I haven't paid attention to the stories."

"Is there anyone else who can tell me?"

"There is an infrequently used well a few streets from here. If you go there just before noon, I will arrange for someone to meet you." As she turned to leave, he called out to her. "Wait! You didn't tell me your name."

She smiled. "I'll tell you tomorrow, after I've met your contact."

He shook his head, laughing, before turning serious. "Don't get your hopes up. People who are taken to the palace aren't always seen again."

Emily nodded, but her stomach twisted at the thought of what that might mean for Eliot.

Emily arrived at the well with plenty of time to spare. She took a seat on the hard stone wall and brushed the sand from her skirt, lamenting the lack of comfort in this city. Despite the closely packed buildings and the regular sweeping, the sand got everywhere.

Desperately missing her books, she fidgeted uncomfortably, and her mind drifted to Eliot. What would the palace want with him?

Perhaps he was too young to work off his portal tax, so they had arrested him straight away. Or maybe he had tried to escape and been apprehended. Or maybe he wasn't here at all and had fallen in the caves. He could be lying in the dark with no one to help.

She shivered and forced herself to think more positively. Soon she would have an answer. She just had to wait for the contact to arrive.

Before long, a middle-aged woman approached, her long brunette hair carefully twisted around golden pins with blue butterflies. She was dressed in grey, like Emily, but her outfit appeared more stylish and expensive, made of a silky, shiny material rather than Emily's itchy wool-like fabric.

"You're the troublemaker looking for the off-worlder," the woman stated, without introducing herself. "Why are you interested?"

"I'm looking for my little brother. I think he may have travelled here before me."

"Oh, a boy. Then you're no trouble at all. The newcomer everyone is talking about is a girl with yellow hair. Rumour is she's from a powerful world that could destroy us all. The mages are taking it very seriously, but she's under the protection of the prince at the moment."

Emily tensed at Alice's description, alarmed people thought her dangerous. It might not be a good idea to admit to knowing her. "How do you know all this?"

"My employer works in the palace. She's a two-star mage. All the talk has been of this girl and her companions. The Royal Mage himself has travelled to South Parsa to search for them."

"There were others?" Emily pressed, her hopes surging at this new information.

"Apparently. No one is sure, though. If they came through a portal in the south, it must have been one of the temporary ones that open in the wilderness. Even the Royal Mage can't scour the entire desert. My employer is worried about having to travel there to help in the search, but if these people are scouting Parsa to attack, they need to be found."

"Can a portal lead to here and the southern desert?" Terrified of the answer, Emily held her breath. There was no way Eliot would be able to survive in the desert alone. And if Alice was here, then it would be up to Jaime and Jordan to find him and look after him.

Her stomach churned at the thought of Jaime coping on an alien world amongst unfamiliar people, but with Jordan, they might be alright. Eliot had really warmed to him, and Jordan's confidence set everyone at ease.

"Not likely. There's no known route between North Parsa and South Parsa through any portal. These dangerous off-worlders must have arrived through different portals or possess advanced knowledge in navigating the portal realm."

Emily exhaled with relief, but confusion replaced her concern. If officials were searching in the south, there had to be a possibility Eliot could have ended up there. There must be something special about the portal from Earth that meant it could lead to both kingdoms, but this woman wouldn't be able to tell her more about that. "Do you think my brother could have ended up somewhere else in North Parsa?"

"Perhaps he was taken to the palace for questioning. If the mage on duty decided he was suspicious, he would have teleported him straight there. You'll just have to wait to see if he is released."

Emily's mind flashed back to her arrival and the odd man in blue. She'd been sure he wasn't a soldier, so he must have been the mage on duty. He hadn't been there when she'd arrived, so that fitted – he'd teleported Eliot to the palace, then returned later.

Or it could have been someone else … But this was her best hope yet. She had to believe that's what had happened to Eliot.

"How do I get to the palace to look for him?"

"You can't go to the palace uninvited," she said with scorn. "Even mages must earn two stars before they're allowed to study in the palace." She looked down her nose at Emily as she spoke, and the extent of her undertaking started to become clear.

"Then what can I do to find him? I can't just do nothing."

The woman narrowed her eyes, as if summing Emily up. "You would be better off waiting, but if you're desperate, the only way in is to gain work with a two-star mage. All other jobs are reserved for mages and members of loyal families. Do you have any particular talents?"

"Erm, I'm good with languages."

"What use is that to a mage? Any mage can cast a spell to understand any language anyone speaks."

Emily deflated, her eyes dropping to the ground. What else could she do?

"Look," the woman said with a softer expression. "There's a mage library inside the town walls, if you can get there. Lots of one-star mages visit and occasionally higher levels."

"Thank you. I'll try there." It would cost more than Emily could scrounge to pay the tax to pass through to the centre of the town. However, not far from where she resided, a gap in the wall permitted her neighbours to sneak through. Concealed by the buildings, it was small and unknown to the guards, therefore little risk.

After a few dead ends, Emily finally found her way to the library. The directions had not been easy to follow, and she'd grazed her hand climbing through the gap in the wall.

But she'd made it.

Even if she looked a little bedraggled and her clothes now stuck to her. There just was no relief from the heat, no matter where she went.

At first, she'd almost missed the library. Squeezed in between the other buildings, it didn't look impressive from the outside, but as soon as she stepped inside, she was overwhelmed, immediately forgetting her dishevelled state.

An enormous cavern opened out before her, with the five upper levels open at the centre. Bookshelves towered across every wall and smaller cases lined the balconies. Craning her neck, she tried to figure out how many books filled this outwardly unassuming building. There must have been hundreds of thousands of volumes, purely devoted to magic.

On the ground floor, chunky walnut tables spread across the room in a disorderly fashion, with books strewn across them. Some were being used by the visitors, but other stacks looked completely abandoned.

For a moment she forgot her reason for being here, swept up in the secrets she could learn. Captivated, she walked further into the room, only to be interrupted by a rude old man.

"Can I help you?" he asked, in a tone that clearly suggested he was not offering assistance. He'd taken one look at her ugly grey robes and decided she didn't belong there. "Only mages are permitted in the mage library. Unless you are here to collect a book for your master?"

"Yes, that's why I'm here," she answered, desperate not to be kicked out.

The old man didn't look at all threatening in his faded blue robes, but she didn't want to risk being barred from her only route to the palace. Besides, she had already fallen in love with the library and longed to run her fingers over its intriguing volumes.

"Is that so?" The old man cast his eyes over her outfit. "What is the name of the book?"

Quickly glancing at the nearest table for a title, she selected a simple text. "Magic in Cooking," she replied, as assertively as possible.

He glanced at the book, raising an eyebrow.

Emily's heart fluttered. He didn't believe her.

"You can read this?" Picking up the book, he scrutinised her so intently his nose wrinkled.

She nodded, her cheeks warming.

He pointed at another three random books. "What are those called?"

After she had correctly answered each question, he peered at her with even more suspicion. "Who are you?"

"I'm Emily. I arrived in Parsa recently."

"How is it a common labourer can read magical texts?"

Luckily for her, the language was not that different from the Farsi she'd been studying for the last several years and it was much easier to read than speak, but she wasn't going to tell him anything about Earth. It probably wasn't a coincidence that this culture was so familiar, but it must have deviated many centuries ago. In that time they'd forgotten about Earth and portals had become more rare.

"I only became a labourer because I had no money to pay the portal tax. My arrival was an accident. I'm actually looking for work."

His frown relaxed. "Do you serve mages on your world?"

"Oh yes," she lied. "I organise the books for the library there."

He nodded. "You'll have to tell me about it sometime. I thought I knew all the worlds with libraries."

"Oh, it's not a large library, nothing like this," she said in her most flattering tone. "This is the best library I've ever been in."

"Of course it is. This is North Parsa. This library is second only to the palace library. And don't even think about that one. You would have to be a two-star mage just to enter."

He paused, looking at the messy tables in disgust. "We could do with extra help tidying up this place. Mages just don't respect the library anymore and never bother to put anything away. I can only pay you a few silver coins a week, mind. Donations are a little low this year."

"That's plenty," Emily replied enthusiastically. Even if she weren't using the position to find someone to help her get into the palace, she would have worked here for free. With her accommodation and food covered, she would save her earnings for the portal tax back home, though she had no idea what that would cost.

"Good, you can start straight away. Go and sort out that pile before it topples over and crushes someone." He pointed at a stack of books currently defying gravity with their height.

Emily worked diligently for the rest of the day, completely skipping lunch. She made a note of texts that looked interesting but didn't dare to stop to read during her first day.

Whilst she worked, she kept an eye out for any two-star mages, but she didn't know how to identify one yet. Most of the visitors dressed in simple blue robes, with the occasional variation in colour and the infrequent dress or tunic, but none stood out. However, she was in the best place to find answers to her questions, and that knowledge spurred her on.

She couldn't help but feel that the old man was watching her, but no one else took the slightest bit of notice. They almost went out of their way not to make eye contact.

At first, she wondered how anyone located anything in the dishevelled stacks, but eventually observed the mages casting spells to summon the texts they required. This didn't appear to help when they were looking for more obscure knowledge, though, which kept the old librarian quite busy.

Late that afternoon, Emily was busy filing books away on the upmost floor when a relatively young woman started screaming hysterics.

"What do you mean you don't have the book? I came all the way from the palace. I have important things to do!"

Emily peered over the balcony to see the librarian bow his head. "I'm sorry. All copies are currently loaned."

The woman stared daggers at him, then her rage getting the better of her, she let loose a concussive force. With a huge thud, tables overturned, and books hurled across the room, crashing into the bookcases.

The room shimmered blue as several mages cast shields around themselves, but the old man wasn't fast enough. Mouth ajar, he flew back into a pile of unsorted volumes, scattering them across the floor.

Emily's eyes widened as he clambered to his feet and hurriedly apologised to the woman.

"My sincerest apologies. I have similar books, which I will find at once." With a hasty bow, he scurried off to fetch another book, faster than she'd seen him move all day.

Emily frowned at his change in attitude and scrutinised the woman more closely.

The man had spoken down to many of the mages, both men and women, in the time she had been here. The only difference she could see were the two gold stars on her robes, whereas the other mages had one or none at all.

Was it that simple? They wore their stars for all to see? And with two stars, she could enter the palace.

Emily shuddered. This wasn't the kind of woman she wanted to approach for help.

But the rest of the mages were well behaved. They couldn't grow a massive temper just because they gained an extra star.

Resisting the strong urge to read up on the mage class system right that moment, she made her way over to the introductory level shelves on the first floor and sought out a book that explained the mage society. She found a childish-looking volume entitled *How to Progress with Magic* and hid it away in her clothes for later reading. Perhaps it would tell her where to find a more amicable two-star mage.

The rest of the day proceeded without any further drama, and she sneaked back to the other side of the wall with just enough time to buy groceries and prepare dinner.

After dinner, Emily returned to her empty room and delved into the book she had borrowed. It taught her a lot about the class system, but much of it she already suspected.

Magic was everything in Parsa – the more stars a mage had, the better their life. At the top of the mage hierarchy was the Royal Mage, the only mage to earn five stars, though he never needed to display his stars. The mage symbol, a double-edged star, was enough to signify his importance.

Below this, very few mages achieved four stars. These mages were usually tied to the same bloodline, held important positions, and reported directly to the Royal Mage. They made decisions in his absence and led various functions, including the magic school. The book referenced the Royal Mage's sister having reached four stars after she married and became queen as a notable example to aspire to.

Three-star mages tended to be given land ownership, with the expectation that they would be able to defend it and the workers from thieves and bandits. Two stars were allowed to work in the palace, but usually had to ingratiate themselves to a higher-level mage in some way to reap the benefits of Parsan society. The book suggested two-star mages should make the most of the palace library to study further, venture to other worlds to improve their magic, or enhance their status through marriage.

Fed up with the suggestions for self-improvement, Emily flicked to the chapter on notable characters. Here, it had an exceedingly amicable profile on the former queen and two more on her children.

She frowned at the sketches of the prince and princess, slightly intimidated by their regal expressions and otherworldly beauty, but even more so by the speed at which they'd progressed through the magical curriculum, surpassing mages twice their age with their skill and magical strength.

Contrarily, the book did not flatter the king or his nephew with their three stars, highlighting the importance of magical heritage and study over royal blood.

Several pages were given to the Royal Mage, emphasising his many impressive magical deeds, his dedication to study and selflessness in protecting Parsa from invaders. The only mage ever known to teleport across half a world, he had never lost a duel and had single-handedly defeated almost an entire army in the catastrophic invasion a generation ago.

Despite his valour, the enemy still succeeded in killing three royals before escaping without a trace, and the book warned of an inevitable future repeat.

It all came across as rather biased and Emily's stomach churned at the thought of fitting in with these people enough to gain entry to the palace, even before the threat of an impending invasion. However, it reassured her that there were plenty of mages and studying was of paramount importance. Sooner or later, another two-star mage would enter the library. She just had to be patient.

Although she wasn't much impressed with the book's content, she was still grateful for the knowledge it imparted and tucked it carefully away in her bedsheets so it wouldn't be discovered. She couldn't imagine what sort of trouble she would be in if she lost the book or got accused of stealing from the library.

The book did raise further questions though. None of the soldiers at the portal had worn stars, so they couldn't be mages. That might explain why Alice had been treated differently and her presence was known about. If the mage that had teleported Eliot to the palace worked for this Royal Mage, perhaps he'd been taken to another part.

But what a powerful mage wanted with Eliot, Emily couldn't guess. He didn't need to protect this world from a little boy.

Eager for the next day and the answers it would bring, she turned in early and was fast asleep before her roommate returned.

CHAPTER 14

DEEP IN THE DESERT

Muffled voices and shuffling footsteps woke Jaime from his slumber. Confused, he glanced around the wooden hut, until his parched lips and hunger reminded him of his desperate situation.

Still fast asleep, Jordan's taut features betrayed his troubled thoughts, despite the bravery he put on when he was awake.

Jaime could only imagine how he felt, though he was starting to get some idea of the loneliness Jordan had suffered recently. Jaime had never been away from home so long, and never anywhere so remote. He'd not realised just how much he counted on a brother being around. But he couldn't bring that up with Jordan. Jordan had never had that and Jaime didn't want any pity from him.

Jaime crept to the entrance of the shelter to uncover the cause of the commotion. To his delight, a caravan of camels approached, with humans riding them. Poor Jordan wouldn't get to see any aliens today.

Sneaking to the edge of the shelters to see more clearly, Jaime surveyed the newcomers. There were only four of them, but they possessed seven camels, fully laden with sturdy and heavy-looking bags. Well organised, they busied themselves with different chores, but swaddled in their scarves and flowing clothes, he couldn't tell much about them.

One retrieved water for the group, filling up their various vessels while another lit a fire and prepared some cooking pots. The other two attended to the camels, offloading the heavy bags so the animals might rest.

He couldn't decide whether to move closer or wake Jordan first, but that decision was soon made for him with a tap on the shoulder and a whisper in his ear. "They look friendly enough. Shall we see if they can spare some food?"

His stomach rumbled at the suggestion, but he was still wary. "Maybe one of us should hang back … just in case."

"You stay here if you're scared. I'm going to say hello." Without waiting for a response, Jordan headed towards the campfire.

"Jordan!" Jaime hissed, but it was too late. He had to decide whether to follow him or hang back and watch. There wouldn't be much he could do on his own if they turned out to be hostile, so he decided to join his friend and hope for the best.

"Hello!" Jordan called out to the man by the fire.

The man turned around and gave a peculiar harmonious greeting of his own, but it was not something either of them could understand. However, his tone was friendly enough and his expression welcoming.

"May we join you?" Jaime asked, sensing that Jordan might not observe the pleasantries of a polite introduction in his starved state.

To his surprise, Jordan sat by the fire and leaned back as if joining a well-known friend.

The man said something else they couldn't understand, then called to his companion returning from the well.

Short and stocky, the figure approached and pulled down their scarf, revealing a soft, feminine face with full lips. She exchanged a few words with the man, then poured some water into the cooking pot. They looked quite alike, with similar wide eyes, the same dark, frizzy hair and dark skin, so they must be siblings.

The woman strode towards Jaime, put one hand on his head and one on his chest and muttered a few strange words. He would have stepped back, but she moved so quickly and confidently he merely stared bewildered at her.

Seconds later, she smiled at Jaime. "You're very pale, aren't you?" she said. "Here, have this scarf. You'll need it when the sun is up. I'm Eliza, by the way."

Thinking about it now, his skin did feel dry and burned, but he hadn't noticed over his hunger, thirst, and exhaustion.

The woman unwrapped her soft cream and shiny pearl striped scarf from her neck and handed it to him. Surprisingly soft and well made, it showed no signs of any fraying, despite having been exposed to the harsh desert conditions.

"I'm Jaime and this is Jordan. What did you just do?"

"I cast a spell of understanding. Now you can understand my language and we can understand yours."

Jaime frowned at her strange explanation. Clearly, she spoke English, though that was a little odd if they were on a different world.

"Hungry?"

Jaime nodded energetically. "Starved."

"Let's get some food into you then." She winked at Jordan, and putting her hands in her pockets, she retrieved some dry bread and handed them both a small roll. A little sweet and peppered with tiny seeds, the bread didn't taste strongly of anything at all. However, in their starved state, they couldn't devour it quickly enough.

Kneeling by the fire, Eliza crumbled some powdery substance into the boiling water and a warming aroma beckoned Jaime closer. He dropped down beside Jordan, only now realising the first man had disappeared. Out of range of the glow of the fire, the man was laying out the traps. Curious, Jaime continued to watch and noticed one drip. Then it clicked. The sticky substance they'd both tried earlier was meant for the traps, not for eating.

His attention returning to Jordan and Eliza, he listened half-heartedly, quite happy for all the focus to be on Jordan, even though he occasionally heard his name mentioned.

"So, Jaime, what are the two of you doing in the middle of the desert with no camels and no food?"

"We didn't intend to be here, we kind of just stumbled into it." How much should he tell her? Would she think him mad if he told her they'd arrived through a portal?

"You found a portal?" Her eyes lit up and Jaime worried she could read minds.

He tried to play it cautiously. "A what?"

"A portal. A doorway between worlds. They're so rare out here, but occasionally one will open up somewhere remote and people appear from some distant world or another." She grabbed at his clothes, inspecting the zips, and apparently finding denim fascinating. "You're clearly not from any of the known trade worlds, with garments so foreign. Can you show us where you arrived?"

"No, the portal kept moving. We both came out in different places."

"Oh, that's a shame." Her face fell and her attention shifted back to Jordan.

"Wait! There are other portals?"

"Of course. Where do you think we're coming from?" She stopped to peer into the cooking pot and stirred the soup for far longer than necessary, as if enjoying the suspense.

Trying to contain his impatience, Jaime asked calmly, "You've been to another world?"

"We're returning from Aveya, where they have the finest silks and cloths. The scarf you're wearing is Aveyan, made by the most talented craftspeople. This one will suit you." Eliza pulled out a diamond-patterned ruby-red scarf and handed it to Jordan. Oddly, she rested her hand on Jordan's forehead and muttered the same strange words she'd first spoken to Jaime.

Jordan merely grinned at her. "Thanks, but we haven't anything to give you."

"That doesn't matter," she said, smiling. "You'll return the favour when you can, won't you?"

"Sure," Jordan said, admiring the scarf.

A little more worried about owing a complete stranger a favour, Jaime tried not to let his concern show. "Do you think there will be a portal back to our home somewhere?"

"Not around here. Your best chance is to travel to North Parsa. That's where most of the portals are and usually where new people end up."

"Okay, which way is that?"

Eliza laughed, then looked at him with pity. "That journey takes months. You'll need to join a trade mission to survive that expedition."

"Will you be going that way?" Jordan asked.

She smiled warmly back at him. "No, we do the shorter journeys. They're much more profitable and much less dangerous. You're welcome to accompany us. We can always use an extra pair of hands."

"Dangerous?" Jaime repeated, catching the word Jordan would miss.

"Yes, it's a long way through the desert, across immense mountains and more desert. The elements alone make the journey perilous. And then there are the wild animals ..." She leaned forwards to stir the pot, letting the words hang in the air.

Jordan interrupted the ominous silence. "Do you think our friends will be in the north?"

Jaime straightened. Was that what Jordan had been talking to Eliza about? He might need to pay more attention to Jordan in the future, in case he said something he shouldn't.

"Most likely. It's been generations since anyone has come through a temporary portal in the south from a new world. How did you find your way through?"

Jordan explained how they had arrived, fighting an invisible current in the bright white light, as Jaime's thoughts wandered to the new challenge ahead. It was clear they would have to travel north, but a couple of days in this desert had been enough of an ordeal.

How would they survive months?

And what if the others weren't there, and were lost in the desert? Or maybe they were safe at home still, wondering where Jordan and him had disappeared to.

The return of Eliza's companions roused him from his thoughts. They brought back the traps, which now contained odd sandy-coloured lizards, with six legs rather than the usual four.

One of the men held up his catch. "Barbecued or stewed?" His long brown hair spilled out from his scarf now, revealing a short beard, small cognac eyes and dark olive skin. The other man also sported lengthy stubble and dark olive skin, but his grey eyes and faint eyebrows gave him a peculiar, unbalanced appearance. Neither looked much like Eliza or her brother. They must be from Aveya.

"Er, barbecued," Jaime replied warily.

After snapping the creature's neck, removing its guts and sticking a spiked stick through it, the man handed him his dinner and gestured for him to hold it over the fire.

He did as he instructed and Jordan did the same, but Jordan managed to anchor his skewer in the ground so he didn't have to hold it over the fire.

"So, what is Aveya like?" Jaime asked.

"Much more hospitable than this place, but just as hot," the man with grey eyes answered.

Eliza frowned, tossing a bone aside.

He smiled apologetically. "Travelling through such a vast desert isn't appealing to many, but we can expect a good price for our silks and cloths in South Parsa. It's well known as a bustling trade centre for many worlds. If we can't get a decent price there, we'll continue on to another world through one of the other persistent portals nearby."

The other man chimed in. "Eliza has told us of the spices we can buy in South Parsa, which will fetch a small fortune back in Aveya. We couldn't turn down an offer to travel with her, given her gifts."

"Gifts?" Jaime echoed.

"Since magic doesn't work on every world, it is useful to have an interpreter who knows the local language, and Eliza has a natural gift when it comes to communication."

"Magic?"

"Yes, that is how you understand us and we understand you now."

It was a simple enough explanation, but Jaime didn't really believe what they were saying. He could just about accept that a rift in space existed, linking their worlds, but not people who could perform magic. It must just be an expression for some innate gift. They spoke English. Somehow.

Jordan caught his puzzled expression. "Can your magic do anything else?"

The two Aveyans exchanged smirks, then turned to Eliza. Without hesitation, she raised her hand towards the fire and shot flames out of it.

Jaime dropped his meal and leapt to his feet.

Jordan broke out into a huge grin. "Can many people do that?"

Eliza shook her head. "Not so many in the south, but if you travel to the north there are many mages there."

Rather disconcerted, Jaime retrieved his skewered lizard, decided it was cooked enough and bit into it. It tasted fairly pleasant, a little like dry turkey.

Eliza's brother dished out the soup and they tucked into the best meal they'd had in days.

Jaime watched Eliza suspiciously as they ate, but nothing about her suggested technology of any kind. She wore nothing on her wrists under her billowing sleeves that could explain the emergence of fire.

Eventually, he summoned the courage to ask more. "This magic, how do you use it?"

Eliza smiled at him, her eyes dancing. "Only those born with magic can cast spells." Concentrating hard, she held out her hand, palm upwards. Flames leapt forth, dancing in her hand.

Jaime leaned forward, his eyes meeting hers in silent question. She dipped her head, so he reached out, then recoiled as the heat scalded his hand.

Eliza laughed, then closed her palm and the fire vanished. It was no trick. The flames were real, and there was no other explanation for their appearance.

He glanced at Jordan, who watched them both with a broad grin. Jaime could only imagine what was going through Jordan's mind. It probably wasn't concern about a world where people could cast magic or what that might mean for their chances of survival.

Though Jaime had to admit that running into Eliza was about the best thing that could have happened. They weren't equipped to cross the desert alone. But now they were headed to a city of magical people, they may have bigger challenges to face.

CHAPTER 15

North Parsa

On her fourth day in this extravagant palace, Alice awoke earlier than usual, eager to meet the Royal Mage. Yesterday, he'd postponed their meeting in order to venture to the south, so today he ought to have news. He'd not specified a time, so she wanted to be ready whenever he deemed her worthy of his attention.

The thought of him appearing in her chambers had her fumbling through her wardrobe, seeking something suitable for outside the palace, but also something that wouldn't make her stand out too much. Her options were limited, but she found some boots and a plainish trouser combination, the wispy fabric not as robust as she'd like.

Wandering onto the balcony, she observed a pair of armoured soldiers setting up for a lengthy battle, and from this distance could just about tell which was Darien and which was Javed before they put on their helmets.

Obviously the better fighter, Javed had a clear advantage in size and power. Nevertheless, she still admired Darien's technique and perseverance in duelling with a superior opponent.

The more she watched, the more she saw how Darien used his opponent's strength against him. Instead of meeting every blow, he dodged more and attacked from different angles, forcing Javed to keep moving and denying him the chance to strike with force.

The pair reminded her of Jaime and Jordan. Where might they be now? Were they lost on Parsa, looking for her, or back at home wondering where she'd disappeared to? She'd happily sit through one of their LARPing matches just to see Jaime's friendly face and have a chance to talk with him.

A gentle knock on the door announced a visitor, and with her heart speeding, Alice rushed across the room.

Taking a deep breath, she pulled open the door, then relaxed at the sight of Yasmin.

"Did I wake you?" Yasmin asked timidly.

Alice shook her head. "I'm watching Darien and Javed duel."

"It's more fun if you give them things to dodge," Yasmin said with a mischievous smile. Leading the way back out to the balcony, she peered over, then muttered a few words under her breath.

Vines stretched out from the garden and entwined Javed before either of them knew what was happening. Darien landed an unencumbered blow across Javed's shoulder, sending him tumbling.

Javed's angry voice reached them even up in the tower. "You cheat!" he shouted, before launching forwards with a rather vicious attack, knocking Darien backwards.

Alice gritted her teeth, but Darien didn't falter. He quickly returned the strike and darted away from the next. He'd learned well.

The observation turned her attention to Yasmin's studies. She clearly had no sword training, but she must have a decent education. "Yasmin, why don't you study at the magic school?"

Yasmin screwed up her nose. "I don't need the school with my uncle's tuition."

"But aren't there mages you'd like to study with?"

"I prefer to study alone." Yasmin cast a new spell, sending rocks hurtling at Darien and blinding him to Javed's next blow.

"You're the cheat!" Glancing up towards the balcony, Darien spotted the two girls, and forgetting to be a good host, cast a pool of cold water to appear over them. Too busy laughing, Yasmin failed to deflect the spell, and the two girls ended up soaked and shrieking.

Retreating inside, Yasmin cast a spell to dry them, then escorted Alice down to breakfast.

As they ate, a message arrived from the Royal Mage informing them he was ready to see Alice. Even with Yasmin's reassurances that her uncle would wait, Alice couldn't finish her breakfast fast enough, and was soon following the messenger to a small room on the other side of the palace, close to the base of the Mage Tower. Inside the small hexagonal room, the Royal Mage waited, scribbling in a journal.

Despite her nerves prickling again in his presence, hope that answers would be forthcoming swelled her chest. She stared at him expectantly, but he didn't seem to be aware she had arrived. She coughed to announce herself, then blurted out her question before her bravery evaporated. "Have you had any luck finding my friends?"

He looked up slowly, then glanced past her, as if expecting someone else. "Alice, thank you for coming. I'm afraid I haven't had any success locating your friends, but I have instructed the South Parsans to look out for them and ordered my own mages to search the desert. If they are in the south, they will be found."

Alice's heart sank. She'd been so hopeful he would find them with all his power. Perhaps she was the only one who had fallen through the portal after all.

Unlike Yasmin and Darien, who always teleported her by linking arms, the Royal Mage did not need to touch her. Instead, he waved his arm and swirled the air about them, as if moving the world rather than themselves.

She barely felt a thing as the familiar walled enclosure blurred into view, soldiers already bowing before them. Sand still whipped around her feet as the Royal Mage strode towards their destination at such a pace she struggled to keep up.

Fortunately, it was only a short distance and then all her attention was drawn to that otherworldly intrusion. The portal was beautiful, shimmering in the air, still and untouched by the world.

The silvery disc gave no clue of what lay beyond, neither of the dazzling dry river, nor the worlds it led to. Mesmerised, Alice contemplated what adventures or dangers she might face if she just stepped through.

Holding both hands towards the quivering oval, the Royal Mage began uttering strange incantations. The portal responded by shimmering brighter and more dimly in a cycle, its colour shifting, first to a hint of red, then to a blue tinge before returning to brilliant white.

After several minutes, he beckoned Alice closer and moved one of his hands in her direction, concentrating intently with his eyes closed.

Alice obliged, though wondered if she should be doing anything else. The man hadn't explained much. She shifted uncomfortably, glancing around for answers.

Most of the soldiers patrolling the area had retreated to the entrance, though a few stayed within the walled enclosure, watching with guarded expressions. A man in blue robes, his three stars shimmering under the slowly ascending sun, kept his eye on the militants, as if daring them to interfere.

Another few minutes passed before the Royal Mage lowered his arms and looked at her curiously. "There is definitely no way back that way. The current is too strong."

Alice tensed. Was she truly stuck here?

He turned back to the portal, his pupils wide. "Though I now recognise the flavour of the river and portals around your world, so I will be able to find another route. It is only a matter of time. Now back to the palace."

Without asking if she was ready, he swept his arm again, and she appeared back in her chambers with more questions than answers.

His words echoed loudly in the silent room. *There is no way back that way.*

Could there be another route through another portal?

Her mind flicked back to the two maps. There were so many portals in Parsa, but if there was a route home, wouldn't there be reports of it back on Earth? Perhaps that had been the only portal and now it was gone.

Her skin tingled, but it was the way the Royal Mage had spoken with such certainty and such intent that prickled her nerves. What would he do once he found a route? She didn't want mages and soldiers turning up in her hometown.

Her hopes dashed, she slumped into a chair on the balcony, not even cheering up when Yasmin visited. If the people here couldn't help her with all their magic, she'd have to find another way. But she'd been told not to leave …

Absent-mindedly, she picked up one of Yasmin's books. Yasmin had taught her some of the language, but she understood little, appreciating the beautiful calligraphy more than the meaning the words tried to convey.

Unfortunately, spells didn't work on translating written text. There was so much here she didn't understand, so much she couldn't be a part of. Other worlds would be the same. Though their royalty probably wouldn't be so generous.

Tempted to throw the book over the balcony, she halted as a red flower caught her eye. Not in the garden courtyard far below but blooming in front of her very eyes on the balcony wall. As she watched, more appeared – yellow, purple, and blue – weaving themselves along the entire length. She spun around, searching for the conjurer.

He lurked behind her, his eyes gleaming with mischief.

As her eyes met Darien's, he dropped into a bow. "Good afternoon, Alice. Would you care for a walk around the garden?"

She ground her teeth and returned to the book. "Not really. I'm sick of being stuck here."

Darien's face fell. "I understand how you feel, but it is much safer for you in the palace."

Alice scowled. "There's nothing to do here but watch Yasmin study."

He leaned on the balcony wall, surveying the courtyard below. "That's not entirely true. If I were you, I'd enjoy my free time. You never know when things might change."

Alice sighed. "At least with all your duties you get to meet interesting people."

"You can, too." A grin stretched across his face. "I think it is about time we had another ball. You could meet plenty of people then."

Alice blinked, then studied his expression. He seemed perfectly serious. "You would hold a ball just to cheer me up?"

He shrugged. "What point is there in being prince if I cannot hold a ball to cheer up my friends?"

Alice couldn't help smiling at his cavalier attitude, but she shook her head. "There must be more important things you have to do."

"There is nothing more important than the welfare of my people and their allies. A royal ball will cause a great deal of excitement and remind people of the significance of North Parsa. Perhaps that will bring your friends to our doors."

Alice's gaze drifted in the direction of the nearest portal cluster. How could she attend a ball when she didn't know where her friends were?

Darien's brow wrinkled. "You're still worried them?"

"Of course I am."

"Meet me in the garden after breakfast tomorrow. I might be able to do something about that."

The next morning, Alice found Darien beside a crystal-clear pool surrounded by tall amber and green bushes, providing seclusion and quiet. Of course, Yasmin was nosey enough to come along, so the three of them found themselves loitering by the water, discussing what could be done.

"I have an idea," Darien started. "And for once you could actually help, Yasmin, if you could see past your pride enough to aid a friend."

Yasmin appeared rather put out by this, narrowing her eyes at him, but waited for Darien to continue.

"There is a man who knows a considerable deal about portals, and is charged with monitoring the portal traffic for all of North Parsa. He might just be able to assist Alice."

Yasmin screwed up her face.

"You would be more persuasive than me in this situation, Yasmin, but I will do all I can to aid Alice, even if you won't."

Alice kept quiet, waiting to see if Darien's blatant manipulation would work.

"I will help, but I won't make empty promises," Yasmin replied.

"I would never expect you to," Darien swiftly responded. "Just follow my lead."

Linking arms, they whisked off to the portal cluster where Officer Gul usually patrolled.

On arrival, Alice got a few strange looks, but everyone seemed captivated by Yasmin. Since she generally didn't leave the palace much, she must have been a rare sight in all her finery, shimmering brighter than the sky against the ochre sand.

Although similar to where Alice had first arrived, this place was much bigger and full of activity. As they walked, people disappeared and appeared through each of the portals, paying a fee as they did. It was all very efficient and surprisingly calm, given the number of people. Police stood guard at each portal, and more still kept a watchful eye on proceedings.

Darien led them towards a group of men who all nodded and called "Sire" in respect to Darien. It felt odd to Alice, seeing all these men salute this young man, and she realised she hardly thought of him as a prince when they were alone.

Their leader merely said, "He's inspecting visitors from the third portal."

Appearing to understand, Darien led them away from the men.

The maps didn't do the portal cluster justice. They passed several portals in the few minutes they walked, each with a dedicated guard, who each greeted Darien in turn.

Within the centre of the cluster, but further to the edge, a mage in blue robes watched everything. He looked rather out of place here, but Alice supposed he was here to keep an eye on everything on behalf of the Royal Mage and could quickly raise the alarm if anything happened.

Finally, they approached Officer Gul, who was more at ease here surrounded by his men than he had been in the palace. However, he still stood out with his chocolate brown hair brushing his strong angular jaw, unlike the short cuts of the other soldiers.

He dipped his head to Darien, then seeing Yasmin, bowed low. "Your highness, it is a pleasure and honour to have you visit us." Turning to Alice and bowing again, he continued, "My lady, it is good to see you looking so well. Parsa agrees with you."

Outside the palace, and with his tall height, broad shoulders and the sword hanging from his side, the officer was more imposing, but it was impossible to be afraid of this charming man. Alice smiled but couldn't help thinking that – in his mid-twenties – he was a little old for Yasmin. Curious how he had become head of the portal police at such a young age, she suspected the sigils on his uniform had something to do with that.

"Officer, my sister has heard many tales of your knowledge of portals and the worlds they lead to, and is impressed by the treasures you have so generously given. She has come here today to seek your wisdom, and to find hope for her friend."

Alice observed Yasmin as Darien spoke, expecting her to at least scowl, but her expression remained perfectly pleasant.

"It is my honour to help the princess and her friend," the officer replied formally.

Darien stared pointedly at Yasmin and eventually she chimed in, talking as sweetly as Alice had ever heard. "My friend Alice is looking for a way home. She comes from a world that rarely links to Parsa and no one can offer her a way back."

Officer Gul smiled weakly. "Princess, no one knows the portal realm better than I, for I have been watching and conversing with those who come and go for half my life. I shall find a route to Alice's world. You have my word." He clasped his hands behind his back. "I would be glad to share my knowledge with the princess at any time."

Alice smiled at his awkward invitation, wondering how long he had been waiting for this moment. From out of the corner of her eye, she observed Darien poke Yasmin in the back.

Despite her reluctance, Yasmin appeared the perfect princess, maintaining her cheery sweet tone. "I would be very happy to hear about your experiences of the other worlds." Another poke. "Tomorrow at the palace, before dinner would be delightful."

"As you wish, princess. I shall be there and look forward to it."

Alice could hardly keep a straight face at the officer's unashamedly broad grin.

"Thank you for your time, officer. We shall leave you to your duties." Darien must have decided to end the interaction on a high point, not so willing to push Yasmin any further.

"Thank you, Prince Darien, Princess Yasmin, Lady Alice," Officer Gul said, bowing deeply again, before they teleported away.

"Now, was that so difficult?" Darien asked Yasmin once they were back at the palace.

Yasmin scowled. "Yes. Now I have to spend time with him tomorrow."

Alice kept quiet, watching Yasmin carefully. Despite her protests, she had been even more charming than Darien and that couldn't have been the first time she'd used her charm to her advantage.

"How do you expect him to keep you informed on his progress finding Alice's world if you don't talk to him?"

That one seemed to stump Yasmin. Clearly, she couldn't keep relying on Darien.

When she didn't answer, Darien continued. "Why are you so afraid of him, Yasmin? You're a talented mage. There's nothing he could do to harm you, and if he tried, he'd have me to deal with."

Yasmin pushed Darien playfully. "I don't need you to protect me like that, little brother. Why do you like him so much?"

"He's a skilled soldier, a good leader, knowledgeable and extremely loyal."

Alice couldn't help thinking he was listing his own traits and began to like Darien even more. He evidently didn't care if a person had magic or not. He was planning a ball for her, after all.

Yasmin, on the other hand, confused her immensely. She had been nothing but nice to Alice, and obviously relished her company, so her disdain of commoners made no sense.

Yasmin contemplated his words for a few moments. "How do you know?"

"I just do. Trust me. The world is a lot bigger outside the palace, and the portals bring both danger and fortune."

To Alice's surprise, Yasmin kept her word and met with Officer Gul before dinner the next day. He must have really intrigued her, or Darien's words must have had some effect, because Yasmin invited Officer Gul back the following day, then the day after that.

Each day, Officer Gul brought a new gift. Nothing as valuable as the blue crystal, but items that met with Yasmin's approval. On the fifth day, he presented her with a beautiful hairpin from a distant world and was visibly delighted when she wore it to dinner.

Even Darien seemed surprised, taking Alice aside after to dinner to discuss Yasmin's change in attitude. She flushed as a dozen pairs of eyes followed her all the way to the door and sighed her relief when they slid into one of the smaller parlours, currently empty.

Darien turned to her with a gleam in his eye. "I had no idea Navid was such a romantic. Has Yasmin really been meeting with him every day?"

Alice nodded. "He visits before dinner, bringing a new gift each time."

Darien frowned, then reached forward, tucking a wayward strand of her hair back into place. As he did, his hand brushed her cheek, warming it even more. "I hope she's not neglecting you. Remind Yasmin not to look too happy with him, especially when our uncle dines with us."

"Why shouldn't Yasmin be happy with him?"

"He's not a mage." Darien rubbed his forehead. "It shouldn't matter, but our uncle won't approve of her associating with him. She should be more discreet."

Alice crossed her arms. "You introduced them. Shouldn't you warn her?"

"I doubt she'd listen to me, but she's besotted with you. I wonder what you've done to her." He stepped closer, searching her eyes for answers she didn't have, then abruptly stepped back, his breath catching. "I'll remind Navid, you remind Yasmin."

He disappeared before she could object, and as Alice walked back to find Yasmin, she realised the problem. She'd have to convince Yasmin to conceal her feelings from her beloved uncle.

As if she didn't have serious problems to worry about.

Palace politics would have to wait. It was time to venture out into the city and search for herself. The royals had done what they could, but they obviously didn't understand the main population, where Emily might easily blend in. She'd certainly not want to attract the attention of mages or soldiers.

CHAPTER 16
NORTH PARSA

On the morning of her tenth day, Emily slid her hand under the covers to retrieve her latest book, only to freeze as her hand met nothing but sheets. Alarmed, she pushed herself off the bed and shoved her hand in deeper, frantically searching until she tore off the sheets completely.

The book was gone.

Across the room, her roommate's tidy bed lay empty. But she couldn't have stolen it from under her. She couldn't have even known it was there.

Her heart beating rapidly, she returned to the library. If someone had discovered her theft, it was best she found out the consequences right away and stopped the news from reaching her mistress.

The building was quiet as she entered, with only a few mages seated at the tables. None acknowledged her presence, which suited her just fine. However, the librarian coughed and gestured at a pile of books on his desk.

Attempting to walk normally, she approached the desk, until her eyes landed on the top book. A very familiar book.

"In these libraries you worked in," the librarian said, "do people take books wherever and whenever they please?"

Her cheeks heating, Emily shook her head, though she was relieved to find her book unscathed. "No. I'm sorry. I thought it would help me understand—"

He chuckled. "Just don't do it again. I can show you how to check books out properly if you can be trusted." Emily held her breath as he glanced at the stolen book. "I suppose if that's what you're interested in and you came back, you're not one of those thieves who occasionally visit."

She exhaled slowly and picked up the stack, keen to show she was worth his trust. She desperately needed to find a way into the Royal Palace, but if the dramatic woman was anything to go by, she would have little luck in convincing a two-star mage to take her there. Before she turned away, she risked a question. "Do many two-star mages visit this library?"

"We get the occasional two-star in here looking for something obscure that can't be found in the royal library, but it is not very often. As soon as a mage earns their second star, they forget we exist. Now get back to work. I'm not paying you to gawp at mages."

He narrowed his eyes at her until she filed a book away, but she found his grumpiness quite familiar and was beginning to like the old man. However, she was not willing to risk upsetting him further, so she retreated upstairs to a more remote part of the library. She'd still have a good view if any two-star mage entered, but by now she was worrying one would never visit.

There were plenty of mages in the city, but they were not forthcoming with help. Wearing blue robes might make them more receptive to her, and she probably had enough to buy different clothes now, but she had nothing to offer for their assistance.

Perhaps if she found one of these obscure books, she'd have something to bargain with ...

She'd seen a few whilst tackling a long-abandoned stack of books in a forgotten corner, so she headed over, energised by her new plan.

It didn't take her long to find a peculiar book in a completely different language. Full of dense text she didn't understand, with what looked like the occasional spell, she hoped this would be enough to intrigue a two-star mage. But the only way to be sure was to check with the librarian.

Normally hunched over a desk on the ground floor, he instantly leapt to his feet and grabbed it from her. "This is one of the ancient texts of the old religion. You can tell by the golden tree on the cover."

His usually condescending voice trembled with excitement, piquing the attention of much of the room. "The prince will be interested in this. We should send it to the palace at once."

Immediately, several young female mages volunteered to make the journey.

"Ah, so now you're interested in helping. Can't put a book back on a shelf, but you can take one all the way to the palace, can you?" He took his time choosing a volunteer, apparently enjoying it immensely.

Knowing whoever he chose might be able to get her into the palace, Emily didn't take her eyes off him. It wasn't exactly what she'd planned, but if it was a way in ...

"Emily will go," he finally declared.

Her eyes widened and her mouth went dry. Had she misheard? Why would he choose her when she wasn't even permitted to enter the palace?

"But she can't even teleport!" a volunteer objected.

"I shall teleport her there. I may be old, but I can still teleport someone the short distance to the palace."

After a brief moment, when Emily was sure he would change his mind, he moved closer, and authority seized his voice. "Ask for Prince Darien. Tell them you have an urgent delivery from old Adar. Don't give it to anyone else. The prince will want to meet you." His brow creased. "And try to stand up tall." He put his hand on her shoulder.

She tensed as the library slid out of view, to be replaced by an empty stone room with a bare stone desk. The teleportation didn't feel as bad as she'd imagined, merely a gentle tug at her core, though she breathed out a sigh of relief.

She turned to ask Adar where they were, but he disappeared again before she could say a word.

Great. She was trapped in a room without a door, with no one to explain what to do next.

She might be in the palace, but her situation hadn't improved. Somehow, she'd found a book that was *too* interesting.

A bell on the desk appeared her only option, so she summoned her courage and gave it a ping.

Instantly, a man in blue robes appeared.

Quickly noting he displayed two stars on his robes, she tried to be as polite as possible. Standing up tall, as Adar had instructed, she repeated the words he had told her.

"What is the delivery?" the mage asked in a bored tone.

"It's a book."

"Is the prince expecting you?"

"Er, no." Holding the book to her chest, she remembered what the old man had said. "It's from Adar."

With unimpressed eyes, the man glanced over her and placed a purple crystal paperweight on the desk. "Put your hand here."

Biting back her questions, she obeyed, trying to decipher his vacant expression as she waited for further instructions. The crystal felt cool to the touch, but otherwise there was nothing special about it.

Retrieving the crystal with his gloved hand, the man seemed satisfied. "The prince will see you when he is ready. Wait here." He disappeared abruptly, leaving her alone again in the doorless room.

Where was she going to go?

With a sigh, she took a seat on the hard stone floor, leaning against the wall. There was nothing she could do about her predicament, and getting annoyed wouldn't help. At least it was cool in here. And she did have a book to read.

Consisting of considerable blocks of text, it was no mere spell guide. Without an index, it was unlikely to be a textbook either. On the contents page, the word for chapter – *kafli* – looked familiar. Nothing like Farsi, yet potentially belonging to one of the ancient languages she had been studying before being dragged to this primitive world.

Portals must have brought people here from all over Earth. Though if they'd all forgotten about Earth, the portals must have disappeared long ago.

Adar had said this was one of the ancient texts of the old religion, so was this the language of the other culture their magic had originated from? She'd read about the two cultures, one represented by a star and another by a tree, but she'd never seen a different language before.

Armed with this new knowledge, she tried to find more similarities in the language, though it was slow work. Without anything to take notes with, she kept forgetting what she had just translated. She managed to figure out the book was a historical account of the ancient culture identified by the golden tree, but it would take weeks or months to decipher correctly.

Many hours slipped by whilst she read, though the passage of time was difficult to determine in this windowless, featureless room. One thing she was certain of was that she had missed dinner. She was going to be in big trouble when she returned to her lodgings. Though, if she did get arrested for not paying back her debt, she could hardly be in a worse cell than this.

As her exasperation at her uncomfortable situation caused her attention to lapse, she became aware of someone else in the room.

Quite a sight to behold after being stuck in the dull grey chamber for so long, his bright blue silky clothes shone at her, and his handsome face was a welcome sight for anyone.

"Can you read that?" he enquired in a voice that seemed to purr.

She recognised the prince immediately from the profile she had skimmed, but he didn't seem as intimidating as it had described.

On stiff limbs, she pushed herself up, using the wall for support. "No," she said. "Well, I can decipher some of the words." She studied his youthful face. He was certainly attractive, but surprisingly approachable for someone of his status.

His eyes flickered between her and the book, as if he couldn't decide which was most interesting, causing Emily to blush.

"I am told you are non-magical, yet you work in the lower mage library?"

She had never heard it called the lower library before, but she supposed from the palace that would be a useful distinction. "Yes, I sort books there, but I have no magical talent." She waited for some look of disgust or condescending remark, but instead his eyes widened in surprise.

"Fascinating. And you have uncovered an interesting text long thought lost. Adar was right to send you to me." A wrinkle formed on his brow. "You look familiar. How long have you been in the city?"

Emily's heart clenched. She should have realised that someone might recognise her from the posters that had popped up everywhere. "Many months. But I've only been working in the library a short time."

Still looking puzzled, Darien nodded. "Where are you from?"

"Er – a distant world. It's called, er, France."

"Have you ever heard of a world called Earth?"

"No. But portal travel is rare where I'm from."

He held out his hand. "I have something to show you."

Glad to be leaving this room, she took his hand without hesitation.

Their destination was a small study, with a decent number of bookcases and a couple of comfortable chairs beside an ornately carved table. Emily took a moment to steady herself, though it barely felt like she'd moved at all.

"This is my private study, where I keep my private book collection."

She barely stopped herself from reaching out to examine the nearest book. From their delicately embossed spines, she could tell they were exceptionally rare and unusual compared to those in the lower mage library. Their peculiar lettering stood out even to her, and the designs were far more complicated than the typical spellbook or historical text.

The prince developed an amused expression on his face. "You really care about books, don't you?"

"I spend a lot of time reading." Slightly under-representing her enthusiasm, she struggled to take her eyes off the texts.

"Perhaps you can help me."

"Me? Help you? How?" She couldn't imagine what use she might be, but if it got her into the palace, that was a massive step closer to finding her brother.

"There is a large mage library here in the palace, full of treasures waiting to be found. Evidently you have an eye for unusual books, so you can search the library for me and bring them here. In return, you can read as much as you like."

Emily couldn't believe her luck. "Don't I need to be a mage to access the library?"

He smiled mischievously. "Normally, yes, but I'll make special arrangements for you. It's good to challenge the mages from time to time." He paused. "It would be better if you looked the part though."

He walked over to a large wardrobe and pulled out some simple blue robes. "These will do. Instead of stars, they bear my personal symbol, so everyone will know you work for me. Best to wear them only when you're in the palace."

Emily carefully placed the book on the table and examined the robes. Silky to the touch, they were far superior to the rags she currently wore. Instead of stars, a golden lion cub rested on its haunches, which made sense given the lion denoted the royal family.

She peeked at his own robes adorned with a similar symbol, but the cub wore a crown. He displayed no stars, which made her curious.

"Something wrong?" he asked, seeing her puzzled expression.

"It's just there are no stars on your robes." She spoke quietly, not wanting to offend him.

"Only those who serve the Royal Mage wear stars. I serve the crown," he said firmly.

This was an attitude Emily had not expected, but it shed some light on her reading. Some divide existed between the crown and the mage society, perhaps explaining why the prince treated her so differently compared to the other mages she had met.

"What should I call you?"

Although the prince seemed more trustworthy than those other mages, Emily couldn't risk giving him her name. She didn't want to disappear in this palace too. As much as she wanted to see Alice, she'd just have to find another way to meet up with her. Eliot was relying on Emily to find him and discover the mystery of his disappearance. For all she knew, Darien was complicit in his abduction.

"My name is Jane."

"You can call me Darien. You had better return home. It's getting rather late."

Wondering if she would be allowed back in, Emily fidgeted.

"Ah, you probably didn't mean to be kept out this late. Will you be in any trouble?"

"Well, I might get arrested," she half joked. When he raised his eyebrows, she explained further. "I'm working to pay off debt as well as for my lodgings, so I might be kicked out for not preparing dinner this evening."

"I see. Well, don't worry. I shall send you with a letter of apology explaining it was all my fault. I'll also pay off all your debts. You answer exclusively to me now. You can keep working at the lower mage library, too. There might be more interesting texts hidden in that mess."

He stepped closer and gently took her hand. "Close your eyes and think of your room."

She hesitated only a moment before doing as he said. The memory of her room surfaced vividly in her mind, so real she could reach out and touch her bed.

Suddenly, gravity skipped a heartbeat. Startled, she opened her eyes.

Back in her room, her roommate was already asleep, so it must be very late. Only a light warmth on her hand told her she hadn't dreamt the entire encounter.

Quietly, she prepared for bed, contemplating how she might search for Eliot from the palace library. She was a massive step closer, but the palace itself was huge. It would take ages to search, and that was only if she managed to sneak around undetected ...

CHAPTER 17
NORTH PARSA

With the sun threatening to make its appearance, Emily fetched water and prepared breakfast as normal, diligently attending to every little detail in nervous anticipation of the disciplinary she was sure to face when her mistress awoke. As much as she missed home and family, life here wasn't so bad, and she'd started to get used to the strange rhythms of desert life. She'd hate to have to adjust to another household or spend her tiny savings on new accommodation.

As she placed the full plates on the table, a loud knock sounded on the front door. Emily rushed to answer it before it disturbed her mistress.

Outside, an official-looking soldier stood proudly, smartly dressed in a tunic bearing the prince's own lion sigil. Her mouth gaped at this formal display on her behalf.

"Is the master of the house available?" he asked.

"Er, the mistress is not available," she started to reply. Unfortunately, her attempts to be quiet had failed and her mistress stormed over and cut in.

"What is all this, and where have you been?" she snapped.

"Perhaps this will help clear things up," the officer interrupted, holding out a letter bearing the royal seal. Only then did Emily realise the letter would ask for Jane, not Emily, and her heart sank. How much trouble would she be in for her deception?

The mistress read, her eyes darting between Emily and the soldier several times, but she didn't say anything.

When she finished, the soldier held out a bag of coins. "My prince hopes you will accept this reimbursement for the inconvenience of borrowing your labourer, both yesterday and for the foreseeable future. This should also pay off all her outstanding debts."

Madame Olsta grabbed the bag and gasped at the money within. "Of course. It is a pleasure to serve the prince."

The soldier straightened and turned to Emily. "The prince would like to meet with you this morning to show you your new duties, if you consent."

Emily turned to her mistress, who now scrutinised her closely, her hand moving to her throat.

"You work for the prince now. You should do as he asks." Her commanding tone gave way to what could almost be described as awe. "Dinner will be waiting for you when you finish, *Jane*."

Emily bit her lip, deliberating on how Madame Olsta would use this lie to her advantage, but it didn't matter at this moment. "I am ready to go now," Emily replied, glad to be done with her chores.

He offered his arm, as if to teleport.

"But you're not a mage," she said, seeing no stars on his outfit. "I thought all those with magic worked for the Royal Mage?"

He cocked his head to one side, letting a lock of black hair fall forwards to brush his cheek. "You've been reading some poor literature. I thought you were being employed for your discerning literary skills."

Emily's face heated. "Sorry, I didn't mean to judge. I'm quite new here."

"Clearly." He smiled. "I used to be a mage, but I was never very good. Prince Darien offered me a better role, and I took it gratefully. You might not know this, but mages can be very snobbish and not much fun to be around."

"I can only imagine."

They teleported directly to Prince Darien's private study, which was currently unoccupied but extremely welcoming with its comfortable chairs, thick blue rug, and pleasant aroma of freshly baked bread.

"Prince Darien will be along when he's finished training," the soldier said. "He thought it would be useful to show you the way from here so you can come and go as you please."

Emily agreed. "He's not like regular mages, is he?"

"No, Prince Darien is unique. He certainly has the power to become a great mage, and the intelligence and perseverance to go with it, but he's never been at all snobbish. He spends a lot of time on other worlds, so perhaps he's seen so much he's risen above all the petty arrogance. Though he would do better not to provoke the mages, which he seems to do for sport." The soldier paused, his eyes darting to the door. "Well, I'd better be getting back to my regular duties," he said quickly, as if worried he shouldn't have said that much. "Help yourself to breakfast whilst you wait."

Emily soon tucked into the food arranged on the small table but was somewhat disappointed to be missing the freshly cooked eggs she'd prepared such a short time ago. The furnishings were much more comfortable here, though, and she eyed the bookshelves as she ate.

Not wanting to get the books mucky, she searched for somewhere to wash her hands. A curtain in the corner looked like it might lead somewhere, so she poked her nose around it, and discovered a room designed for entertaining. She imagined the prince stretched out on one of the chaise longues amongst a group of important dignitaries, indulging in cuisine from worlds she couldn't imagine.

A twinge of guilt shot through her. She shouldn't be snooping around the prince's rooms after he had been so nice to her. Then again, that was the reason for her being in the palace. She'd have to get used to the experience.

Ignoring the guilt, she crept through the room to a short set of stairs leading to a smaller chamber with cloak hooks, wardrobes, and washbasins. Hurriedly washing her hands, she decided that was enough exploring for now, and returned to the study, her heart racing. She didn't want to be kicked out on her first day here.

She ventured over to the bookshelf housing the book she had delivered. Similar covers adorned others, each featuring the golden tree. She gently opened one of the volumes with a more unusual cover and flicked through the pages. Its contents appeared to match that of the first book, written in that same complicated language, so it was likely from the culture of the golden tree, too.

She pondered the books' significance. Could Darien read them? The text didn't seem to contain many spells, so was he merely a collector of ancient rare books?

From what she had discovered about him, she didn't think so. There must be some useful information in them, but she couldn't guess at his purpose.

The texts on the next shelf were more familiar. Written in the mage language resembling Farsi, their colour had faded with age and many of the words were spelled oddly. Some words she didn't recognise at all and must have become lost over time, or introduced after the inhabitants had left Earth.

She began to read one of them, assuming it might tell her more about the books on the previous shelf, if Prince Darien had organised them with a purpose in mind. Any clues she could find would make her job easier.

The book turned out to be an accounting of an ancient tribe that used to inhabit the mountains south of the capital. Although not geographically specific, the author had determined from various accounts that the tribe relied on trade through the local cluster of portals, but had chosen the mountainous region to settle for its defensibility and access to fresh water. A simple people, they did not have the irrigation the region possessed today.

By all accounts, the area was regularly raided by opportunistic bandits, and it was not until much later that a union between two magical tribes provided a strong enough force for a fortress to be built.

Emily rubbed her sore neck, confused at Prince Darien's interest in this book. Even she knew the stories about the foundation of the capital, from her days spent in the lower mage library and casual conversations with neighbours.

Determined to discover its secrets, she read on, but nothing jumped out as important. The book detailed the tribe's customs, their family life, the clothes they wore, the food they ate and the religion they practised. They followed one of the ancient roots of the current magic culture, denoted by the silver five-pointed star, so the text told her nothing she didn't already know.

She glared at the pages, her neck stiff, until the words started to blur, only looking up when Prince Darien sauntered in.

"I see you are already getting familiar with my library," he said approvingly. He looked a little flushed, as if he had been exerting himself.

Despite her curiosity, Emily didn't feel like she should be questioning him about his other activities. "Yes, I thought it might help to know what type of books you're looking for."

"Good thinking. I knew I hired the right person. Many mages rely on magic so much they forget to think. I want you to use your intuition and bring me anything you think unusual, the older the better. Over the generations many histories have been lost, but this city has stood for centuries. Old texts might still be found in one of the libraries, if you look deep enough."

Emily smiled, glad for his approval, but more pleased at the promise of autonomy. That would make it much easier to slip away when the time came.

"Put on your blue robes and we'll head over to the library."

Oops, she had forgotten to change. Becoming so used to wearing her ugly grey outfit, she no longer thought about clothes. "Er—"

The prince held out a hand and robes suddenly appeared.

A useful trick. He'd never have to worry about forgetting anything.

"If you ever need any, you'll find spares in the wardrobe," he said.

Not wanting to keep him waiting, she swiftly slipped them on over her current outfit.

Prince Darien nodded, then led her down the tower. Since she had arrived by teleport, she had no idea how far up they were, but they spiralled down several floors. The rooms here were fairly open, so probably weren't hiding her brother. However, she paid attention to each and every one, just in case it held useful information.

"I apologise for the lengthy walk. I keep these rooms near the base of the tower so I can entertain my non-magical guests without them spending all day climbing, but there aren't any suitable spaces lower down. Fortunately, the mage library is near the bottom of the Mage Tower, so that won't take long to reach."

Sure enough, after they reached the base of the Royal Tower and followed a wide stately corridor linking the two towers, it was only a short climb to the entrance of the mage library.

This library put the lower mage library to shame, and she instantly understood why few of the higher-level mages bothered visiting once they had earned their second star.

At least five times as big, it must have filled the entire width of the tower. Bookshelves were no longer limited to lining up the walls, being dull in colour, or regular in shape. Golden bookcases spiralled from the ground into the air, and branched out, as if the bookcases themselves were trees with books instead of leaves.

Golden desks gleamed without any trace of abandoned texts. As she watched, a mage left a table and his book floated back to the appropriate place, the branch bending towards the volume as if welcoming it back.

She gazed in wonder at the spectacle until reality hit. How was she supposed to retrieve any books without a ladder in sight and no magic to summon one?

Before she could ask the question, Prince Darien whisked her over to a stern-looking woman. Introducing her as Jane, he informed the librarian she would be working there for him for the foreseeable future.

The librarian did not look happy at all. "This is most irregular. I shall have to inform the Royal Mage of this." She vanished, her three stars shimmering in the air for a second longer, as if to remind everyone of her importance.

Emily watched the stars fade away, and with them, her hope. This was not a place she could ever belong. The lure of secrets hidden in the pages of ancient texts did nothing to overcome her fear of the magic barring her way. Even the bookshelf trees themselves bent away from her as if to protect their precious knowledge.

"I'll leave you to it, then," Prince Darien said. He must have seen her panic-stricken face, because he put a comforting hand on her shoulder and whispered in her ear, "Just follow your instinct." Then he left.

Unlike the lower mage library where everyone ignored her, any time she went anywhere near a mage in this place, she received an angry glare. She wished she was back in the old library. For all its wonders, this was not a place she wanted to be.

Even if it was closer to Eliot.

Steeling herself, she set to her task. In the absence of an indexing system, she deduced that the rare books would be in the most remote places, though she might just have been giving herself an excuse to get away from the annoyed stares.

Unfortunately, she had no idea how to reach the lower branches, let alone the higher ones. Some branches stooped low, but as she approached, they lifted themselves out of reach, almost teasing her.

Or maybe they just moved out of the way to stop people from walking into them.

She played a game with the trees, turning away as if she wasn't interested in the books at all, then walking backwards until she reached a branch, but every time it gracefully retreated from her grasp.

Eventually, frustrated, she paused to lean against the tree and come up with a new plan. As she did, the tree shimmered, starting from where she had leaned and rippling up through the trunk and throughout each branch.

Worried she had hurt it in some way, she checked where she had leaned. Only then did she observe the tiny writing on the tree itself.

It didn't take her long to discover the words detailed the topics of the books in each tree, though each tree had a certain character to it, presenting the information in different ways, rather than just providing a factual list.

The first shared friendly colloquialisms, but with her lack of mastery of the language, she struggled more with this tree than the bland list on the next. The third simplified its language and repeated words so often, it seemed to be patronising her.

She spent most of the day reading the trunks, trying to decipher the layout of the library. However, she accidentally revisited one tree and discovered the text had changed in the short time she had circled around the neighbouring trees. Somehow the tree had understood that she'd been looking at the other trees and adapted its offerings to match her new interests, much like her annoying computer that kept advertising things to her she had already bought.

It was going to take considerable time to make sense of this place, and magic wouldn't speed that up. She sighed and renewed her determination, telling herself her patience would be rewarded.

Lunch was served on a balcony so high she didn't spot it until the aroma of freshly baked bread and lightly seasoned meat wafted down. Luckily, a staircase spiralled upwards at the back of the room, so she didn't have to starve for lack of magical ability.

Now she thought about it, though, she hadn't seen any mage teleport in or out of the library. They used the same stairs to reach the food terrace. She could only conclude that teleportation was not permitted in the tower.

After the server refused to acknowledge her, she helped herself to some bread and cheese and perched alone on a table far away from the crowd. Turning her gaze to the library below, she ignored the angry stares of the mages and reminded herself she was here for a reason.

From her vantage point, she admired the view of the golden forest from above, observing how the higher branches of trees intertwined, some sharing books between them. This gave her a new idea, but she'd have to figure out how to reach these books to see if she was right.

By the end of the day, she still hadn't convinced a tree to give her a single book. She had tried grabbing one off a table after a mage finished with it, but she was much too slow to succeed.

A commotion at the entrance of the library eventually caught her attention, and she realised the soldier messenger who'd fetched her this morning was the cause.

"How dare you come in here?" a three-star mage shouted at him.

He grinned back, unfazed, seemingly enjoying the attention. He was more like Darien than he realised.

Not wanting to be the cause of more drama, Emily hurried over to join him and they escaped the library before more vicious insults could be thrown.

"How was your first day?"

Unable to think of a positive thing to say, she debated her answer. If she admitted to finding nothing, she may end up dismissed before she'd even had a chance to search for Eliot.

"That good?" he continued.

"Not a great place to be without magic."

"You'll get used to it," he said, though from what she'd seen, she had no idea why he thought that.

"Prince Darien wanted me to show you the way back to your house so you can come and go as you please. It'll take a lot longer than teleporting, but he insisted you be free to go to whichever library you need without having to wait for transportation."

Emily sighed in relief. Clearly, Prince Darien didn't expect results any time soon.

Once outside, they crossed a spacious courtyard featuring a totally out-of-place tropical garden, with beautiful columns and pointed archways. As grand as the interior of the palace, no surface was without an intricate geometric pattern. She studied them closely, contemplating their origins, until a huge lion padded up right in front of them.

She froze, her heart catching in her throat, but her escort didn't seem bothered. He sauntered forwards to greet the lion and extracted a treat from within his short cloak. When the lion could coax no more from him, it approached Emily, brushing her arm with giant whiskers. He sniffed at her, exhaling hot meaty breath, then wandered off to join others.

The soldier grinned at her. "Don't worry about the lions. Once they've got your scent, they won't show you any interest, unless you bring them treats."

Closing her gaping mouth, she followed her guard through the gate into a wide street lined by tall buildings, which led into the centre of the city. The streets grew gradually busier until they reached the heaving centre, still alive with the buzz of trade despite the late hour.

Not unlike the markets she visited near her lodgings, the only real difference was the people. Dressed more finely and predominantly in blue, a robed figure would occasionally appear or disappear, fresh groceries in hand.

Winding their way through the streets, they approached the city walls several minutes later, but the streets here were still busy. Confused, she turned to her guide. "Why is it so quiet near the palace?"

"Only the prominent mage families live near the palace and they need not walk anywhere. Behind the palace, the royal gardens take up most of the inner city, so city life skews towards this gate. As you know, the population long ago spread beyond the city walls, in this direction in particular."

Emily nodded, familiar with the extent of her neighbourhood, despite the number of ruined structures. "Why are there so many abandoned buildings if the city is growing?"

"There was a large invasion about a generation ago, which destroyed many of the buildings outside of the wall. Most of the population found safety within the city, but decided not to rebuild." He smiled reassuringly at her. "North Parsa is regularly attacked, almost every generation, but always the invaders are fought off, so you needn't worry. The mages spend their entire lives training to ensure we have the best defence, and the soldiers are no less dedicated."

The reality of her situation hadn't really sunk in until he said it out loud. Reading about historical battles was quite different to living in a city which expected regular attacks. It was only half an hour or so to the palace from her accommodation, but that was an age to someone who could travel instantaneously. If the city came under attack, would she have time to get to safety?

She shuddered as she imagined her neighbours crowding the gate, seeking protection within the walls.

But they wouldn't be here if they didn't have confidence in their safety.

Her escort left her at her door, leaving her with mixed feelings. Now she'd gained access to the palace, she was much closer to finding her brother. And working for the prince, she could roam far more freely. She didn't even have to pay the tax on the gate.

Soon, she would find Eliot. She could almost see him as she closed her eyes.

CHAPTER 18

NORTH PARSA

The day after Emily's encounter with the prince, she first went to the lower mage library to apologise to Adar for not showing up the previous day, but he didn't seem bothered at all. He barely glanced at her before he spoke. "My dear, I have sent people to the palace who have not come back for days."

Emily's eyes widened. Hopefully they hadn't been waiting in that dull, furnitureless chamber for that length of time. If so, she was quite lucky.

"Yes, the prince and I go way back. That's how I knew he would be interested in that book. And you." He glanced at her grey dress. "I received a message that you'd be working for him now."

Emily nodded. "He wants me to find more books for him."

"Don't let me stop you then."

Finding the lower mage library much more homely than ever before, Emily decided to spend the morning there. In the afternoon, she would head back to the palace, and in the evening she could look for her brother. With fewer people around at that time, she would probably attract less attention.

After tackling a haphazard bookshelf in a dusty corner of the smaller top floor, she stepped back to admire her handiwork, only to frown at the books still jutting out unevenly. Although the irregularity was hardly enough for anyone to notice, she hadn't worked all morning to accept less than perfection, so she moved closer to examine the supposedly uniform collection of texts.

A few moments' scrutiny revealed the shelves of this part of the bookcase were not aligned with the rest. The edges were just slightly further back, something she would never have noticed from the previous arrangement. Frowning, she gave the shelves a push and felt a slight movement.

Her heart quickening, she shoved harder, but the bookcase went no further. There was only one explanation.

Running her fingers along the sides of the case, she searched for anything that might be a mechanism holding the bookcase in place, but all she felt was smooth wood. Yet another mystery she couldn't solve. Could this only be solved with magic?

If it had moved that first time, then surely not.

Certain there was something hidden behind the bookcase, she searched more widely, scouring the adjoining bookcases, but still found nothing. In despair, she glanced around, but there was little up here beyond the shelves and a few lamps to see by. Most of the lamps were fairly plain, but the nearest had an unusually long and intricately twisted stem. An odd design to be hidden up here out of sight.

Holding her breath, she reached out and pulled. Her heart stopped as the lamp shifted down and a click sounded behind her. A moment later, she pushed the bookcase back into a darkened chamber.

Behind the case was a tiny space, crowded by a small desk and chair. The walls were bare stone, and the only object of interest was a book lying on the desk. She opened it carefully, discovering beautifully inked calligraphy in a language she hadn't seen before. The writing stopped two-thirds of the way through the book, which appeared to be an unfinished journal judging by the regular headed entries.

Since she had nowhere better to keep it, she didn't dare take the book out of its hiding place, but she copied some of the letters onto spare parchment so she could search for the language later.

Aware anyone could visit this section of the library at any time, she hastily turned to leave, but her foot connected with something small and metallic that rang out against the stone. She stooped to pick it up and discovered a ring adorned with a beady-eyed falcon, its wings outstretched. Without thinking, she dropped it in her pocket.

Before someone noticed her absence, she quickly replaced the bookshelf and headed to the lower level. She almost jumped out of her skin when she opened the door to the darkened steps and found a young woman on the other side. It wasn't like mages to use the stairs here, especially two-star mages, but she was probably just on edge after finding that room.

Moving out of the way of the unusually short-haired mage, she kept her head down as she returned to the ground floor, then made her way to the palace. No one would be sneaking up on her there, and she longed for the privacy of the prince's private chambers.

Enthused by her discovery, Emily decided to try the palace library again. There must be a way to access the knowledge without magic, she just had to find it.

Standing before a tree housing much of Parsa's history, she reached up on tiptoes, but still the branch was out of reach. Annoyed, she edged closer and muttered under her breath, "Won't you just give me one book? Any of yours would be better than those in the lower library."

To her surprise, the tree dipped its branch and delivered a book into her hands. If she hadn't been in a library, she would have laughed. Was it that easy? She just had to ask?

Armed with this new information, she soon had several books, though none that would interest the prince. He might have mentioned how to get started, but then if he knew what he was looking for, he could hire any mage. Only deep research would yield the clues she needed.

Her hopes lifted, she headed to the prince's private study with the new material. To her surprise, the palace had come alive in the late afternoon. Mages lingered in the corridors and numerous people bore foreign insignia on their colourful outfits. Her assumptions about the palace being quieter in the evening must be wrong. She'd have to wait until morning to search these rooms. Though with so many people around, Eliot could hardly be hidden here.

As she weaved her way to the other side of the palace, the sensation that she was being watched grew, but when she turned, all she'd seen was a flash of blue or a wisp of caramel hair. Or perhaps that was her imagination. Being surrounded by snippety mages always set her on edge.

Deep in chronicles of Parsan history and age-old spellbooks, Emily was soon drawn back to the prince's private collection. His books were far superior to any others she had discovered, with their beautiful calligraphy, detailed writing, and unique viewpoints, making her wonder how he had found them. Most of the books in the two main libraries were derivative, presenting old spells in new ways, adding a few new tricks here and there.

The first book she'd started reading here caught her eye. There didn't appear to be anything special about the information it contained, so why was it here?

It began to nag at her, so she retrieved the book and started to read it cover to cover. If she could deduce its importance, perhaps that would reveal new topics to search.

Now more familiar with the modern mage culture, she realised a few rituals described were no longer practised or mentioned in any other text. She focused on these, determined to figure out their importance. More spiritual than anything, the extra rituals taught how to cleanse a troubled soul, clear the mind before battle, or to thank the forest for bountiful hunting. She could see why they had been left out of the modern spellbooks, but not why they would be important to Prince Darien.

She must have missed something.

Turning back to the beginning, she started to read through again. In her tiredness, she began to skip words, and the translation became nonsense. She now read that the first chief's son, who was born without magic, magically blessed his grandson, who in turn went on to save the tribe from their most hated enemy. She frowned and read it again, doubting her translation, but it definitely said the first chief's son had performed the blessing.

Flicking back a few pages, she double-checked that he had indeed been born without magic. There on the family tree, he was clearly marked as unmagical. More texts on the unfortunate cases of non-magical children being born to magical parents were referenced, so there was no way the reference was a simple slip-up. But perhaps she had misunderstood the blessing.

Determined to discover the truth, she found an entire chapter devoted to the blessing, which clearly required magic, so the only explanation was that the non-magical man had somehow gained magic.

She stared at the pages for a few moments, following the information to its logical conclusion. If *anyone* could gain magic, the mages would lose their superiority.

Regardless of whether there was any truth to the story, Emily closed the book, satisfied she had learned the reason for its place in the collection. She still didn't understand why the prince would be interested in such a story. Nor why he would keep something that threatened his power.

Stretching as she stood up, she realised she had got rather carried away with her reading. Darkness seeped in through the window, and shadows stretched towards her.

Her eyes darted to the clock. Unlike a regular clock, the three hands tracked the sun, the lone moon, and the binary moons around the planet. If the largest hand pointed directly upwards, it was midday, and if it pointed directly down, it was midnight.

To her dismay, the large hand had already passed the midnight position. She really didn't want to travel back to her house in the dark at this time of night, but a long time remained until morning. Tiredness gripped her limbs and already she was fighting to keep her eyes open.

The soft rug beckoned invitingly, but then she remembered the comfortable room next door with all its chaise longues. She crept through and collapsed onto the lavish recliner, pulling velvety cushions around her, and fell straight asleep.

Voices in the entrance chamber below woke her shortly before dawn. Not knowing whether she should be in this room at all, she darted back into the study. In her tiredness the night before, she had left out some books, so she hastily returned them to the nearest bookshelf.

The seriousness of the voices as they moved into the next room caused her to hesitate.

"The treaty is important. I want you to support your cousin as much as possible," an unknown voice said.

"Of course, Father. I understand the importance of the alliance and securing the south for the future of all Parsa."

Emily recognised the second voice as Darien's, so the first must belong to the king. She relaxed, before realising they might not want her to hear the conversation. Though if she left now, they'd probably hear the door close.

"You should consider finding a bride, too. Have you not found a suitable princess on one of these worlds you keep visiting? The only way to secure the future is through powerful allies, and the best way to do that is through marriage." Despite Darien's young age, the king sounded serious, and for the first time, Emily felt sorry for him.

"I know, Father, but the worlds we connect to are not powerful. They are filled with simple traders, farmers, and hunters."

When she was sure they weren't coming into the study, she peered through the gap in the curtains, shifting her position until she could see the two men. Darien stood stiffly with his arms crossed in front of him, looking more miserable than she'd ever seen him, but she couldn't see the king's expression from her vantage point.

"Don't let your arrogance get the better of you," the king chided. "You're sounding like a common mage. Parsa is only as strong as the allies that come to her defence in times of war. You are too young to remember the battle that took your mother from us, but don't forget that army is still out there and could strike at any time."

Darien lowered his eyes to the floor. "Yes, Father, I won't let that happen again."

A long silence passed before the king spoke again. "I hope you're not getting distracted by the blonde girl. The Royal Mage suggests you are getting a bit too attached and that it would be better for him to keep an eye on her."

Emily tensed. She'd not seen any blonde mages, so that *must* be Alice. But why was Darien interested in her?

"He only says that to get at the information she possesses. She is from an advanced world. They don't have magic, but they have technology. Technology that can help us defeat our enemies." Darien now stared down his father, but the king turned and walked across the r oom.

"And how do you suppose you will obtain that information?"

"With the mind-sharing spell."

The king stopped dead in his tracks and turned back to Darien. "Hmph. How do you expect to gain enough trust to use that?"

Confident now, Darien's tone became more cunning. "She already trusts me. She's totally infatuated with me and so naïve. By the time of the ball, she'll be completely in love with me. I'll suggest it will help her get home and she'll have no reason to doubt me."

Horrified, Emily sank back, letting the curtains close. Never would she have suspected the prince of such manipulation, but then what did she really know of him? He'd seen her skill and decided she would work for him without asking her thoughts. Now he planned to steal Alice's memories.

No matter what Darien thought, Alice wasn't that naïve. But then Darien was more charming than most ... She had to find Alice and warn her.

"Hmph, you really are your uncle's nephew. I don't know what happened to my blood at all," the king replied evenly, resuming his walk across the room.

"I've got your skill with a sword," Darien said, turning to face his father.

"You wish. I've seen you practise and you're not half as good as I was at your age. Your cousin puts you to shame."

"He is older and bigger!"

"Excuses won't save your life on the battlefield. Now go and train before I fetch my sword and give you a real lesson."

"The soldiers would enjoy seeing you fight," Darien replied.

"Don't tempt me. Now go."

Darien dipped his head before disappearing, though Emily couldn't miss the mischief in his eyes. Everything was a game to him. Perhaps even Eliot's life.

She stayed still until she was sure they were both gone. Her illusions entirely shattered, she remembered why she was here. She had been so distracted by the wealth of information in the library she had wasted valuable time she could have used to search for her brother.

Completely taken in by Prince Darien's charm and totally dazzled by his apparent trust in her, she hadn't realised just how much he was using her and Alice to advance his own goals. They were nothing to him but a way to find ancient magical secrets and new technology.

She wouldn't be a part of that. From now on, her research would focus on accounts of off-worlders and where prisoners might be held.

CHAPTER 19

NORTH PARSA

Finally, after waiting days for a chance to slip away, Alice found an opportunity to sneak out of the palace unnoticed whilst Yasmin was busy with her uncle and Darien had disappeared off-world.

If her friends had made it to the city, she would find them, even if it took all day. All she had to do was get past the guards at the gate. There was a chance they might not stop her, but they'd certainly inform the palace of her departure, and she didn't want anyone coming after her. Not when they'd all made it clear they thought she should stay put.

Her heart already speeding, she dressed in the plainest clothes she could find and swiftly descended the tower. At every turn, she expected someone to appear and demand to know where she was going, but she didn't meet a single soul. She might be the only person in the entire palace who couldn't teleport.

Once she reached the base of the tower, she listened intently for any voices, then crept towards the kitchen. Nudging open the door a crack, she peered inside. A few people busied themselves tidying away the freshly cleaned dishes, but they were at the other end of the room and not looking her way.

With a deep breath, she tiptoed inside, then darted to the nearest door.

She was in luck. A blast of cool salty air surrounded her, and despite the dim light, she made out several loose cuts of meat.

After stuffing what she needed in her pockets, she hastily backtracked through the kitchen into the corridor. One task down, now onto the next challenge.

Walking as calmly as possible into the familiar courtyard, and holding her head high, she showed the palace guards little attention. They'd seen her plenty of times before, though rarely on her own. However, she'd need a distraction to get through the gate.

Before she could lose her nerve, she made her way over to one of the storage buildings by the edge of the courtyard. Inside, torches on the walls cast a warm glow on the piles of neatly folded clothes.

She hesitated as her doubts rose. This plan could get her into serious trouble. It could get someone hurt. Though mages shouldn't have any difficulty putting out fire before it spread too far. And it was the only thing she could think of that would distract the guards long enough.

There was nothing for it. With a deep breath, she yanked a torch from the wall, and held it against the simple navy tunic on the topmost shelf. It smouldered, but to her immense frustration, did not catch fire.

Clenching the torch tighter, she moved it to the wooden shelf, willing it to burn. For a few seconds, the wood merely glowed, then fire surged across the shelf and flames licked the walls.

Staggering back, she dropped the torch on the ground. For a moment she stared at the scene, captivated by the flickering display. Until the smoke thickened, stealing her breath away and stinging her eyes.

With her hand over her mouth, she fled the building.

Keeping out of sight, she sprinted towards the gate, hiding behind the various bushes until the soldiers detected the fire. Despite the short distance she'd run, she struggled to catch her breath, and her heart pounded in her chest.

Before long, smoke billowed into the sky, raising calls of alarm from the guards. Both the officers from the palace entrance and the outer gate ran towards the fire, leaving Alice with the opportunity to slip through unnoticed.

Unfortunately, she had forgotten about the final obstacle.

A low growl and fierce yellow eyes froze her to the spot, just in front of the gate.

The lions.

Trembling slightly, she slid her hand into her pocket and retrieved the meat she'd stolen from the kitchen. She dropped it on the floor in front of the lion and waited.

Still, it stared at her, so she backed away a couple of steps. Finally, it lowered its head and sniffed her offering.

As soon as she saw it bite the meat, she carefully walked around, then sprinted through the gate and down the cobbled street towards the city. She didn't stop running until she had turned several corners and was completely out of breath.

When she could run no more, she leaned on a building to catch her breath and glanced back up the street.

No one pursued her. The street was empty.

Adrenaline surged through her. She had succeeded in reaching the city unnoticed!

Once recovered, she examined her surroundings. Tall, ochre buildings bordered a broad cobbled street, decorated with mosaics around the doors. There were no trees, but mesh screens reached between the buildings to provide shade. Even so, all her running had left her unpleasantly flushed.

After she'd traversed a few streets, people started to appear, many wearing blue robes, but also dresses embroidered with the patterns she had seen in the palace. Most of the men wore tunics, but a few she would describe as dresses. A few glanced her way, pausing to stare, before moving on.

Was she that odd in her trousers? Or was it the lightness of her hair that attracted the attention? If her clothes were the cause, she ought to have no problem finding Eliot, Jaime and Jordan in their jeans, but Emily would probably blend in with her cotton skirt.

The further away from the palace, the more varied the people and their outfits became, though many still glanced curiously at her.

Lowering her gaze, she continued to where she thought the main marketplace was, trying to reconcile what she had seen from the palace with the labyrinth she now wound through. Soon, she passed people selling their wares and longed for a scarf to cover her hair, but she had no money. She'd been completely dependent on the palace for everything.

A busy market square selling all manner of food seemed her best chance for answers. If her friends had ended up in the city, they would have to eat. Her hopes rising, she headed to a fruit vendor just finished with a customer.

"Hello," Alice said. "I wonder if you can help me."

The woman frowned at her. "Have you lost your way to the palace?"

"No, I'm looking for some people. Perhaps you've seen them in the market. Three teens my age and a younger boy."

The stall keeper shook her head. "We've all seen the posters. Trust me, if anyone saw them, they'd be dragged to the palace for the reward."

"Could they have come through a remote portal somewhere?"

"Not here. All the portals are guarded. You'd be better off asking a mage though. Isn't the palace helping you?"

"Yes, but I thought I'd check, just in case they hadn't thought of something."

The woman folded her hands. "The mages know far more than us folk. You should get back to the palace before they start to worry about you."

Alice nodded. "Thank you. I will." Deflated, she headed out of the square to wander through unremarkable streets, none with any clues. At least she knew now that Darien had told the truth about the portals, and the people had been looking out for her friends. It seemed that they weren't here after all.

Perhaps they hadn't found the portal and only she was lost. Unless they were on other worlds, but she couldn't hope to visit those alone. The portal police would never let her pass.

As she wound her way back to the palace, an old woman beckoned to her from the doorway of a large house. Wearing a simple long cobalt dress with a deep-blue rope belt, she stood with a slight lean. "You're the girl that everyone's been talking about," the woman said. "Have you found your friends yet?"

"They're not in the city," Alice replied.

The woman beckoned her closer, her grey hair falling across her face. "Are you sure about that?" She smiled, revealing tiny dimples and a crease in her brow.

Alice strode forward. "Do you know something? Please tell me."

The woman nodded and hobbled backwards into the house, holding the door open.

Alice hesitated. The woman appeared harmless enough, but she'd seen enough of magic to know she wouldn't stand a chance against a mage.

"Don't you want to find out where they are? I have tea brewing." The woman leaned more heavily against the door, as if she was having trouble standing, raising a twinge of guilt from Alice.

"Can you just tell me now?"

Without answering, the woman pulled a cane from behind the door, leaned awkwardly on it and disappeared inside.

Alice bit her lip. It would be odd if this woman knew something when no others did, but what if she'd been to another world? She couldn't let any information slip away. Not after all this time.

Against her better judgement, she stepped inside.

Smaller than she had expected, the room was comfortably decorated and dimly lit by a few shell sconces. Two brown sofas hugged the walls, with a small ebony coffee table in between. A russet rug filled most of the floor, and similar tapestries hung on the wall. From a door at the other side of the room, a pleasant mint aroma wafted.

The woman stopped before reaching the door and turned back to Alice, gesturing at the sofa. "Please take a seat while I fetch the tea."

The room showed no signs of magic, but if the woman didn't know anything, Alice didn't want to waste time here. "Please, can you just tell me if you've seen them?"

"Of course I've seen them, dear. Though the girl had green eyes. Someone must have got the poster wrong. I have their address written down."

Alice's heart skipped a beat, and she rushed forward. "Are they here, in the city?"

The woman gestured at the sofa again before limping into the kitchen.

Alice's mind raced. Had they been within her reach this entire time? But why hadn't this woman informed the palace to claim the reward?

She dropped onto the sofa, lost in thought, only to be distracted by the soft click of the front door. Immediately, her head snapped up. The door had closed itself.

Her heart accelerating, she darted over to the door and tugged.

The door stayed closed.

She was locked in. Trapped.

The old woman re-entered the room, her lips drawn into a tight smile, and all trace of her limp gone. She placed two cups of tea on the table, reinforcing the minty aroma. "There's no way out, so you may as well have a drink with me. We can have a nice conversation."

Alice surveyed her again, contemplating her options. "What do you want?"

"I just want to get to know you. Then I'll tell you about your friends. Isn't that fair?" Her eyes on Alice, the woman sipped her tea.

Alice moved to stand by the opposite sofa. "What could you possibly want to know about me?"

"Tell me about where you're from. We don't get many people like you here."

Alice's brow tightened. She might have looked out of place in the city, but with all the portals here, she could hardly be that much more interesting than all the other travellers. Something else was going on here. "Who do you work for?"

The woman's eyes widened. "What a peculiar thing to say. I am merely a lonely old woman looking for someone to talk to."

Alice glanced at the kitchen door. "Are you sure you've seen my friends? Emily would be wearing trousers, like me."

The woman nodded, and Alice's heart sank. There was no way Emily would start wearing trousers in a place like this. At once, she strode to the kitchen door, but the handle slid away from her before she reached it.

Her stomach lurched at the sudden shift, and she blinked to adjust to her new surroundings. Instead of a door, she now faced the Royal Mage and a spacious, finely decorated room that must be inside the palace.

"Alice, thank goodness you're alright. Didn't Yasmin or Darien tell you it's dangerous to leave the palace on your own? What were you thinking?"

Alice's mouth gaped. "How did I get here?"

"One of my loyal subjects thought you might be in trouble and I teleported you here. What were you doing, going into the house of a stranger?"

Alice shifted uncomfortably under his penetrating gaze. "I went to see if any of my friends had reached the city."

He sighed. "I thought I'd made it clear that we're doing everything we can to help. If your friends are nearby, I'll find them. Now, what did the woman want?"

Alice shrugged. "She wanted to know about my world."

"What did you tell her?"

"Nothing!"

He frowned. "Are you sure?"

Alice nodded. "She told me she'd seen my friends, but she lied. Though she knew the posters had Emily's eye colour wrong. How would she know that?"

"I've told many people what you told me. For a reward of that size, word spreads quickly."

Alice nodded. That made sense. But she couldn't help feeling there was more to it than that. The woman had clearly lured her into the house for a reason.

"I'll call for some tea and you can tell me everything," the Royal Mage said. "You must have been very frightened."

Alice trudged behind as he led her to a cosy seating area. Tea was the last thing she wanted right now, but she was grateful to be out of that house, so she slumped into the chair without protest.

A huge crash a few floors below had her leaping to her feet again.

"Wait here. I'll see what that is about."

She watched as the Royal Mage left the room, then sagged back into the chair, wondering how much more her heart could cope with. Her mind raced back to the old woman and the strange situation she had found herself in. Nothing made sense.

Why would the woman need to trap her?

Her eyes meandered to the door, and with a sickening lurch, a terrible thought crossed her mind. Could the woman have been working for the Royal Mage? Perhaps she'd informed him herself and he'd brought her back to the palace to keep her out of the city.

But for what reason? To stop people learning about her world?

She leapt up, sprinted across the room, and reached for the door handle. Holding her breath, and with a shaking hand, she twisted the handle and pushed, but it didn't budge.

She dropped her hand in dismay and leaned on the door. The world threatened to swallow her up.

Until she heard shouting from the other side.

"Yasmin, what are you doing, storming in here like this?"

"Uncle, Alice has gone missing. I think she's left the palace. You must help me find her!"

"Yasmin!" Alice yelled, banging on the door. To her surprise, it swung open, and she lurched forward, almost falling to the floor.

Yasmin's wide eyes met hers. "Alice! What are you doing here?"

Alice ran to Yasmin, and in her distress, wrapped her in a hug, under the watchful eye of the Royal Mage.

"You see, Yasmin. There is no need to panic. I have already found Alice."

"Alice, you're trembling. What happened to you?"

Unsure what to say, she shook her head.

"Don't worry about anything." Yasmin put her arm around her, a steadying comfort. "I'll take you back to your room."

As they reached the familiar small receiving area at the entrance to the Royal Mage's chambers, Alice stopped in shock. The door to the corridor had been completely blasted off its hinges and was resting across the table.

She glanced at Yasmin. "Won't you get in trouble for that?"

Yasmin smiled back sheepishly. "It's only a door."

Alice shook her head, then noticed the mage cowering behind the desk. Sheet white, he nervously glanced between Yasmin and the missing door. He didn't dare say anything as they passed, merely shrinking behind the desk.

The route to Yasmin's practice room, the teleport to her chambers and the next teleport to Alice's room were less distressing, but Alice collapsed on the bed as soon as they arrived.

Yasmin scrutinised her with concern in her eyes. "Promise me you won't leave the palace alone again."

Alice exhaled deeply. There was little reason to visit the city again. Her friends weren't there. Nor was she reckless enough to try a portal without a guide. "I promise."

Though was she any safer in the palace?

She slid closer to Yasmin and lowered her voice. "Yasmin, I think your uncle locked me in that room before you found me."

Yasmin sat up abruptly. "Why ever would he do that?"

She bit her lip. She couldn't think of a solid reason, but the door had definitely been locked.

Hadn't it?

Or was her hand so shaky she hadn't twisted the handle enough?

"I'm not sure, but the door only opened when you were there. And how would the woman who trapped me in her house have known that Emily had green eyes unless he'd told her?"

Yasmin's face darkened. "There are plenty of spies in the city who could have found out. My uncle has had plenty of people searching. You should be thanking him rather than making silly accusations." Her eyes narrowed. "What has Darien been telling you about him?"

"Nothing! Darien said he would help me, too. That's why he took me to see him in the first place." Alice spoke quickly, not wanting to stir up trouble. It wasn't exactly a lie, since Darien hadn't really said anything against their uncle. It was his peculiar nervousness that gave away his distrust, but why would Darien have anything to fear from his own uncle? Yasmin and Javed clearly didn't fear the Royal Mage.

She would have to talk to Darien. If he knew something about his uncle's weird behaviour, perhaps she could convince him to explain what was going on. And he probably was her best chance to explore other worlds.

CHAPTER 20

SOUTH PARSA

Rough hands shook Jaime awake and he jerked upright, looking for the threat.

Jordan's worried face blurred into view. "Alright, Jaime?"

Jaime pushed his hair back, off his damp forehead. "What's going on?"

Jordan threw him a clean tunic. "You've been asleep for ages. We'll miss going to the market if you sleep any longer. Eliza's been so good to us, we can't laze about all day. We need money and answers."

Jaime blinked sleep out of his eyes and glanced around the room. They'd made it to the city of Mekenas, the capital of South Parsa, the evening before. Unfortunately, the warm welcome had done little to quell Jaime's worries, and after weeks in the desert, the bed was a little hard.

Above him, a camel mosaic stared at him with accusing eyes. He should be more grateful. But there'd been no news of newcomers, and a family that relied on trade from portals ought to be well informed. Their friends probably hadn't made it to Mekenas. At least not yet.

As Jaime threw on his clothes, Jordan pushed open the shutters, letting a gentle cool breeze seep inside, a hint of ginger on the air.

"Yeah, I know," Jaime said. "It's not going to be that easy though." He removed his watched and stuffed it into a drawer along with his phone. The hands informed him it was three in the morning back home. "We should keep these to ourselves so we don't attract unwanted attention."

"Sure." Already sporting his new tunic, Jordan strode to the door. "I'm starved. Come on. I can smell breakfast."

They followed the smell of spiced meat down to the dining hall, Jordan two strides ahead the whole time. They saw no one, but shouts reached them from distant corridors, the house already bustling with activity despite the low sun. The buzz was almost familiar, yet everything about the house was odd, reminding Jaime just how far from home they were.

Eliza sat on her own at the table, a purple fruit in her hand. At their entrance, she gestured for them to join her. "I thought we were going to have to send someone to find you."

Jaime's stomach squirmed with his embarrassment, but Jordan slid in next to her, completely unabashed. "It's been a long time since we've had somewhere comfortable to sleep. How can we thank you?"

"You can help us take our goods to the market, then you can look for someone travelling north from there. Unless you want to stick around? We'll be heading off-world again in a few days."

Jaime shook his head. "Thanks for the offer, but we have to find our friends." He glanced at the piles of vibrantly coloured fruit and cured meat, too guilty to enjoy breakfast. What if they were starving somewhere?

Piling his plate high, Jordan didn't seem bothered.

A short time later, they found themselves winding through narrow alleyways following Eliza and a few of her brothers. The rough wooden wheels of their hand-pushed carts rattled against the stone, just one of the noises of this bustling city. At times, the wheels got stuck in cracks and it took two of them to heave the heavily laden carts back on track.

Glad he didn't have to navigate his way through this labyrinth, Jaime was lost after just a few turns. He wouldn't even have found his way back to Eliza's house. There seemed to be no order to the place.

People sold food in apparently isolated corners and the tools of all varieties of crafts spilled out of miscellaneous doorways. The only commonality throughout the route was that everyone called out to greet them and everyone appeared to know Eliza's family well.

As the street widened, shouting filled the air, but this was unlike the hubbub in the narrow streets. Scared and urgent, the voices grew, until people ran towards them, shoving past in their haste to escape. In the opposite direction, smartly dressed men in charcoal-grey tunics, much like the guards at the wall, rushed into the fracas.

Ahead of them, Eliza shouted for everyone to get back, but Jordan surged forwards out of sight.

Cursing Jordan's impulsiveness, Jaime struggled past the crowd that now pressed back into the passage, failing to keep up.

The unmistakable sound of metal upon metal and further shrieks froze Jaime in his tracks. But only for a moment.

Desperate to see what had become of his friend, he shoved past the last few people to the entrance of a spacious square.

In the centre, amongst numerous market stalls, a man lay unmoving on the floor. Another, dressed identically in a smart red tunic, stood with his back to the fallen man, his sword held out in front of him. He confronted a group of scruffy men in simple desert robes.

Kneeling beside the fallen man, a young woman in her early twenties looked rather out of place in her silky red gown and cloak.

To Jaime's horror, Jordan ran to the fallen man, picked up his sword, and joined the defending man as the four attackers closed on them.

Jaime stood rigid, his warning failing to escape his throat. What was Jordan thinking? The desert must have affected his mind.

At Jordan's arrival, two of the attackers quickly broke away, and hastily started shoving jewellery into bags. Jordan lunged forward, attacking with vigour and confidence, as if they were still messing around on the LARPing field.

Jaime's heart leapt into his throat. Those blades were real, and any wound could be fatal here. There were no hospitals or ambulances. He winced as Jordan's sword clanged against his opponent's, ringing out throughout the square.

With their bags full, the two thieves sprinted for a street at the far side of the square, distracting the two remaining attackers from their fight. Jordan managed to knock his opponent's sword out of his hand. Jaime held his breath. It had to be over now.

Thankfully, the final thief surrendered, and the guards in charcoal seized them. More guards restrained the two thieves who had attempted to flee. Jaime tried to push through the crowd to reach Jordan, but more red-tunicked men, dressed like the injured man and his companion, poured into the square, keeping the crowds back. As Jaime watched, two of them carried the wounded man away. The others stayed, guarding the woman.

He examined her more closely now, realising she must be very important. In addition to the well-dressed men guarding her, her silky crimson gown shone in a splendid fashion, even without the shiny gold belt flattering her curvaceous figure. Upon her deep-red unruly hair, she wore a tiara with a dazzling ruby at the centre.

At that moment, he caught Jordan's eye and tried to call him over, but a guard got in the way. Impatiently, Jaime waited, unable to get any closer under the watchful eyes of the guards in red.

Eventually, Jordan sauntered over, looking quite pleased with himself. "I've got an invitation to the palace. You can come as my guest."

Jaime didn't know what to say first. "Are you crazy? You can't just jump into a sword fight. This is real life. You could have been killed!"

"What was I supposed to do? I saw the princess in trouble and had to do something."

"We should be keeping a low profile," Jaime argued, frowning at Jordan's thoughtlessness. "People will wonder where we're from. Wait … did you say princess?"

"Yeah! I saved the princess. No doubt this invitation is the first step in receiving my reward. We could be rich!"

Jaime shook his head. "You could have been hurt."

Jordan shrugged. "The princess has magic. Didn't you see her heal her guard?" Jordan bounded forwards and gave him a hearty shove. "Cheer up. We don't have to tell them where we're from. We could say we're from Aveya or another one of those worlds they trade with. We can't keep relying on Eliza. Think of how useful the reward would be in getting us north."

"Yeah, I guess." It was hard to argue with Jordan when he was like this, and he did have a point.

"Look, I've already got some coins to buy some fancy clothes for dinner. Let's go shopping."

"Okay, but let's talk to Eliza so we know where to get a good deal."

"Good idea. I knew I kept you around for something," Jordan replied, before bounding off in Eliza's direction.

Jaime scowled, but that was the only appreciation he was going to get for trying to keep Jordan out of trouble.

CHAPTER 21

SOUTH PARSA

As they entered the palace, Jaime had to admit that Jordan had done well. So many people congregated here that news of foreigners couldn't be missed. And with the wealth on display, the princess could certainly afford to reward Jordan with considerable money. Money that would help them organise an expedition north.

Two guards, dressed in the same red uniform as the guards in the square, flanked the door, but they greeted the boys with a friendly bob of the head and waved them inside, far more welcomingly than Jaime expected.

With an insufferable grin, Jordan skipped up the steps. Hopefully the victory wouldn't go to his head. They needed to be on their best behaviour.

A tan-skinned woman with long dark curly hair approached them almost immediately. Wearing a closely fitted red tunic and tight black trousers, she dressed little different to the guards they had seen earlier, but she greeted them with an eager smile. "You must be the hero who saved the princess," she said, bowing to Jordan. "Please follow me."

The stairway led to a long thin corridor, with portraits of royalty adorning the plain ochre walls. All the subjects shared large dark eyes, full lips, and broad noses, indicating an unbroken family line for at least a dozen generations. Jaime had thought the princess extremely odd with her deep-red Afro hair combined with her dark complexion, but many of the portraits showed these same traits. At the end of the row, he recognised the princess between two men of similar age, perhaps her brothers, though they had jet-black hair.

In a larger room beyond the corridor, a few dozen people mingled in groups, enjoying drinks and canapés. Amongst them, the princess stood out in her sleek red gown and glittering tiara.

Beside her was one of the men from the portraits, looking much younger in person, probably only twenty-two. Though the princess herself could only be a couple of years older. Certainly dressed well enough for royalty in his fancy-cuffed glittering ruby tunic, the prince was also heavily bejewelled, from his gold gilded ears to the rings adorning his fingers.

Their escort led them over to the princess and introduced them as the hero from the market and his friend. "This is Princess Safia, our most beloved ruler, and her brother, Prince Otis."

All words escaped Jaime as he took in the golden lids, long lashes and glittering lips of the youngest prince. He wore more makeup than the princess, though somehow it suited him. Judging by the rest of the room's occupants, this extravagance wasn't typical.

Prince Otis smiled warmly and grasped Jordan's hand. "My dear friend. Thank you for intervening earlier today. It would have been a terrible tragedy if my sister had been hurt. Thievery of this magnitude is generally quite rare, but there has been an increasing number of attacks from off-worlders on trade caravans, and it now looks as if they are growing more bold. I shall have to increase the number of guards in the market."

"It's the least I could do," Jordan replied, beaming under the attention. "Do you spend much time in the city?"

"Of course, we're not North Parsans." Prince Otis's eyes gleamed as his hand brushed a golden lion claw hanging from his neck. "The city has much to offer and citizens are welcome to visit the palace."

With practised deftness, he swiped a glass from a passing server. "Forgive me. I didn't properly introduce myself. I am the trade master of South Parsa. I am responsible for all the trade routes, markets, and taxes. It's an important but occasionally unpopular job." His eyes landed on Jaime, and he looked curiously between him and Jordan, but before he could say anything else, Jordan opened his mouth.

"You're not a prince?"

Jaime squirmed, but the prince smiled back, unoffended.

"Yes, I am also a prince, but that hardly means anything, does it? My sister is the ruling government official and manages all of that business. She's quite effective at diplomacy too."

"Hush," the princess said. "How can we reward you for your bravery?"

"We're looking for our friends and a way home," Jordan said. "We came through a portal in the desert, but it moved too fast for us to get back through. We think our friends might have found their way into the desert too."

Princess Safia frowned and exchanged glances with her brother. "There is a rumour of people from a new world arriving in the north. What world are you from?"

"One that has never heard of portals," Jaime said quickly. "How long ago did these people arrive in the north?"

"A few weeks. But I've never heard of a portal that connects to both the north and south of Parsa." She peered closer. "You do fit the description of the missing people."

Jaime's heart leapt. "People are looking for us?" That could only mean that they were safe and well, not lost in the desert.

"It would seem so."

"Can you help us reach them?" Jordan asked, "We'd be forever grateful for any assistance."

The princess pursed her lips. "The journey north is no easy undertaking. Nor is their kingdom somewhere you want to end up."

"We must find our friends, especially if they are in danger," Jordan said.

"Your concern warms my heart. Jordan, you should return tomorrow morning to meet with the head of my guards. We may be able to help you reach the north. And we can always use someone of your bravery and skill."

Jaime tensed at the thought of Jordan putting his life at risk again. Though it would probably be rude to decline straight away. Before Jordan could throw himself into another reckless situation, he replied, "Thank you for your kindness and generosity. We will consider your offer." He glanced around, almost expecting to see the people who haunted his dreams. "How many people are being looked for?"

"Aside from you two, two others. A young boy and a girl. You two are the first to reach our city. If I hear anything about others, I will send word to Eliza's house."

Jaime nodded. That meant only one of them had been found. "Has there been no news of any arrivals here in the south?"

"Many people travel through our portals, but none are lost."

A bell cut off their conversation, calling them into the next room for the main meal. Quite a formal affair, the meal promised to impress.

Dozens of people dressed finely in a wide range of clothes represented a variety of cultures. Clearly, they placed a great deal of importance on maintaining strong relationships with the people from the different worlds.

Ushered away from the royals, Jaime and Jordan had no chance to ask more. They were seated with a group of traders debating which world offered the best opportunities. Jordan quickly joined in, singing Aveya's praises as if he had been trading there all his life. He still had the scarf Eliza had given him and proudly showed it off to demonstrate the fine workmanship.

Jaime sighed. He'd rather ask more about this northern kingdom that everyone kept warning them about.

After dinner, they were escorted back to the entrance where their driverless chariot awaited. Jordan bobbed along, quite pleased with himself. "I'm going to come back in the morning to meet the head guard and see if he can help us."

Jaime's brow tightened. "Do you really think that's a good idea? We should probably move on as soon as possible and not get too involved."

Jordan leapt into the carriage and held out his hand to pull Jaime in. "Of course it's a great idea. Who better to help us?"

Jaime took his hand and jumped up beside him. "We don't know anything about them. You don't want to be indebted to them and end up stuck here, do you?"

"You're too pessimistic. It won't hurt to see what they have to offer."

Jaime stiffened as the carriage pulled away and sped through the shadowy gate, with no signs of stopping for traffic. The horse somehow found its way through the narrow winding streets, racing at impossible speed. In the dark, every sudden lurch felt like a near crash, but no one called out and the carriage remained upright.

Jaime pushed himself back into the seat, attempting to relax into the unpredictable movements. Beside him, Jordan didn't seem to notice the journey.

Jordan's face twisted into a scowl. "Why can't you appreciate anything I do? This is better than anything you could have planned." His voice raised. "I *earned* this. I risked *my* life. I invited you to share in *my* reward. You should be thanking me. But if you don't want to come tomorrow, you can stay with Eliza." He crossed his arms and stared off into distance, ignoring Jaime completely.

Jaime clenched his jaw and clutched the edge of the seat, his knuckles turning white as buildings appeared before them and twisted away just before they collided. Now was not the time for a calm discussion.

When the horse veered into Eliza's property and slammed to a halt, he breathed an audible sigh of relief. He took a moment to steady himself, but Jordan was already striding into the house.

Jaime followed more slowly, and by the time he reached their shared room, Jordan was already in his bed, facing the wall. He slumped onto his own bed, debating what he should say. After a while, he decided to wait for morning, when Jordan might have calmed down.

By the time Jaime woke, Jordan was nowhere to be found, so he headed into the town to see if he could find some traders heading north whilst Jordan had his meeting at the palace. Hopefully, Jordan would consider the consequences of his decisions before he acted. He certainly couldn't want to stay here.

A little fame was all he wanted. Jaime could allow him that. And if he got tangled up with those guards, Jaime would just have to help him out. These people couldn't be that unreasonable to keep Jordan here.

Jaime's optimism slowly diminished as trader after trader informed him they would not be travelling north, no matter how much profit could be made. One older man said he might consider the journey in a few months, once his sons had come back from their current missions, but only if he couldn't make enough money here in South Parsa.

Deflated by his lack of progress, Jaime returned to Eliza's house to see if Jordan had had any better luck. When he arrived, one of the camel keepers greeted him with a letter. The palace seal of crossed golden swords set his heart racing and he tore it open immediately.

The message was short, written in Jordan's scruffy handwriting. Jaime read it twice, only looking up as his hands started to shake.

It couldn't be true.

He dropped his hands to his side. Stared vacantly at the wall for a few moments. Spun around. Checked the letter again. Stuffed it in his pocket, then sprinted into the street.

Running as fast as he could, he wound through the streets more erratically than the masterless horse had the previous night. The correct route eluded his memory, so he followed the uphill paths whenever he could, knowing the palace stood above the town.

Three times he almost knocked people over in his desperation to reach the palace before Jordan did something utterly stupid. Twice he found himself at a dead end, his thoughts racing as fast as his heart.

What if he didn't get there in time?

Almost breathless now, and frustrated that he kept going wrong, he turned once more up a winding path, slightly wider than the previous streets. This one opened onto a walled street, one he recognised as bordering the palace.

His vision blurred as he pushed himself faster, consumed by one thought. A gate offered him a way into the entrance courtyard, and then he was hurtling up the steps, past the bemused expressions of the guards.

He practically fell into the fiery ombré entrance chamber, but he hadn't reached Jordan yet. Gasping for air, he glanced around, looking for a clue where to go.

"You must be looking for your friend," spoke a voice from somewhere in the room.

Spinning around, he discovered the same woman from the previous evening, wearing the same fitted red tunic. "Yes!" He sucked in a deep breath, his heart pounding loudly. "Where is he? I must speak to him."

"You're too late," she replied calmly. "The royal delegation has left. You should have received a letter explaining this."

"No— I mean yes, but I still need to talk to him. Can you tell me which way to go?"

Her stare turned glassy. "Of course not. Even if I did know the route, I could not reveal it to you."

"Who can I ask then?" Jaime cried.

"Only the royal family and their most trusted advisors know the routes, and they do not share them with anyone. You were there in the marketplace. Do you want thieves and marauders attacking the princess?"

Jaime's heart plummeted. "No, I suppose not."

"Now, please see yourself out. The palace is not a guest house."

His adrenaline abandoning him, he stumbled back outside. He did not doubt that no one knew the route the royal delegation would take through the desert, and it would be impossible to find the convoy on his own.

So what was he supposed to do now? Carry on without Jordan?

CHAPTER 22
NORTHERN DESERT TRAIL

Jordan hadn't had much choice about leaving Jaime behind. The opportunity had been too good to pass up and there was no way they could take Jaime with them. He just wasn't cut out to be a guard.

And he'd only hold Jordan back. He'd proved that already, trying to convince him not to collect his reward.

But it wasn't Jaime's fault. That was just the way he was. Plenty sensible for normal life, but here they had to risk a little to get ahead. And what a prize he'd earned. As a royal guard, Jordan would be in the inner circle of royalty, and taken right to the northern palace. No worrying about searching for traders or trying to earn money. He'd earned his way with his sword and his bravery.

After demonstrating his skills to the head guard, there'd been no time to tell Jaime in person, so he'd hastily written him a letter. The mission had all been planned and prepared for, and it was just extreme bad luck one of the princess's personal guards had been injured the previous day.

But their misfortune was Jordan's gain. There could be no better reward.

He wasn't too worried about Jaime. With Eliza and her family, Jaime had plenty of prospects to earn some money and live comfortably until Jordan returned. He might even find them a portal to return home if he had any sense.

This way, Jaime wouldn't get in the way of Alice and him either, so the circumstances had their upsides ... he grinned at that thought.

Not that the journey would be easy. Sitting at the campfire, chewing on something that was more gristle than meat, he already missed the fine food of the city. He took a swig of refreshing liquid from his dwindling supply, only to spit it out again when Kasan, the most enigmatic of the guards, materialised right beside him.

Tedric, a younger and more talkative guard, smirked at him from across the fire. "So, they don't have magic where you're from?"

Shaking his head, Jordan glanced suspiciously at Kasan. Summoning fire was one thing, but disappearing and reappearing at will? *That* was highly disconcerting. Nevertheless, he had to admit it was useful for Kasan to teleport ahead and scout the route or check for water. But he could find another place to reintegrate ...

Tedric adjusted his meal over the fire. "You'll have to get used to it. Where we're going, magic is practically revered and the whole mage caste teleports around. Many can sense their destination so precisely they can materialise within a crowd. Kasan's still working on that," he said with a wink.

A scowl darkened Kasan's already stern face. "The mages of North Parsa devote their entire lives to magical study. No one compares to them." He dropped down beside Jordan, helped himself to some slightly overcooked lizard, and met Tedric's smirk. "I don't see you working on your teleportation skills."

Jordan's head snapped back to Tedric. "You can perform magic too?"

"A little, but Kasan is right about the north. They have entire libraries bursting with information." He gave a mischievous grin. "Perhaps we can pick up a few books whilst we're there."

Jordan tensed. Northern mages didn't sound like the type of people to be trifled with. If Kasan envied them, they must be capable of unimaginable feats.

"Are you regretting your decision?" Princess Safia asked.

"No," he replied with confidence. Unlike any princess he'd ever imagined, Safia often showed how much she cared about her people. Since he had first seen her healing her wounded guard, he had observed her tending to the camels, helping with the food preparation and talking with the other guards as if she were one of them. If she could handle the desert, so could he. "This is the best way to find all my friends. If they turn up in the south, Jaime can be there for them. If they're in the north, I'll find them and bring them back to the south and we can find a way home together."

"You must be very close to travel all this way on the off-chance they are the ones looking for you."

He flushed, realising the scale of the undertaking he had embarked on for a girl he had a crush on, her friend and her friend's brother. Tendrils of doubt crept into his mind, reminding him of other lost friends. Friends who had quickly forgotten Jordan when his world had collapsed.

But he'd been the one lost then, not them. He wouldn't be that fickle. "I can't just wait to see what happens. I have to do something," he finally said, his chest tight. These were the types of doubts Jaime usually voiced and he'd never had any problem ignoring them before.

Unprepared for these emotions, he changed the subject to more pressing matters. "Why can't magic conjure water?"

Safia smiled at him. "It can, if you're skilled enough. I can summon water in an emergency, but it drains my strength considerably, especially in such a dry environment. Many of the mages in North Parsa can do it with less difficulty, so they have an advantage over us already. Ironically, it is much easier to summon fire than water, though I suppose it is always easier to destroy than create, and flame, once sparked, easily spreads."

As Safia was explaining, a young woman Jordan had never seen before teleported in. Somehow, she knew exactly where the group rested, despite their route being kept secret.

Safia jumped up to greet her and the two of them hugged like sisters, though they couldn't have looked more different. Safia was curvy and dark-skinned with fiery red curls, whereas the newcomer was slender and olive-skinned with straight black hair.

"I'm sorry I missed you at the palace," the new arrival said to Safia. "There have been some interesting developments in the north, and I thought I ought to find out as much as possible." She looked enquiringly at Jordan, making his skin crawl as he was exposed as the outsider to the group.

"This is Jordan, my new guard," Safia explained. "He saved my life yesterday. You can talk freely in front of him. He's from an undiscovered world and wants to get back to it as soon as he's located his friends." Safia turned to Jordan and said in a tone that conveyed great affection, "This is Torvia, my most talented and loyal subject."

With overt curiosity, Torvia contemplated Jordan. In his uniform, he didn't think he looked that different from the other guards, but Torvia evidently found something interesting about him.

"There's a newcomer in the north, too. A girl. All the palace is abuzz about her arrival and the interest the royals have shown in her."

Jordan's heart skipped a beat. "Do you know her name?"

"She's called Alice."

"Yes!" he exclaimed, a grin spreading across his face. This was his proof he'd been right to join them. "That's who I'm looking for. Was there another girl too, and a boy?"

Torvia shook her head, glancing at Safia. "No, just the girl with yellow hair."

Jordan's face fell, his euphoria abandoning him as quickly as it had arrived. At least he had found some good news. Perhaps Emily and Eliot were in South Parsa after all, and would reunite with Jaime, whilst he went off to rescue Alice.

"Do you know why they're interested in her?" Safia asked.

"There can only be one reason. She must be from a technological world." Torvia turned to Jordan. "Do you have advanced weaponry on your world?"

"I suppose ..." he replied, his thoughts elsewhere.

Safia and Torvia exchanged a meaningful glance, worrying Jordan. "Are your kingdoms at war?" he asked.

"We have no intention to go to war with anyone, especially North Parsa," Safia answered. "But we must be vigilant when our rivals seek out new technology." Safia turned to Torvia. "The Royal Mage already visited. He'll send his mages to keep searching. Torvia, I want you to go back to South Parsa and find another boy called Jaime. Keep an eye on him and see if you can find out what the Royal Mage wants with him."

"Yes, princess." Torvia bowed her head, then turned her attention to the fire and the food that remained. Kasan moved aside as Torvia sat with them, and handed her a well-cooked lizard.

Jordan watched her for a few moments longer. It would be good for someone to look out for Jaime, but there was something strange about this woman. And he could only imagine how Jaime would react if she teleported into his room. Jaime was hopeless with strangers, especially girls, let alone magical ones.

If only Jordan had known about this Royal Mage sooner, he could have warned Jaime. But then he probably would have had to stay with him. He'd just have to trust this Torvia. After all, she worked for Safia, who appeared to trust her. "What will this Royal Mage do with Jaime if he finds him?"

"He will *not* find Jaime," Safia said. "The Royal Mage is not as powerful as he thinks, nor does he have the support he believes. You need not worry about that."

"But he has Alice already. What will he do with her?"

Torvia reached for another skewer. "Alice is under the protection of Prince Darien. He too will want to find new portals and technology to enhance his power, influence, and wealth. There's quite a bit of competition between them." She turned to Safia. "Princess Yasmin just seems to want a friend for herself. I don't think she's a threat to us, despite the potency of her magic."

Jordan's breath hitched. Was Torvia a spy? He tried to contain his awe as he continued. "What do you mean, a threat to you? Aren't you going to be allies through your marriage?" The whole point of this journey was for Safia to meet her groom and secure an alliance with the north, so he was confused at this new revelation.

Safia eyed him with interest. "Life on Parsa is complicated, especially in the north. The Royal Mage wants greater control over the south and the portals here, and will seek to gain it in any way he can, even if it means marrying off one of the North Parsan royals."

Torvia exchanged a sympathetic glance with Safia, and Jordan started to appreciate how different things were here. Safia might be entering into this marriage of her own free will, but it was entirely for diplomatic reasons.

Safia squeezed Torvia's hand before she continued. "He doesn't understand the marriage won't give my new husband any power by South Parsan law. Only the council of elders can choose who rules and what roles they will take, depending on their virtues of course." She sighed heavily. "Not that laws matter to him. No one disagrees with the Royal Mage, perhaps not even the king of North Parsa. The Royal Mage is the most powerful mage in all the known worlds. He can teleport straight to South Parsa in one jump, so we have to be very careful what we do."

Jordan's stomach churned as they described the Royal Mage. "This Royal Mage is in the south looking for Jaime?"

Safia shook her head. "He has returned to the north, but his mages will continue to search." She gave him a reassuring smile. "Don't worry, Torvia will look after your friend."

Jordan glanced back at Torvia but was not reassured. She might be good at snooping around palaces, but nothing he'd heard suggested she could protect his friends from this terrifying man. His stomach knotting, he wished he could turn back now and warn Jaime. "Will Alice be safe in the north?" he asked, not optimistic about the answer.

Torvia and Safia exchanged glances again, and it seemed neither one of them wanted to respond.

It was Safia who eventually answered. "It appears Alice has made quite an impression, so it will be difficult for her to go missing. The Royal Mage tends to respect customs and royals, even if their power is not as great as his own. As long as she remains a guest of the royals, she will be relatively safe."

Jordan gulped. That was not very reassuring. He had to get to Alice before she disappeared. Though if he was to save Alice, he would need as much information as possible. "So, in the north, how do they decide who becomes king?"

"Generally, the eldest son inherits the throne on his father's death, but coups are not unheard of."

"But in the south, the council of elders decided you would become queen?"

"Yes. They decided I possessed the best attributes for ruling. My elder brother is an excellent soldier and leader, so is the ideal general of our army. Unfortunately, he has little patience for politics. My younger brother, on the other hand, is an exceptional diplomat and can settle the angriest of trade disputes, but does spend a bit too much time enjoying the benefits of his position. He's also not so enthusiastic at dealing with issues he considers boring, such as infrastructure and housing."

Jordan's thoughts drifted back to the portraits in the palace as she discussed her family. "But the ruler is always a member of the same family?"

"It has been, but it doesn't have to be. The council of elders could potentially choose someone else from among the prominent leaders if they thought they would be the best person for the job."

"But there wouldn't be anyone suitable," Torvia said. "Most people don't know anything beyond their trade."

"True, it would be difficult for someone to gain the broad education royal children receive, so the job stays within the family. Most occupations are like that," Safia finished.

"Then who chooses the council of elders?" Jordan asked.

"They are elected from the different trade bodies and craft guilds. All the members are eligible, and each receives a vote, but usually the eldest and most experienced members are selected, hence their name." Safia smiled. "You're very curious about government."

"Er, I just wanted to understand the world and where we're going. Will it really be as dangerous as people suggest?"

"No," Safia said. "They have fewer freedoms in the north and it is much more heavily policed, so there won't be an attack like in the marketplace yesterday."

"What about this Royal Mage?" The man sounded terrifying, and Jordan was in no hurry to meet him.

"If we anger him, there's nothing you could do. Not even my brother's entire army could protect me. They say he wiped out an entire army with a single spell. Best to keep on his good side."

His throat uncomfortably dry, Jordan swallowed. "How can people live in a place with a leader like that?"

"He protects them from their enemies, so most people benefit from his presence. Only criminals, his opposition and people like my younger brother need to worry about him. Can you believe they punish a man for loving another man? If Otis had been born there, he would have probably disappeared long ago. Or worse." Safia sighed. "There is a small resistance of lower-level mages and non-magical people, but they don't have much power. All they can really do is smuggle unfairly convicted people out of the city. It's a miracle they haven't been discovered yet."

Jordan glanced at Torvia. "And tell you about their kingdom?"

Safia smiled. "Offending the sensibilities of powerful mages isn't a crime in our kingdom. We can offer them a better life. And in return why shouldn't I find out about the family I'm marrying into?"

Jordan nodded, but he didn't envy Safia.

Though she didn't seem at all put off. Their elders had chosen their ruler well.

CHAPTER 23
NORTH PARSA

The following morning, Alice woke early and headed to the courtyard garden. It wasn't at all coincidence that she found herself with a good view of Darien and Javed as they emerged to train. Her best chance of convincing Darien to take her to other worlds relied on catching him alone, but she couldn't resist the opportunity to watch him fight.

They wasted no time, Javed lunging at Darien barely a moment after they had secured their helmets. The blows rang throughout the courtyard, even more deafening than from her balcony, and for a heartbeat Alice worried about Darien's safety. However, whenever he failed to block Javed's attack, his light armour flashed blue, as if magic shielded him too.

It wasn't long before they were interrupted by the arrival of Officer Gul, looking rather ragged in his slashed and blood-stained tunic. He walked stiffly, with something clutched under his arm. With a sidewards glance at Javed, he bowed to Darien.

She ducked back into the shrubbery to avoid being seen, whilst trying to get a better view of the object Officer Gul concealed under his arm, but Javed's gaze had already flicked to her. Even so, he paid her little attention, quickly finding another soldier to spar with.

When she looked back, Darien and Officer Gul had already vanished. Disappointed, she headed in to breakfast, debating whether she should tell Yasmin what she'd seen.

To her surprise, Javed appeared just as she sat down. "I hope you're not worried about Officer Gul. He shouldn't have turned up like that."

"Not at all," she said quickly. "He looked like he'd already been healed."

Javed nodded, though his eyes darted to the door, where Darien had appeared.

"Given up on training already?" Darien asked.

Javed's face twisted into a puzzled frown. "Of course not. You know where to find me if you want to continue."

"Don't be like that. Stay for breakfast." Darien strode forwards and took a purple berry pastry whilst Javed slid into a chair, not looking too pleased at the invitation.

Alice stared at the peculiar behaviour. How could Javed have happily pummelled Darien with a sword only minutes ago, only to turn into a meek, obliging subject now? With a frown, she turned to Darien. "How is Officer Gul?"

His eyes slid to Javed, who already nursed a twisted pyramid lattice oozing with orange fruit.

"I saw him in the courtyard," she said firmly, bringing Darien's attention back to her.

"Did anyone else see?" he asked.

Javed straightened. "You shouldn't keep secrets from Yasmin. She'll find out, anyway."

Unbothered by Javed's warning, Darien reached for another pastry. Flame consumed it before it reached his mouth.

Alice jumped, then froze as she beheld Yasmin's furious expression. A hand pressed on her shoulder, and she found herself at a new table in the corner of the room, with Javed beside her.

She spun to face him. "What are you doing?"

"Trust me, you don't want to be in the way."

Alice glanced back at Yasmin as she bore down on Darien, her hand already glowing. Darien calmly reached for another pastry, which only seemed to infuriate Yasmin further. As her scowl deepened, sparks flew from her clenched fists.

"How dare you sit here whilst you send Navid to dangerous worlds on your personal errands?"

Darien frowned. "That is his job—"

"It is not his job to risk his life at your personal whim. He serves North Parsa, not your ambition."

A smirk spread across Darien's face. "That's what bothers you, isn't it? That he might have learned something you don't know. Not that you care anything about why he risks himself."

Flame erupted from Yasmin's outstretched hand, setting the entire table alight.

Alice jumped up in shock, but Darien only looked in dismay at the burning bread. She turned to Javed. "Shouldn't you do something?"

He shook his head, then spoke quietly. "They both outrank me. Besides, Darien never loses his temper, not even when it would benefit him." He sighed. "Yasmin has enough temper for them both."

"Navid is not your errand boy. If you're too afraid to go yourself, don't send anyone at all," Yasmin growled.

This time the flame lunged for Darien, meeting the blue shield and wrapping itself around him until the amber burned away.

Alice staggered back from the intensity of the blaze, staring incredulously at Yasmin. She should have known Yasmin had such power, but seeing her use it on a person, her brother, was another thing entirely.

Darien pushed himself upright, bristling at Yasmin's insult. "I am not a coward. And Navid acted of his own accord."

Alice glanced nervously at Javed. Just how well did he know Darien?

Yasmin scowled. "Don't tell me that. He brought you something. What was it?"

"If you want to learn the secrets of other worlds, *you* seek them out. Don't tell everyone else what they can and can't do." With a final glare, he disappeared before Yasmin could retaliate.

Nevertheless, she hurled another fireball at where he'd been standing, before turning to Alice and Javed. "Get out, Javed."

He inclined his head and swiftly teleported, leaving Alice to stare warily at Yasmin. She forced out the words, "What happened?"

Yasmin scowled. "Navid refused to tell me. He says he is honour-bound to keep Darien's secrets." She scoffed. "Darien doesn't deserve such loyalty."

Alice glanced away, unable to hold Yasmin's fiery gaze. Javed hadn't been worried at their argument, so she shouldn't worry either, but—

Yasmin strode over and took her hand, her skin surprisingly soft and cool. "I'm sorry if I scared you. Darien just has a way of irritating me like no other. He needs to start taking his responsibilities seriously, especially when the lives of others are at stake."

Alice nodded. "I'm sure he didn't intend for Navid to be injured." She halted at Yasmin's severe stare. "But you're right. He should be more responsible. Did you have to throw fire at him, though?"

Yasmin scrunched up her face. "I'm a mage. It's what mages do." Her eyes darted to the scorched table. "When they're not cowards."

Alice bit her lip. "He can't be a complete coward. He sword fights with Javed—"

Yasmin snorted. "Mages duel with magic, not swords."

Realising this was one of those unwinnable arguments, Alice sighed. "Why did you snap at Javed?"

Yasmin rolled her eyes. "Javed couldn't wait to get out of here, nor hide the scorn on his face. He'll be out training with Darien already. Go look."

"I will. Maybe I can find out what Navid brought Darien."

Alice soon found Javed in the courtyard garden, but he was no longer training. Nor was Darien with him. Sitting on a bench, Javed watched the soldiers spar, though he paid little attention to any in particular. As soon as he spotted Alice, he gestured for her to join him.

"Yasmin thought Darien would be here," Alice said, remaining standing.

"I think this time Yasmin went a little too far," Javed replied. "She should know Darien would never risk Navid's life for anything trivial."

"You could have said that."

"And get fire thrown at me?" He shook his head. "I'd rather stay out of their arguments."

Alice frowned. With his magic, Javed could have at least tried to calm down the situation. "Do you know what Navid brought Darien?"

"Some treasure from a faraway world, I'd imagine. Navid meets a lot of people in his role, and somehow coaxes out all sorts of secrets."

"Darien wouldn't tell you?"

"I didn't ask. Perhaps if Yasmin had asked rather than demanded, Darien might have told her."

Alice crossed her arms. "You don't think Yasmin was right to worry about Navid?"

Javed shrugged. "Yasmin has never cared about commoners before." His brow creased. "Perhaps you've changed her mind about them."

Her skin tingled as a mage materialised at her side, one she remembered from the evening of her second day here, and unforgettable from the scar on his face. "Excuse me," Ahmad said, dipping his head to Javed. "I hope I'm not interrupting."

"Darien isn't here," Javed said lazily.

"I see that," Ahmad replied. "Do you know where I can find him?"

"I am not his keeper."

Alice's eyes widened. It was not like Javed to be rude.

"Of course not, your highness. I am sorry I bothered you."

"Wait!" Alice called. "Do you know what happened?"

Ahmad dipped his head. "When furniture is incinerated in the royal breakfast room, gossip spreads faster than fire." Concern spread on Ahmad's face as he stepped closer. "Were you present? I hope you weren't caught up in the clash."

"I'm fine. I'd like to talk to you though, if you wouldn't mind."

"Of course." Ahmad held out an arm. "Shall we tour the garden? The blooms are lovely this time of day."

Javed jumped up. "Shall I accompany you?"

Ahmad smiled at him. "That won't be necessary. It is clear you are not in the mood for conversation." He waved his hand and a blast knocked two sparring soldiers off their feet. "Your prince needs someone to duel with," he called out to them. With what could only be described as a mocking bow, Ahmad backed away and held out his arm again to Alice.

Not knowing whether to be shocked or amused, Alice joined his side, but couldn't bring herself to take his arm. This man was rather unusual, but he certainly wouldn't have stood by whilst Darien and Yasmin were fighting. "Why are you looking for Darien?" she asked.

"Contrary to what people may tell you about mages, it is not normal for mages to attack royals at breakfast. I merely wanted to check on Darien. His magic is not as advanced as his sister's."

"Darien was not hurt." Alice bristled at the insinuation. "Yasmin is royal, too, and she had good reason to be angry. It was an argument not an attack."

"I am pleased to hear that. May I ask what caused such a disagreement?"

Alice hesitated. Neither Darien nor Yasmin would want Yasmin's affection for Navid to be widely known. And it was Darien's business whether he shared the secrets Navid had brought him with Ahmad. She could hardly imagine Ahmad would share them with Yasmin. "It was an argument about Darien's lack of responsibility towards magic," she said.

"Ah. The princess's standards are too high. Darien is not a bad student."

"The Royal Mage said he is."

"Another mage who has dedicated his entire life to the pursuit of magic. Darien is the crown prince. He has other responsibilities."

Alice smiled. Finally someone who didn't disapprove of Darien. "When we first met, you asked me what I thought of the Royal Mage. May I ask the same question of you?"

Ahmad laughed. "The answer to that question is extremely complicated."

"Well?"

Ahmad stepped off the main path into a grassy area surrounded by tall leafy plants, most deep green, but some with pink and purple tinges. "He may not be the friendliest of men, but he protects us all and he takes his job very seriously."

"Is it true he defeated an entire army?"

Pain flashed across Ahmad's face and his voice tightened. "Yes. Without the magic in his blood the city might not be standing now. He lost his own sister in that battle."

"I'm sorry if it brings back bad memories."

"It was long ago ... yet some wounds never fully heal." He sighed and led her to a bench overlooking a small pond. "All those who died secured the future of the city. The queen's children have grown up in peace ever since."

"But this enemy could come back."

"If they dare, Kavir will protect us once more."

"Why do they keep returning if they keep losing?"

Ahmad shrugged. "Why does anyone? They want the city for themselves. All the riches and all the portals. It's no secret that the city has prospered far beyond any other, and over the generations we've gathered more magic than any mage can ignore." He shook his head and let out a strange laugh. "If any of our ancestors met Darien, they'd think him a god with all the magic he can perform. So don't you worry about Darien's magic."

"I'm not, but I wish Yasmin was a little less hard on him."

"You have more influence over Yasmin than I. I hear the two of you are almost inseparable." He flicked a stone in the pond. "Though I wonder what Darien has done to make you take his side."

"I'm not taking anyone's side. I just don't like to see them fight."

"If you ever have any reason to worry, call for me immediately. Any server will be able to get a message to me."

"I don't think anything will go that far. Yasmin wouldn't want to harm Darien."

"Sometimes magic can be unpredictable, especially when emotions are charged. She wouldn't be the first to lose control of her magic."

Alice swallowed heavily. But if there was one thing she knew about Yasmin, it was that she'd never let her magic get out of control. "Thank you for the offer, but I'm sure it won't be needed."

With a nod, Ahmad stood. "Shall we walk back to the palace?"

"You haven't said anything complicated about the Royal Mage. What did you mean by that?"

Ahmad's face turned serious. "Is there something you wish to ask me?"

"Well, er – when he rescued me from the city I got a strange feeling. Like maybe he didn't want me to leave his chambers. Does he, er, ever keep people there against their will?"

Ahmad's brow wrinkled. "Only our enemies. He can be very odd, but if he had intended to keep you there, that is where you'd be. All I meant is that he's not the easiest person to get along with, but he is a valuable asset to the kingdom."

Accepting she wasn't going to get any more out of Ahmad, Alice returned to the palace. Until things calmed down, she probably wouldn't be going off-world. And right now, Darien and Yasmin probably needed her more.

CHAPTER 24
NORTH PARSA

Emily peered down the dark steps, trying to discern anything ahead. Without any light, she couldn't even see how far the stairs descended.

After finding nothing in the library about where Eliot might be held, she had no choice but to explore, and where better to search for prisoners than below ground?

Placing her hand carefully on the cold wall, she began her descent. No one had seen her enter, so there would be no one to come to her rescue if she fell.

Or got lost. Or got captured.

But there were no other options. She couldn't trust Prince Darien. If she told him what she was doing, she might as well tell him she was looking for Eliot, and that she was from the world he was interested in. The prince might help her, but more likely he would want her memories. For now, that cost was too high. She didn't want magic messing with her mind.

There were no books on memory spells in the libraries. She could only conclude that those spells were too advanced for the two- and three-star mages who visited, or that they were not permitted for regular mages. The king had not been impressed by Prince Darien's plan, but he had not forbidden it either, so she didn't doubt the prince had access to that type of magic.

Her footsteps echoed off the hard stone as she moved down into unknown depths. This was certainly the type of place she'd imagine prisoners being kept, but the door had not been locked or guarded. Nor had any magic blocked her path.

After what seemed an eternity, but was probably only minutes, the steps ran out and she found her fingers sliding across smooth wood. A door?

She fumbled around until she found a handle, then pushed the door open.

Cold air swept towards her, filled with an assortment of strange smells. Salt, spice and an earthy, nutty smell wafted past, not unpleasant, but not what she was expecting. Ahead, a gentle flickering lit up large crates and barrels.

A storeroom?

She followed the chamber to the next door, and the next, her hopes diminishing with each one. There was nothing here but stores of food.

Eliot had to be held somewhere else.

The only places she hadn't looked were the higher levels of the two towers. The mages would never let her climb further up the Mage Tower, so she knew little about what might be up there. She'd never seen anyone on the stairs of the Royal Tower, but if anyone caught her, she'd have nothing to explain her presence. If she was going to venture higher, she needed to know which tower held captives.

Trying to be satisfied that she'd at least ruled out a large part of the palace, she headed back up the steps.

The buzz of conversation greeted her even before she opened the door. It seemed a crowd had gathered in the main corridor, slowly moving towards the Grand Hall. She managed to sneak out and close the door behind her with no one noticing, but there was no chance she could try any other doors.

Instead, she made her way through the corridor to the Mage Tower to try the library once again. There must be something that documented where prisoners were kept, she just wasn't searching in the right place.

As she turned to leave, a flash of blonde close to the main hall doors caught her eye.

Alice?

Her heart leapt and her feet propelled her forward. She ignored the angry stares as she pushed past, trying to reach the front.

Guards at the door turned their heads to her, but she kept going. Just a glimpse would settle her worry.

Hovering at the threshold, she peered inside, searching through swathes of people in their finest, a spectacle far from the sensible attire of the city. More filed past her, taking seats at each of the tables, but none so dazzling as the people headed to the highest table.

And there she was … dressed like royalty in her sparkling blue gown. Happy and smiling to the young woman beside her. Prince Darien was there too, holding out Alice's chair, almost fawning over her.

So many emotions bubbled up, threating to overwhelm. Relief that Alice was fine, anger that she could sit here without a care in the world, but most of all, a desperate longing to run across the room, ignoring the guards that now moved towards her.

But if she joined Alice, Emily's cover would be blown. She'd no longer be able to search the palace for Eliot.

She hesitated a moment more, watching the young woman, most likely the princess, scowl at the prince as he ignored her and took his own seat.

There was no way to warn Alice about Prince Darien's plan right now, but there was plenty of time before the ball. When she'd found Eliot, her cover wouldn't matter. Now she knew Alice ate here, she could shove past the guards and run across the room any day.

Happier than she'd been in many days, she made her way up to the library. A few discussions with the trees resulted in a book documenting the history of crime and punishment.

Gruesome descriptions filled the pages, but she skipped straight to the end, where a short chapter reflected on the past and the improvements of the modern age. Nowadays, most criminals were exiled or sent to work on another world where they could be closely monitored and not pose a risk to the citizens of Parsa.

Finding the sudden change highly suspicious, Emily pushed it aside. Eliot surely couldn't have been sent to another world.

Out of the corner of her eye, she noticed a mid-twenties two-star mage watching her, a familiar caramel bob framing her pointed chin. With none of the usual disgust on her face, the mage observed Emily with intense curiosity. As soon as she saw Emily notice her, she looked away and left the room.

Confused by the woman's bizarre behaviour, Emily packed up her bag of notes and set off for the vague normality outside the palace. Used to the journey now, she barely paid any attention to the winding streets or the familiar figures. That is, until a hand grabbed her from behind and teleported her into a dark room.

Panicked, she shoved the mage away, then tried to run, half tripping over her skirt in the process.

"Calm down!" a voice ordered, before a fireball emerged above them, revealing the caramel-haired mage from the library.

"What's going on? Why did you bring me here?" Emily demanded, failing to hide the shaking in her voice.

"Listen. My name is Shirin. I needed to get you to a safe place to talk. Where we won't be overheard." The woman stepped back, giving Emily her space.

"What do you mean?" Emily's voice returned to normal as her initial panic subsided, though her heart still pounded.

"You've been snooping around the palace. Looking into books about prisoners. That could get you into trouble."

"How do I know *you're* not the one going to get me into trouble?" This woman couldn't have been following her for no reason.

"You should know by now the palace is where all the power is. That is what you should fear." As she spoke, her fireball flickered ominously. Was she doing that on purpose?

Emily glared at her. "But you're a mage. You serve the palace."

Shirin flicked her hair out of her eyes and contemplated Emily for a moment. "There are some of us who don't like the way things are run. Some of us have disappeared without a trace, so we keep our existence a secret. You will end up disappearing too if you're not careful. What exactly are you looking for?"

Emily hesitated, but she was running out of options. She could really use the help of a two-star mage, especially one who didn't approve of people going missing. "I'm looking for my brother. He disappeared and I suspect he might be in the palace."

"Why do you think that?"

"He came through a portal on the same day the blonde girl did, and someone told me a mage might have teleported him there."

Shirin pursed her lips. "Why would they be interested in him?"

"I don't know, he's just a little boy."

"Strange ... Well, if he's being held in the palace, he'll be at the very top of the Mage Tower, in the Royal Mage's section."

Emily gulped. "How do I get in there?"

"You don't. Even our most powerful mages wouldn't dare think of doing that. Unless ..."

"Unless what?" Emily moved forward, desperate for any help.

Shirin looked her over, as if assessing her capabilities. "You'll have to get past the mage on duty. There are lots of books in there. Perhaps you could use that as an excuse."

"Can't you help me?"

"No, not a chance. No one crosses the Royal Mage without a death wish. Only his nephew dares to defy him. You should convince him to get you in."

Emily blanched. Could she get Darien to do that?

It took Emily a few days to build up the courage, but the next time she saw Prince Darien, she casually approached him. "So, a mage mentioned the Royal Mage has his own collection of books. Have you looked through those?"

Prince Darien glanced sideways at her. "A mage talked to you? You must be more intriguing than you look for them to overcome their fear of talking to commoners."

She stared blankly at him, waiting for a proper answer.

How had she never seen through his charm before?

"I've perused them a few times, but they're mostly just advanced level spellbooks for four- and five-star mages. The Royal Mage isn't a collector of rare texts."

"It could be worth a look," Emily pressed.

"We'd have to walk almost to the top of the tower."

Emily nodded. "You can take me?"

He sighed. "Tomorrow, after breakfast."

Hardly able to contain her glee, she assented.

Early the next morning, Emily waited for Darien in his study, half convinced he would change his mind. Despite hardly touching her breakfast, her stomach was heavy with apprehension.

Even when she reached the Royal Mage's library, she would still have to find a way to sneak away to search an entire third of a tower without getting caught. It sounded impossible, but she'd made it this far. She could almost visualise finding her brother.

Eventually, Darien appeared and escorted her up the Mage Tower. It took a lot longer than she expected and she was out of breath by the time they reached their destination. This room followed the theme of the palace library, but the central golden tree was purely decorative. The books rested in normal shelves along the walls. Nevertheless, the tree was beautiful under a sea of silver stars.

The mage behind the desk was not pleased to see them. "The Royal Mage has asked not to be disturbed," he announced.

"That is fine," Darien said pleasantly. "I've actually come to look for a book. Well, my assistant here is going to find it for me."

The mage turned his attention to her, his eyes widening in recognition. He must have seen Emily in the palace library and knew she was no mage. "No, no, no, she can't come in here. Why must you always disobey the rules, Prince Darien? Please take her away." His tone shifted from superior to pleading, as if he were scared of the trouble he might wind up in but didn't want to forcibly defy Darien either.

"It will be fine. Just think of her as me," Darien said, walking further into the chamber.

The mage shifted uncomfortably in his seat. "No, I won't let her stay."

"Carry on." Darien motioned to her.

Step by step, Emily tiptoed past the mage, expecting him to stop her at any moment, whilst Darien seemed amused by his inability to figure out what to do.

"What is going on here?!" a voice boomed from the top of a short flight of stairs at the other end of the room.

All eyes shot towards the towering figure projecting the outburst.

Emily froze under his furious gaze, immediately understanding why everyone feared the Royal Mage.

"How dare you bring a commoner in here?"

"My lord, I'm sorry," the indecisive mage called.

"Out!" the Royal Mage yelled at him and he wheeled around, shooting through the exit as fast as his legs would carry him.

"Your insolence has gone on long enough, Darien! This is not your private palace. You are not above the law." The Royal Mage's features twisted with rage as he bore down on the pair of them.

"Uncle, she's just a girl fetching me a book," Darien said quietly. All the colour drained from his face and his charming demeaner had never seemed so far away.

Emily slowly retreated towards Darien. This had been a terrible idea.

"Silence! It's time someone taught you a lesson, you spoiled child. I am the power here, and you either obey me or you are my enemy."

Emily froze again, unsure of what was happening. This was no regular dispute. A normal man would never call his nephew his enemy. Her eyes sought the exit, so far away now.

"The crown is the rightful power," Darien yelled back. "It serves all the people, not just those with magic."

The Royal Mage laughed cruelly. "When have you ever helped the people, *Prince* Darien? That crown is a symbol of failure. Never once has it stopped invaders wreaking havoc in the city. Your father wastes time on fruitless alliances with inferior people. They won't stop the Iybryrians taking everything you hold dear. Have you forgotten they took your own mother?" The Royal Mage lowered his voice. "And you, crown prince, what have you done but shirk your inheritance and waste your gifts? With your magic you should be an inspiration, not an embarrassment to the kingdom."

Darien burst with rage, red faced and barely able to speak. "This is treason!"

The Royal Mage laughed. "You don't know the meaning of treason. Swear your loyalty to me now. Stop this foolish behaviour and I shall permit you to ascend the throne when the times comes."

"I am the rightful heir. You should be swearing your loyalty to me and my father."

Her legs shaking and her heart pounding, Emily resumed her wobble towards the door. Perhaps she could sneak out unnoticed while the pair were absorbed in their argument.

Once again, the Royal Mage laughed. "Girl!" he shouted in Emily's direction.

Cold shot through her, rooting her to the spot.

"Since you're here to fetch a book, fetch this one for his highness." A book appeared in his hand, and he held it out to her.

Shaking uncontrollably, she took the heavy volume and handed it to Prince Darien. Numerous family trees identified it as a genealogy book, detailing the family history going back dozens of generations.

"Tell me what you see on the most recent page," the Royal Mage instructed.

Prince Darien flicked the book open to the marked page, whilst Emily peered at it from the side.

It was clear straight away. Darien's father had inherited the throne from his older brother, even though his brother had a living son. Prince Javed was the rightful king but had been too young to claim the throne for himself. The secret had been kept from their entire generation, no doubt supported by the Royal Mage because his sister became queen.

Darien's face lost all colour, then he threw the book to the ground. "This is a lie!"

"This is the truth. I made your father king and if you want to inherit the crown, you will need my support. For that, you will start taking your magic seriously, and show me the respect I deserve. No more shirking your lessons and galivanting off-world. If the city is to be attacked, you will be here to defend it." The Royal Mage spoke calmly now, as if all was resolved. Turning to Emily, he said, "You, girl, come with me. I have some questions for you about your service to Prince Da rien."

Emily blanched, and her legs refused to move.

"No!" Darien shouted, stepping in front of Emily.

"No? Did you just say no to me after all I've just said to you? Foolish boy. Your magic is no match for mine. It's time you learned that."

Cobalt lightning shot from his hand, rushing towards Darien, before ricocheting off a sapphire shield.

Emily staggered back as a dark cloud followed in the lightning's wake. Several wisps brushed past her as it converged on Darien, numbing her skin where they touched. She rubbed life back into her arms as the cloud enveloped Darien, dimming his shield, until no light escaped.

Suddenly, gold sparks flashed throughout the cloud, dazzling the room. Emily shielded her eyes with heavy arms, until a loud thud sent a shiver up her spine.

The Royal Mage sharply recoiled his arm, his eyes black. Darien lay on the floor, his eyes closed.

Breathless and drained, Emily stared at him. She wanted to lean down and help, but her limbs wouldn't obey.

Hard fingers wrapped around her arm, and the Royal Mage pulled her across the room and up the stairs. She glanced back, just before he pulled her out of sight of the prince.

Darien lay there unmoving, and his uncle was just leaving him there. What kind of man would do that?

Emily's feet turned to lead. This was her fault. She'd convinced Darien to do this, knowing full well she wasn't accepted in the palace. And now she was at this man's mercy.

Repressing a shudder, she followed him deep into his private chambers, as reality slowly dawned on her. She'd never had any chance of sneaking in here.

But at least she was being taken to the place her brother was being kept, even if that meant imprisonment.

CHAPTER 25

North Parsa

Concerned by Yasmin and Darien's continuing feud, Alice decided to try talking to Javed again. He probably knew them best. And perhaps he could even be persuaded to take her off-world. It wasn't that she didn't believe Darien had spread the portraits of her friends, but there had been no news in quite some time.

By now she was starting to worry she'd never get home. After all this time here, moving to a new town didn't sound so bad. A few hours travelling was nothing compared to being stuck on another world.

The royal siblings' quarrel also reminded her of her own sister. Their arguments were never this dramatic. Though if they could use magic, perhaps they would be more like Yasmin and Darien. The thought spurred her on to redouble her efforts.

Annoyingly, Darien had disappeared straight after breakfast, so she couldn't ask him, even if his mood improved. Yasmin had taken the opportunity to accompany Officer Gul on a tour of the crystal caves on Stratis, leaving Alice in the courtyard garden. Since Yasmin technically wasn't allowed to leave the palace without a formal escort, Alice had the job of covering for her, though she couldn't imagine anyone asking about Yasmin's whereabouts.

To Alice's disappointment, most of the soldiers had vacated the courtyard garden and Javed was nowhere to be seen. She'd spent too long helping Yasmin select an outfit for her off-world adventure. Despite several times suggesting something more practical, this didn't seem to be in Yasmin's vocabulary. Eventually, Alice had convinced her to wear some long sturdy boots and to tone down the decorative embellishments, but Yasmin still stood out as a very wealthy woman, even if people couldn't recognise her immediately as the princess of North Parsa.

Alice suspected Darien would approve of Yasmin's new behaviour, but she wasn't going to be spilling Yasmin's secrets to anyone, not when Yasmin had only just started to exercise her freedom. Perhaps after a few more adventures, Yasmin would be less supportive of the restrictive aspects of this society and lose some of her prejudice. Then she might start to see Darien's worldview.

Amongst the beautiful fragrant blooms, a dragonfly flitted past Alice's head, reminding her of when she first arrived. Over a month must have passed, and she was still no nearer to finding her friends or a way home.

She told herself to have faith in all those who were helping. There was nothing else she could do. Still, thinking of them made her a little homesick and she would give anything to be able to visit a mall right now. Or to shoot her bow.

A door at the edge of the courtyard garden, nestled up against the central palace building, caught her attention. Perhaps there were other training areas where Javed might be. Cautiously, she pushed open the door, and found a smaller courtyard lined by two long rows of buildings on either side. They looked a little like stables, though the doors were full height and fully closed.

Further along the courtyard, she spotted an open door and headed over. Instead of finding a horse, she discovered Javed polishing his armour.

"Alice! What brings you out here?"

She stared open-mouthed at the peculiar sight for a moment. "I thought I would get some fresh air and explore a bit. I noticed these buildings and thought they might be stables."

Javed laughed. "There are no stables in the palace grounds, Alice. We keep some on other worlds, but they're no use here. We mages teleport everywhere and the soldiers stay in the city until they're needed off-world."

"Could you take me to some?"

"Take you off-world?" Javed shook his head. "That's not a good idea. Is there something you need?"

She sighed. "I was hoping there might be some news about my friends. Or a way home."

"There's no need to go off-world for that. Any news will be brought to the palace."

She nodded, though she was disappointed at Javed's rigid response. Somehow, she had to get him to open up to her, but she knew little about him. Her eyes followed his diligent movements. "Don't you have people to do that for you?"

His hands paused for a moment. "Yes, but I find it quite relaxing to do it myself sometimes. Have you become fed up of being Yasmin's fashion experiment?" His lips twitched into a smirk as he resumed polishing.

"No. Well, a little. Do you have archers on Parsa?" Hoping he wouldn't ask any more about Yasmin, she twisted her hands together nervously behind her back.

"Of course, the practice range is in the next courtyard. Would you like a tour?" Reaching a topic he found interesting, he set down his armour.

"Yes, please," she answered at once, bouncing onto her toes. As she realised she was behaving like her little sister, she stopped abruptly. That thought sent a pang of guilt through her. What would Natalie be doing now?

She'd probably be in less trouble without trying to follow Alice. She was more bold than Yasmin, despite Yasmin's power and position. Perhaps when Alice returned, she could take Natalie somewhere, just the two of them. She could even teach her to shoot. She'd always asked about archery.

Javed carefully stowed his armour and led her to the next courtyard, where archery targets stood, riddled with holes. The distance was not challenging compared to what Alice was used to, barely two-thirds of the sixty metres she regularly shot outdoors.

"Where are the bows kept?"

"In that building there. You won't find them that interesting."

She followed his gaze, tempted by the treasures within. "They're more interesting than ribbons and dresses."

"True," Javed admitted, changing direction.

In her eagerness, she got ahead of him and pushed the door open.

Javed rubbed his jaw. "That door should be locked. I'll have to have words with the master of arms to make sure he checks it's properly sealed."

Ignoring him, Alice charged inside to examine the bows. Simple – yet beautiful – one-piece wooden recurve bows with no trace of embellishments awaited her. Since they were designed for soldiers, most were too heavy for her, but that didn't bother her. She picked up one of the lighter bows and a full quiver of arrows.

"What are you doing?" Javed exclaimed.

"I'm going to shoot a few arrows," Alice replied in a no-nonsense tone, heading towards the target area. No one, not even a magic-wielding prince, was going to keep her from archery.

"You can't do that. You'll hurt yourself," Javed said, in both surprise and concern as he ran after her.

Disregarding his protests, Alice nocked the bow. It would take a lot more effort to draw and she was out of practice, but it felt good to hold a bow again.

When she released the arrow, it soared towards the target, firmly implanting near the centre. Not bad.

She knocked another arrow, ready to improve her aim.

"How did you do that?" Javed exclaimed.

"Just like this." Alice shot the second arrow to meet the first, slightly closer to the centre.

Javed stared at her, wide-eyed. "But women can't shoot."

Not at all bothered by his attitude, as long as he didn't interfere, Alice shot another and another, getting closer and closer to the bullseye. She didn't see the need to answer him in words.

"Are ... are you a soldier or a hunter?"

Considering her answer, she drew her arm back. She decided to stick with the truth. "I just shoot as a hobby."

"You're a decent shot. Better than many of the soldiers. I didn't know women could be strong enough to shoot a bow."

A glare was all it took to silence him, and soon he fetched a bow to join her. He was a fairly decent shot himself, but it was nothing like shooting with Jaime. Alice had little in common with Javed, and they talked sparingly. With Jaime, she could talk about anything or nothing for hours.

In her element, the afternoon flew by, and all too soon Javed suggested they head inside to prepare for dinner.

Reluctantly, she agreed, but she must have pulled a face at the thought of climbing all those steps because Javed said, "I'll teleport you to Yasmin's rooms. I wouldn't want her to scold me for making you walk."

Alice smiled, and swiftly dismantled her bow under Javed's watchful eye.

"You know, you might be a good influence on Yasmin. Perhaps even on Darien."

Her cheeks warming, she led the way into the equipment building. "I fully intend to make sure Yasmin challenges North Parsa's silly expectations."

Holding the door open for her, Javed raised an eyebrow. "You don't have to worry about Yasmin. She's quite capable of defeating any of my soldiers with her magic."

Alice dropped the arrows into place with a thud. "That's not what I mean."

"I know what you mean, but Yasmin has a lot of responsibility. You can't expect her to change so suddenly. Especially if you're not going to stick around."

Suppressing the pang of guilt, Alice changed the subject. "What possible influence could I have on Darien?"

Javed shrugged. "You're not like the mages and women around here. It's quite ... refreshing."

She shook her head again. "You should travel more. Darien's not so narrow-minded. What does he do all the time, anyway?"

With the wave of a hand, Javed sealed the equipment room door, then glanced towards the palace. "As the crown prince, he has a lot to learn, and many people to meet with. The king expects Darien to act competently on his behalf already, just in case something happens to him." He pushed his hair back with one hand. "Their arguments can be quite dramatic."

Alice raised her eyebrows.

"Nothing like Yasmin's temper, but enough to clear a room."

Alice's own temper flared. "Perhaps you could stand up for him instead of cowering in a corner."

Javed's eyes widened. "My magic is no match for Yasmin's and I'd only enrage her further. Besides, Darien would probably punish me himself if I challenged her." He lowered his voice. "He really cares about her, especially as he never knew his mother."

"But you said Darien should fight back."

Javed sighed. "Magical duelling is often how mages settle disputes, so he will lose respect if he doesn't participate."

He held out his arm, but she wasn't done questioning him yet. "Do you think him and the Royal Mage are doing everything he can to find my friends and a way home?"

Javed nodded solemnly. "I'm certain of it."

"Why?"

His eyes darted back to the palace. "New worlds bring new opportunities. There is little else as exciting."

"Even worlds without magic?"

"Every world has something to offer."

"Are there ever worlds that aren't welcoming?"

"Sometimes. But we have excellent traders. I'm sure we'll come to some agreement with your world. Now, I'd better teleport you back before Yasmin comes looking for you."

She pursed her lips but consented. Javed's hand barely brushed hers as he teleported her outside Yasmin's room. He bowed before leaving, but Alice hardly noticed, her thoughts on his words instead. If the North Parsans couldn't trade what they wanted, would they send soldiers?

They weren't invaders, so she probably didn't have to worry about that, but what would happen if people back home found out about magic? They'd stop at nothing to find a portal.

That couldn't happen. Despite North Parsa's imperfections, this place was too special to be ruined by an influx of careless people from Earth.

Satisfied she had some answers now, she knocked on Yasmin's door. Javed might have settled her doubts about the North Parsans finding her a portal home, but he'd done nothing to help her with Darien and Yasmin's quarrel. She would just have to convince Yasmin that leaving the palace was worth the risks, and Yasmin couldn't keep begrudging Darien for that choice. Hopefully, she'd had a good time with Officer Gul.

CHAPTER 26
North Parsa

Alice found Yasmin pacing her room, a fireball burning in her hand.

"Where have you been?" Yasmin said. " I've been looking all over the palace for you. I thought you might have wandered off and fallen through another portal!"

"I was just shooting arrows with Javed."

Yasmin stopped in her tracks. "With Javed? You poor thing. You must have been so bored. Where was Darien?"

"I haven't seen him all day."

"We'll have to quiz him at dinner, but first you have to hear about the crystal cave." Her eyes gleamed as she recounted her adventure. She'd picked up a few decorative crystals as souvenirs, but generally they were worthless, without any magical properties.

Extremely annoyed Officer Gul hadn't appreciated her outfit, Yasmin ranted that he had the audacity to suggest she wear something more discrete, at which point Alice strongly resisted the urge to remind her of their morning conversation. However, it was totally surprising that Yasmin even cared what he, a commoner, thought in the first place. Then she'd gone on and on about how Officer Gul had told her this and he'd shown her that, and how Darien was right about how knowledgeable and loyal he was.

Alice shook her head, glad Yasmin had found someone to excite her. Darien was quite the matchmaker, it seemed. "Do you think you'll go off-world with Navid again?" she asked.

"He told me about a world with waterfalls. I'd love to see those. But…"

"But what?" Alice pushed.

Yasmin shook her head. "I have a lot of studying to do."

"Navid might take you somewhere with magic you could learn. And a little break now and then wouldn't hurt."

"Perhaps." Yasmin turned to the wardrobe. "We should get dressed or we'll be late."

A little sick of hearing about Officer Gul by the time they went down to dinner, Alice scoured the entrance hall for Darien, but he was nowhere to be seen. Not looking forward to an evening of gushing from Yasmin, she pulled her towards the Grand Hall. However, a flash of flame had her staggering back in alarm.

Beside her, Yasmin didn't flinch as the Royal Mage stepped out of the conflagration, a deep scowl on his face. After all their awkward encounters, Alice realised she'd never seen the man angry before, and it was quite unsettling.

"Is something wrong, Uncle?"

He glanced at Alice before giving Yasmin his full attention. "You will have to tell me, Yasmin. I hear you have been travelling off-world with a portal police officer and this isn't the first time you've been seen with him."

Yasmin's eyes lowered immediately. "I'm sorry, Uncle. I should have said I was going off-world."

"Yes, you should have, but that is not what concerns me most. Why are you spending so much time with a portal police officer?"

Yasmin glanced at Alice, so she smiled back encouragingly. "He knows so much and as the Royal Mage-in-Waiting, it is important for me to understand other worlds and the people on them."

The Royal Mage's gaze sharpened. "It is entirely inappropriate for you to spend so much time with someone of his status. You should know that. It could damage your future prospects and that would be a terrible tragedy for someone of your magical inheritance."

He paused as a few mages appeared nearby, who – upon seeing the serious nature of their conversation – scurried into the dining hall. "There are plenty of mages who would happily escort you wherever you wished to go. I hope you will consider that next time you decide to venture off-world."

Yasmin opened her mouth to speak, but then merely nodded.

A pang of sympathy shot through Alice. All Yasmin's prejudice was rooted in her fear of disapproval from her uncle. Still, Alice was disappointed Yasmin hadn't stood up to him. With all her power and her family's general adoration, she couldn't believe Yasmin would put up with such restrictions.

Though magic wouldn't have helped Alice with her own parents. Or the cheat in the archery competition. Yasmin had to stand up for herself. Or have a friend to help her out …

Alice took a deep breath. "Perhaps *you* could take Yasmin somewhere?"

The Royal Mage fixed his beady eyes on her, so Alice stood taller, willing herself not to wilt.

"I can't do everything for Yasmin. She knows what is expected of her. She must learn to be responsible for her behaviour and stop shunning the mages if she's to have any hope of leading them." Ignoring the watering in Yasmin's eyes, he ushered them into the hall before they could say anything more.

Alice slid close to Yasmin. Looping her arm through hers, she whispered in her ear, "Don't listen to your uncle. He's wrong about Officer Gul and I'm sure you could arrange to meet off-world more discreetly."

Yasmin shook her head. "He's right. I should be more responsible. I should be spending my time with mages, not commoners."

Alice frowned. "Navid is not less worthy of your time because he doesn't have magic."

"It's my job to lead the mages, not attend to the other affairs of the kingdom."

Alice sighed. Yasmin's brainwashing was going to take a lot of undoing, but there was no way she was going to let her give up on Navid.

To her delight, she spotted the king exchanging curt words with the Royal Mage, which only deepened his scowl. Unfortunately, Ahmad, the head of the magic school, interrupted the conversation before Alice could hear what they were saying, and they all took their seats in silence.

Despite the Royal Mage's foul mood and the awkward atmosphere, Ahmad appeared positively cheerful. Apparently, being scarred by the Royal Mage hadn't rendered him skittish.

After a few uncomfortable moments, the king's gaze settled on an empty seat. "Is Darien not joining us this evening?"

"I have told you many times, you are too lenient with him," the Royal Mage answered.

"Missing the occasional dinner is no trouble," Ahmad said. "He keeps a busy schedule."

Under her breath Yasmin muttered, "He can go off for days without anyone complaining."

Before Yasmin made matters worse, Alice edged closer. "Perhaps next time you could go with Darien. No one could complain then."

Yasmin turned up her nose. "He could have at least mentioned that he was going somewhere."

Ahmad smiled at Yasmin. "This wouldn't be the first time he's made it back later than expected. Keeping track of time on other worlds is challenging for the best of us."

"Enough of Darien," the Royal Mage said. "Let us change the topic."

After dinner, they both decided it would be very sisterly to check up on Darien. Yasmin teleported them right outside his chambers, knocked on the door, then shoved her way inside, barely waiting for an answer.

Alice followed right behind, then almost walked straight into Yasmin, who had frozen at the entrance to Darien's bedchambers. Concerned, Alice peered around Yasmin, and her heart almost stopped. Darien lay on the floor beside his bed, his cheek swallowed up by a thick rug, his eyes closed and his skin ghostly pale.

Yasmin ran to him, calling his name, but he did not stir. No sooner had she reached him than she started casting a spell, her face contorted in both concern and concentration.

Alice stood paralysed, a wave of nausea washing over her. What could she do?

After a few moments, she slumped down beside Yasmin, watching the shallow movements of Darien's chest. He was breathing, so he was alive. And there were few mages more capable than Yasmin.

Eventually, Darien started to stir, and murmured confusedly for Yasmin to stop annoying him. Satisfied, Yasmin levitated him onto the bed, then turned to Alice, her face taut. "He was hit with a really potent draining spell. He's lucky to have made it back."

She put her arm around Yasmin, but the princess remained rigid and inconsolable.

"Darien is always going off on his own, with no protection. He's a decent mage and knows plenty of spells, so whoever did this must be extremely powerful and incredibly evil. No one on Parsa would ever dare attack a prince in this way."

Alice swallowed the lump in her throat. Perhaps Darien *was* wrong to be so cavalier. If this could happen to him – someone who could summon fire, cast shields and teleport – what chance did she have going off on her own? What chance did her friends have?

A knock on the bedroom door made them both jump.

"Excuse me." Ahmad dipped into a bow as he entered. "I didn't mean to startle you. Is the prince hurt?"

Yasmin narrowed her eyes at him. "Why are you here?"

Surprise flickered in Ahmad's eyes, but he didn't show his offence. "The door was open—" His eyes on Darien, he moved closer. "A mage informed me the prince was seen returning in a concerning state."

Yasmin jumped to her feet. "You know where he went?"

Ahmad shook his head. "Unfortunately not. Darien likes to keep these things to himself. Does he need a healer?"

"He'll be fine. His magic was drained, but he isn't hurt."

Ahmad pulled a vial from his tunic and set it beside the bed. "That will restore his energy when he wakes." He grimaced. "Though no potion will restore his pride."

Yasmin nodded. "Thank you, Ahmad. I will stay with him tonight."

"I'm sure that won't be necessary. I can call a server to attend him—"

"No," Yasmin said firmly. "I will watch him. You may go."

Ahmad dipped into a bow. "You know where to find me if you require my services."

After a restless night, Alice awoke early in the morning, and found herself missing the familiar sound of clanking. She imagined Javed sitting alone cleaning his armour, waiting for someone to duel with.

Preoccupied with Darien's situation, she tiptoed up to his chambers and knocked on the door. It swung open before she had time to worry about what she would do if no one answered. Darien must have magicked open the door, because Yasmin slept deeply in the chair beside him.

"Good morning, Alice. Do you think we should wake Yasmin?"

On hearing her name, Yasmin jerked awake and glanced around with wide eyes, before focusing on Darien. "Are you feeling better? I've never seen you like that before."

"I'm fine," he said, though he neither looked it nor sounded it. His usual charisma was absent, and his tone was flat and lacking its usual energy. His skin was almost grey, and the life seemed to have been sucked out from him. "I merely had an unlucky encounter with a powerful mage. I'll be prepared next time."

"Next time!" shrieked Yasmin. "Why would you go back?"

He reached out and squeezed Yasmin's hand. "It's my responsibility, Yasmin. I'll be fine, you don't need to worry about me."

"Tell me who did this and I'll send mages to arrest them."

Darien's hollow eyes flicked to Alice and back. "This is not your business. You're safer if you don't know."

"I insist you tell me. I have a right to know about dangerous worlds."

"It was my own fault, Yasmin. Please, let it be."

Yasmin pursed her lips, looking even more worried than the previous evening, presumably imagining what might happen if Darien was caught off guard again or couldn't make it home.

Alice, her face as tightly drawn as Yasmin's, shared her concern. Perhaps Darien was a little too reckless, but in this moment, she just wanted to reach out and take his hand too.

His eyes fell on the potion on the bedtable. "Who brought this?"

"Ahmad visited last night. He thinks it will restore your energy."

If it were possible, more colour drained from Darien's face. "Who else knows what happened?"

Alice bit her lip. "Only the mage that saw you and informed him."

Contemplating the potion, Darien nodded. "I see. Now, if you don't mind, I'd like to get dressed."

Alice and Yasmin exchanged glances before Yasmin took Alice's hand and teleported them straight into her chambers.

"I need your help," Yasmin pleaded, taking her hand.

"Anything."

Yasmin called for a server and requested their breakfast be delivered to her chambers, before explaining to Alice. "We could be here for a while. I'll need to get a book and a few things from the Mage Tower, but we can do the spell here."

Yasmin headed for her crystal circle that allowed her to teleport straight into her rooms in the Mage Tower. "Useless servers have been knocking my crystals around," she complained, before putting the circle back together and teleporting out of the room.

Only a few minutes elapsed until she returned with a strange assortment of things. She handed the single book to Alice and asked her to find the protection spell.

After spending so much time watching Yasmin study, Alice had learned some words, but the Parsan language was so difficult. She flicked through the book to what she thought was the right spell as Yasmin laid out various items. "Is that a rabbit foot?" she asked, incredulous.

"Yes. Do you know this spell?"

"Of course not, but they're supposed to bring luck on my world." Alice watched Yasmin with fascination. She'd seen her prepare many spells, but none with this assortment of ingredients.

"Interesting. Do you prepare them in chamomile?" Yasmin continued, her hands moving diligently.

"No. Are you going to eat it or cast a spell with it?"

"This is a complicated spell and we need all the correct ingredients," Yasmin said sternly.

Adopting the same serious expression, Alice focused all her attention on Yasmin.

With all the ingredients laid out, comprising bright fuchsia petals, a frothing green liquid and some amber dust, Yasmin retrieved the rare blue crystal Officer Gul had gifted her. She obviously thought of the gem differently now, as she set it down with gentle reverence.

She tied the rabbit's foot to the crystal, then submerged them in the jade potion before pouring in the shining powder. A pungent mossy smell tinged with chamomile and vanilla emanated from the mix, reminding Alice of the damp forest.

"Normally, this spell would be cast on the rabbit's foot, but the crystal will absorb and amplify the spell and the protection will last forever," Yasmin said.

"Wait, are you going to give Darien your crystal?"

"He needs the crystal much more than I do, and he did earn it spending all that time and effort trying to introduce me to Officer Gul." She finished tearing the petals, and with but a glance, the liquid began to stir itself. "Now the spell."

Alice handed her the book, and Yasmin gave her a hopeless look. "Fertility spell?"

"Oops." Alice's cheeks burned.

They both giggled, then the seriousness of their situation swept over them.

"Hold my hands and repeat after me," Yasmin instructed.

Alice looked doubtfully at the pages of incomprehensible text and back to Yasmin. "Will it mean anything if I join in?"

"It means something to me."

Alice did as instructed, and they began the lengthy spell.

We call upon the ancestors, blood of our blood. Infuse this crystal with your power.

We call upon the land and sun, givers of life. Nourish this crystal as the flower.

We call upon the sands of time, twister of fate. Bless this crystal in this hour.

As they chanted, the crystal grew brighter and brighter until it burst into flame. Shocked, Alice almost let go of Yasmin, but Yasmin squeezed her hands tightly.

When they finished the enchantment, all the items that had been tied to the crystal had burned away, but the crystal itself was unscathed.

"Shall we test it?" Yasmin asked.

"How?" Alice contemplated the crystal, but it looked no different to her, other than a lingering glow.

"You could put it on and I could try to cast spells at you."

That didn't sound appealing – so much so that she screwed up her nose in the same way Yasmin did.

"I'll just cast a tiny spell. How about an itching spell?" Yasmin fixed a chain to the crystal, melting the metal into an intricate swirl around the gem, and handed it to Alice.

Hesitantly, she looped the chain around her neck. "Okay, a small spell."

With only the slightest movement of her hand, Yasmin cast something, and the crystal glowed gently. "Did it work?"

"I didn't feel anything."

Yasmin cast another spell, this time causing the crystal to glow brilliantly.

"What was that?" Alice shrieked.

"What?" Yasmin's eyes widened. "Did it hurt?"

Alice shook her head. "No, but you made the crystal react strongly. What spell did you cast?"

"Just a four-star disablement spell I've been practising," Yasmin said, avoiding eye contact.

"You went from an itching spell to *that*?"

"Well, the crystal worked, didn't it?" Yasmin looked up at her from under heavy lids. "We should present it to Darien before he gets into any more trouble."

"Will it protect him from all spells?"

"It will counter most spells, unless they're strong enough to defeat my magic and the amplifying effect of the crystal. Of course, since I cast the enchantment, I can defeat the protective spell much more easily." She smiled mischievously as Alice handed her the crystal.

They returned upstairs, walking instead of teleporting, and knocked on Darien's chambers. This time there was no answer, and the door was locked, the telltale blue shimmer preventing them from teleporting inside.

They spent the rest of the day trying to find him, revisiting his chambers every few hours, but no one had seen him.

"Maybe he's just resting," Alice suggested.

"Maybe," Yasmin said. "I hope he's alright. I've never seen him like that."

Alice took her hand and guided her back to her chambers. No matter what Yasmin said about her brother, the shock of finding Darien unconscious on the floor had clearly affected her considerably. Perhaps there was hope for the siblings yet.

CHAPTER 27

NORTH PARSA

The next morning, they finally found Darien at breakfast, with his colour returned to normal. While he seemed to have plenty of energy, he was much quieter than his usual charming self, and he slid into his seat without a word. The last thing Alice expected to see was Yasmin hugging him fiercely, but that's exactly what the princess did before sitting down to breakfast herself.

Looking slightly annoyed at all the fuss he was receiving, Darien pushed Yasmin gently away. "Yasmin, stop it," he said calmly.

"You can't always be so reckless," Yasmin said. "What would you have done if you hadn't made it back? What would North Parsa do without a crown prince? What would I do without a brother?"

Darien took her hand in his. "Yasmin, you don't need to worry about me. It was just a little accident. My life was never at risk."

"You're not invincible, Darien." She pushed the crystal into his other hand. "I want you to have this. It's enchanted with a protection spell. Don't ever take if off."

Darien's eyes widened. "You don't know what this means to me." Finally relenting, he wrapped his arms around Yasmin.

The scene tugged at Alice's heart, and she glanced away, her cheeks warm. She was supposed to be searching for a way home, not getting caught up in this mysterious family.

A few days later, Yasmin and Alice were quietly sitting at breakfast, hardly touching their food, when Darien strolled in.

"Morning, ladies. Why are you looking so glum? Shouldn't you be debating the final touches on your outfits for the ball?"

Alice's mouth dropped open at the transformation. She'd completely forgotten about the dance and all the news it was likely to bring. Yasmin glared at him as if he had said something offensive.

Darien picked up a pink fruit, tossed it in the air, then took a large bite. "Actually, may I borrow Alice today?"

"Where are you taking her?" Yasmin asked, frowning her concern.

"Don't worry, Yasmin, I'm not going to take her anywhere dangerous. I just thought she might like to get something special for the ball." Totally reinvigorated, he winked at Alice.

"Off-world?" Alice asked. She'd about given up hope.

Yasmin eyed him with suspicion, as if she thought Darien didn't know the meaning of dangerous. "As long as you don't get into trouble. I don't want to have to send mages after you."

Before Yasmin could dissuade Darien, Alice chimed in. "Sounds like fun." Wherever they went, it would be worth the risk. It was time she saw other worlds for herself. And she could think of no better guide than Darien. "When are we leaving?"

"As soon as you like."

She wolfed down her pastry and looked expectantly at Darien.

The corners of his mouth turned up at her eagerness, but he swiftly finished his own breakfast and escorted her out of the room. "We'll need to find you some more suitable clothes. I prefer to travel a little less conspicuously."

With a spring in his step, he led her to a small room at the base of the Royal Tower, not far away from where they had been eating. The door opened before them with an exaggerated flourish of his hand.

Hit by a peculiar mix of cactus blossom and sandalwood, Alice entered the long, thin room slowly. Wardrobes towered along an entire wall, with a few doors left ajar, showcasing a wonderful arrangement of outfits. Many of the garments were suitable for day-to-day wear in the desert, but others had been designed to cope with much wetter and colder climates. A tingle of excitement shot up her spine as she imagined their destination.

Moments later, an odd-looking lady with dishevelled hair appeared, eyeing up Alice as she approached. "Prince Darien," she said, bowing. "How may I help you today?"

"This is Alice. I'd like you to help her find a comfortable and warm outfit, please. No sigils."

"Of course," she replied, with a knowing expression.

Immediately, Darien vanished, presumably to change his own attire.

"This way please," the woman said, leading her to a wardrobe full of simple and plain yet warm dresses. She could imagine Yasmin's disapproving expression if she had been presented with such outfits.

She settled on a dark green dress with long tapered sleeves and matched it with long black leather boots. The woman adjusted the outfit to fit Alice, and although she possessed a little magic, she was nowhere near as talented as Yasmin. The fabric just didn't hang as well in the flattering way that Yasmin achieved with every item.

Alice tried to manoeuvre it into a better position, visualising how Yasmin would have fitted it, and somehow it stayed in place. She was still fidgeting in front of the mirror when Darien teleported back in.

Dropping her hands, she stared in awe at his transformation to dangerous and capable mercenary. In his full black ranging outfit, not a trace of blue or gold could be seen. He no longer fitted in with the ostentatious North Parsan royalty, but his bearing still screamed regality.

She'd seen him in full armour and with a sword before, but that was just for practice. With his sturdy leather coat and boots, and tough tunic and trousers, she had no doubt he was capable of surviving the roughest and most inhospitable conditions. Even more, the black outfit complimented his hair and accentuated his dark brown eyes, drawing attention to his handsome features. She really couldn't image him blending in anywhere, no matter what he wore.

He nodded in approval of her outfit, but pulled out an ivy green cloak from a wardrobe near the door. Without a word, he swept it around her shoulders. A little magic fastened the cloak in place, then he gently adjusted her hair to fall over the cloak. As he did, his hand brushed her neck, sending a pleasant shiver through her body.

"Perfect," he said, admiring her new look. "Shall we go?"

She nodded and took his outstretched hand. A second later, they emerged within the portal cluster she had previously visited.

Noticing them arrive, Officer Gul marched towards them. "Prince Darien, Lady Alice," he said warmly, and he dropped into a bow.

"How are things today, officer?"

"Very good, your highness, all peaceful trade and plenty of taxes."

Darien guided them away from the other portal police. "You've been spending less time at the palace lately."

"Yes, sire." Officer Gul glanced at the floor. "I think Yasmin may not have enjoyed her time outside the palace as much as I had hoped."

"Nonsense. She enjoyed it immensely. Isn't that so, Alice?"

Alice gritted her teeth. Did everyone know about Yasmin's excursion? "Yes, she relished it. She's just been a little distracted lately."

A slight look of guilt flicked across Darien's face before he regained his composure. "That may have been my fault. Don't take it personally, Navid."

When the officer failed to respond, Darien pushed further. "Is there something wrong?"

"No, sire, not at all."

"You're among friends here, Navid. Did something happen?"

"No sire, everything was perfect," he said stiffly.

"So, she's a little different to what you thought?"

Navid hesitated, so Alice smiled encouragingly at him.

"Don't worry, Navid, no matter what happens, you'll always have a place at the Royal Palace. You're a loyal officer and an excellent leader. We need more men like you."

"Yes, sire. Thank you, sire."

Darien raised his eyebrows, waiting for him to continue.

"It's just ... she's so royal. All the time. I thought she'd be more sensible away from the palace."

Alice couldn't help smiling at the description. But would that put him off?

"Have some patience, Navid. She rarely sees anything beyond the palace walls. Looking like a princess and behaving like a mage is all she's ever known."

"Yes, sire. You have wisdom beyond your years." A small smile spread across Navid's face as his shoulders relaxed.

"Now, what of the search for Alice's world?"

The officer's face fell. "I was sure a route would have been found by now, but it is proving more difficult than anticipated. I have sent more men to search a promising portal, so it is only a matter of time."

This news might have upset Alice a few weeks ago, but she found herself glad for more time on Parsa. There was no rush to get back, and she had confidence that either Officer Gul or the Royal Mage, with all the power and knowledge between them, would find a way.

Darien placed his hand on Navid's shoulder. "I have faith in you, Navid. No one knows more about portal navigation than you."

"Thank you, sire. Though I suspect you may know more than you let on, with all your off-world adventures."

With Navid back to his cheery self, Darien grinned. "Prince's prerogative. Now, I'm taking Alice for a little adventure and some shopping. Keep up the good work."

"Yes, sire. Alice." He bowed, but Darien was already heading to a portal.

Almost running to catch up with him, Alice found her nerves tingling with apprehension as they approached the portal. Hanging unnaturally in the air, it shimmered and twisted in stark contrast to the still desert around her.

Darien must have noticed her nerves, since he put his arm around her and said reassuringly, "This is a simple trip and the current will be very gentle."

A wall of light slammed into them as soon as they crossed the threshold, but true to Darien's word, no current threatened to pull her off her feet. With a firm arm around her, he guided her to an oval only a few paces away.

As soon as they emerged back into normality, humidity stole her breath away. In her thick dress, the heat was stifling. She glanced at Darien to check nothing had gone wrong.

"We'll be teleporting to a secret portal to get to the next world," Darien explained. A moment later, they emerged before a new portal tucked between tightly packed spindly trees cradling a shallow pool, the rocks moss green.

"Hold on tight, this journey is a bit more difficult."

As he guided her through, a dry river crashed into her, threatening to pull her under. She wavered, losing her footing, until Darien tightened his grip and steered them across the current. This time the dazzling light dizzied all her senses, and she buried her head in Darien's chest until it was over.

When the current no longer churned around her, she opened her eyes. Lush greenery, so absent from Parsa, filled her view, and a cool breeze tousled her hair. Fragrant blossoms beckoned, dancing in the wind.

Darien looked down at her with concern in his eyes. "Are you alright?"

"Yes, I'm fine." She pulled away and straightened her clothes, but he put his arm back around her and teleported again.

Now in a small clearing, surrounded by tall evergreens, Alice could hear voices in the distance.

"This way," Darien instructed, leading them past another portal. No one guarded this doorway, despite its proximity to civilisation.

"Where are we?"

"A little undiscovered gem, known to locals as Camfis. There is an excellent marketplace here and they're more than happy to accept Parsan gold." He raised his hand, then stopped just before reaching her face. "May I?"

"May you what?"

"The people here speak a different language, one Yasmin wouldn't have given you with her spell."

Alice nodded. "Go ahead."

His fingers rested lightly on her face as he uttered those strange, guttural words, still incomprehensible.

"Yasmin didn't need touch to perform the spell."

Darien's hand recoiled sharply. "Yasmin's spell-casting is extremely advanced. She spends enough time perfecting her craft."

Alice's stomach clenched. She hadn't meant to upset him. But he never normally cared about such things. Did he think she did? "Too much time. Perhaps we should have brought her with us."

Resuming their walk, Darien smiled. "The people here wouldn't know what to make of her." He glanced sideways at her. "I'm surprised you were so willing to visit another world without knowing anything about it. Do people on your world travel often?"

"Yes. We can't travel to other worlds, but there are lots of different countries."

"Do you travel by horse?"

Alice laughed. "Not anymore. The quickest way is to fly."

Darien's eyes widened. "That's not possible. People can't fly."

"You can levitate things!"

"Other people, a small distance, but not ourselves. Many have tried, but the closest anyone has got is by controlling the wind."

Alice shook her head. "You can teleport though, so you don't need to fly."

He glanced skyward. "Still, I've often wondered what it would be like to soar above everything. When we find your world, I think I might visit."

"My people wouldn't know what to think of you."

Darien grinned. "You'll have to be my guide."

A few minutes later, the trees parted before a beautiful small town. There was nothing ostentatious about it, but all the buildings stood proudly in immaculate condition, as did the surrounding walls. A river meandered through the centre, as well as diverting around the walls, forming a defensive moat, but mostly looking picturesque. From the pristine state of the grey stone walls, there didn't appear to be much need for the heavy defences.

They walked straight towards the main gate, accessed by a well-worn wooden drawbridge. From the looks of the rusty chain, this had not been raised in a long time.

The people they passed were friendly, calling out to greet them as they ambled by, and there was no sign of any royalty or any mages. They could easily be walking through a European medieval city with the outfits people donned.

The woman wore beautifully woven dresses in a rainbow of colours, matching their long flowing hair, which varied from darkest black to lightest blonde. The men were similarly colourful with their stockings and tunics, though these were less patterned.

Darien led the way to the marketplace, having to slow his pace for Alice to keep up whilst she marvelled at all the wonders on offer. It was the noisiest place she had been in a long time, with people shouting their offerings and calling out to their friends. All manner of goods were being traded, from colourful spices to fine furs, filling the air with pungent exotic aromas. So much was on offer, she couldn't guess what Darien had brought her to buy. No one could surpass Yasmin's dressmaking and she needed little else.

Before long, they turned into a quieter street near the centre of the town, with jewels and precious metals of all kinds overflowing the stalls as far as the eye could see, glinting in the temperate sun.

Darien leaned closer. "There are no magical people on this world, but occasionally a rare magical crystal will turn up, which is useless to anyone here. A trader keeps an eye out for me, in return for a small fee. We'll visit him first, before we find something suitable for you to wear at the ball."

A tall, tawny-haired trader saw Darien approaching and called out to greet him. "If it isn't my favourite customer! I have some rare crystals saved up for you to peruse."

"Eric, it's always a pleasure to do business with you," Darien replied, as the trader retrieved the secret crystal collection. Far more beautiful than any she had seen, they dazzled with their shine. A variety of different colours, generally roughly cut and varying from the size of a pea to a tennis ball, they gave no indication of their magical properties.

As Darien hovered his hand close above them, three of the crystals started to glow, two purple and one green. Darien's expression gave nothing away about the value of the gems as he negotiated a price, though he couldn't conceal which were special.

They haggled for almost a minute before settling on several gold coins. He paid a further two for the trader's continued service in finding and reserving crystals for his next visit.

"Is the green crystal rare?" she asked Darien.

He turned to her with a quizzical smile. "Yes, how did you know?"

"I've seen lots of purple crystals in Yasmin's chambers."

"Ah. Yes, purple crystals are the most common, but they're still extremely useful at absorbing or reflecting magic. Green ones, however, are excellent for enhancing healing potions and spells."

As they wound away from the crowds, Darien glanced sideways at her. "I can hardly picture Yasmin without you anymore, but you never talk about your family."

Startled at the abrupt change in topic, she took half a step away. Despite spending so much time with his family, it seemed a little odd to talk about hers. Thinking about them remined her how long she'd been gone and left an unpleasant heaviness in her stomach.

She shrugged. "There's not much to tell. We're a normal family, without needing to worry about magic, portals, or invading armies." She met his gaze. "You should spend more time with Yasmin. You obviously care about her enough to introduce her to Navid, but have you ever talked to her about him?"

Darien's eyes hardened. "Such topics are difficult to discuss with Yasmin."

"You might find she's changed and is more willing to talk."

Darien shook his head. "Yasmin knows what is expected of her. I should probably try to be more like her."

Alice stopped dead at his sudden change in attitude. That was the last thing she expected to hear from him. Grabbing his hand, she pulled him aside. "You don't mean that, do you?"

He gave her a puzzled look. "You saw what happened to me. I have to be more careful."

"Careful, yes, but you don't have to turn into Yasmin."

Darien grinned and squeezed her hand. "Maybe not that cautious. I couldn't stay in the palace all the time." He kept hold of her hand as they meandered along the cobbled streets, until they reached a display with a fantastic assortment of jewellery.

"Darien, how about a new necklace for your sister, or perhaps your beautiful companion," the trader called out as she spotted Darien, then Alice.

Surprised the trader knew Darien by name, Alice surveyed the glittering treasures on display. One of the best collections she'd seen, the jewels must have fetched a fine price.

"I'm looking for something extraordinary. Something striking for my companion to wear at a ball, something that will bring out her beautiful blue eyes." As he said this, his dark eyes met hers, and she couldn't help but blush. This ball wasn't just about receiving news from far away worlds now. Darien had organised it for her, and now he was buying her expensive jewellery. Something more was going on.

The trader led them along the display to an even more expensive collection and selected a gold necklace with a leaf design. Blue stones with golden spines formed each of the leaves. "How about this one? The gold will shine as spectacularly as her hair."

Alice contemplated the design. The leaves were gorgeous, but so tiny they were hardly noticeable. On seeing her reaction, the trader selected another, a simple gold chain with a large oval topaz.

"These might be beautiful on a plain woman, but they would do not do Alice justice," Darien said, making Alice blush all over again.

"Very well. I don't have anything to match her beauty, but this is my finest treasure," the trader said, pulling out a necklace from within a cabinet.

The necklace was comprised of a similar design to the first, but with larger, more detailed leaves. At the bottom of the necklace hung a brilliant blue sapphire, set into a golden leaf with gold filigree detail. It was that unusual, Alice gasped.

"That's the one," Darien said, surrendering a handful of gold coins without haggling at all.

Alice shifted uncomfortably to have so much spent on her, but she supposed he could afford it.

Next, they sampled some of the local cuisine. Fish appeared quite popular, freshly sourced from the local river, but meat from the surrounding woodlands was also plentiful. The food was simple, but its freshness made up for that.

They meandered from store to store, finding delight after delight, until Alice noticed the sun approaching the horizon, even though it felt like they had only been here a few hours.

"Should we be getting back?"

"We've got plenty of time. The sun sets here much earlier than it does in North Parsa. It's only lunch time there, so we can stay longer and still be back before this evening's meal."

"Is there a good spot where we can watch the sunset?"

"Certainly. Let's go down this quiet street so we can teleport away without startling anyone."

Moments later they looked back on the town from high in the hills. To the west, the river joined a lake, which turned into a pool of liquid gold with the setting sun. Beneath them, a soft carpet of grass dotted with purple flowers stretched out to the forest.

"How do you think this place compares to North Parsa?" Darien asked.

"It's beautifully quaint and so friendly," Alice replied. "And so safe. I can't imagine there being any need for any portal police here."

"True, it has charm in its isolation. North Parsa needs its police or it would be overrun, not to mention the portal taxes ..." He trailed off, staring into the distance.

"There are a lot more people in Parsa to protect," Alice volunteered. It couldn't be easy to inherit the responsibilities of such a kingdom. She could see why he liked to escape to places like this.

Darien sighed. "True, but are all the people actually being protected? The palace towers above everyone, but the city walls are still half in ruin from the Iybryrian invasion a generation ago. The markets are half empty and taxes keep being raised to make up the shortfall, but where does all the money go?"

"Maybe you can do something about it?"

"Perhaps. But this is political talk. We're supposed to be enjoying the sunset."

With the dying sun, the little warmth seeped away and Alice couldn't help shivering. Darien, being the perfect gentleman, removed his cloak and wrapped it around her, pulling her in close. Heat rushed through her, and a fluttering spread through her chest.

There really was no end to the worlds Darien could show her, her very own magical prince. But he was more than that. She'd never been so intrigued by someone or so concerned about their wellbeing. This man had the weight of a world on his shoulders, a portal realm for a playground, yet he chose to spend his time with her.

And she longed to be closer.

Leaning into him, she felt his warm breath on her cheek, and his steady heart beating in his chest. He tilted his head towards her, his molten eyes meeting hers. A jolt of electricity rushed through her, and she broke their connection, her eyes falling on his soft pink lips.

An overwhelming urge to kiss him overtook all her senses. Darien was kind, loyal, adventurous. Confident. Kissing him would be like nothing she could imagine. And he was so close.

Could he feel the same way about her?

She had to know.

He seemed surprised as her lips touched his, but was soon kissing her back, sending a new wave of heat coursing through her. She expected him to politely pull away after a couple of seconds, but he entwined his hand in her hair and pulled her closer, kissing her more passionately and forgetting any sense of decorum.

The world melted away, until it was just her and Darien, together in a perfect haven. But all too soon it ended. As Darien pulled away, his eyes burned into hers and she felt she might drown in those mysterious pools of liquid cocoa.

Coming to her senses, she realised he looked lost and confused, for once not in control of everything. She blinked. That was a revelation. The kiss left no doubt that he desired her, but he didn't seem happy about it.

He slowly got to his feet and offered his hand. "We should get you back to the palace."

They returned to Parsa in silence, Alice reliving the last few moments in her mind.

Did he regret the kiss?

By the time they arrived at the palace, Darien was his usual self again and politely excused himself to prepare for dinner. Alice contemplated telling Yasmin but thought it better to wait to see what happened next. Darien might not want something so private shared with his sister.

Instead, she would talk to Yasmin about something that had been bothering her for a while. "Yasmin, why is the Royal Mage so accepting of me when I don't have magic?"

Yasmin glanced up from her spellbook and frowned. "My uncle may be strict when it comes to North Parsan laws, but you're not a North Parsan. Your world could become a valuable ally if we can find it, so that makes you important."

That made some sense, but the Royal Mage surrounded himself with mages and barely spoke to any diplomats from other worlds. "You don't think less of me because I don't have magic, do you?"

Yasmin dropped her book, bounded across the room, and wrapped her arms around Alice. "Of course I don't! You're the sister I never had and my favourite person in all the worlds."

Smiling at Yasmin's confession, Alice returned her hug. Yasmin had become like a sister to her too. Their relationship was so different from the one she had with Natalie, and with a pang of sadness she started to regret that they hadn't been close like this. When she got home, she'd have to change that.

She gently extracted herself from the embrace. "But what about Officer Gul? You were reluctant to even talk to him."

Yasmin flushed. "That's completely different. You heard my uncle. I have a responsibility to pass on my magic to a new generation, which means marrying an equally powerful mage."

Alice screwed up her face. "Do you really intend to do that? Your uncle isn't married and doesn't have any children, so why must you follow the rules when he doesn't?"

Yasmin smiled. "You're as bad as my brother! I want to have children and I want them to have everything I have had, so I can't really complain."

Alice sighed, wondering about Darien's thoughts on the matter. After all, he was the one who had introduced Officer Gul and Yasmin.

Trying to sound casual, Alice turned her gaze to one of Yasmin's spellbooks. "Your brother doesn't want to marry a powerful mage?"

Yasmin shrugged. "Darien thinks he can do whatever he wants, but he will have to marry a gifted mage, or someone important from a powerful world to secure an alliance. He'll learn that one day."

Alice pushed the spellbook aside. She had been right not to mention the kiss, but instead of feeling disappointed, she felt conflicted. She didn't want to marry Darien, but she couldn't forget the thrill of the kiss, nor the feeling that he, a charming magical prince, wanted her.

CHAPTER 28
SOUTH PARSA

Days after Jordan's departure, Jaime sat alone on a hill near the palace. Although he'd kept busy helping Eliza's family, and undertaking delivery work in the market, he found himself sitting here for an hour or so each day, wondering whether he would ever see his friends or his home again. There had been no sightings of them, and no further word from the palace, so South Parsa no longer held purpose for him. He had to believe they were all in the north, but getting there was proving problematic.

With a sigh, he stood and started his journey back to the house. Eliza's family had been very welcoming, and he spent a lot of time with them, but he missed building things and tinkering with his own family. After Eliza's departure on a new trade journey, he had been a little mopey, so to pay back their kindness, he'd offered to teach her two younger brothers how to shoot a bow during the evenings.

It was at these times he most missed Alice. He would have quite happily put up with being beaten, and even being teased about it, just to hear her voice. Even to be surrounded by his annoying brothers, instead of the throng of strangers he now weaved around, he would have given anything.

Over and over, he replayed the day of Jordan's disappearance in his mind, trying to figure out what he could have done differently, not able to accept there was nothing he could have done. Now, Jordan's fate lay with strangers, and he had no way of knowing how he fared. Nor even how far he'd travelled.

Perhaps Jordan had been right to jump at the opportunity.

And it was Jaime's fault he was stuck here. Too cautious to do what was needed. If only he'd accompanied Jordan to the palace, they might never have been separated.

Now Jaime was the one in need of rescuing. He scowled at that thought.

But he hadn't given up on finding his own way north. Sooner or later he'd convince someone the journey was worthwhile, even if he had to pay them. Unfortunately the desert expanse put off all but the most determined, so he'd have to look elsewhere for someone bolder. He just didn't know where yet.

A few steps down a dusty, lesser-travelled passage between old buildings, a door flung open, blocking the narrow street. He waited for someone to exit, but no one appeared.

Confused, he tried to push past it, but it wouldn't shift. Nothing wedged it open, so there was no reason why he shouldn't have been able to move it. Nothing in the dark room offered an explanation either. He turned around to follow a different path. There were many routes through this labyrinth.

After only a few steps, another door opened in front of him. Opening outwards, it trapped him in the street. Rather more annoyed, he gave it a strong shove, but this too wouldn't budge.

This was very odd. He possessed nothing worth stealing, carrying only a few coins around with him. The rest of his earnings he saved and hid in his room.

He had no choice but to turn around again and enter the dark chamber to find out who was messing with him.

Peering inside, he squinted at the wall, looking for any hanging lamps. The faint outline of what might be a lamp rested only a few paces away. Steeling his nerves, he tiptoed towards it. Until the door slammed behind him and all light disappeared.

A moment later, four lamps lit up simultaneously, dazzling him with sudden brightness. He froze, unnerved by the sense that someone stood behind him, despite his certainty that the room had been empty when he entered.

Catching his breath, he spun to discover a slender, dark-haired woman, casually observing him from beside the wall. She had not been there a moment ago.

Looking quite plain wrapped in her sand-coloured cloak, something about her unsettled him, or perhaps it was the manner in which she observed him. Her amber eyes stared at him unblinking, burning in unison with the fire lamps, but she leaned against the wall, as relaxed as Eliza in her family home.

After a few moments, she walked towards him, passed him, and proceeded into another room.

Hesitation rooted him to the spot. What kind of person greeted someone this way, not saying a word? Though if she were going to harm him, she probably would have by now. Following was the only way he would get answers. And a way out.

"I've been watching you," she announced coolly as he caught up with her in another empty room.

The hairs on the back of his neck stood up. "You mean in the street?"

"For several days now. You're not from here, are you? Or one of the known worlds."

His worse fears confirmed, he nodded. But what did she want from him?

She'd probably been planning this for days and he'd been totally oblivious. He'd become so comfortable in his routine that he'd forgotten his fears about someone wanting information about a new world.

She'd had him trapped from the moment he walked into the narrow street.

Thankfully, he'd hidden his phone and watch in his room to avoid attracting attention.

She pulled out his watch. "What is this?"

His stomach clenched. She must have been in his room. He glanced around for another exit. There didn't appear to be anyone else in the building, so perhaps he could surprise her and push past her to escape. Small and slender, she didn't look like she would be able to stop him, and she was only a couple of years older than him, though her confidence had made her seem older at first.

"Or this?" Watching him intently, she pulled out his phone.

Fortunately, the battery was dead, so the phone didn't do anything, but it was still so foreign compared to anything else in the city.

Maybe he would get away with playing dumb. "Er, I bought them at a market on Aveya. The bracelet is supposed to tell the time and the metal thing is an interesting paperweight. At least, that's what the seller told me."

A frown formed on her brow as she scrutinised the objects, until amusement lit up her face. "So, this tells the time on your world. Your days must be so short!" More seriously, she asked, "What powers it?"

Jaime twisted his hands in his sleeves. "I don't know, I just bought the thing."

She stepped closer, not held back by being shorter than him, even in her heeled boots. To be so confident, she must be capable of wielding magic.

"You're lying," she said in a threatening tone.

Jaime gulped. Just what was she capable of? "I really can't help you. You can torture me, but I don't have anything to tell you."

The woman laughed. "Torture you? Who said anything about torture?" Slowly, she removed her long tan cloak, revealing a rather attractive figure. "I'm here to trade. All I want is a little information. New trade worlds are big business. There must be something you want too."

"It doesn't matter. There's no way back to my world. I'm stranded here. All I want is to travel north to find my friends."

Her eyes widened in surprise. "I might be able to help you with that, if you help me."

"How can you help? Who are you?" Her clothes gave nothing away. With her leather trousers, long boots, and simple tunic, she could be from any world, but he hadn't seen her in the market and his intuition told him she was no mere trader. She didn't appear to be South Parsan either, with her long straight ebony hair and paler olive skin. She must be familiar with the town, though, to have followed him completely unnoticed and trap him in this building.

"You can call me Torvia. My job is to help people. You could say that I'm a trader, but I deal in more specialised commodities."

"But how can you get me to the north?" She didn't look capable of surviving the desert, let alone facilitating their journey. Unless she had hidden wealth …

"Is that what you really want?"

"Yes, but I can't help you find my world or understand any of this," he replied, gesturing at the phone and watch.

"That's too bad. But I'm sure you have something to trade. Something from your world you can build?"

Jaime thought it through. She was the first person who had expressed any interest in helping him reach the north, so he couldn't afford to turn her down. Perhaps in her travels she'd discovered the route. But he mustn't give her technology, having no idea what that would lead to.

"You don't trust me, do you?" Torvia said. "I'll give you a good price for anything, more than fair."

"It's not the price," Jaime said quickly.

"Then what? Do you want to set up your own business? I would be a good partner. I know all the right buyers."

"No, it's just that technology can be used to do harm and I don't want to be responsible for changing the balance of power on a foreign world."

Her laugh set him on edge. It wasn't that funny. "It's your world too, now. And South Parsa is peaceful, with thievery the only real crime. Besides, I'm not asking for weapons."

"How do I know you're not an enemy of South Parsa?"

"You think a lot." She started to circle him, making him feel he was being hunted. "I think I'm going to enjoy working with you."

Surprised at her deduction, Jaime raised his eyebrows. "Working with me?"

"Yes, you'll learn to trust me and we'll get you to North Parsa." She stopped midway between the torches, half obscured by shadow. "How would you travel on your world?"

Jaime couldn't answer that, could he? If she had the secrets of air travel, she might change the whole world. But then it didn't look like she would take no for an answer.

Perhaps that was something he could do on his own though. A hot air balloon might be possible if he put his mind to it. It would certainly be an easier and quicker way to travel. And there were plenty of expert craftspeople in the city who could help with the basket and canvas.

But could he make that journey on his own? Without directions and without a compass?

That gave him an idea. A compass probably wouldn't change the world, but it might be interesting enough. She had found his watch fascinating.

"How do you know which way is north?"

Her brow wrinkled in confusion. "The sun and moons point east and west when they rise and set and the stars guide the way at night."

"Then I shall show you how to make a compass, which will always point to the north, and you can tell me how you're going to get me to North Parsa."

"Okay," she said eagerly. "We should go to the workshop." Lunging forward, she grabbed his arm, and a wooziness washed over him.

"What just happened?" he exclaimed, reaching out to steady himself.

Shock stiffened his limbs as his vision returned. Why was there a bookcase behind him? Why were there workbenches across the room? Why was the room a different shape?

His hand tightened around the solid wood, and he breathed in stale, musty air. Something very strange had happened, and now he stood in a room overflowing with odd contraptions strewn across various workbenches. Bookshelves or shelves of tools lined every wall and lights hung from the ceiling instead of the usual torches on the walls. A few of them weren't lit, but fire sprang forth as soon as Torvia waved her hand.

"We came to the workshop." Torvia looked at him with concern. "Do they not have magic on your world?"

"Magic? Did you do something to me?" She couldn't possibly have moved them in the blink of an eye.

"Clearly not," she answered for him. "You must have seen others use magic. Eliza is excellent at translation spells. She must have used one on you for you to understand our language."

"That was just a few small flames and a language spell!" Jaime collapsed on to a stool. Eliza had never mentioned anyone like this woman. Though as traders, it made sense that they'd know each other.

That didn't excuse Torvia sneaking through her house to steal Jaime's belongings though. But perhaps Eliza didn't know Torvia did such things. "What else can you do?"

"Plenty, but you're here to make a compass first. We're trading, remember?" She dropped onto the stool next to him, concern in her eyes. He must have looked a troubling sight.

"Right, but why do you need technology if you have magic?" He glanced around the room for clues, but nothing here appeared magical.

"Not everyone can use magic, magic can't do everything and magic doesn't work on some worlds."

"Wait, can you teleport me to North Parsa if I give you something worthwhile?"

"Sadly not. Further distances require more magic and no one can travel that far. Well, almost no one … But there are other ways, so let's see what you can show me."

Feeling a bit more optimistic, Jaime began to search for items to build a compass. He felt a little silly worrying about a watch, knowing she could teleport at will. No wonder she had laughed, but what else she was capable of?

The workshop seemed to lack any kind of system. Strange half-built devices with unclear purposes littered the worktops, and judging by the layers of dust on some of them, they had lain abandoned for some time. Eventually, he found a small bowl in a drawer that just wouldn't close after he dislodged the contents, and a jar of metal needles on one of the shelves. Nails of all description filled several pots, so hoping some were made of iron, he grabbed a few and placed them on the worktop next to the bowl.

Now he needed something buoyant to put the needle through. He hunted around but found nothing.

Torvia watched him intently, though she seemed to enjoy watching him work more than being interested in what he built.

"I need some water," he informed her.

"Will wine do?"

Jaime frowned as she pointed to a rack of dusty old wine bottles in the corner. A peculiar addition to a workshop, but he knew nothing about the type of person who normally worked here. "I suppose …" Fortuitously, the bottles were stoppered by cork, ideal for his compass.

Using the rather unusual corkscrew resting on the rack, he unstoppered a bottle, poured a little of the fruity red liquid into the bowl and cut off the end of the cork. He offered the remainder of the drink to Torvia, but she merely pulled a face. He tapped the needle with the iron nail to magnetise it, then pushed the needle through the slice of cork and placed them into the bowl of wine.

Holding his breath, he waited for the needle to spin, but it just sat there.

Maybe it was already aligned north?

He poked it to point in a different direction, but still it didn't move. He felt a little stupid but persevered with a new nail.

Suddenly it occurred to him that magnetic fields might not work the same in this world. However, this time the needle slowly spun and settled pointing towards Torvia.

Torvia peered down at it. "What does that mean?"

"Either you're wearing something magnetic or north is that way."

She prowled around the table, keeping her eyes on the compass. The point didn't follow her, so Jaime relaxed, feeling quite pleased with himself.

"It doesn't work," she announced, shattering his pride. "North is the complete opposite direction."

"Oh, it aligns itself with the magnetic field, so it could point north or south. Look." He moved the compass and flicked the needle. It settled back, pointing in the original direction. "South is that way, so north is that way."

"Hmm," she said neutrally, so Jaime couldn't tell if she was impressed or not. "What is the magnetic field?"

Relief brought a grin to Jaime's face, and he couldn't help explaining. Unlike Eliza's family, her curiosity was so refreshing, and for the first time in days, he felt like he wasn't alone. That he might have a chance to follow Jordan to the north.

Even if Torvia couldn't teleport them there directly, her talents, magical and otherwise, had to be an asset. All he had to do was convince her it was a journey worth making.

But gold wouldn't do that. Her price was knowledge. And so long as she didn't ask for anything that would cause harm, Jaime was happy to oblige.

Over the next few days, he spent the mornings working at the market, saving up his money for supplies. In the afternoons, he walked over to the dark, empty building where he had first met Torvia. There she would spirit him over to the workshop in total secrecy, where he would build something else that might be worth her help.

Every day he arrived at the abandoned building a little earlier, eager to see Torvia and spend the hours chatting away. They talked about everything. Her curiosity was insatiable. She wanted to know about the animals on his world, the clothes, the people, religions, everything. Every day that went past found him slipping deeper into the routine of life in the south, his despair at being trapped here beginning to abate.

Only when he was alone did doubts creep in. A small voice that told him he was no closer to the north than he had been since Jordan's departure. A voice that told him he'd never leave. That he was caught in another trap.

CHAPTER 29

PARSAN MOUNTAINS

After what felt like an eternity, mountains loomed in front of the convoy, providing a welcome change of scenery. The days still dragged on as they trudged closer, but Jordan focused on the peaks as a beacon of hope. Every day they grew bigger, until finally he could see the cracks of ages etched into the rocks, and individual trees emerged out of the seething green.

The transformation was most odd when they finally did reach the trees. He had forgotten what it was like not to have the sun blazing above or the coldness of the night sucking all the warmth away. The gentle coolness kissed his skin, and the shade provided his eyes with a welcome rest.

His other senses, however, were assaulted by a variety of aromas, and he jumped more than once at the gentle rustling of the fauna. After a while, it became relaxing, until peculiar squawks and shrill whistles started to call.

In addition to the unsettling sounds, the forest and mountains brought new challenges. The camels couldn't handle the rocky slopes, so they had to be set free. Safia assured him they would find their way back to South Parsa on their own and were perfectly capable of surviving the desert. Unfortunately, this meant they had to carry all their belongings, food, and water.

After entire days of nothing but sitting upon a camel for weeks upon end, Jordan's legs had forgotten how to walk, so the first few days in this new terrain were slow and difficult. On a difficult incline, he stopped to rest a moment, and took a seat to massage life back into his calves.

Heavy breathing from beside his head caused him to glance up in alarm. Right in front of him, close enough to reach out, stood a giant lizard-like creature. The size of an alligator, but with long limbs, it was far more terrifying than their desert counterparts.

Jordan froze, his instincts abandoning him at the sight of this alien reptile.

It stared at him unblinking, showing no sign of fear. When it opened its cavernous mouth it displayed rows of razor-sharp teeth.

The creature lunged.

Jordan's instincts returned, and he quickly dodged, but he knew it was too late. He closed his eyes a split second before the creature closed its jaw around him.

The force of the blow knocked him backwards, but the sharp pain of teeth was less than he'd anticipated.

Confused, he opened his eyes, then almost vomited.

The creature's decapitated head had fallen into his lap. Blood and other bodily fluids oozed out all over him, releasing a pungent acrid odour.

"You shouldn't wander off on your own," Tedric said, wiping blood off his sword.

Jordan shoved the creature off him. "I know. I only stopped a moment." Of all his companions, he had developed a closer friendship with Tedric, having bonded over their shared love of sports. South Parsa enjoyed a range of pastimes merged from a variety of worlds, some similar to football and basketball, which gave them plenty to talk about.

Jordan had also spent a lot of time practising his swordplay with Tedric, and his skill had improved so dramatically that he was now confident he would be able to beat Jaime with little difficulty. But sparring with an opponent was quite different to a surprise attack from a formidable creature.

Next time he'd be prepared.

Jordan tried to wipe the blood off his uniform, but there wasn't much he could do about the stain. Nor hide what had happened from the other guards, so he soon became the subject of much teasing.

Finally, Safia took pity on him and magicked away all the mess, but Jordan's cheeks still burned.

Safia consoled him with a comforting hand on his shoulder. "Don't let it bother you. These creatures can sneak up on even the most alert guard."

Tedric smirked. "This Alice must be really special for you to go through all this to find her."

His cheeks burning even more, he realised he hadn't thought much about Alice at all. "She's not the only one I'm looking for, but yes, she is."

"So, tell us about her."

The thought of Alice lifted Joran's spirits and he couldn't help smiling. "She's beautiful. Tall and athletic, with shiny blonde hair. She's an excellent archer, far better than my friend, Jaime. She's a good friend too, always looking out for Jaime and joking around with him."

Tedric raised his eyebrows. "Sounds like she might be interested in this Jaime."

Jordan frowned. "No, they're just good friends. They've known each other since they were very young."

Safia smiled. "I don't blame you for wanting such friendship. If I didn't have Torvia, my upbringing would have been very lonely."

Jordan opened his mouth to reply, but he didn't know what to say. True, he envied Jaime and Alice's relationship, but that wasn't why he was interested in Alice, was it?

Tedric clapped him on the back. "Have no fear. As soon as you turn up as a royal guard, she'll forget all about Jaime."

Jordan nodded, though the words sounded hollow. As hollow as the empty desert that stood between them. He didn't want Jaime to be forgotten. Or either of them to lose anything more. If Alice could forget Jaime, what was the point in anything?

As they continued their journey, Jordan found himself searching the dark eyes of his companions for any sign of struggle, any desire to return home, or even to joke around, but they were devoted to their task. Even the mischievous Tedric sparred with deadly seriousness, and although Jordan appreciated his company, he was not Jaime.

The more he thought of Jaime, the more his stomach twisted, a nest of snakes growing and writhing inside him. Jaime had always stood by him and he'd abandoned him without a word, in pursuit of a girl he knew Jaime adored. He'd been awful to Jaime, and he couldn't get those words out of his head when the silence of the world let everything in.

Jaime had pleaded with him to *just drop it,* to spare his feelings, and Jordan had accused him of being jealous. Why was everything so obvious now? He might never see him again and Jaime would never know how sorry he was.

A few days later, Jordan sensed a new threat. As the others moved closer to Safia, he knew this was no false alarm. His heart beating faster, he edged nearer to Tedric, gripping his sword.

A man stepped out from between the nearby trees, dressed in a fur cloak and scaly trousers that looked like they might have been made from the creatures that stalked them through the forest. Despite his simple clothes, his muscular physique and dignified bearing demanded respect.

He walked slowly towards the group with his arms out, indicating he carried no weapons.

To Jordan's surprise, Safia made her way to the front of their group and raised her hand, uttering a strange, guttural greeting. Despite her confidence, the guards still seemed uneasy, shifting as nervously as himself.

After exchanging a few words with the newcomer, Safia turned to the guards. "We're being invited to join the tribe for the evening." Without waiting for a response, she continued forwards with the tribesman.

The guards rushed to join her, and not wanting to be left alone in this unfamiliar environment, Jordan followed swiftly behind.

A strange queasiness swept through him, and he started to notice things that weren't there before. Merely hazy outlines at first, they grew stronger as the trees melted away. The babbling of the river faded, replaced by the sounds of rhythmic chanting.

He halted, but the track continued to disappear right before his eyes, gradually to be substituted with short grass. The others still followed the tribesman, so Jordan tentatively trod on the new, slightly out of focus ground.

The blurry outlines became wooden huts, bordering a clearing with a large fire roaring at the centre. A few paces behind the fire, a silver star topped a totem pole. Other tribe members danced and chanted around the fire and totem in a ritualistic fashion, their faces obscured by shadow.

Jordan watched, fascinated, but avoided getting too close.

Safia was given a position of honour beside the leader of the tribe, and the other guards sat in the spaces between the non-dancers. None of the observers talked, all sitting mesmerised. Colourful paint decorated each of the people, but Jordan could only guess at the meaning.

Unable to understand a word of the chanting, he stared entranced as every person performed their part flawlessly, until the people were no longer individuals, but a wall of flesh and muscle pulsing rhythmically, the colourful skins and paint blurring their outlines, forming hallucinogenic patterns of their own.

He blinked, trying to focus. Carved wood and bone swayed from the men's and women's necks as they bounded up and down, then side to side, circling around the fire and weaving between each other, all the while chanting in perfect time.

Before long, the silver star started to glow, and the fire burned more ferociously. Blindingly intense, the fire roared upwards, shifting to deep red before brightening to molten magma.

To Jordan's surprise, images began to appear in the flames. Distorted at first and difficult to make out, a stag ran through the forest reflected in the fire. The animal stumbled, and Jordan flinched as an arrow pierced its skin. A hunter dressed in red stooped to collect the prize and the vision followed her back to her village.

Jordan glanced around at the observers, but they all watched the apparition with serious expressions. Safia's guards, however, mirrored Jordan's unease, including Kasan.

Other hunters joined the first, but became distracted by a building being consumed by fire. As they tried to put out the blaze, the stag clambered to its feet and ran towards the forest. Only the first hunter continued the pursuit, but upon reaching the trees, she transformed into a deer.

Claimed by the flames, the building crumbled and a silver star flashed brightly in the fire, obscuring the scene. When the star faded, the vision flickered away, the fire diminished, and blackness seeped into the clearing.

Jordan glanced around to see what the others made of the spectacle, but they all still stared seriously into the fire. Even Safia was lost in thought, refusing to make eye contact with any of her people. His throat tightening, Jordan deduced the omen could not be good.

The following morning, Jordan sparred with Tedric as usual, though the night had been anything but. No one talked about the vision, so Jordan's questions remained unanswered and he couldn't get the images out of his mind.

In his distracted state, his foot caught on a root and he crashed to the ground under the weight of Tedric's blow.

"If you wanted to sleep a little longer, you should have just said," Tedric said with a smirk.

Jordan glared back, rubbing his ankle.

Tedric knelt down to inspect Jordan's injury. "Kasan can heal that. Unless you want me to give it a try?"

"Umm ... Maybe this is something for Kasan." Jordan didn't need to wind up crippled, and he'd not seen Tedric cast that many spells.

"Fair enough." Tedric offered his arm and pulled Jordan to his feet. "I wouldn't want to be healed by me either."

"Where does Kasan learn?" Jordan asked as Tedric helped him back to their camp.

"South Parsa has many tutors. Some are mages from other worlds paid handsomely for their services. There are even North Parsan spellbooks for the most accomplished."

"Is the magic that different?"

"Magic in South Parsa uses spells from one ancient culture, often denoted by the silver star, but in the north they have a whole other culture of spells to draw on. They're often more powerful, especially when the two sources are combined."

Jordan's attention flicked to the star on the totem. "Does this tribe follow the same magic as South Parsa?"

"Mostly, but with differences." He sighed in dismay at the empty camp, the only sign of life the fire's smoke entwining with the morning mist. "Kasan must have left already."

"Jordan!" Safia called, emerging from the chief's tent, only one guard with her. "What happened?"

Tedric grinned. "He fought a tree root and lost."

Jordan's cheeks warmed. "We were sparring, and I lost my footing."

Safia smiled. "I can heal that for you. Tedric, accompany the hunters and bring us breakfast."

Lowering Jordan carefully to the ground, Tedric lost his smile for a moment, before bowing his head. Jordan watched as he headed over to the waiting hunters, conveying no doubt despite his previous unease around the tribespeople.

Safia placed her soft hands on Jordan's ankle, muttered a few words, and spread a warmth through his skin and into the tendons. Slowly, the pain subsided, and the swelling reduced.

He beamed. "You're an excellent healer. I can't feel any more pain."

Safia smiled. "It's a simple injury. Tedric ought to have been able to heal it. I'll have to give him some lessons."

"You're not what I imagined a princess would be," Jordan said.

"Oh? Would you imagine a princess letting her guards suffer?"

He shrugged. He'd never really thought about it, but weren't royalty supposed to be self-absorbed?

Safia smiled. "I'd do anything to protect my people. That is why I am the chosen ruler."

"I guess I don't know much about royalty." His eyes wandered to the fire, now blazing again under the watchful eye of a few of their hosts. "Or this world."

Safia followed his gaze. "Tribes like this are scattered throughout the mountains. They're mostly nomadic, keeping to traditions passed down through the generations, and rarely interact with outsiders. We are privileged to be accepted into their camp."

Jordan nodded. "That vision – was that magic?"

Safia inhaled deeply. "The tribes are known for their prophetic visions, but their meanings are often unclear."

"What do you think it meant?"

"There have been numerous prophecies about the fall of North Parsa. So many can't be ignored, but there has always been hope in their interpretations. I've never seen deer represented before."

A cold wind whipped around the camp, ruffling Safia's hair. Jordan resisted the urge to shudder. "There was a woman in red."

"It could mean anything. Perhaps South Parsa will help to save the city or perhaps this has nothing to do with North Parsa at all. Their royal insignia is a lion. I'm not aware of any of kingdoms adopting a deer for a sigil."

Jordan contemplated her seriousness. She truly believed in the prophecies. "The woman in red turned into a deer. Are there any southern families linked with that symbol?"

Safia shook her head. "The trade guilds adopt the symbols of their crafts. We've traded with worlds for deer, but none of those have links to the north." Her expression turned pensive. "Even so, who would hunt one of their own?"

Jordan shrugged. He couldn't answer that. "If North Parsa is going to fall, why bother with an alliance at all?"

"No one knows when it might happen, but if North Parsa falls, South Parsa might be next. I intend to find out all I can about potential threats during my visit. Their city has withstood so many attacks, and their magic has only ever grown, so it's hard to imagine anyone who could conquer their kingdom."

Jordan fell silent. He had never suspected such an answer. He had seriously underestimated the princess.

"Don't worry," she said. "Nothing will happen before we reach there."

"How can you be so sure?"

Safia looked away. "There is another prophecy. My actions could save North Parsa."

"Is that the best course of action for South Parsa?"

She sighed. "It seems no prophet or vision can answer that."

He didn't dare ask anything more. He already felt like he'd overstepped many boundaries and was glad for the return of the hunters and the excuse to busy himself with their catch.

He couldn't help glancing at Safia as she sat with the tribe chief, now understanding her need to know more, but he didn't envy her that responsibility. How could anyone save a kingdom that threatened their own?

CHAPTER 30
North Parsa

Still undecided about whether to talk to Darien about the kiss, Alice watched him devour breakfast as if nothing had changed between them. Ideally, she wanted to get him on his own, but that was impossible at dinner.

"Darien, what are your plans for the day?" she asked.

He smiled pleasantly. "I'm afraid my father is expecting me to accompany him today. Perhaps Yasmin will help you design something to wear to the ball." With a swift bow, he disappeared.

Alice's heart sank. Was he avoiding her on purpose?

Yasmin frowned. "I was going to study with my uncle today. Would you like to join us?"

"No, thanks," Alice said quickly. "I'll head outside for some fresh air." Perhaps Javed would shed some light on Darien's behaviour. It would be nice if she could continue exploring other worlds, but she'd have to be extremely convincing to get Javed to take her anywhere.

She found him in the main courtyard with a group of soldiers crowded around a stall of swords and all things sharp. A man seemed to be showing off his wares, but ignoring the pride of the collection, a magnificent sword with a blue-eyed lion pommel glistening with dozens of crushed crystals.

Curious, she sidled up to Javed. "Are those magical crystals?"

Javed tilted his head. "Are you shopping for someone in particular?"

"Just curious why no one is interested in that sword."

The blacksmith turned to her with a smile. "You have a good eye, but that sword is already bought. A special order by the Royal Mage for his nephew once he comes of age." He glanced at Javed's lion-pommelled sword. "The crown prince can't be outdone by his subjects' swords, can he?"

"It won't make him a better swordsman." Javed raised his voice so all the soldiers could hear. "The same goes for all of you, before you spend all your money." He turned to Alice and started to walk away from the crowd. "I take it your appearance wasn't just to comment on the quality of our swords."

Alice feigned offence with a hand on her chest. "I care deeply about the quality of your swords. So those crystals are magical?"

Javed nodded. "I doubt they'll make that much difference to Darien. Swords don't need crystals to be imbued with magic."

"Is yours?"

"There are ancient spells that help my blade resist and penetrate magic."

"Does it have a name?"

"My sword?" Javed laughed. "Why would a sword need a name?"

"Lots of famous swords have names. You should call it Lion Claw or something."

Javed shook his head. "You are quite something. This sword is simply the prince's sword, the defender of the kingdom."

"Would the defender of the kingdom like to visit another kingdom with me?"

Javed lost his smile. "You want to leave Parsa?"

"Just for a day or a few hours."

"That's not wise. Not all worlds are as welcoming as Parsa."

"But you know which ones would be safe."

"It's best you stay here, Alice. Anything you need can be brought to the palace."

She sighed. "I need to get *away* from the palace. Don't you ever want to explore somewhere?"

Javed smiled his sympathy. "I have responsibilities here. You'd be better off asking Darien. Will he not take you anywhere?"

"He's busy. You must have time outside your responsibilities."

"I'm sorry, Alice." Javed backed away. "Not all of us shirk our duties."

Alice ground her teeth as he returned to his men, who were already testing out their purchases. Now she had no chance to ask him about Darien. Though if he thought little of Darien's adventures, he'd probably not approve of a romance either.

A familiar voice spoke from behind her. "How is it you have all the royals swooning about you?"

Alice greeted Navid with a smile. "I don't think Prince Javed swoons. What are you doing here?"

He gestured to the blacksmith. "Some of my men are raving about their new swords. I thought I'd check out the vendor."

"Does he meet your standards?"

"It would seem so. I never would have guessed you had an interest in weaponry."

"I care about the people who wield the weapons."

Navid raised his eyebrows. "You have an interest in Prince Javed?"

"Not like that," Alice said quickly. "I thought he might like to join me off-world, but it seems he is too busy. Would you like to join me? We could talk about Yasmin."

Navid blinked. "I don't think that's a good idea. Prince Darien could take you."

Alice rolled her eyes. "Is he the only one who goes anywhere?"

"Mages and traders travel, but you don't want to go with any of them."

"How about a trip into the city, then?"

Navid shifted uncomfortably. "That wouldn't be appropriate."

She resisted the urge to punch him. "Are you sure you want to be seen talking to me?"

"We're in the palace grounds." He sighed. "I'm taking enough risks visiting Princess Yasmin. If the wrong people found out about our friendship, it could cause problems for both of us. Please don't ask me to do anything more."

Alice's voice softened. "This is why I can't stand this world sometimes. How can you bear it?"

"This is where I was born. I couldn't imagine living somewhere people didn't respect each other."

"Do you think I'm disrespectful?"

"You're very bold." Navid grinned. "I never thought the royals would appreciate that, but I suppose you are not one of their subjects, so it's not an offence. You could try to be a little more understanding, but I like you regardless. You've brought out something in the royals that I can only approve of."

"You only have Darien to thank for Yasmin talking to you."

"I think your presence helped. Some middle ground they could both relate to."

"They fight a lot?"

"No, too little, really. They've been drifting apart, focusing on their own concerns."

Alice nodded. "Yasmin's uncle keeps her busy and Darien ... has a restless spirit."

Navid smiled. "That's a kind way of putting it." He glanced up at the palace and lowered his voice. "Sometimes I think the Royal Mage *wants* to keep them apart, to make sure they don't unite against him."

Alice's eyes widened. "Yasmin would never do that."

"I know. Forget I said anything."

She stepped closer, throwing caution to the wind. "I think you might be right. Whenever Yasmin tries for more independence, the Royal Mage seems to have a good reason to stop her."

Navid's brow furrowed. "Look out for her, Alice. And Darien, if you can."

She nodded. "I intend to." She bit her lip. "What would happen if Darien had a friendship like yours and Yasmin's?"

Navid grinned. "You've got nothing to worry about there, Alice. Few would question a prince's choice, especially one as unencumbered as Darien."

"But it's different for a princess?"

"Yes." Navid sighed again. "Yasmin could challenge that, but expectations mean a lot to her. And as Royal Mage-in-Waiting, she can't turn her back on magic."

"I see."

"Don't worry about me," Navid said. "I'll encourage Darien to spend time with you next time I see him. A trip off-world always cheers him up."

"Thanks," Alice said. "Yasmin is with her uncle today. Would you like me to pass on a message?"

"No need." A smirk lifted his lip. "I have my own ways to communicate with the princess."

Buoyed up by their conversation, Alice headed into the gardens for some much-needed respite. Somehow, the gardens seemed to have their own climate. The air itself felt more humid, especially in the shade of the large palms in the tropical section.

She followed a narrow winding path to a small pond with fish glistening under the surface, and dipped her feet into the cool, refreshing water. A gentle breeze rippled across the surface, tousling her hair, and easing her stress away. She closed her eyes and took a deep breath, relishing the bird song amongst the steady rustling.

When she opened her eyes, someone was observing her from the shadows across the pond. Dark eyes watched her for a moment more, disturbing in their intensity, before their owner slid into the trees.

More curious than unsettled, Alice swept after the figure, into the more remote area of the gardens, where the slender palms were replaced by bushy ferns. Shoving her way through the overgrowth, she pursued the flash of blue silk into a small clearing with a lion statue in the centre.

The mage waited for her there, her long dark hair curtaining her face.

Alice halted, taking in the peculiar woman. Although dressed in fine blue, she displayed no stars, but something about her radiated magic.

"Who are you?" Alice demanded. "Why were you watching me?"

The mage tossed her hair over her shoulder, a shimmering wall of inky black, revealing an unfamiliar face. "I heard you wanted to leave the palace. Why is that?"

"It's not a crime to leave the palace. Why bring me here?"

"Are you sure about that? Has anyone let you leave?"

Alice frowned. "I have left the palace before."

"With the prince?"

She nodded.

"But he brought you back here."

Alice narrowed her eyes. "What are you trying to say?"

"You don't belong here. Haven't you wondered why they're keeping you around?"

"If you have something to say, say it."

The woman shrugged, her silky dress shimmering as it rippled. This was no ordinary mage. "If I were you, I'd be trying harder to leave."

Alice stepped forward. "You're a mage. Can you help me?"

The woman held out her hand. Ignoring the oddness of the situation, Alice took it. A moment later, sand surrounded her, and the sun blazoned down from on high, making her squint.

Slender fingers clawed at her, and nails scraped her scalp as they tugged back her hair.

Alice shrieked and attempted to twist away. "What are you doing?"

The mage pulled harder, yanking Alice's head to hers, and whispered in her ear. "If you know what's good for you, stay away from the prince."

Alice flailed and grabbed at the woman's arm, but she was already gone.

She'd left Alice alone in the desert.

Alice spun, finding relief in the sight of the palace towers glistening in the distance. But she had no way to reach them, other than to walk in this blistering heat.

By the time Alice reached the palace, night had long since fallen, her skin was red raw and she could barely stand. She staggered towards the gate, falling onto the guard that approached.

To her surprise, he seized her wrists and pushed her against the wall. "What are you doing trying to get into the palace at this time of night?" he growled.

Alice stiffened. Why didn't he recognise her? The firelight lit up the gate enough to distinguish people as they approached, even on the darkest of nights.

"I'm Alice, Princess Yasmin's friend," she croaked, her throat painfully dry.

The guard laughed. "You expect us to believe that? You haven't even bothered to get the right hair colour."

Alice wriggled, enough for her hair to fall forward. Coal-black hair. She groaned. That evil witch! "A mage changed the colour after abducting me," she said wearily.

The guard laughed again. "You escaped from a mage with no magic? Do you think we're idiots?"

Other footsteps approached. "She could be hiding her magic. She needs to be tested."

The man turned her around to face his companion. "Do you think she'd let us catch her this easily if she had magic?"

He shrugged. "It could be part of her ploy to gain entry. We should take her to the Royal Mage just in case."

The guard shook his head. "I'm not waking him up at this time of night. We should interrogate her first."

Alice tried to loosen his grip, but his fingers remained unyielding talons. "Look at my face! You must recognise me."

The second guard squinted closer. "She does look like her, though that could be a spell."

"I don't have magic!"

"We should take her to the prince. He asked to be notified if anyone heard anything about the missing girl."

"Yes! Take me to the prince. He can reverse the spell."

The guard frowned and tightened his grip. "If that's what she wants, we shouldn't take her."

"Then bring him here. Please." The cool breeze raked her sunburnt skin and her legs threatened to give way at any moment.

"We should throw her in a cell until morning."

Alice almost sobbed. "Please, just inform Yasmin I'm at the gate. She'll be extremely angry if she finds out you withheld information from her."

The guard stiffened and glanced at his colleague. "You expect me to disturb *Princess* Yasmin? The sun must have addled your mind."

Alice straightened. "Yes, I expect you to inform the Royal Mage-in-Waiting that her friend has been found. Perhaps I won't tell her how poorly you treated me if you hurry." She yanked her arm away, but still could not pull herself free.

"I'm not going to fetch her."

The other guard shook his head, then raised a hand. Instantly, a blue-robed man appeared beside him. "This woman claims to be the princess's friend. Could you bring the princess's server down to verify her identity?"

The blue-robed man nodded and disappeared without a word.

With a heavy sigh, Alice slumped against the wall, and scowled at the guard who still held her wrist. "You don't have to hold me so tightly. I'm not going anywhere."

He relaxed his grip just in time, as Yasmin appeared beside him. She took one look at Alice and ran forwards to hug her. They teleported mid-hug, straight to Alice's chambers. "What happened to you?" Yasmin's gaze darted from her hair to the red blotches all over her arms.

Tears welled in Alice's eyes, but she blinked them back. "A mage teleported me into the desert and I had to walk back. I didn't realise she'd changed my hair colour until I reached the gate."

Yasmin shook her head, then moved her hands across Alice's skin, leaving a cooling numbing sensation in their wake. "You know it's not safe out of the palace. Who was the mage?"

Alice shook her head. "I didn't recognise her, but her clothes looked expensive."

Yasmin's hands moved to her hair. "She could have been in disguise if she didn't want to get caught. What did you do to upset her?"

"I didn't do anything! She told me I didn't belong here and that I should stay away from the prince."

Yasmin's hands paused. "Sounds like a jealous admirer."

Alice turned, looking Yasmin in the eye. "She said I should be trying harder to leave. That it isn't safe for me here."

The princess's brow wrinkled. "It's safe for you if you stay in the palace. It sounds like she just wants to get rid of you because she has a crush on Darien."

"She was in the palace gardens. She can find me in the palace."

Yasmin shook her head. "She couldn't do anything to you without incurring the wrath of the Royal Mage, Darien or me. I'll make sure the servers know to look out for you."

"We don't even know who she is. How can we stop her?"

"You'll be fine, just as long as you don't wander off alone."

Tired of being told what to do, Alice frowned. "Haven't you fixed my hair yet?"

Yasmin sat back, her eyes thoughtful.

Alice grabbed a strand of coal-black hair and looked questioningly at Yasmin.

"The spell is very strong. Disguises are not my strength. I'll have to get a book."

Her stomach churned. "So, you're telling me this jealous mage is powerful enough to stump you?"

Yasmin shook her head. "I just need to check a spellbook." She vanished before Alice could ask more, and returned a few moments later with a heavy tome. She didn't make eye contact as she scanned the book for a new spell, unsettling Alice more.

"Do you know who this mage could be?"

Yasmin glanced up. "There are plenty of mages who could cast this spell."

"Any who might have a chance at becoming queen?"

Yasmin's lips formed a hard line. "A North Parsan is unlikely to marry Darien. Father would prefer he marry for an alliance with a powerful world. Any North Parsan with a chance would have to belong to one of the important families, and be close to the Royal Mage. They would never dare attacking someone under his protection."

"Am I under his protection?"

"Of course. He always asks after you." She reached into her dress. "He gave me this to give to you when I found you."

Resisting the impulse to throw it aside, Alice took the gold star necklace. She doubted his interest had anything to do with her welfare. Still, he probably wouldn't be pleased if someone upset Yasmin, and would be only too happy to punish them.

Strangely, the thought comforted her. The woman had lured her into a remote corner of the gardens rather than approach her in the palace in view of anyone, so clearly she didn't want to get caught.

"There!" Yasmin's voice jolted her out of her thoughts.

"It's back to normal?"

"As golden as ever."

Alice smiled. "Thank you, Yasmin. Let your uncle know what happened. I'm not going to tiptoe around the palace in fear, but if he wants to make some threats, perhaps the mage will start to be afraid."

Yasmin beamed. "I will tell him. And I will make my own threats. No one is going to attack you and get away with it."

"Isn't there any way I can defend myself? Some magical item that can stun an opponent?"

Yasmin laughed. "Some items are impregnated with magic, but nothing compares to a living, breathing mage. Our power lives in our blood, not in inanimate objects."

"What about crystals?"

Yasmin pursed her lips. "There is the blue crystal I gave Darien, but you'd more likely be a target with something like that. All a mage would have to do is teleport behind you and wrestle it away. Or trap you in ice until you gave it up. Or suffocate you until you passed out." She smiled. "I adore your spirit. You would have made a spectacular mage."

Alice sighed. "I thought you said blood made the mage, not spirit."

"Blood fuels magic and spirit. More powerful mages tend to be more spirited."

Alice's lips twitched into a smile. "That explains your temperament."

Yasmin scrunched her nose.

"Is that why you try to provoke Darien?"

Yasmin's mouth dropped open. "I don't provoke him, but yes, it would be better if he showed more of his magic."

Alice shook her head. "I think he cares too much about you to use his magic against you. And—" She stopped, not wanting to set off Yasmin's temper.

"And what?"

She took a deep breath. "I think he doubts his power because he's constantly been told it's weak."

Yasmin's gaze sharpened. "That's ridiculous. He should know the power of his own magic. If he studied more and used it, he would know."

Alice's voice diminished. "What if every time he studied, he was ashamed because someone told him he was a disappointment?"

Yasmin's face darkened. "That's absurd. He has the best tutors on all of Parsa, the best known anywhere. He's a prince. No one would dare shame him."

Alice stilled. "Someone would."

Yasmin stood, and her voice remained firm. "No one would. You don't know what you're talking about, Alice. Darien is just trying to earn your sympathy and your favour."

Alice sighed. "Perhaps. You could be more encouraging, though. Even if he isn't the best mage, he's still your brother."

Yasmin crossed her arms. "I always encourage him. He is the one that disappoints me."

Alice frowned. "Do you really mean that? You're disappointed in him?"

The princess's face softened. "He doesn't live up to his responsibilities. I work hard and he spends half his time galivanting off on other worlds."

"You could visit other worlds. You've been once with Navid."

Yasmin glanced away. "I'd rather he took his duties seriously. One day he will be king. He can't just disappear on a whim."

"He's not king yet. He's still young and learning. He'll mature eventually and then he will be a better king for all he's experienced."

Yasmin laughed. "He'll certainly be able to charm people to his side."

"Will you at least talk to him about something that isn't how much he disappoints you?"

Yasmin's lips formed a tight line. "If it means that much to you." Her face lit up. "We can always talk about you."

Alice rolled her eyes. They must have something else to talk about.

Then again, Navid had said they were drifting apart. Perhaps it *was* up to Alice to bring them together.

As soon as Darien stopped ignoring her, she was going to have to confront him about that kiss. The upcoming ball was the perfect opportunity, but ... "Yasmin, will you teach me to dance?"

"Of course." Yasmin squeezed her hand. "Get some rest. I'll seal the room and come back for you in the morning."

Her eyelids already drooping, Alice nodded.

CHAPTER 31

South Parsa

Another delivery complete, Jaime wound his way back to the marketplace. A peculiar silence lingered as he reached the normally busy streets, causing him to slow his pace. He glanced around for familiar faces, but all the craftspeople had vanished, and their doors remained closed.

Curious, he skulked forwards, and eventually found tradespeople in the central plaza, but few customers. A tall, dark-haired man in a dazzling blue tunic and cloak caught his eye. It wasn't just that his silky clothing looked expensive, but the star that shimmered on his cloak appeared alive with magic. One moment it glittered gold, then the next, flames licked around the edges. Not even the South Parsan royals had clothes so fine.

Was this a mage of the north?

Jaime crept closer, until he realised a trader cowered before this unusual man. And all around the foreigner, people wore expressions of fear.

Unease rippled through him. This wasn't a man he wanted to meet, but curiosity held his gaze.

Before black eyes met his, a hand on his shoulder made him jump, and a second later the workshop blurred into view.

He spun around to face Torvia. "Who was that man?"

Torvia frowned back at him. "You don't want to think about him. Did he see you?"

He shook his head. "You can tell me, Torvia."

"Forget about him. He's North Parsan and only brings trouble. Anyone who's smart stays out of his way."

Jaime pinched his brow. Sure, everyone had been avoiding him, but that wasn't a good enough explanation. After all he'd told her, she could answer one question.

Now that he thought about it, she'd hardly told him anything about Parsa or herself. He'd been busy giving her everything she wanted, but she'd not revealed anything of her plans to take him north.

Had she used some magic spell on him to trick him into working for her?

His skin crawled. He didn't even know where this workshop was located. Or who Torvia might be working for. But how could he find out if she wouldn't tell him anything?

Perhaps he could use her tricks against her.

"Thanks for looking out for me," he said. "I really enjoy spending time with you. Do you think we can stay longer today? And maybe eat here?"

"If you like," she said nonchalantly, but her expression told him she was pleased by the suggestion. "What would you like to eat?"

He thought quickly about what might take longest to obtain. "Bring a variety of things, all your favourite foods."

As soon as she disappeared, he ran up the stairs to the only door, his heart pounding. With no other way to the north, he couldn't afford to upset Torvia, but the more he thought about it, the more concerned he became about how little he knew about her and what she might be hiding.

The door was the only exit, though he'd never needed to use it before. Grasping the handle, he turned slowly.

Surprisingly, it opened.

It was almost an invitation. Torvia could hardly be angry with him if she'd left the door unlocked. If she returned before him, he could just say he'd gone looking for something to drink. She'd believe that. Probably.

With no windows, the corridor was dark, so he grabbed a lamp from the workshop and proceeded forwards cautiously. The air was cool and damp, suggesting he might be underground.

Sure enough, the floor soon sloped upwards, steadily at first, then more steeply. He passed a few locked doors on his way, but he didn't try to force his way inside. His best chance of finding out his location was to get outside.

A couple of twists and turns led him to a junction with a wider corridor. Both directions looked the same, so he took the right path again, preventing him from forgetting his way back.

A short distance down this passage, he reached a staircase and climbed all the way to the top. Through some promising doors, he found himself on an enclosed rooftop. Clothes and sheets were hung up to dry, but the remarkable expanse of the roof itself gave him his first clue about his location.

At the edge, the view was unmistakable. No other building could have this view over the town.

To his left sloped his favourite hill for contemplation, though he hadn't visited that for several days now. Directly below, the familiar stone path dotted with desert plants arced from the building entrance to the walls that separated the grounds from the city. How could he be here, though?

There could only be one explanation. Torvia worked for the Royal Palace.

His mind raced through all the possibilities, but he couldn't figure out what he thought about this revelation. This was probably better than her working for an unknown enemy, but why had she kept her allegiance a secret?

He knew so little about the royals. Only that they'd taken Jordan away. But if she worked for them, she might know the route they'd taken.

Armed with the truth, he hastily made his way back to the steps, hoping to beat Torvia back to the workshop.

Though he couldn't keep this quiet. He'd have to ask her why she'd withheld her identity from him.

The sound of a slamming door stopped him dead in his tracks. Angry voices drifted up to him from below the rooftop. He was prepared to ignore them until Torvia's name was mentioned. Needing answers, he approached the edge of the roof to peer down at two very well-dressed men standing on a balcony a few levels below.

Even from this high angle, the gilded ears and golden cuffs of Prince Otis were unmistakable. The other man wore a scowl and a much less extravagant deep crimson tunic, but the ruby-and-gold pommelled sword at his side made up for the lack of jewels on his person. He resembled Prince Otis, though he was a few years older and his features were more chiselled. He must be the oldest prince, who'd been absent when Jaime had visited the palace with Jordan.

The older prince took a step closer, his battle-hardened muscles rippling under his tunic. "Neither I nor Torvia have time to keep checking up on you. You must take your duties seriously."

Prince Otis leaned an arm on the balustrade, casually observing the people congregating below. "Even drunk, I am more charming than you. If I need your sword, I shall call for you."

The older prince stared at his brother, his body tense. "I can't worry about both you and Safia."

Otis turned to face his brother. "I thought you supported her plan to travel north."

"I do. But to hide those boys from the Royal Mage ... It's reckless." He shook his head. "If he finds out—"

Otis straightened. "He won't. He has no reason to concern himself with lowly guards, and Torvia will keep the other one safe."

The older prince nodded and joined Otis in looking over the balcony. "Sometimes I wish Safia would spend more time picking her battles."

"Standing up to that bully is why the council follow her." Otis peered sideways at his brother. "Would you cower before him?"

"You know the answer to that. Would you challenge him in our absence?"

Prince Otis shrugged. "He won't come anywhere near me. He'd have to acknowledge my existence then."

Confused, Jaime frowned, but he had delayed enough. Torvia knew exactly who he was, had been sent to hide him, then pretended she knew nothing. He had to confront her now.

Jordan certainly would be upset to hear he wasn't Safia's guard purely because of his skill with a sword, but Jaime should have known to question the decision.

His heart thumping, he returned to the workshop. The room was empty, so relieved, he went back to his favourite workbench. It was only then that he noticed the wicker basket on the end.

Fire erupted before him, causing him to stagger back, and Torvia emerged, her expression furious. She had never appeared so dramatically before, and his knuckles turned white as he gripped the bench.

"I thought I could trust you!" she shouted. "What were you trying to do?"

"I just wanted to see where I am," he answered timidly.

"Why do you need to know? You know this place is secret. You betrayed my trust at the first opportunity!" She didn't give him the chance to reply. A tower of fire engulfed her, and she disappeared.

As did the lights. Every single one of them extinguished, plunging the room into total darkness.

Jaime fumbled around until he found the stairs, and with a hand on the wall, climbed back up to the only door. This time, it was locked. He was stuck.

Stumbling back down the steps, he contemplated his predicament in the dark. Although he felt like he had done the right thing in searching for answers, he did feel guilty he had betrayed Torvia's trust.

But then she hadn't exactly placed her trust in Jaime ...

Whatever the case, there was certainly no way out of the workshop without her, so hopefully she would forgive him.

In the meantime, he busied himself trying to relight the lamps by scratching various objects together to create sparks.

When she returned, easily an hour later, he had successfully relit all the torches. It wasn't necessary to light them all, but he found working kept him busy and made him feel that he wasn't completely useless against her magic.

She appeared rather embarrassed and a little surprised he had managed to relight the room. She stared around in wonder. "Can you use magic after all?"

"No, just a little ingenuity. I'm sorry I left the room. I only wanted to know more about you. Do you work for the palace?" he asked tentatively. He didn't dare confess whose conversation he'd overheard, in case she erupted at him again.

"Yes, I do," she replied calmly.

Now her anger had subsided, Jaime relaxed. "Do you know where Jordan is?"

"Only vaguely, but I can't take you there. You know that already. He's too far away." From under her tunic, she removed a pendant with a ginormous red crystal, similar to the one in the princess's tiara. A strange glow emanated from the gem when it brushed her fingers. She held it out to him.

"Why are you giving me this?"

"Just take it."

He grasped the cool chain and turned the crystal in his hand. The glow quickly faded away until it was nothing but a regular ruby, simply cut and without much of the shine he would expect from a jewel. Though its purpose was hardly decorative.

Satisfied, Torvia held out her hand for it. As soon as it touched her fingers, it lit up again.

Fascinated, Jaime peered closer. "Why does it glow?"

"That is a magical crystal. It responds to magic by glowing, but it can also amplify magic." She whispered a few words to it, and it shone more brightly. After a moment, she returned the pendant around her neck and tucked it beneath her tunic. "I'm sorry I haven't told you anything. I said I'd trade fairly, but here you've been telling me everything and I've told you nothing." She took a seat on the worktop bench. "What else would you like to know?"

He sat beside her. "How did you end up serving the royal family? You don't look like you're from Parsa."

"You're right. I'm not originally from here, but looks can be deceiving. Here is where I belong and where I can do the most good." She sighed. "The place I was born was in a simple world. Food was plentiful, and we traded frequently with South Parsa. My father was a hunter, as were many of my people. My mother was a healer and exceptionally gifted with magic.

"One day, when I was very young, our world was invaded by an unknown enemy. We had everything we needed, and we were a peaceful people, so we couldn't imagine an army like that. Word spread ahead of the invaders that villages were being destroyed, but we had no idea why. They didn't take anything, they just burned everything."

Jaime gasped. "I'm so sorry. What happened to the people?"

Her tone turned sorrowful. "Few people escaped, but those who did tell of a vast unforgiving army with at least a hundred powerful mages. The elders of my village pleaded with South Parsa for help, but by the time the South Parsan army reached my world, it was too late for most of us. The foreign invaders retreated through an unknown portal, leaving behind nothing but scorched earth. Most of the survivors resettled in South Parsa or other worlds, fearing to ever go back home."

Fascinated by her story, Jaime listened intently. "What about you? Have you been back?"

"No. I was brought here by the South Parsan army. Prince Ademir himself took a liking to me and presented me to his family. He told me I reminded him of his younger sister and I ended up growing up with her in the palace as her best and only real friend. When I became older, I found a way to pay them back for their kindness by becoming a spy for them."

Jaime was stunned into silence by her story. No wonder she had been so secretive. And Prince Ademir must have been very young when he'd first gone into battle. He could only be in his mid-twenties now. Their kingdom was more interesting than he'd first thought. "Why are you sharing this with me now?"

"Because you deserve to know what you've been working for. No one knows what happened to that army. It could come back at any time. Through any portal. Besides, I've grown to like you." She leaned towards him, and gently brushed his lips with hers. When he didn't kiss her back, she drew back and looked at him quizzically. "What's w rong?"

What *was* wrong with him? An attractive girl he enjoyed spending time with had kissed him and he couldn't kiss her back. Why did he freeze up in these situations?

Immediately, his mind took him back to the picnic with Alice, and the memory of her floral perfume and dazzling smile dizzying his senses.

"Alice?" Torvia said.

He stiffened. Had he said that out loud? "Erm ..." What could he possibly say?

Torvia's amber eyes flashed, betraying her anger. "Is Alice your girlfriend?"

"No! She's just a friend," he insisted, though that familiar turmoil surged through him.

"I see," she replied, her tone stern. "But if you travel north to rescue her, you'll win her affection."

"I don't want to win her. I just want to find her, and Emily and Eliot, and find our way home. Besides, rescuing her is more Jordan's idea for dating her." He squirmed as he explained all this to Torvia. It sounded daft, even to him. He shook his head, his decision made. "I'm going to make my way north however I can. I can't wait any longer. If you're going to help, it needs to be now."

Torvia contemplated him for a moment. "Okay, I'll help you even though I shouldn't. Pack some food, say your goodbyes, and meet me in the abandoned building before dawn tomorrow."

CHAPTER 32

North Parsa

Emily scraped her fingers down the cold stone wall, feeling for any signs of weakness. She'd scoured every inch of it already, so she knew there was no way out, but her brother could be just on the other side, trapped in identical misery. She couldn't stop trying now.

Even if there was no way out of the palace, if she could just see that he was unhurt, let him know he wasn't alone, that would be worth getting trapped here.

There was no point hoping for a rescue. Who even knew to look for her?

Her stomach clenching, she eyed the stale bread carefully wrapped in a corner of the single thin sheet of her hard bed. She'd learned to ration since the three-star mage who brought her food didn't visit every day, but that wasn't the only way she was starving.

She longed for a smile, a kind word or even a conversation, but there were only questions, every time the same. What was Prince Darien looking for? What was he planning? What was her role in his plot?

The questions left her with no doubt the man was paranoid, but then what did Emily know of Darien's plans? For all she knew, he could be plotting to give magic to an army to overthrow his uncle. After what she'd seen, she wouldn't blame him.

But Darien didn't seem the vengeful type.

She had no illusions that Darien would be able to help her escape her current situation. She didn't even know if he had recovered or whether he was still lying in that room, deathly pale. A shudder rippled through her. If he could do that to his own nephew, and simply walk away, what would he do to her and Eliot?

Perhaps she should have told Darien the truth from the start and neither of them would have got into this mess. How had she been so naïve to think she could sneak into the chambers of the most powerful mage in the world completely undetected, find her brother, and sneak him out on her own?

She moved her hand to the shimmering shield across the door and pushed her weight against it. Totally impenetrable, but all the Royal Mage had to do was cast the right spell and it would appear or disappear.

Too late, she had learned why those who disappeared in the tower were never heard from again.

Was this her brother's fate, too? Were they both doomed to spend the rest of their lives in isolation, without a glimpse of hope?

She collapsed back on the bed, her head still groggy from her last interrogation. Every time, he used a spell, putting her into a trance-like state, and she would answer without really knowing what she was saying.

Fortunately, he hadn't asked her about her background, so he hadn't yet found out she was from the same world as Eliot. He thought of her as nothing more than Prince Darien's obliging worker.

The last time he'd visited, the Royal Mage had seemed quite bored, barely paying her any attention at all, and robotically repeating his questions. He showed no doubt in his magical ability, so he must know she couldn't be lying when she told him all she knew was that Prince Darien sought ancient history books and rare collectibles. She knew of no plot and thus could have no role in it.

But what would happen when he saw no more use for her?

Had this been how Eliot had spent his final days?

She shuddered and hugged her legs closer. She couldn't think like that. But she couldn't take much more of this hell.

A pulse of light from the opaque force made her stiffen. The flash rippled across the surface, obliterating the barrier and revealing her captor.

Before he could cast another spell on her, Emily jumped up. "I have something to confess."

The Royal Mage raised an eyebrow. "What is it?"

"It wasn't Darien's idea to bring me to your library. I asked him to bring me up so I could find my brother."

His eyebrows hitched higher. "You, a commoner without a speck of magic, convinced my nephew to flout all our laws so he could help you find your brother?" He peered closer. "Why would he do that?"

Emily chewed her lip. She didn't have a good answer to that. If Darien was a good man, why would he say such manipulative things about Alice? But the Royal Mage didn't need to know that. And she didn't want him to hurt Darien further. "He's a good man. Please, is Eliot here? I just want to see him."

"Come with me," the Royal Mage snapped.

It was the first time she had left her little room in days, and she found herself hesitating at the doorway. Was he taking her to Eliot or a different interrogation?

Taking a deep breath, she braved the step into the more brightly lit corridor.

The Royal Mage led her along a row of cells, most of which were empty, into a much larger lounge area, disturbingly normal given its proximity to prisoners. Fire flickered from golden lamps, casting writhing shadows amongst soft furnishings and polished wood. Swords gleamed menacingly on the walls.

In the corner, a middle-aged man lurked, his vivid blue tunic bright despite the soft light.

The Royal Mage paused. "Ahmad, what are you doing here?"

Ahmad dipped into an elegant bow. "I was curious about the prisoner. May I watch the interrogation?"

Emily's heart lurched. She'd always been interrogated in her cell before, and never with an audience.

"Have you found out anything from my nephew?"

Ahmad wandered closer. "He maintains that he employed the girl to conduct research for him. He is convinced there is knowledge in old books that will lead to new magic."

The Royal Mage shoved Emily towards a chair. "Is that true?"

She nodded. "I don't know exactly what he wanted, but he was interested in history books."

The Royal Mage glanced at Ahmad. "Can you believe this girl is from that world too?"

"Which world?" Ahmad gestured for Emily to sit down.

"The same world Alice is from. This is Eliot's sister."

Emily's heart quickened and her eyes darted back to the cells. He must be here.

Ahmad peered closely at her. "I detect no magic."

"No. She does not have any."

"What will you do with her?"

"She will be banished, as befits her crime. If she finds a way back and provides us with valuable information about the portal realm, she will have served her sentence."

"Is that wise?" Ahmad asked. "Others could find out about her world."

"She's kept it quiet all this time. And I've found nothing helpful in her brother's memories. Their world is unreachable."

"Darien still seems to think it's possible."

"Then make sure he is followed. I want to know whenever he travels through a portal."

Ahmad dipped his head.

Emily gripped the edge of her chair. "What about my brother?"

"He'll be waiting here for you. If you make it back, you will both be pardoned."

"He's done nothing wrong!"

The Royal Mage reached for her forehead, a sure sign that he was about to cast a spell on her. Emily dodged, moving towards Ahmad. Perhaps he could be some help. "What about what you did to Darien?" She fixed her eyes on Ahmad, hoping he would ask the question. Maybe, just maybe, he'd say something to Darien, and he could find her

.

Instead, the Royal Mage turned to Ahmad. "How is Darien responding?"

Ahmad shrugged. "I've talked him around. He understands you didn't mean to hurt him and he knows it's not in his benefit to say anything. I recommend giving him some space for now. He'll learn not to question you in his own time."

The Royal Mage clenched his jaw. "He is the most obstinate spoiled child I've ever known."

"He's a royal, born into a palace of mages. You must give him some leniency. He never had your upbringing."

The Royal Mage's eyes flashed, making Ahmad shrink back. "He should be making use of those advantages before it is too late."

Ahmad's voice quietened. "He may have years to learn. The Iybryrians suffered heavy casualties last time. There's no reason to assume they will return."

"There is every reason to prepare for their return." Kavir turned back to Emily. "What do you know of the Iybryrians? Where is their world?"

"Nothing," she squeaked. This was turning into a proper interrogation now.

With a sigh, the Royal Mage stood. "Since you're here, Ahmad, you can probe her memories. I want to know everything about her world and anything about what she's been doing here. Erase this conversation when you're done."

Terror gripped Emily as Ahmad reached for her. Now *her* memories were in jeopardy. Too late, she sprang to her feet, only to be dragged back down by a steely grip.

Emily blinked at the man standing before her, her mind still foggy. Instead of her cell, she sat in a dimly lit room with swords glinting on the walls. Puzzled, she glanced around. She'd never been interrogated here before, but the fogginess was familiar enough.

Unlike previously, the Royal Mage held out a glass of clear liquid. "Drink. You'll need your strength."

Not daring to defy him, she brought the glass to her lips and drank slowly. "Why am I here?"

"You are to be released."

Her heart leapt. But why now? She couldn't remember saying anything useful. Or anything at all. Nor could she even remember how she'd got to this room. Dread chilled her core. He'd done something to her memory. "Why?"

"You have agreed to serve the realm by mapping the portal realm. When you return your brother will be released."

"He will?"

"Yes. Do you accept?"

"How will I map the portal realm?"

"You will be sent through a portal of our choosing. Then you will find your way back to us. When you return you will share your memories of the journey and all you have learned."

Emily gulped. "What if I can't find my way back?"

"If you care about your brother, you will."

"He doesn't deserve to be a prisoner. Please, let him go. I'll do whatever you ask, but he's just a child. There's no need to keep him here."

"Do you accept your punishment or would you prefer an execution?"

Emily shook her head. "I'll go." She would find her way back. It was her only option.

"Good. Come with me."

He led her to another staircase where the three-star mage who brought her food waited for her. "Take her straight to the portal," was all he said. Then he cast a spell that transformed Emily's beautiful silky-blue robes into ugly grey. Even the cub sigil disappeared, leaving her completely abandoned for the first time since she had arrived on Parsa. Nothing tied her to Darien, and nothing tied her to the place that had become her home.

The three-star mage marched her down the stairs without a word, giving Emily a shove when she moved too slowly. There was no chance of catching her off guard and sneaking back up.

As soon as they reached the base of the tower, the mage whisked her away to an unknown portal. Without any hesitation, she pushed Emily across the boundary, and kept hold of her collar as they transited through the portal realm.

It was nothing like the first time Emily had experienced this place. The current swirled calmly about her rather than dragging her along. Though disorientated, she could tell they moved purposefully towards another portal, and they promptly exited through it.

The world they arrived at was unremarkable, not too different from Parsa. They teleported once again, and the mage told her to prepare herself.

With no guidance on what to prepare for, Emily took the chance to look for an escape. Unfortunately, nothing in any direction offered refuge. Merely an expanse of sand and rock stretched to the horizon.

It was too late now to attempt an escape. She had no idea which direction they had come from, nor how far the mage had teleported her. She may as well go forwards and meet her fate.

Before her very eyes, a crack in reality began to appear. Shimmering into existence, it grew and stretched, forming an oval.

A portal that only existed at certain times!

Emily tensed. How would she get back if the portal no longer existed?

When the oval became full, the woman shoved her through, almost knocking Emily off her feet. She had only a split second to brace herself against the dazzling, dizzying light, but it never came. She remained on the same world.

She turned around to find the mage staring through her. Seeming satisfied, she disappeared, presumably teleporting back to the portal to Parsa.

Confused, Emily stepped back through the portal, but it vanished before she reached it. At the same time, Shirin appeared and gleefully jumped towards her. "It worked!"

Emily stared in disbelief. "What just happened?"

Shirin grabbed her arm and pulled her to the side. Exactly where Emily had been standing, a new portal poked into reality, identical to the first.

"Convincing, wasn't it?" Shirin said, appreciatively watching the portal.

Emily's knees wobbled as a new oval formed. Almost lost for words, she turned to Shirin. "Please tell me what's going on."

"I faked the portal! She pushed you into my illusion and now you're safe. I knew as soon as that silly old mage came down from the tower jabbering about how 'Prince Darien had done it now' that you'd never escape the tower. I followed the Royal Mage's personal server for days until she came here and scouted out the portal to send you through. I waited here for you and set up the illusion, so she would think you had gone through and would leave. You must tell us everything you can about the Royal Mage's chambers. No one has ever been rescued from there before."

Tears prickled Emily's eyes. She hadn't been forgotten, and there was still hope for Eliot. "Okay, I'll tell you everything I know, but you have to help me get my brother out of there."

Shirin's eyes widened. "He's still in the tower?"

"He's holding him until I provide memories of new worlds." She shivered at the thought of her brother being interrogated by that man.

"I don't know how we can get to him, but I know someone who might be able to help. You should lie low until she's back in North Parsa. I'll take you somewhere safe."

Emily backed away before Shirin could teleport her. "Aren't you a North Parsan mage? Why are you helping me?" Shirin looked the same as the other mages Emily had met, other than her short hair.

"We're not all bad," Shirin replied. "Most of us are decent people, but a few ruin things for everyone." Her eyes flashed with excitement. "But you are something else, trying to rescue someone from the clutches of the Royal Mage. And getting Prince Darien to help!" She grinned. "How did you manage that?"

"I'm not sure. He wasn't convinced there'd be interesting books in the Royal Mage's library, but he still listened to me." Her eyes fell on the stars on Shirin's robes. "But don't all mages work for the Royal Mage? You're wearing mage clothes and you're obviously skilled at performing magic."

Shirin shrugged. "He leads the mages, but we don't all follow, at least not all the time. Only the more accomplished and richer families benefit from his rule. We want more of the freedoms they enjoy in South Parsa. There's not much hope, but it can't hurt to dream ..." Her eyes glazed over as she spoke, and a smile spread on her lips. "Every little defiance is a small victory."

Emily's tension abated slightly at Shirin's positive spirit. She did seem different to the mages Emily had met, and genuine in her desire to help. She took Shirin's outstretched hand. But ... "Is there anywhere safe from the Royal Mage?"

Shirin's eyes flashed. "Just you wait."

CHAPTER 33

SOUTH PARSA

Unable to sleep, Jaime found himself making his way to the workshop far too early. Stars still shone above, and an unusual silence hung over the city. To pass the time, he meandered past his favourite hill for contemplation, but today it held no solace for him. He was too keen to get going.

Despite his worries, he looked forward to the journey. Even if he had conflicted feelings about Torvia, she was still the best travelling companion he could think of. And he couldn't wait to see Jordan again.

Hopefully soon they'd both be reunited with Alice, Emily and Eliot.

As he passed the palace, the lone moon sank below the horizon, casting the city into deep shadow. A few lights flickered in the occasional window, but their glow didn't reach Jaime. It would get darker before it got light.

Eventually, twilight started to push back the darkness, and he arrived at the abandoned building. Meeting there, he was sure they would be teleporting somewhere, but he had no idea what their expedition would involve. Torvia couldn't teleport them across the entire world.

Contemplating the possibilities, he spent the next few minutes pacing back and forth.

"Worried?" Torvia asked, her eyes glinting brighter than the dawn. He hadn't noticed her appear.

"Just keen to get going. How are we going to travel?"

"Some walking, some teleporting, some portal hopping. The usual." She offered him her arm, and with a deep breath, he took it.

A moment later, they were deep in the desert, with sand stretching all around as far as the eye could see. He couldn't even tell which direction the city lay.

The deafening silence struck him louder than the endless sands, his last few weeks in the bustling centre quickly fading as if a dream. He turned to Torvia to ask where they were but stopped on seeing her exhaustion. Her skin ashen, she could barely stand. "Here, let me take your bag," he offered.

She didn't argue, which worried him. If she was so exhausted from one teleport, the journey was going to be extremely perilous.

"What now?" he asked, trying to keep the concern out of his voice.

"We walk."

The sun had made its appearance and set the sky on fire, making navigation straightforward. He didn't dare ask how far they needed to walk, but he was curious about their destination. "Have you been to North Parsa before?"

She turned and fixed him in a pitying stare, making him feel stupid. Of course she'd been there. How else would she know the way?

Less bothered than he thought he'd be, he tried again. "What's it like?"

"North Parsa is very different to South Parsa. Magic is rare outside the royal family and the mage society. The portals are closely guarded and trade heavily taxed. We'll have to disguise you to avoid attracting unwanted attention."

"What will happen to my friends if they ended up there?"

Exhaling loudly, she halted. "I should have told you this before, but I didn't know I could trust you. Promise you won't be mad."

"Er, I promise I won't." Failing to disguise the panic in his voice, he said, "Please just tell me."

Torvia wavered, and for a moment, Jaime thought she wasn't going to say, but then … "Alice is a guest in the palace. Prince Darien seems to have taken a liking to her and rumour is he's helping her find a portal home."

"That's great news!"

Torvia looked at him quizzically. "You're not mad I didn't tell you?"

He shook his head. "I understand why you didn't. I'm just glad you're telling me now. How do you know she's there?"

"I was at the palace when she arrived. It's part of my job to know these things." She began to walk again, and Jaime followed with a spring in his step.

"But what about Emily and Eliot?" he asked.

"I didn't hear anything about any other newcomers. Though if they fell into the hands of the mages, they would be keeping it quiet."

Jaime's stomach twisted. "Tell me about them."

"The mages? They are a group of magical people that answer to the Royal Mage. With their own school and laws, they consider themselves above everyone else. They don't have a problem letting people know that either." She adopted a scowl. "The royal family are the only ones who don't answer to the Royal Mage. There's supposed to be a balance of power between the Royal Mage and the king, but the current

Royal Mage has far superior magical ability and enjoys exercising his power even over the royal family." She shrugged. "Though they're all intermarried and live in the same palace." As she spoke, her eyes gleamed with excitement. "You should see the palace. There's nothing like it on all of Parsa or any other world. The twin towers reach high into the sky and glitter like jewels. And then there's the garden with such exotic plants, and everything is guarded by magnificent beasts."

Whilst Torvia recovered, they continued to chat about North Parsa – until Jaime's stomach rudely interrupted. Torvia laughed and suggested they stop for food.

They ate quickly, neither one wanting to delay their journey, and shortly they were marching through the desert again, Torvia reclaiming her bag.

"Do you do this journey a lot?" Jaime asked.

"Yes, but it's quicker on my own. I can teleport much further when it's just me."

He smiled sympathetically, guilty at the extra burden he caused, but nevertheless fascinated by her abilities. "You said we'd be going through a portal. Is there one that takes us north?"

"Not exactly. This is a secret route you mustn't tell anyone about. It takes us through a few different worlds until we reach one that links to the north. No one knows how to find this route. If North Parsa were to find out, South Parsa would no longer be safe. Princess Safia travels the long journey across the desert and mountains to make sure this secret is kept."

Jaime nodded solemnly, surprised at the extent of her trust. Not that he'd be able to recount the journey. "What do you mean South Parsa wouldn't be safe? Would North Parsa attack?"

"Not directly, but they want to control all the portals on this world and if their armies and mages could travel here easily, they could do whatever they wanted and no one would be able to stop them. It would only be a matter of time before the flow of trade stopped, and the people lost their livelihoods."

Jaime grimaced. That would surely ruin South Parsa. Eliza's family relied on portal trade, so they'd probably have to leave. The city would become soulless and deserted without people like them.

"I think we can teleport from here," Torvia announced.

Jaime observed nothing different about this particular spot compared with any other, but he couldn't guess at the mysteries of teleportation. Magic was something that defied all logic.

Torvia didn't need to ask him this time. He took her arm straight away, and the desert blurred out, then back into focus. It was hard to tell they had moved at all, apart from the lack of footprints behind them, but Torvia proceeded with purpose when they rematerialised. She took a few enthusiastic steps forwards, then collapsed into the sand.

Horror gripped Jaime as he moved her bag out of the way, and gently shook her. "Torvia, are you okay?"

No response.

Trying not to panic, he retrieved some fruit and water. "Torvia, wake up!"

"I'm okay," she replied faintly.

"Here, drink this," he instructed, handing her the water.

She gratefully took it, then nibbled on the fruit he offered. "Thanks," she said, trying to sound cheerful. "Can you see a cave?"

He surveyed the scenery, but little had changed. "No, just sand."

"Not far enough then," she said, her face falling. She tried to clamber up, but swayed, almost falling back into the sand before Jaime caught her.

What could he do? The sun had reached its full height now and scorched hotter than his previous journey with Jordan. They couldn't stay out here, but Torvia clearly couldn't walk, and teleporting again was out of the question.

Her brow scrunched, Torvia reached into her robes, clutched her crystal pendant, and whispered a few words. The gem glowed brightly, and a little colour returned to her cheeks. "Fetch my bag."

As soon as he brought it to her, they lurched once again, then both collapsed into the sand.

Slightly nauseated, he glanced around once more to find the scenery had changed. In a rockier part of the desert now, a large rock face loomed in front of him.

The location of the cave?

He turned to ask Torvia but discovered her completely unconscious. It was up to him to find the entrance. And he had to be quick. This heat couldn't be good for her.

If it was here, it was not obvious. He hugged the wall as he followed it along, scrutinising every patch for any sign of an opening, but nothing stood out.

Finally, he found an area where the rock face overlapped itself and, in the gap, a small ingress hid, totally obscured from view. He squeezed through to check the gap led to a cave before fetching Torvia, but in his haste, he almost stepped through the portal hidden inside. Entirely different to the one he had stumbled through on Earth, it proudly hovered in the air at knee height, shimmering brilliantly.

Half expecting it to disappear, he watched it for a few moments, transfixed by its oddity. An urge to touch the rippling surface took hold, but he resisted. This was no time to indulge his curiosity. A few twists and turns through the passage and he arrived in a small sandy area ideal for resting.

It was little effort to retrieve Torvia and carry her inside, though he lamented not being able to do anything else for her.

A couple of hours passed before Torvia jerked upright. "What happened?" she asked, blinking awake.

"You passed out again. You managed to teleport us to the cave entrance, and I brought you inside."

Rubbing her eyes, she surveyed her surroundings. "Thank you. How long have we been here?"

"A few hours."

Her eyes widened in alarm. "We should get moving."

Concerned by her pallor, Jaime frowned. "Eat some food first. You should get your strength back."

She nodded slowly. "Good idea."

Relieved by her recovery, Jaime's curiosity returned. "Where does the portal go?"

"Somewhere you're not going to like. Go through that passage and retrieve a couple of outfits."

Jaime looked in the direction she indicated but couldn't see anything. He'd explored all around the cavern whilst she slept and had found no other way out.

"Just walk that way," she insisted.

Deciding not to argue, he walked over to the edge, putting his hands out as he reached the wall. Instead of meeting rock, his hands passed straight through. Astonished, he snapped them back and glanced accusingly at Torvia. "This wall was definitely solid."

"If you say so." She smiled back mischievously.

Shaking his head, he stepped through the fake wall to find a new passageway. Struggling to follow it in the dark, he called back, "How far does this go?"

"Sorry, I forgot you can't perform magic." A small ball of light swept past him and darted around the next corner. He chased after it before the darkness closed in again.

When he caught up with the fireball, he stood in another cooler cavern, with smaller chambers used for storage. Most were filled with clothes, but some other objects attracted his attention, including a telescope. On closer inspection, he found some thick fur coats and trousers and guessed the next place was going to be very cold.

He jumped as Torvia's voice sounded behind him. "What's taking so long?"

"Do you mean these heavy fur outfits?"

"Yes, you'll be glad for them. There are some waterproof boots over there too."

He examined the clothes. They looked difficult to walk in and a little on the small side.

"What are you waiting for? Put them on and we can go."

The colour still had not returned to her cheeks, so leaving now didn't seem wise to Jaime. If this new world was going to be cold, they might need her magic to keep warm.

Unfortunately, she was too stubborn to admit she needed rest, but Jaime wasn't too proud to admit he'd be hopeless without her. "I think we should rest more," he said firmly. "I didn't sleep well last night and that walk through the desert was pretty tiring."

She gave him a suspicious look, but agreed. More tired than he thought, he fell asleep almost immediately.

He woke to a sharp poking in his side.

"Finally! I thought I was going to have to waste the water to wake you."

"What?" Jaime replied sleepily. Where was he?

Torvia stared straight at him, her brow scrunched. Dressed in her winter outfit, she was packed and ready to go. "You've been asleep for hours!"

Sitting up, he soon found his own furs thrown at him.

"Put those on."

Not wanting to annoy her further, he slipped the coat on and pulled the trousers over his current pair. But in attempting to shove his foot into the boot, his suspicions were soon confirmed. There was no way he could fit into these.

"What are you staring at?" Torvia snapped, the fire back in her eyes. "Oh, sorry." She waved her hand and his foot slid into the now perfectly sized boot. A little more kindly, she handed him his bag and led him to the portal.

"Hold my hand," she said, more pleasantly now.

"Why?" Jaime breathed sharply, memories of his first portal encounter resurfacing.

"I don't want you to get lost."

Placing his hand in hers, he followed her hesitantly into the portal. This one felt different. The shimmering white light still blinded and the eerie silence still deafened, but no current swept him away. A gentle tug on his hand pulled him forward, and he discerned the blurry outline of a slender figure.

Even sight didn't work properly in this strange place.

At his next step, a current whipped at his feet and he tensed up, preparing to be dragged along. However, Torvia squeezed his hand and guided him towards a more stable white landscape.

A moment later, a thousand icy knives stabbed at his face and through his clothes. Never having imagined cold such as this, he recoiled away from it.

"Come on!" Torvia shouted. Still holding his hand, she dragged him forward.

Unable to comprehend anything but white, his brain ceased to process this reality. Frigid wind whipped at his face, blinding him further. With every breath, ice stabbed into his lungs. Each step was an immense effort. Yet he couldn't stop stumbling in the snow.

As they pressed forward, the relentless cold sapped his strength evermore. They had to turn back. This was much worse than months in the desert. They had no chance of surviving this.

"Climb." Torvia shoved him towards an impossibly steep hill, pre-empting his protest. She was his guide and his only chance to survive. He'd placed his trust in her, and it was too late to back out n ow.

Clambering upwards, using his hands to pull himself forwards, he failed to keep up. Terrified of losing her in this blizzard, he tried his hardest, but his body just wouldn't obey. His limbs were freezing stiff, and it would be only a matter of time before he couldn't move at all.

He struggled forwards and upwards, forwards and upwards. One step after another.

His knees buckled. So he crawled. Forwards and upwards.

Eventually, his arms seized up and he collapsed into the snow.

His mind fled back to the desert and the warm soft sand. He should have stayed there. He should have gone with Jordan.

A glittering palace formed in his mind. A palace where Alice waited and Jordan arrived to rescue her, only to find her married to a prince instead. He imagined Emily and Eliot held prisoner by the mages, and even in his delusional state, he knew he had failed them all.

A warming sensation on his shoulder roused him from his troubling dream and brought him back to his waking nightmare. The warmth spread throughout his body, loosening his limbs and rejuvenating his spirit.

"Come on, we're nearly there," a voice spoke to him.

All he knew was to keep climbing, so that was what he did. Step by step, he pushed forwards until the steepness of the slope began to abate and he no longer needed to use his arms.

At the top of the hill, their glimmering salvation awaited. A new portal to some other world. Linking arms, they heaved through together, the blinding light welcoming them into its embrace.

CHAPTER 34

NORTH PARSA

Much to Alice's disappointment, she failed to catch Darien alone over the next few days. Darien continued being as polite as ever, but he'd never seemed so busy.

One morning, he'd declared to Javed that he would help spruce up the city in time for the arrival of his bride, so she would find a kingdom worthy of an alliance. Many soldiers were roped into painting houses and performing minor repairs, and somehow, he managed to convince several low-level mages to assist, too. After investing some of his own funds into regenerating the public spaces, reports of new traders and heaving marketplaces reached the palace.

From her balcony, Alice could see the walls being repaired, the ruined houses being rebuilt, and green spaces popping up in the place of abandoned buildings. The buzz soon spread throughout the palace and Darien was taken aside by the king before dinner one evening to discuss what was going on.

Finally, the day of the ball arrived, and the air of excitement in the palace was palpable. Even the servers at breakfast were chattering amongst themselves.

Alice hadn't given up on Darien just yet. He might have started to think an arranged marriage was his only choice, but that was not the Darien she knew. He *was* still enthusiastic about the ball he'd arranged for Alice.

Yasmin had pulled out all the stops in designing her gown. More gold than blue for once, she glittered like a jewel. Tiny sapphires adorned the dress, and when they caught the light, she appeared to glow. Alice settled on the traditional cobalt, but Yasmin made sure it was the most extravagant dress Alice had ever seen, aside from Yasmin's golden gown.

Yasmin beamed at her creation. "Are you ready?"

Almost blinded by Yasmin's outfit, Alice nodded.

Yasmin looped her arm through hers, teleported them to the entrance foyer, then strode towards the Grand Hall, scattering people out of their path.

Alice's breath caught at the dramatic change, and she flushed as so many eyes turned their way. The most splendid tapestries now hung from the walls and the windows were draped with the most expensive shimmering curtains. Above them, stars twinkled, casting the room in a golden light.

Along one wall, elaborately carved tables painted in gold held the highest quality food and drink from a vast range of cultures. The tabletops were not of uniform height, which gave a peculiar organic feel to the display. Occasionally, a table would stretch out above the others, allowing for multiple tiers of dishes. Small tables suitable for eating and relaxing lined two other walls, while the third opened onto the garden courtyard.

Through the doors, a steady flow of people arrived, bringing with them the fragrant blossoms and flowery scents of the garden courtyard beyond. From high-level mages to high-ranking soldiers, the room brimmed with glittering stars and medals. Yet none had brought Emily with them.

Alice followed Yasmin across the hall, skirting the central space vacated for dancing, separated by an intermittent border of flowers and plants. Exotic birds with red, blue-and-gold plumage and long curved beaks perched in the corners of the border on specially designed displays, bobbing their heads at her as she passed.

Seeking out friendly faces, Alice only recognised Javed so far. He currently talked with a group of soldiers and had clearly put a lot of effort into dressing up for the occasion. Aside from dinner and breakfast, Alice had only ever seen him whilst training, so had never seen him in his formal military clothes. Barely twenty-one, he had few medals to display, but his deep-blue double-breasted tunic was adorned with the sigil of the royal house and his two mage stars. As the orphaned nephew of the king, he was also entitled to wear his own sigil, the crouching lion.

Finding him much more imposing in his formal outfit, Alice couldn't help drawing comparisons with Darien. Taller and broader, Javed usually wore a serious expression under his sensible short hair, giving the impression of an honourable knight. Darien, on the other hand, was much leaner and rarely serious, yet still had the same commanding presence. Not to mention his ability to use his compelling charm to his advantage whenever the situation suited.

They made their way over to Javed and the soldiers, though Alice found herself leading the way. Remembering how often Yasmin told her how boring Javed was and how he thought little of Yasmin's interest in fashion, she anticipated quite an awkward conversation.

As they approached, the soldiers all bowed deeply to Yasmin, and Javed performed a small bow befitting his station, something he would not normally do.

"Princess Yasmin, Alice, you both look extraordinary," he began.

Yasmin beamed, even if his compliment was mere politeness. Alice did her best attempt at a curtsey as Yasmin somehow managed to dip elegantly under her gown.

"You don't look too bad yourself, Prince Javed," Alice said, admiring the sword medal pinned to his chest.

Javed straightened his tunic, and slid a disapproving glance at a group of giggling girls nearby. No doubt they were hoping to be asked to dance. "There's nothing like a royal ball to bring out the best in everyone." He smiled, then glanced towards the banquet. "The food is superb. Have you tried any?"

Missing the easy charm of Javed's cousin, Alice shook her head.

Javed led them towards the culinary delights, whilst everyone else moved aside, giving them a far wider berth than necessary. Yet the guests congregated around them, observing from a distance.

As they ate, a musician plucked a haunting melody on an instrument much like an elongated guitar, but with the softer sound of a harp. The notes chimed out the musician's melancholy, perhaps a song of a lost love, before another joined and filled the room with answering hope.

With no sign of Darien or even Officer Gul, Alice and Yasmin whispered to each other whenever they could, Yasmin pointing out which of the high-ranking soldiers and mages were suitable for dancing.

Suddenly, in the exact centre of the room, the Royal Mage appeared in a burst of flame, eliciting a murmur of approval from the mages in the room. His outfit stunned too, the deep blue appearing to be consumed by golden flickering flames. On his cloak, the golden Royal Mage symbol burned ferociously.

Alice stared as he strode over to a group of high-level mages, who each bowed or curtseyed. One she recognised as Ahmad, but the others she hadn't seen before. A beautiful girl around Yasmin's age stood with them, her silky dress dotted with stars that occasionally fizzed out, only to be replaced by new ones.

"Who's that?" she whispered to Yasmin.

"That's Ahmad's daughter, Rosana. She thinks she's special because my uncle gives her private lessons." Yasmin wrinkled her nose. "It's only because of her father."

Alice bit her lip. She knew better now than to suggest they talk to someone of whom Yasmin disapproved. Though perhaps she was only bitter because her uncle had gone to speak with them first.

The king's entrance was much more subtle, but he marched towards Yasmin first, greeting her with a kiss before acknowledging the soldiers. "Yasmin, you have outdone yourself once again with your dress. I cannot imagine how you will surpass this one."

Yasmin beamed, even as his attention turned to Alice. "Alice, you too look wonderful. I hope my children have been looking after you."

She nodded her agreement before he headed off to greet more soldiers, mages, and foreign dignitaries, at a pace that suggested he intended to converse with everyone in the room before the evening ended.

Finally, Alice spotted Officer Gul hovering around the food with a few other high-ranking portal police. He repeatedly glanced towards Yasmin, so Alice smiled encouragingly at him, but it appeared he wasn't brave enough to approach in their present company.

To her surprise, the Royal Mage joined them next. "Yasmin, you are looking exquisite today. Would you do me the honour of the first dance?"

"Of course, Uncle," Yasmin said, her face lighting up. Taking his arm, she let him lead her into the centre of the room.

The music changed to accompany the dancers, a bass plucking out the steady beat and a few violin-like instruments accompanying their sweeping movements. The original instruments decorated the song with a few elegant trills, building to a wild crescendo, only to begin all over again.

Despite her familiarity with the dance from her lessons with Yasmin, Alice stared in fascination at the surprising grace of the Royal Mage and the magnificent sight of all the couples together, moving in perfect harmony to the emotive music.

A soldier in their group stepped forwards and bowed, holding his hand out to Alice. "Would you care to dance?"

There was no sign of Darien, and this was one of the soldiers who met with Yasmin's approval, so Alice consented. By the time they reached the dance area, many other couples had joined in, so Alice began to relax and enjoy herself, allowing the soldier to whirl her around the room. She supposed the dance was much like a waltz, not that she'd ever waltzed before.

At the end of the first dance, most people swapped partners, and to her horror, the Royal Mage strode her way. "May I have the next dance?"

Alice had no chance to object as he took her hand and moved her into position. Fortunately, his arms were so long he didn't hold her so close. He swept her around the floor so confidently she barely needed to think about where to put her feet, not even when he twirled her. Instead, she worried about why he danced with her at all.

Out of the corner of her eye, she observed Officer Gul sweep in towards Yasmin, and tried to be happy about that.

"Is there any news on the search for my world?" Alice asked.

"I'm afraid no route has yet been found. Though may I say that palace life suits you? Have you considered you might be better off staying here?"

Alice blinked at the unexpected statement, unsure of what to say. "Yasmin has been extremely welcoming and Parsa is fascinating, but I can't stay."

"No?"

"I have my own family to get back to. They won't even know what's happened to me. And I can't just live in a palace for the rest of my life. What would I do with myself?"

"A beautiful girl like you could marry a high-level mage or a high-ranking soldier and continue to live a life of luxury. Yasmin really has been much happier since you've been here. Perhaps you could even marry a prince."

Alice blushed, hoping her thoughts weren't that obvious. She remembered how she had been treated when she wasn't with Yasmin and how the mages viewed Officer Gul and those like him. "The palace is fine for those with magic," she said pointedly.

"Ah, mages can be a little snobbish when it comes to magic, but you shouldn't let that put you off. With a friend like me, you needn't worry about that at all. If anyone ever upset you, a word is all it would take to silence them."

To her relief, Darien interrupted at that moment, teleporting right into the Royal Mage's path. He swept his shimmering cloak behind him and dropped into a flamboyant bow, flashing a charming smile. "Mind if I cut in?"

The Royal Mage's eyebrows twitched, but he replied with perfect politeness. "Of course. I should have known I couldn't dance with the most beautiful girls all evening." Drawing Alice in close before he surrendered her, he whispered quietly in her ear, "Remember, anything you need, come to me first." As he let her go, he turned to Darien, and in a peculiar tone said, "My compliments on your efforts to reinvigorate the town."

"What was all that about?" Darien asked, his suspicious gaze following the Royal Mage.

"I'm not sure. He wanted to express how glad he is that I'm making Yasmin happy, I think." It was such a weird conversation that she put it to the back of her mind. However, she did notice that the Royal Mage only danced with a couple of other high-level mages throughout the evening.

Alice melted into Darien's arms as soon as he offered them, and they spent the next few hours dancing together, despite the annoyed stares of most of the women in the room.

"I've been thinking about how to help you find your way home," he stated out of the blue.

"How?"

"There's an old spell that might aid us in reliving your memories, to see exactly how you got here."

"Why didn't you mention it before?" Alice exclaimed. Her feet faltered as she digested his words, but he guided her back into position. However, he hesitated to reply, so Alice glared at him.

"It's tricky and probably wouldn't have worked until I located a rare clear crystal. I was hoping the Royal Mage or Officer Gul would have discovered a way home for you by now."

"Do you have the crystal?"

"I discovered the crystal today, but didn't have a chance to find you before the ball. We can give the officer more time, though. He's never let me down before." His eyes darted to Officer Gul, and Alice happily observed that he still danced with Yasmin. It seemed the Royal Mage wasn't bold enough to drag them apart in front of everyone.

"What will happen if it doesn't work?"

"Maybe nothing, or maybe I'll see something else you don't want me to see," he answered, his brow furrowed.

"I have nothing to hide. We should try it." Although she enjoyed dancing with Darien, the thought of sneaking off with him to perform magic was even more compelling.

"Alright," he replied. He spun her around, then teleported right out of the middle of the dancefloor. It wasn't quite what she'd had in mind when she thought about sneaking away – most of the room would have seen them disappear together – but it was too late to say anything now.

In Darien's chambers, memories from her previous visit flooded back, and she scarcely suppressed a shudder at the thought of him lying unconscious on the floor.

"Don't worry, nothing can go *that* wrong," he said, reading her expression. He retrieved a clear crystal from a magically sealed chest, then knelt in the middle of the floor, waiting for her to join him.

Her heart accelerated at the prospect of magic. Of finding answers. Of Darien sharing her thoughts.

After a deep breath, she settled down in front of him, her eyes locked on his.

"All you need to do is open your mind and think back to the day you came through the portal." He wrapped a silver chain loosely around them several times, before attaching the ends to the rare clear crystal. The gem didn't look that impressive and didn't glow when touched, unlike Darien's other crystals.

A thought flickered across Darien's face, and he reached out towards another cabinet. With one sweep of his arm, a group of purple crystals flew towards them and settled in a circle on the ground, encompassing both of them.

"Are you ready?"

She nodded, though it was hard to focus on the portal and her arrival when he was this close to her.

He leaned forward, put his hands gently on each side of her face, then started the incantation.

Fogginess swept through her mind and memories of her two lives randomly surfaced, quickly to be replaced by new ones. It was a dizzying, jumbled mess, and even she couldn't tell what some memories were. Yasmin's face mingled with Darien, then Jaime, Emily and Natalie appeared amongst a backdrop of school, home, and the palace.

"Focus, Alice," Darien said.

She tried to focus on her journey, but instead of her own world, she saw herself meeting Darien for the first time. She had been so entranced by his appearance and startled by his use of magic that she hadn't really noticed the man behind it all. But what had he thought when he first laid eyes on her?

Instantly, the memory shifted viewpoint. She was seeing herself through Darien's eyes and hearing his thoughts!

She couldn't help but smile when she discovered how beautiful he thought she looked, despite her peculiar clothes. Then the memory blurred and Officer Gul stood in front of her, or rather Darien. "The girl carries a strange device with her. It's clear she's from an advanced technological world," the officer said.

She felt Darien's delight as he answered. "How advanced? What does the device do?"

Officer Gul shook his head. "I'm not sure, but it seemed important to her. She kept looking at it as if it would give her answers and it repeatedly lit up with an odd blue glow."

"What were you doing at that portal in the first place?"

"One of my men informed me the mage on duty had vanished, so I went to see what was going on, but no one remembered anything unusual."

"Never mind. There are other ways to retrieve memories."

Alice blanched at this revelation. Darien was interested in her because of her *phone*? That couldn't be why he'd befriended her, could it?

Immediately, the memories raced ahead to a conversation with Darien's father, but they started to flicker, and darkness crawled at the edges. She saw the king, but couldn't hear his voice as he walked across an unfamiliar room. However, Darien's words were clear, in a cunning voice that made her skin crawl.

"... the mind-sharing spell" – the image flickered again, but Darien's voice continued – "infatuated ... so naïve ... the ball."

Alice's stomach turned to lead, and the voice started to fade, but she willed it back, focusing all her attention on Darien. She had to know.

His words were distant, but she heard them clearly. "I'll suggest it will help her get home and she'll have no reason to doubt me."

"Alice, stop!" Darien shouted, this time loud and clear from outside her mind. His voice was panicked as he failed to prevent her from accessing his thoughts. It didn't matter, though. Too enraged to hold on to the memories, the spell broke.

"You lied to me!" she yelled. "You're just using me so you can get hold of technology from my world." Anger surged through her, a wave of energy that – once departed – left her tingling all over. At the same time, furniture shattered into pieces, and crystals hurled into the walls. Instinctively, she ducked and put her hands over her head, but it was already over.

Her hands shook, and she suddenly felt drained, as if the memory spell had sapped all her strength. Darien himself thudded against the wall, his protective crystal hanging loose and glowing dimly. He stared at her, his mouth gaping, and only then did she realise she was unharmed and kneeling right in the epicentre of the explosion. Had the spell backfired that much?

"You have magic?" Darien said, still staring at her in incredulity.

"... What?"

Suddenly, all her memories shifted into perfect clarity, perhaps because of the spell. She saw herself in the Royal Mage's workshop picking up the crystal. Recalled it glowing in response to her touch. The Royal Mage had seen. He'd known. And he'd kept it quiet all this time. No wonder he'd offered to help her.

Still tingling, Alice stood and walked to the nearest crystal. It began to glow before she even touched it. Darien didn't move. He just watched her, his eyes bulging.

What should she do now?

Alice's first instinct was to find Yasmin. She would understand.

Unless she was involved, too?

She soon shook off that thought. Yasmin had been nothing but genuine towards her and had chided Darien for using people. Why hadn't Alice paid more attention?

Storming from the room, she began the long climb downstairs, her heart pounding and her mind racing. Yasmin would still be at the ball, but Alice would rather return there than be alone with her terrifying new discovery.

Darien's memories flashed through her mind over and over as she descended. How could she not have figured him out before? He'd asked so many questions about her world. About technology. And she'd thought him charming.

She sped up, half tripped over her dress, and collided with the wall. Then the truth hit her. If she had magic, she could learn to teleport. She wouldn't have to walk these stairs or be afraid of mages anymore.

She could be one of them.

A shiver shot through her. It wouldn't be enough to protect her from Darien or the Royal Mage, but she had Yasmin for that. There was no limit to the things they could do together now.

Sooner than expected, she reached the hall and hovered in the doorway. Little had changed since her departure, and Yasmin still danced with Officer Gul. Conscious of her red face, Alice took a deep breath and strode towards them.

Officer Gul noticed her first, stepping aside with a bow. "Please excuse me. I've just realised I must talk to someone before he leaves."

Alice watched him head towards other officers, then turned her attention back to Yasmin. "Can we go somewhere else?" She didn't even care that she'd be the subject of much gossip, leaving the ball twice in the same way.

Yasmin nodded and teleported them back to her chambers.

"What happened?" Yasmin asked. "I saw you leave with Darien. What did he do to you?"

Yasmin stared open-mouthed as Alice told her about the spell, and her face darkened as she learned of Darien's plot. But when Alice revealed her own magic, Yasmin squealed and wrapped her in a hug.

"You'll have to study with me properly now you can actually cast spells," she said authoritatively. Her tone turned menacing. "But first, we should pay Darien a visit."

Alice's stomach twisted at the idea, but it was the best way to find out whose side Yasmin was on.

She needn't have worried. They had scarcely appeared in Darien's chambers before Yasmin started yelling at him. Though she stopped abruptly when she saw the state of the room.

Darien himself had hardly moved and was now standing by the wall staring at a crystal in his hand.

A flicker of guilt rushed through her, but after all he'd done, Alice was glad her magic had had some effect on him.

"You did all this?" Yasmin asked, and Alice nodded.

"You must be incredibly powerful to do this without a spell." Seeing Darien's condition, Yasmin's rage subsided a little, and her volume decreased. "What did you think you were doing?"

Darien looked up, his eyes wide. "It's not what you think. She only saw fragments of the truth. Alice, please listen to me. There's more going on than you know. I wasn't just using you. I care about you too."

Alice scowled at him as Yasmin voiced her thoughts. "Oh, shut up Darien. Come on, Alice. He's not worth it." Before they left, Yasmin sent a crackling hex at him, which he barely bothered to deflect.

Back in Yasmin's chambers, Alice collapsed into a chair and exhaled loudly.

"Sometimes boys can be really stupid," Yasmin concluded, breaking the silence.

"Agreed." The sting of betrayal and her embarrassment at being taken in so easily began to subside now she was with Yasmin, and the excitement of being able to cast her own spells took over. She'd be able to leave the palace more easily now and may even be able to venture off to other worlds once she'd learned some defensive spells.

She could actually go look for her friends, rather than waiting for others to do it for her.

CHAPTER 35

A FOREST WORLD

Jaime woke abruptly as Torvia moved away, the heat of her body no longer warming him. He had no concept of time, though the firewood they'd collected had almost burned through. Darkness seeped through the cave entrance, and owls hooted in the trees, but that didn't mean anything. They were on another world, and time probably didn't align with Parsa.

Still cold from the icy world despite the furs he wore, he massaged life into his stiff limbs.

With the flourish of her hand, Torvia coaxed the fire higher, spreading a comforting warmth throughout the cave. "Let's heat some food on the fire."

She must have been too weak to cast the spell before. "Are you alright?" he asked. "I'm sorry if I slowed you down."

She smiled and tossed him a biscuit. "I'm fine. You did well to keep going without magic. Sometimes I forget how difficult the elements can be."

Just the thought of that place had him pulling his furs tighter. "You worried me more in the desert."

Torvia bit her lip. "I'm used to travelling alone. I'm sorry if I snapped a little. Being drained like that—"

"You don't have to apologise. You're the one helping me." He huddled closer to the fire. "Do people live on this world?"

"Perhaps. I've not explored far from the portals, but I've never seen any sign of anyone. There's plenty of wildlife though, so it can be a good place to stay for a few days." Seeing his expression, she added, "We won't be here that long. It will take a few teleports, but we can rest in between. It's fairly safe here."

"Why couldn't we teleport on the icy world?"

"It would be far too easy to get lost. There's nothing to mark out the portal or anything else, even if I could see through the blizzard. Every time I visit, the snow has shifted into a new landscape. If we teleported only a few paces wrong, we might completely miss the portal and be lost for hours."

Jaime shuddered. Minutes had been long enough in that hell. There was no way they could have survived hours. "How do you know where to find these portals? I mean, the first time you used them."

"Many are known by a few people. The one in the desert on Parsa is familiar to a few traders, but no one dares use it because of the strong likelihood of ending up on the inhospitable world we just departed."

"We could have gone somewhere else?"

Torvia bobbed her head. "We could have carried on in the portal realm and left through a different portal, but that would have been extremely dangerous. There is no guarantee of finding a way back or even knowing where you might end up. It's best to stick to common routes unless you're desperate."

"Do you think if we'd continued we could have eventually found my home?"

"It's impossible to say. There are more worlds than anyone has counted and the portal realm is only traversable in a few areas. Eventually, the river would have scooped you up and spat you out onto some unknown world with no hope of getting back through."

"Like the portal that brought me here," Jaime muttered. "But how did you know the second portal would lead here instead of somewhere else?"

"I used to visit here with a close friend of mine. An accomplished hunter and skilled mage, he taught me a lot, more than how to find my way here." She smiled. "Spells can be used on portals to tell you where they might lead, but they don't always work. He searched for a new world to hunt, and – curious about what might lie behind the ice world – he found his way here. One day I stumbled through another portal from a world that connects to North Parsa and recognised this world, so it was only a matter of time before I found my way between them. I don't think there is anyone else who knows about the complete path outside South Parsa, except you now."

He frowned. "If you weren't sure where you would end up, why did you go through the portal in the first place?"

"Let's just say I really needed to disappear, or I would have been in a lot of trouble." She smiled mischievously and leaned forwards to stir their stew.

Once the food was cooked, they tucked into a simple yet gloriously warming meal and Jaime began to feel more alive again, the frozen nightmare fading into the past.

Now more relaxed, he peered outside. Completely untouched by humans, the forest loomed all around him in the pale glow of dawn. A pair of yellow eyes, unfazed by his presence, stared back at him from a nearby tree, evoking a small shudder. It was peaceful, yet ominous, as if more animals lurked just out of sight, waiting for the sun's ascent.

"Shall we move on?" Torvia asked, offering her arm.

He took it gladly, and a moment later, they materialised in a similar clearing. He glanced covertly at Torvia to check her condition, before noticing it was quite a bit brighter here. They mustn't have traversed as far as the desert jumps but had travelled east towards the rising sun.

"We can rest here for a while, then carry on to the next place," she announced.

They carried on like this a few times, stopping in a sheltered area at each jump.

One of the stops was much higher up in the mountains where vegetation was sparse, providing them with a magnificent view of the surroundings. Perched on a rocky outcrop above a thundering waterfall, Jaime surveyed the scene.

Bubbling water surged over the crest, hurtling down to plunge into the murky pool far below. Swells crashed against slate rocks before winding through the vast mountain range, and effervescent white met russet soil between silvery grey stones, contrasting against the mosaic of green beneath the cerulean sky.

As he marvelled at the scene, battling his vertigo and sense of insignificance, he realised Torvia was watching him. "Something amusing?" he asked.

"I've never brought anyone up here. I'd forgotten how spectacular the view is. Watching you is like seeing it again for the first time."

He grinned. He had never been the adventurous type, but travelling with Torvia made him feel at ease.

A couple of jumps later, they rested for a well-deserved meal. Torvia located some interesting fruit from a nearby copse, and handed Jaime a pink lime-shaped fruit, twice the size of any regular lime.

After one bite, his face instantly twisted with regret. More sour than the sourest of candies and totally repulsive, the pulpy insides oozed down his face. "What did you give me that for?" he spluttered, still spitting out bits of fruit.

Torvia couldn't stifle her laughter. "Oops, did I give you the sour one?" She offered him another fruit, which he eyed suspiciously, only trying it after she bit into an identical one.

After their buffet of local fruits, Torvia filled up her bag with the sweetest variety, presumably to trade somewhere, then turned to Jaime with an air of expectation. "Are you ready for this?"

She'd never asked if he was prepared before, and he was quite used to teleporting by now. Apprehensively, he took her hand, and they snapped to their next destination.

Totally gobsmacked, he stared at the apparition before him. No doubt Torvia observed him, seeing it again through his eyes, but he could not tear his eyes away.

He knew he stood on the same world. The sounds of the forest and its woody scents had changed little throughout their journey, but the sight before him did not fit with his other senses.

Stretching across the entire horizon and looming high into the sky, a whole other world ascended. Shades of red and orange streaked across the giant orb, caught in a dance, a snapshot in the timescales of the turbulent planet.

Dizziness washed over him, as if gravity had suddenly changed direction and pulled him into the sky, towards the giant red marble. Brighter and more vivid than any picture, it instantly reminded him of Jupiter, but seeing it up close struck wonder into his heart. They weren't on a planet. They were on a moon orbiting the gas giant.

"Amazing, isn't it?" Torvia finally said. "The first time I saw this, I was fleeing through an unknown portal, running for my life. I almost thought I had died and gone to the afterlife."

Still gazing at the spectacle before him, Jaime couldn't reply. Filaments of gold, copper and bronze streaked out from the bands, twirling around in a violent storm, right in front of him, yet so far away.

How many people would give everything just to be here?

It must have been like seeing Earth from space for the first time. Except instead of looking at his home, he marvelled at a distant world from some unknown place in the universe. He didn't even know if he stood within the same galaxy.

A sudden loneliness gripped him and he glanced away, finding Torvia's comforting face. Possibly the only other person on this entire world, and the only person who could lead him back to Parsa, she beamed at him.

He grinned back. "Thank you for trusting me enough to show me this place."

She gave him a squeeze and he felt awkward all over again, but as she pulled away, she left a comforting warmth that stayed with him even in the cool mountain air.

"Say goodbye to this world. The next jump is to the portal and then we're in North-Parsa-controlled territory."

His gaze stayed skyward as he took Torvia's hand, and they teleported to the next destination. In the shadow of the colossal planet now, which occupied much more of the sky, the giant seemed to press towards him.

Tearing his eyes away, he realised Torvia had removed her cold weather gear. He followed her into a half-crumbling makeshift wooden shelter that had seen better days and received some rather ugly grey robes. He changed outside and stashed his comfortable desert clothes inside his bag, but there was no room for his winter furs.

A moment later, Torvia popped out of the shelter wearing similar attire. Although hers too were plain and unfashionable, the clothes didn't quite disguise her attractive figure. As she slid a knife into a strap above her boot, she looked far more capable than Jaime knew he appeared, and he couldn't help but stare in admiration.

He quickly discarded his winter furs inside the shack, and rushed to catch up with Torvia, who had already slipped through the trees. Even with her leading the way, he missed his footing more than once, mesmerised by the vision above.

This moon really was full of marvels, but for Torvia this was just another journey. What else might she have seen? The portals opened up an entire new universe, one Jaime was only just beginning to glimpse.

A few tight turns later, and after clambering up some rocks, they reached the next portal. Even this had a slight pink hue to it, as if it had somehow captured light from the neighbouring giant.

Without a word, they joined hands and crossed the shimmering threshold. Immediately, a current tried to force Jaime back through the portal. Bracing himself against it, he pushed forward, squeezing Torvia's hand.

Their journey was short, and in no time at all they emerged into a ravine with steep rock walls on each side. Jaime craned his neck, wondering how they would get out of it. A second later he found himself at the top, looking down on their former location.

Magic was going to take some getting used to.

Like the previous world, this place seemed deserted, but in a much more extreme way. With no trees and no animals, the world felt empty.

Only rocks and dirt surrounded the portal. Even the air smelled of dust.

He looked expectantly at Torvia.

"I thought you would want to admire the view before we carry on." She smirked, clearly enjoying this trip.

"Thank you," he replied sarcastically, but fully appreciating the experience. "Let's go then."

"One more thing." She waved her hand in front of his face.

"What did you do?" he asked, puzzled. Was that a spell? A strand of hair fell in front of his face, black instead of its usual light colour. He grasped at more of his hair, all black, and stared questioningly at Torvia.

"It will fade after a few days, but this way you won't stand out so much."

Wondering what else she was capable of, he took her arm for the next jump.

This time, they appeared in some sort of farm. Signs of irrigation streaked through the fields and where the land was too rocky, giant chickens roamed in irregular pens. Although indications of civilisation littered their view, no people emerged. The world was quiet, save for the scattering of dirt with the wind and the occasional flapping of feathers.

Following a vague track, they meandered downwards, through arid farmland, and eventually more buildings entered their view. The further they went, the more densely clustered the dwellings became, until a small village emerged cradled in the rock.

Torvia led him down a different path at that point, towards a more remote building. "I'd like to visit a friend first," she explained.

The wooden house they veered towards appeared identical to the others, with little decoration other than simple shutters, but it was set apart from the rest. A chicken darted across the front yard, clucking as it disappeared around the side of the building.

On their approach, an extremely well-dressed young man walked out of the door. Jaime didn't get a good look at him before Torvia practically punched Jaime in the chest in her haste to teleport him away.

Further up the hill now, they looked down on the building, shielded from sight by rocks. From their vantage point, they observed the man take a few steps before he teleported away.

"So, who was that?" Jaime asked.

"That was Prince Darien, the crown prince of North Parsa! He shouldn't be here."

"Is there something important about this town?" Jaime surveyed the area but saw nothing remarkable.

"There are some who resist the oppressive rule of North Parsa, and this is a safe place to meet and to hide out if necessary. If Prince Darien is visiting, he must be aware of the rebels. It's too much of a coincidence otherwise."

Torvia peeked further around the rock, her entire body stiff. "Let's go see if we can find out why he was here."

She didn't knock as she entered the building, but as they passed through the door, under sprigs of lavender and sage, a jingling sound announced their presence.

An old woman with grey hair and a slight hunch ambled into the room. Wearing a loose flowing slate dress that was bound with a simple rope, she smiled at Torvia. "Torvia, how lovely of you to visit in these troubling times." Her eyes slid to Jaime for a moment, betraying a flicker of curiosity.

"Troubling?" Torvia said. "Some might say it is a great victory that the north and south of Parsa are about to be joined."

"Yes, all signs point to a prominent union between the north and the south, but there will be much strife and loss before that happens." The old woman rolled up her sleeves and scrutinised Jaime. "Who have you brought me, Torvia?" Without waiting for a reply, she grabbed Jaime's arm and examined his hand. "Fascinating. No magic, yet he has an important role to play."

Torvia contemplated Jaime with equal curiosity, making him think this woman might have some gifts for prediction.

"Do you see something?" he asked.

"So, you want me to read your fortune, do you?" With surprising strength, the woman pulled him to a small table and pushed him into a chair. Slowly, she lowered herself into the chair opposite, and requested both his hands. Again, she clutched them with superhuman strength, and her eyes rolled back in head as she chanted an eerie incantation with a peculiar rhythmic rasping tone.

Jaime had never believed in fortune tellers, but then he had never seen anyone teleport or summon fire before, so he stared, intrigued.

The woman started rocking and shuddering, making the hair on the back of his neck stand up. "Five can give you the power you need. Seek the forbidden texts of the true star. He who is your rival will be your salvation."

Suddenly, she jumped and dropped his hands. She had been clutching them so tightly that red marks remained on his skin. He glanced at Torvia to see what she made of this message, but she seemed to be lost in thought.

As far as he was aware, he had no rival, and he wasn't in need of any power.

The woman got up from the table and retrieved something from a dusty old drawer. "Here, take this talisman as a reminder of your destiny." She handed him a silver five-point star attached to a chain. Not wanting to offend her, he put it around his neck.

"How are the others?" Torvia asked the woman.

"That is not the question you want to ask." She eyed Torvia knowingly. "You saw the prince, didn't you?"

Torvia scowled. "Yes. How long has he known?"

"Longer than you think. But you needn't worry about that. He doesn't know where to find anyone. He merely visited to ask if someone had been rescued. Someone I think your friend might be interested in."

"Me? Alice was here? She was rescued?" He glanced nervously at Torvia, but her expression remained neutral.

"No. The prince knows her by the name Jane, but I believe you know her as Emily."

Jaime's heart leapt. Now only Eliot was missing. "Emily is here?"

"Yes. She got into a little trouble in the palace and was rescued by the others. It seems the prince was concerned about her, but she had been keeping her true identity a secret."

Torvia sneered. "The prince cares about no one, unless it furthers his ambition. What did he want with her?"

"Some things never become clear, especially to those who have chosen not to see." The old woman glared at Torvia, her eyes full of scorn.

"We should visit there immediately." Ignoring the cryptic riddle, Torvia headed for the door. Keen to see Emily, Jaime followed.

"Wait, Torvia! You have more in common than you know. You must learn to overcome your prejudice, lest history repeat itself."

Torvia shook her head. "I know all I need to know about North Parsans." She whirled for the door, clearly annoyed at the discovery of an enemy in a place she thought secret and safe.

CHAPTER 36

THE SECRET OASIS

E mily peered out of the window of her tiny room in the desert shack, chewing on nails already bitten to the quick. Since she'd arrived at this hidden oasis on a world unknown to the North Parsans, her hope in Shirin and the resistance had risen, but there was little to do here whilst she waited for Shirin's promised help to arrive.

Unlike most days, a gradual stream of people headed into the communal hall. Finally, something to distract from her failure to rescue her brother.

Following them in, she wondered how many people could belong to a secret resistance. The ability to disappear in the blink of an eye probably helped keep them from being discovered but they couldn't all teleport. Perhaps portal travel to the adjoining world was so common that no one noticed the extra traffic.

Unless the portal police were part of the resistance?

Emily glanced around the hall, barely large enough to comfortably fit the fifty or so people who gathered, many sitting chatting in groups, or drinking mint tea. Some worked on various crafts, others practised magic. These were nothing like the proud portal police. But the police could probably be bribed easily enough.

Many of the occupants wore the North Parsan blue – mages and commoners alike. But no one displayed golden embellishments or house symbols to impress. Few people her age were present and even fewer older than fifty, though one elderly man sat alone in the corner, mumbling to himself.

She wandered over to talk with him, stepping over women weaving tapestries and men carving wood into intricate designs. The man was working on his own beautiful carving of a young lion. "That's an impressive design," she said.

He glanced up at her for a moment, then lowered his eyes back to his craft.

She tried again. "Have you been in the resistance for long?"

Squinting his almond eyes at her, he dropped the carving. "Who are you? You don't belong here." Before she could answer, a flash of light blinded her, and the man vanished.

Emily spun around, her eyes drawn to a tall woman limping to the other end of the room. She'd not been there a moment ago, and she was the only person alone. Confused, Emily stooped to pick up the old man's carving. The wood was unusually heavy, yet perfectly smooth.

Shirin weaved through the crowd, following Emily's gaze. "Don't worry about him. A powerful memory spell addled his mind long ago."

Emily frowned. "He transformed into that woman?"

"Yes, he's quite talented. He must have been an accomplished mage in his time, but now he trusts no one and keeps to himself."

"Can't someone reverse the memory spell?"

Shirin shook her head. "Many mages have tried, but it's just too strong."

Emily's blood chilled. She didn't need to ask who might have cast such a spell. But was this just to hide the change in succession or were there other secrets?

A hush fell over the room as a young woman entered, far more formidable in appearance than any other visitor and completely oblivious to the reaction she caused. Despite her plain desert clothes, something about her suggested danger, and it wasn't just the blade poking out of her belt or her fiery amber eyes. That confidence could only belong to a talented mage, and judging from the room, the most powerful mage present.

Captivated by the woman, Emily almost didn't notice the black-haired man follow her in, but as soon as she did, her heart skipped a beat.

"*Jaime!* Is that you?" She rushed forward, oblivious to the crowd.

Jaime's face lit up, but he didn't seem surprised. Something about him was different, besides his hair, but whatever it was didn't stop her from enveloping him in a hug as soon as she reached him. It was unlike either of them to be so forward, but she was just glad to see a familiar face after all this time.

As he wrapped his arms around her, all her tension evaporated.

She was no longer alone.

A thousand questions rushed through her mind, but the least important one of all spilled out first. "What happened to your hair?"

"Apparently, I needed to fit in better," he explained, with his usual mischievous grin.

Unable to take her eyes off him, Emily stepped back for a better view. "Where have you been?"

"It's a long story. I think it can wait until the important stuff is out of the way first." He turned back to the young mage, who watched them closely.

Emily glanced between them, her curiosity growing. How could Jaime know this striking young woman?

"Thank you, Jaime," the young mage said with a smile, before turning to address the room. "On our way here, we stopped to visit the fortune teller, and almost ran into Prince Darien himself."

Gasps and whispers filled the room.

"Apparently, he came to check on Jane," she explained, fixing her unsettling eyes on Emily.

Emily's cheeks flushed. "Call me Emily. That's my real name."

"Perhaps you should tell everyone what happened," Shirin suggested.

Emily tossed her hair over her shoulder, and ignoring the tightness in her throat, began her story.

"When I arrived on Parsa, my brother went missing and I soon suspected he had been taken to the palace. I found work in the lower mage library whilst I looked for a sympathetic mage to help me into the palace, but then I discovered an unusual book, and was ordered to take it straight to Prince Darien. He employed me to search for more rare books, both in the lower mage library and the palace mage library."

A few murmurs spread through the room, so she cleared her throat.

"It took me ages to search the palace, but one morning I overheard Darien plotting to steal my friend's memories of our world and knew I had to hurry and find Alice too."

Jaime shifted uncomfortably, obviously wanting to ask more about Alice, but he patiently held his tongue, waiting for the full story to unravel.

"That's when Shirin found me and suggested I convince Prince Darien to help me get into the Royal Mage's chambers."

She repressed a shudder and was driven on by the rapt attention of the crowd. She *had* promised Shirin she'd share everything she'd seen in return for help rescuing Eliot. "The Royal Mage was furious when he discovered us and revealed Prince Darien isn't the rightful heir to the throne. Then he brutally attacked the prince, leaving him unconscious on the floor."

Numerous gasps filled the room.

"That's the last thing I saw before I was imprisoned. The Royal Mage interrogated me about the prince's intentions, but I had nothing to give him. All I knew is that he was interested in ancient history magic books. Eventually, the Royal Mage told me I could serve Parsa by finding routes through portals, but Shirin rescued me before I was lost forever."

Silence filled the room and several moments elapsed before a middle-aged man spoke. "We knew something had happened between the Royal Mage and Prince Darien that day, since the batty old mage came down early from his shift babbling about Prince Darien having 'done it now'. The prince was scarcely seen for a few days after, but we had no idea the Royal Mage would attack his own nephew."

Emily listened intently, relieved to hear that Darien had recovered.

"What does this mean? Will there be a feud between the mages and the crown?" another woman questioned. A murmuring spread throughout the room, but all eyes remained on Shirin.

"No, not even the crown possesses the power to stand up to the Royal Mage. And Prince Darien is alone," Shirin explained. "He will learn to follow the Royal Mage, just as all the other royals have and all the mages do."

"What if we convinced him to join the resistance?" a younger voice said.

"It's too risky to expose ourselves. There still aren't enough of us to overthrow the Royal Mage and all his devoted followers. Prince Darien will choose to follow him as well," Shirin argued.

Many people nodded their heads in agreement, but Emily wasn't so sure. "If you gave Prince Darien another option, he might support you."

Shirin shook her head. "It's too dangerous to approach the prince. If the Royal Mage found out about any one of us, he would discover us all through his interrogation spells."

Nausea gripped Emily as Shirin's words took her back to her cell. She didn't need to be reminded about those spells. And what mage could hope to resist such power?

Eventually, the debate subsided, and the groups went back to their activities, leaving Emily with a chance to catch up with Jaime. He filled her in on his arrival in South Parsa, Jordan's departure, and his unexpected friendship with Torvia.

"Your ordeal sounds far worse than mine. I'm really not looking forward to reaching North Parsa," he finished.

"It wasn't all bad," Emily conceded. "There were some amazing things in the palace, and if the resistance does overthrow the mage caste system, it could be a wonderful place."

"We should hurry and get there before this Prince Darien tries to steal Alice's memories."

Emily's face fell. "It's too late. He planned to do it on the day of the ball, which has already passed. I'm sorry. I couldn't go back after they caught me. As soon as the wrong person saw me, I'd be imprisoned again, or worse."

Jaime's face flashed with shock, and he replied rigidly. "It's not your fault. If only I had got here sooner."

Emily took his arm and led him away from the crowd. "It's not your fault, either. I don't think Darien would hurt her. Physically, at least."

Jaime stared off into the distance for a moment, his face contorted with worry. "Are you sure Eliot's in the palace?"

Emily nodded. "The Royal Mage admitted to it. He thinks keeping Eliot will ensure I return with secrets of the portal realm." Mentioning his name sent a new shiver down her spine. Eliot was still alone and had no idea they were coming for him. "But I can't go back now, knowing about the resistance."

"Then how can we rescue him?" Jaime asked, voicing both of their thoughts.

Emily didn't have an answer, but Torvia answered from right behind them. "Our best chance will be when everyone is distracted and the Royal Mage is not in the tower. Princess Safia will arrive in North Parsa in a couple of weeks, and since the Royal Mage is the only one who has travelled to South Parsa, he will welcome her to the palace. That's our greatest opportunity."

"You'll help us?" Emily asked, astonished this lithe stranger wanted to assist them.

"Of course." Torvia grinned. "Resisting the Royal Mage is what we do, and sneaking around the North Parsan palace of is one of my favourite activities."

Emily glanced at Jaime again. He and this mage were closer than she'd first realised.

Shirin, too, looked curiously at Jaime before she joined in. "There will be extra security, so it will be much harder to get around the palace. You won't be able to use a disguise in the Mage Tower, either. I can try to help, but it will be easier if you take your second-star exams, Torvia. Then you'll be able to move freely around the palace too."

Torvia didn't look convinced, so Shirin continued. "You'd easily be able to pass them with your skill."

"It's not that," Torvia replied. "If I take them, they'll know my true appearance and may start to ask questions about my background. If they figure out I'm not North Parsan, I may be barred from the Mage Tower indefinitely."

Shirin shook her head. "They'd never think that. You could fool anyone. But if you need, I can convince my cousin to say you're her sister. She's been off-world for years and has no plans to return."

Emily held her breath as Torvia contemplated her decision. With her long dark hair, confident bearing and rumoured skill with their spells, she fitted in a little too well. But was Torvia really as capable as people thought? And why would she risk being captured by that man for a boy she'd never met?

After several long moments, Torvia dipped her head. "I'll take the exams. Then we'll see about rescuing your brother." She turned to Jaime. "We'll head to the city now."

Emily jumped forward. "What about me?"

"You're safer here."

"But I know where Eliot is being kept. I can help."

Torvia's lips formed a thin line. "We'll return when a plan is formed. Since no one knows who Jaime is, he can help find Alice, but you would be too conspicuous."

"You will return though?" Emily's throat tightened. All her hopes had rested on this mysterious mage, but she'd never imagined she'd be left out.

Torvia took her hand. "Try to be patient. You'll be no good to your brother if you're caught."

Emily nodded, but it was hard to watch Jaime walk off with this stranger so soon after they'd found each other. This exile was almost unbearable. The Royal Mage had chosen his punishment well.

CHAPTER 37
NORTH PARSA

It was hard work learning even basic spells, especially as Alice still didn't have a good grasp on the written language, but she was determined to make the most of her newfound skill. Frustratingly, most spells she tried didn't do anything. She consoled herself by practising the few incantations that did succeed, but even Yasmin thought there was something peculiar about her magic.

She flicked ahead in the spellbook Yasmin had suggested, and to her surprise, she spotted a fireball spell. "Casting a fireball is basic?"

Yasmin shrugged. "All North Parsan mages learn to cast fire early on. It's quite fundamental and doesn't require much thought, so long as you don't want to direct it anywhere."

The memory of Darien casting a fireball flashed in her mind, and everything he had done flooded back. With a scowl, she turned back to the page, forcing herself to focus. The spell appeared fairly simple, but she wanted to get the technique exactly right. "Will you teach me?"

Yasmin's face lit up, and she practically dragged Alice to her crystal circle. "Let's go to the Mage Tower so we can practise."

Alice followed eagerly, never more pleased to see Yasmin's sparse spell-casting room. "So, what do I do?" she asked.

"Focus and visualisation are more important than the words themselves. Eventually you won't need to use them, but for now they will help you focus. Hold your hand out like this, try to visualise the fire, then say 'orta'."

Alice did exactly as instructed, but nothing happened.

Yasmin frowned. "I was sure you'd be a natural after what happened with Darien."

Alice tried again a few times, but still nothing happened, not even a flicker of flame.

Yasmin waved her hand, and the spellbook flicked ahead to another page with an illustration of fire, but the words looked slightly different. "Try this one instead, pronounced 'brenna'."

As soon as Alice spoke the word, flames shot out of her hand, threatening to consume the book in front of her. She staggered back in alarm, but the flames disappeared as abruptly as they had appeared.

She glanced at Yasmin, who frowned again. "It seems you have more affinity for certain spells." She sighed. "Often, foreigners find one of the root cultures easier to master, but I've never seen such a difference so early on."

A smile spread across Alice's face. She didn't care which spells worked, as long as some did, and now she could cast fire.

The following days were filled with more spell-casting and study. Once, at breakfast, Darien appeared in the doorway, but Yasmin cast a barrier at the door to stop him from entering. He didn't try to push past it, and Alice hadn't seen him since. Still embarrassed, she tended to avoid the formal evening meals unless she knew Darien was definitely not going to attend.

Another morning, she had returned to find her room full of flowers and jewels, and Yasmin had taught her a hex that had filled Darien's room with locusts. She rarely thought about him anymore, and when she did, she chided herself for being so naïve. She hadn't seen Javed much either, assuming he breakfasted with Darien, and she didn't have time to shoot now she was busy studying.

However, the more Alice learned about magic, the more she wanted to get out of the palace and explore her new universe. No one could say she was helpless anymore. And her friends might be hiding on one of these neighbouring worlds, unaware she was the one looking for them. Now Alice knew what Darien and the Royal Mage were like, she wouldn't blame them if they were avoiding North Parsan mages.

Tearing her eyes away from the words already starting to blur together, she glanced at Yasmin, whose brow was screwed up in concentration. "Yasmin, can we go somewhere?"

Yasmin looked up from her spellbook and stared blankly at Alice. "Where do you want to go?"

Alice slammed her book shut. "Anywhere. Take me through the portal I came through. I'd love to see another world and maybe my friends will be there."

Yasmin frowned. "That portal doesn't go anywhere. People can only arrive through that one."

"Then another one. There must be a world you enjoy visiting." Alice approached the desk, where Yasmin kept some of the gifts from Officer Gul, and picked up one of the crystals. "What about Stratis? Can we go there?" It sounded like the sort of place that might be well travelled.

Yasmin glanced at the crystal and pursed her lips. "It's extremely dangerous to go off-world without an escort, and you're only just beginning to learn basic spells."

Alice rolled the decorative crystals in her hands, contemplating Yasmin's reluctance. "I've been off-world with Darien. You'd be just as good an escort *and* you know more magic. You'd protect me, wouldn't you?"

"Of course I would, but it's still risky." Yasmin returned her attention to her spellbook.

"You're not worried about your uncle, are you? I don't think he'd ever punish you and he can't accuse me of damaging your marriage prospects."

Yasmin scowled but had no retort. Perhaps this trip could be good for Yasmin too, teaching her to challenge her uncle's overbearing nature and unrealistic expectations. He still hadn't mentioned anything about Yasmin dancing with Officer Gul at the ball, so there was still hope.

Alice lost her smile as she remembered Darien's pitiful attempts. But she could do better than him. "Please, Yasmin. I desperately need to get out of the palace. Away from Darien." She slumped onto a chair, her head down, trying to look distraught. She felt a little guilty manipulating Yasmin, but at least she had learned something useful from Darien.

Yasmin sat beside her and put her arm around her. "I suppose we could go somewhere, just the two of us."

Alice beamed at her. "Can we go now?"

"As long as you promise not to get me in trouble. Let's find some suitable clothes." She walked over to the crystal circle and held out her hand to Alice.

Alice bounded after her before she could change her mind, and a moment later they stood in Yasmin's chambers in the Royal Tower. Her excitement taking over, Alice opened Yasmin's largest wardrobe to find some clothes that might be considered suitable.

A regiment of silky bold royal ensembles dazzled her. Doubt numbed her excitement, and she turned to Yasmin. "Do you mean you will wear something plain?"

Turning her nose up, Yasmin summoned shimmering azure silks into a whirlwind around her. Within seconds, they had wrapped themselves into a stunning dress trimmed with gold. By Yasmin's standards, it was rather plain, but she would shine as brightly as any crystal among normal people. To her credit, she did retrieve a pair of sturdy, yet stylish, black boots with small gold studs down the sides, and the dress was a little shorter than usual.

Shaking her head, Alice headed towards the door.

"Where are you going?"

Alice glanced back. "I'm going to find some plain trousers and some boots of my own."

"Nonsense, I can make you some trousers and summon your boots." With a wave of Yasmin's hand, Alice's boots appeared before her, then Yasmin turned her attention to her outfit. Despite her request, the trousers formed with gold stripes down the seams and a golden band at the waist. Alice tried to covertly pick at the gold thread, but it was inseparable.

"What are you waiting for? Put them on. Or are you having second thoughts about going?"

Alice swiftly threw the clothes on before Yasmin could change her mind. Now was not the time to critique Yasmin's wardrobe. Once ready, Yasmin held out her hand, and with a jolt of excitement, Alice took it.

When the world flashed back into focus, she found herself faced with that peculiar shimmering light, but she didn't have time to contemplate the portal before Yasmin pulled her through. She tensed as the disorientating light enveloped her, but Yasmin squeezed tighter and guided her through the blinding abyss.

It was a couple of minutes before she stumbled out into a rocky terrain, her heart thumping at the prospect of travelling to another world. After the dazzling luminance of the portal realm, it took a few moments to adjust to the dim ambience. Then she looked around in eager expectation.

Her face fell at the rocky expanse all around. There was nothing exciting about this place, nothing alien, and not even any sign of civilisation. "Is this world populated?"

Yasmin smiled. "There's a small town, but it's not very impressive. The only reason people come here is for the crystal caves. Shall we go there now?"

Alice nodded and the rocky scenery disappeared, replaced by dazzling purple. So much purple, it took her breath away. Everywhere she looked, the cave wall glistened with crystal, and the cavern was at least as big as her house. Even the ground glinted violet, and as her gaze followed the passage, there was no end to the spectacle as it twisted around the corner.

Shifting firelight reflected in the crystals from numerous torches positioned along the path, all ablaze with abnormal intensity. Every second, the light revealed a new cluster or a new formation, adding to the wonder.

She turned to see Yasmin smiling at her.

"Isn't it wonderful?"

Totally speechless, Alice nodded.

Ambling through the caves, they admired the different shapes and crystal formations, dancing with the reflections of the firelight.

"Yasmin, why didn't you stop to talk to Officer Gul before you came through the portal?"

Yasmin bit her lip, and her face became a peculiar rose colour in the filtered light. "I didn't want anyone to realise who we were and send someone after us."

Alice shook her head in disbelief. Only a glimpse of Yasmin would be needed to identify her. It was baffling how oblivious Yasmin was to that fact.

A dark figure around the next corner stopped her dead in her tracks. Blocking the path, and with features shrouded by his cloak and the shadowy passageway behind, he caused Alice's heart to pound.

"Hello, sweetheart. How nice of you to join us."

Yasmin moved closer to Alice, as the torches in the passageway ignited. All the blood drained from Alice's face. Could Yasmin handle this man? She couldn't tell what magic he might possess.

"So, you have magic," another voice growled from behind them.

Alice spun around, finding a second cloaked man clearly visible as he looked them over with a greedy smirk. Her heart leapt into her throat. They were cornered. Whatever happened would be her fault, and no one knew to rescue them.

Her eyes darted to Yasmin, who calmly surveyed the pair of middle-aged ruffians. She tried to remember that Yasmin was a powerful mage, but all sense abandoned her as the second man fixed his small grey eyes on her. His features were hard and unforgiving, betraying no signs of mercy. With scruffy grey clothes, the legs caked with mud and patches where the material was well worn, they were far from the soldiers of North Parsa.

The man stepped forward, his chainmail tunic jangling in time with the shivers that shot down her spine. These men were prepared for a fight.

Taking another step, the first man lowered his hood, revealing his stubbled angular jaw, but it was the sword at his side that caught Alice's attention. Could Yasmin defend them against steel?

Instinctively, she gripped Yasmin's arm in warning, but Yasmin still showed no fear. Instead, she tossed her hair and glared at the approaching man.

"Yasmin, shouldn't we get out of here?" she whispered.

The first man turned to Alice, fixing her with his gaze. "Why would you want to leave so soon? For a small fee, we can show you around." He glanced over them again, his attention captured by Yasmin's shimmering dress. "You can clearly afford it."

Scowling at the man, Yasmin crossed her arms. "Do you know who I am?"

Alice winced. That was probably the worst thing she could have said. She had forgotten Yasmin was so sheltered, unaware of how to act outside the palace, but she couldn't think of any words herself. Nothing could undo the look of amusement on the man's face as he closed in on his prey.

The man behind them shuffled uncomfortably close too, and now Alice didn't know which one to look at. "You're a spoiled rich mage with more money than sense. I can help with that."

Yasmin spun around, her hair brushing Alice. "I am the princess of North Parsa and the future Royal Mage. You should show me some respect."

Alice's breath stopped. What could she do? They were unarmed and helpless and the men knew it.

Both men laughed. "The princess of North Parsa never goes anywhere without an escort. Now you will have to pay double."

Yasmin stared down the first man. "We will not be paying anything. Now let us leave."

The men smiled and took another step closer. "I'm afraid we cannot allow that. We both have families to feed, so think of this as just another tax."

Yasmin lifted her hand, and inspected her nails, speaking almost with a bored tone. "If you don't stop blocking my teleportation, I will stun you."

Alice's heart clenched. They really were trapped here, at the mercy of these two strangers, and Yasmin would never consider paying. She probably didn't even carry any money.

Alice glanced past the man to the passage behind. Could she push past them and run for it? There must be a way out. But would she be able to drag Yasmin with her?

Probably not.

Again, both men laughed.

With a sigh, Yasmin flung out her arm, shooting a bolt of cobalt lightning at the first man. He deflected it just in time, but the streak ricocheted at the cave wall, shattering numerous crystals. Blood rushed through Alice's ears, dimming the sound of crystals crashing to the ground.

She flinched as the second man attacked, but Yasmin was ready for him, and his feeble fireball bounced harmlessly off her dazzling shield.

Her face twisted in rage at the sneak attack, Yasmin blasted the men with a massive shock wave that knocked them both off their feet. Hundreds of crystals shattered, raining down from the roof, deafening and paralysing Alice.

Yasmin turned to Alice. "Shall we leave?"

Alice stared at the scene in disbelief. The two men now cowered under the crystal hail, all thoughts of challenging Yasmin evaporated. Crystals harmlessly scattered to Alice's side, bouncing off a shield she hadn't even notice Yasmin cast.

Alice nodded, and soon they arrived back on North Parsa. Yasmin didn't loiter on their return journey, so mere moments elapsed before she was back in the safety of the palace, contemplating her ordeal and Yasmin's power.

Her heart still raced as she sank onto Yasmin's bed, images of the two men flashing across her mind.

"Are you okay, Alice?"

Alice nodded, but she wasn't entirely sure.

Yasmin sat on the bed and put her arm around her. "I knew I shouldn't have taken you anywhere. It's just not safe outside the palace."

Bewildered, Alice turned to stare at Yasmin. "I'm fine. I'm just a little shocked. But you weren't scared at all. You don't have any reason to be, though, do you? Those men were no threat to you."

Yasmin smiled. "Those were merely opportunistic thieves, preying on defenceless tourists. They were little threat to anyone."

Alice leaned into Yasmin as she contemplated what might have happened if she hadn't been there. She would be no match for anyone. Casting spells in the safety of the palace with Yasmin to guide her was nothing compared to using them on actual people off on some foreign world. Alice was little better off than she'd been shortly before she'd discovered her magic. And she'd been naïve enough to think it would solve all her problems.

Yasmin gave her another squeeze. "There are much more dangerous people to worry about, but you don't have to worry about anything here in the palace."

Darien's unconscious form flashed in Alice's mind, and icy fingers gripped her heart. "If there are far more dangerous mages that intend harm, can't they just teleport into the palace whenever they like?"

Yasmin shook her head. "The palace has certain defences, invisible to most. As soon as someone new crosses the threshold, mages are alerted, and strangers are investigated. It's too dangerous for most mages to teleport somewhere unknown anyway, so most newcomers have to explore before they can teleport."

Alice eyed Yasmin's flushed cheeks and the gleam in her eye. "You were enjoying antagonising those men!"

Yasmin bit her lip.

Alice laughed. "You enjoy exercising your power."

Yasmin turned even redder. "Those men deserved it."

Failing to hide her smile, Alice shook her head and reached for a spellbook, determined not to be so helpless. Next time she ventured off-world with Yasmin, she would fight by her side. "Will you teach me that shield spell?"

Yasmin beamed and summoned a whole pile of books towards them. With renewed vigour, Alice immersed herself in her studies, keen to learn as much from Yasmin as possible. She couldn't imagine what she would do without her, nor remember how she had filled her life before magic.

CHAPTER 38
The Secret Oasis

Several days after Jaime's visit, the aroma of fresh bread and eggs filled the hut as Emily cooked breakfast, desperate to be of some use. Lamenting her loss of access to the mage libraries, she contemplated whether she might find something that could help the resistance if she still had that privilege.

Heaps of advanced spellbooks filled both libraries, but Shirin already had access to them. The Royal Mage did too and had probably trained his entire life with them. Not to mention that magical strength came from a mage's blood, so knowing a spell wouldn't necessarily help a mage if their adversary possessed stronger blood. That explained why all the higher star mages were limited to a few families, but only exasperated the resistance's desperate situation.

When everything was cooked, Emily joined Shirin in her private room. Seemingly the most important person here, at least with Torvia gone, Shirin had a few luxuries that others didn't.

Shirin smiled as she entered and gestured for Emily to join her at her surprisingly ornate wooden table. Instead of four legs, the surface was supported by a carved falcon with its wings outstretched. The resistance may lack magic, but it had plenty of other talent.

Emily placed the plate of bread and eggs on the table and seized the opportunity to find out more. "Shirin, do your family have similar abilities to you?"

A brief look of grief washed across Shirin's face before she answered. "My brother was as gifted as I am with deceptive spells, but was caught stealing from a much more accomplished mage." She sighed, taking some bread. "Our mother was sick, and we couldn't afford to pay for the medicine she needed, so he tried to steal it. Since our father died in an invasion long ago, money had always been tight, but we'd managed until then. My brother was taken to the palace to answer for his crime and never seen again. Our mother died a week later and there was nothing I could do for either of them." She forced a smile. "That's when I started to poke around the palace a little more and found out about prisoners being used to explore the portal realm. Apparently, the Royal Mage thinks if people care enough for their family, they'll find their way back, just like he did." She shook her head. "I doubt I'll ever see my brother again, even if he never gives up." She dipped a piece of bread in runny yolk. "A little later, I discovered the res istance."

"Oh, I'm so sorry, that's awful." Her throat constricting, Emily poured Shirin a glass of juice. Knowing that such suffering had allowed Emily to be rescued made her feel a little guilty, but she couldn't change what had happened. Only what might happen next. "Do you know if the Royal Mage's family have always been Royal Mages?"

Shirin blinked rapidly, tracing a finger across her lip. "Royal Mages have usually been part of the royal family, but I'm not sure who the current Royal Mage's parents were. His sister, who was also a talented mage, married the king, so they can't be that closely related." She dropped her hand to her side. "Come to think of it, I'm not aware of any mage family that claims kinship with the Royal Mage – which is odd, given the prestige and power it would give them." She stared vacantly at her plate, soaking up the runny egg with her bread.

Emily continued to eat her breakfast as she waited for Shirin to remember, but after a few minutes, she interrupted. "Maybe he didn't come from North Parsa at all?"

"Perhaps, but who would know, and what does it matter?" Shirin's attention snapped back to her unfinished breakfast.

"Maybe you could ally with other powerful people from his birth-world."

Shirin dropped her fork. "No one has ever thought of that. But how would anyone find out where he is from? It must be a distant world if no one is aware of it."

"There might be some record or a journal from the time he appeared which I could look for."

"Perhaps, but it is too dangerous for you to go back to Parsa."

"What if I were in disguise?" She bit her lip. Magic wouldn't work in the palace library, but she could wear a wig to help her blend in. "I'd only have to be careful in the palace, and no one would look at me there."

Doubt flashed across Shirin's face. "You're safe here—"

"Please let me help, in return for everything you've done for me. I can't just wait here and do nothing. Besides, I know the palace and the libraries well enough not to get caught again."

Shirin shook her head. "You don't have magic to defend yourself if someone suspects you to be an imposter."

"I'll wear the right outfit this time and I know how to talk to the book trees to avoid suspicion."

Shirin's lips formed a hard line. "You should wait for Torvia. She's best at sneaking around." Before Emily could push her further, Shirin started to clear away the dishes, but at least she had given Emily hope.

Another few days passed before Torvia appeared and Emily could put forward her plan. As reluctant as Shirin to start with, Torvia eventually agreed that understanding where the Royal Mage came from could only help their cause, and the resistance was desperate for assistance.

With a shiny blue two-star mage cloak provided by Shirin and a jet-black wig, Emily faced the portal back to Parsa, her fists tightly clenched. If anyone recognised her, she could find herself back in that tower, with no hope for escape. They'd not make the same mistake again. And under that truth spell she might end up incriminating Shirin and Torvia, her brother's only hope.

Torvia placed a comforting hand on her back. "You don't have to do this."

Her voice steady, Emily replied, "I do." There was no way she was going to sit around waiting whilst strangers risked their lives to save Eliot. If there was something that could improve their chances, she was going to find it.

Torvia gave a curt nod. "If anyone recognises you, I'll get you out of there."

Before her nerves could change her mind, Emily strode into the portal, and a few moments later, her heart pounding wildly, she ascended the familiar stairs to the mage library. Without a word to Torvia, she strode inside, her head held high, the long black hair of her wig flowing down her shoulders.

Selecting a familiar tree, she confidently asked for the book she desired, and the tree obliged. Only a slight tremble of her hands would have given away her fear. She clasped the book to her chest and turned back to survey the library. No one paid her any attention. Only Torvia observed her from outside the door.

Her heart galloping, she sought an empty table far from the other mages, and letting her hair fall over her face, she opened the volume and began to read.

An account of the royal family, it detailed unions going back dozens of generations. Each union contained a description of the king as he inherited the throne, his life achievements, his wife and his children. On the most recent pages, she found the current king, King Baraz.

It told her he had inherited the crown from his father after his father had been killed in an attack on the city. His younger brother had died in a more recent battle, so King Baraz had become the guardian of his brother's son, Prince Javed. His wife had tragically died whilst he drove the attackers away, leaving him with two children to raise, Princess Yasmin and Prince Darien.

Emily considered this information carefully. If the Royal Mage's assertion that Prince Javed's father was the older brother was to be believed, then this entry couldn't be true. Which should she believe? The book or the man?

If the book was the lie, then how many other books here contained lies? Could magic have altered them all? If so, then she may never find anything of use.

Hoping that something might have been missed, she carried on searching the text for any clues, regardless of whether they might be true. She could always cross-reference it with other sources to find any inconsistencies to help her separate fact from fiction. Unfortunately, the book was disappointingly vague and said little about the queen or where she originated, only that she'd studied diligently and shown considerable talent from the moment she'd arrived in the city.

Emily flicked through the pages for anything more about the queen's background, but it was as if she'd appeared out of thin air. Odd for a royal to have so little written about them – unless they were purposely hiding something? Perhaps there was something for Emily to find if she searched hard enough.

Similarly, few entries detailed the king's life achievements, compared to the more descriptive past monarchs. She presumed it just hadn't been updated recently and might only be filled in once his life was complete.

Even less was captured on the current Royal Mage. Previous Royal Mages were listed, along with their relationship to the king and similar details about their life achievements. They appeared less likely to marry and have children, so the role was rarely inherited. The current Royal Mage had a page only listing him as brother-in-law to the king.

She stared at his picture for a few moments, resisting a shudder, then slammed the book closed. Her body tensing, she glanced around in alarm, but no one seemed to have been bothered by the noise.

Undeterred, she continued her search. She felt a slight thrill at being back in the palace, doing something useful again, and even more so that no one knew she was here. Not even Jaime knew she was back on Parsa.

She resisted the urge to seek out her brother, knowing full well where that would lead. Jaime would find Alice, so Emily's time was best spent here. It was up to her to discover something they could use against the Royal Mage. There were so few days left until Princess Safia arrived, and she did owe them her freedom.

However, as the days passed by, her enthusiasm slipped away. There simply wasn't any information here. It was as if someone had wiped away every specific detail about the Royal Mage from history.

On the day before Princess Safia's arrival, Emily realised she was looking in the wrong place. Of *course* the Royal Mage would have removed anything that could be used against him, but what if something remained hidden in the lower mage library, lost in all the chaos? He couldn't have altered every book in existence, and something may have been deposited there over the years.

Annoyed she hadn't thought of that sooner, she swiftly changed into her normal clothes and made her way there using the money Shirin had given her to pay the portal tax.

Currently in magical disguise, with straight jet-black hair and a deep tan, she debated whether to tell the old librarian who she was. So much was at stake, she couldn't afford to make any mistakes.

After much contemplation, she thought it best not to raise suspicion. With her two-star cloak, Adar would do anything she asked, anyway.

Before she arrived at the lower mage library, she ducked into a deserted alleyway and waited a few minutes before putting on her mage cloak. Hopefully, if anyone noticed her, it would look like she had teleported into the street before visiting the library.

Upon entering the building, she hesitated, alarmed by the lack of people. It took her a few moments to realise everyone must be preparing for the arrival of the southern princess. Except for the old librarian, who was currently filing books away, muttering to himself as he went.

A pang of guilt twinged through her at the huge pile of books that had reappeared since she'd stopped working here, but she reminded herself it wasn't her fault or her responsibility anymore. She had far more important things to worry about now.

She coughed to get his attention, then realised she'd have to be much ruder to pose as a two-star mage. "Excuse me, I'm looking for a book," she said as haughtily as possible.

The old mage turned and scurried towards her. "I don't recognise you. What family are you from?"

"Neither myself nor my family make a habit of visiting this place. Now, will you find me that book?" she declared, her heart pounding.

The old man blinked at her but didn't seem suspicious. "Of course, just tell me what you're looking for."

She had tried to think of a clever way to ask for information on the Royal Mage without attracting attention but hadn't been able to think of much. With little time left to search before Eliot's rescue, she hoped the old man's loyalty to Prince Darien would make him less inclined to discuss her request with mages loyal to the Royal Mage.

Just as she was about to ask, inspiration struck her. "I'm researching possible links between my ancestors and the Royal Mage. Do you have any books that can help with that?"

"No, I don't. The Royal Mage was not born on this world."

"How can you be sure?"

He frowned at her and proceeded in his more usual condescending tone. "I am not merely a keeper of books. I have kept knowledge and records of the goings-on of this world for longer than you have been alive."

Knowing he would get to the point eventually, Emily persisted, trying to suppress her annoyance. "Then can you tell me about where he's from?"

"Why are you so interested?" he asked, narrowing his eyes.

She couldn't think of a reason for a random mage to start asking questions about her leader, but Prince Darien might. "I'm not, really. Prince Darien suggested I should look into it. He said you had been very helpful finding an interesting book recently and that you might be able to find some useful information on the Royal Mage. But ... if you don't have anything, I won't waste any more time." She turned to leave, hoping the old mage wouldn't notice her heart thumping so loudly or call her bluff.

"Now wait a minute. I didn't say I couldn't help. I record important information in my own journals. It was very unusual for a foreigner to become the Royal Mage, you see. Follow me."

She followed as he led her upstairs to a dusty old bookcase she had never found time to search when she worked here. Books were still scattered in front of it, waiting to be sorted.

Adar stared at them as if he had forgotten what he was looking for, then summoned a journal from deep within the pending avalanche. With irritatingly slow fumbling, he finally found the page he sought. "Ah, here it is, the arrival of Kavir and his sister." He flicked through a few pages. "His disappearance and Nasrin's marriage to the king's brother."

"Wait, did you say the king's brother?" Emily tried to peer at the writing herself, but Adar brought the book closer to his face.

"Yes, that is what I said. The king at the time was already married, you see, so his brother – our current king – was the best option for an advantageous marriage." Panic flicked across his face as he lifted his eyes to hers. "You didn't hear that from me though, and if you repeat it in the wrong company, you may end up with your memory altered." He stood up straighter, wrinkling his nose. "You probably shouldn't tell that to Prince Darien, either. He can get a bit precious about his inheritance and wouldn't be too happy to hear Prince Javed should be on the throne if the proper succession had been followed. Not that it makes much difference to the rest of us though, eh?"

Before Emily could interrupt to steer him towards the Royal Mage's origin, he leaned forward, his eyes twinkling. "She was a real asset to the royal family though, the Royal Mage's sister, I mean. Wherever they came from, they had stronger magic than has ever been seen before on Parsa. Did you know the Royal Mage can teleport directly to South Parsa in one jump? And now that magic strength is part of the royal descendants. Prince Darien will become the most powerful king in history. It's a lot to live up to, eh? No wonder he's a bit power-mad."

Emily smiled at his conclusion on Prince Darien and seized the opportunity to cut in as he paused to take a breath. "But where were they from?"

"Ah, they were from a world that has since been destroyed and abandoned. Let me find the right notes."

He flicked through more pages. "Hmm, it doesn't say. But if I remember correctly, they arrived in South Parsa first and made their way here. No one from the south knew the extent of their power when they arrived, though I suppose it might not have been fully developed at that point. The southerners must have been disappointed they let such talented mages slip through their fingers, but no mage can resist the allure of our city."

"What did you mean when you said the Royal Mage disappeared?"

"Ah that's common knowledge. An altercation with another mage resulted in Kavir being lost through a portal. Took him three years to find his way back, but when he did, he knew secrets the rest of us couldn't dream of. There's no one with more knowledge of the portal realm."

Emily nodded. No wonder he thought others could build on that knowledge. "Thank you. I shall tell Prince Darien you have been of help."

She contemplated searching through the rest of the books for the remainder of the day but knew she would find nothing. Instead, since this might be her last opportunity, she retrieved the journal from the secret chamber. Deciphering the journal would have to wait, but she couldn't help but think it was important.

Satisfied she had discovered something about the Royal Mage, she returned to the safety of the oasis, replaying the conversation in her mind.

Was there anything helpful amongst the information? If the Royal Mage's world had been destroyed and abandoned, there would be no one there to help the resistance. Still, she was fascinated at how quickly the Royal Mage had found his way to North Parsa and embedded himself into the royal family.

She supposed she ought to tell Torvia since she came from the south and might know about worlds that had been destroyed, but she pushed it to the back of her mind to focus on Eliot's rescue. Tomorrow it was time to put their plan into action.

CHAPTER 39

NORTH PARSA

Jaime fidgeted in his new crimson tunic. To enter the palace, he was posing as one of Safia's bodyguards, which meant he'd be joining the royal contingent in the desert. Emily would be accompanying Torvia and Shirin in climbing the tower to search for Eliot. Jaime didn't like the idea of splitting up, but Torvia would look after Emily. And Emily just wouldn't accept being left behind.

After waking early, he was ready and prepared for when Torvia arrived with Emily. In his days here, he had familiarised himself with the city, but he couldn't imagine what it would be like inside the palace. Torvia seemed confident they'd be fine though, and she'd had no trouble passing her two-star exams.

"It's time," Torvia announced.

"Good luck," Emily said with an encouraging smile. "Say hello to Alice for me." She didn't even sound nervous.

"You too," he whispered back, before giving her a quick parting hug. The next time they saw each other, they'd all be back together ... if everything went well.

They left quietly, Jaime eager to see Jordan again, and even more impatient to see Alice. At this moment, his eagerness eclipsed his apprehension at being surrounded by mages in the Royal Palace.

One teleport later, Jaime and Torvia arrived in the midst of the desert. Barely twilight, there was little to see, but a group of silhouettes shifted towards them, slowly and purposefully.

Torvia cast a fireball in the air and uttered a short spell, causing it to glow green and then furious red. A similar fireball shot above the approaching travellers, shifting from crimson to blue. Jaime scanned for Jordan, but he couldn't tell him apart from the others in this low light. He had to be there, though.

Moments later, Safia emerged and greeted Torvia with an embrace. They exchanged a few quiet words before turning to Jaime.

"Torvia has told me of your predicament," Safia said. "I am happy for you to accompany us as one of my guards. However, you must do nothing to raise suspicion during the banquet, because there will be no way I can protect you. Do you understand?"

"I understand," Jaime replied, matching her serious tone.

Safia gave a satisfied nod, then her eyes flickered to Torvia. "You don't *have* to do this."

Torvia smiled. "Don't worry. We won't get caught, and even if we do, it can't be traced back to you. It's about time we tried something against the Royal Mage." Torvia's eyes flashed with excitement, sending a shiver down Jaime's spine.

Safia sighed and turned to a tall figure loitering a few paces behind her. At her gesture, the man bounded forward, so familiar, yet so different. In his professional uniform, Jordan looked much older and much more serious. However, when he reached Jaime, Jordan's face broke into a huge grin and the pair fell into their traditional shoulder to shoulder hug with a clap on the back.

Jordan kept his arm around Jaime as he pulled him away from the group. "I hear you found Emily! *And* you have a plan to rescue Eliot and Alice." He shook his head. "I thought I was doing all the rescuing."

Was that resentment in his voice? Jaime shrugged him off, getting a better look at him and the deep lines on his dry skin. Two months in the desert couldn't have been easy. "I was lucky Torvia found me and decided to bring me along. But you didn't take any chances. You jumped at the best opportunity. You were right to leave."

Jordan blinked a few times. "Yeah, I knew that. You look good, though." He scratched the back of his neck. "You'll have to tell me all about Torvia and I'll tell you about Princess Safia." He pulled Jaime back towards the princess, who was still deep in conversation with Torvia.

"So, tell me more of my betrothed, Torvia," Safia requested.

"You don't know anything about who you're marrying?" Jordan said.

Jaime rolled his eyes. How much trouble had Jordan got himself into during his journey?

To Jaime's surprise, Safia smiled warmly at Jordan. "Few people have made the journey between the two kingdoms, and none I trust more than Torvia."

"Prince Javed is an excellent and devoted swordsman, and a fairly decent mage."

Safia smiled at Torvia. "But what of his character?"

"He's disciplined, obedient and friendly. He'll make a decent husband."

Jaime wondered if these were traits Torvia herself thought important, or whether they were Safia's values. She certainly didn't sound impressed.

"Thank you, Torvia, for that *detailed* description."

Torvia frowned at Safia's obvious dissatisfaction. "It's hard to put into words, exactly, but I think he'll fit well into South Parsa. I suppose he's fairly attractive too, if that's what you care about."

"High praise from you, Torvia. You've put my mind at ease at least."

Jaime raised an eyebrow. Torvia definitely hadn't been shy with him, so it was odd she struggled to talk with Safia about her future husband. Nevertheless, he had more serious things to worry about right now.

Disconcertingly, Jordan appeared to be more interested in Jaime than the conversation. "What are you staring at?" Jaime asked.

"Nice hair. You could try a bit harder to fit in though."

Torvia smiled. "I can fix that." She waved her hand in front of his face.

"Much better," Jordan said. "You could almost pass for a South Parsan."

Jaime glanced down and saw his hands had developed a sudden tan, though only matching the palest of Safia's guards.

"What about your hair?" Jordan continued. "It's a bit long for a soldier."

Torvia immediately pulled out a knife, making Jaime raise his hands in defence. "Can't you alter that magically too?"

Torvia shook her head. "This way is much easier."

Jaime backed away. "There must be something you can do with magic."

Jordan smirked. "Now we know how he distracts his opponents. Don't worry, Jaime, you'll still look pretty without it."

"It's not so long compared to many North Parsans," Torvia said, sheathing her knife. "Most won't notice."

Jordan shook his head. "It's a good thing you didn't join us in the desert, *princess*."

Jaime sighed. "We'll be in the palace *one* day. I want to give Alice a chance to recognise me."

"Uh-uh." Jordan pounced and ruffled Jaime's hair, much to his annoyance. "It is *so* alluring. Alice won't be able to stay away."

His cheeks heating, Jaime shoved Jordan off him, but at least his hair had remained intact.

After one final goodbye, Torvia teleported back to the city, leaving Jaime and Jordan to enjoy one last desert sunrise while they tucked into a simple breakfast. Strangely relaxing, it was like the last day of a holiday.

Shortly after sunrise, a new fire blazoned before them, more intense than their morning spectacle, and a whirlwind swirled around the entire group, whipping up the sand. The crackling of electricity surrounded them, and a rainbow of colours glistened in the storm.

Was that glass?

Jaime glanced at Jordan, who stood open-mouthed beside him. His friend's eyes told him Jordan hadn't expected this either.

Finally, as the central blaze died away, a man emerged, the flames still licking his cloak. The Royal Mage.

The man cast his eyes across the group – eyes that still smouldered with the brightness of an inferno, much unlike the dark eyes Jaime had seen in South Parsa. Ice ants stampeded down Jaime's spine. No wonder everyone feared this man.

The Royal Mage strode towards Princess Safia, his silky cloak billowing, and bowed. "Princess, I hope your journey was as pleasant as one through the desert can be. All of North Parsa awaits your arrival, and your betrothed is eager to meet you."

Jaime strained to hear the conversation, but hung back with Jordan, not wanting to get too close to this fearsome man.

Safia, however, replied confidently. "Thank you, your highness. The journey has been long, but uneventful. I look forward to the legendary hospitality of the north, and meeting my betrothed."

The Royal Mage glanced around at the guards before returning his attention to Safia. "Princess, I would be glad to personally assure your safety if you wished to teleport to the palace ahead of your guard."

She smiled back. "That won't be necessary. I shall arrive with my escort in due time."

Jaime stared at Princess Safia with respect. How could she remain so calm in this man's presence? Her magic surely couldn't rival his.

"As you wish. I shall alert your betrothed. He will want to escort you through the city." They both bowed, and then, with a flash of flame, the Royal Mage was gone.

Jaime and Jordan exchanged glances but were rendered speechless. This was the person they were going to rescue Eliot from?

As promised, Safia's betrothed was to be found waiting for her outside the city limits a few hours later, standing proudly in military regalia, alongside the Royal Mage. He was surrounded by his own escort, all finely dressed, but only one matched him in stature.

Safia's betrothed dropped into a formal bow. "Princess Safia, you are even more beautiful than described," he said in a pleasant and welcoming voice. He didn't look at all like the Royal Mage, with his short dark hair and large warm eyes, which relieved Jaime immensely. He'd begun to picture all North Parsan mages like the Royal Mage, but this prince was not so intimidating at all, even with the sword at his side.

The Royal Mage stepped forward, his eyes back to their normal black. "Princess, this is Prince Javed, nephew of the king of North Parsa. It is his deepest wish to unite the north and the south, and join you in the south as your husband."

Prince Javed beamed. "It will be my honour to do my part in uniting all of Parsa, and I am delighted you have decided to visit the north before we marry. I will personally show you everything you desire to see."

The princess gave away no emotion, but kindly replied, "Thank you, Prince Javed. I intend to see all the north for myself, so your invitation is most pleasing."

"May I also introduce my cousin, Prince Darien, who is as keen as I to establish good relations with you and your people."

The other extravagantly dressed man stepped forward. Although not in a military outfit, he could easily have been mistaken for their leader, given his confident bearing and the richness of his silky-blue golden-embellished tunic and cloak. Jaime scrutinised him intently but found no hint of his evil nature.

Both annoyingly handsome, and clearly aware of their impact, the two princes could have been brothers, though Prince Darien had longer hair and a straighter nose. Jaime detected a little smugness in him, but noted with satisfaction that Darien looked a little scrawny next to his cousin.

Jaime glanced sideways at Jordan, to gauge his reaction, but he still stared at Prince Javed, his eyes taking in the man's military posture and the lion-pommelled sword at his side.

Bowing deeply, Prince Darien greeted Safia. "Princess Safia, welcome to North Parsa. If there is anything I can do to make your stay more pleasant, please inform me at once. I look forward to a future in which our two nations work closely together. May I also say you have chosen your husband well. In all the worlds, I could think of no other more dedicated."

No more than eighteen, Prince Darien's apparent ease surprised Jaime, and he had to remind himself what he was actually capable of. Not what he expected from Emily and Shirin's description, in person he seemed younger, friendly and the perfect gentleman. Certainly not someone who would go around stealing people's memories.

"Thank you, Prince Darien," Safia replied.

After the pleasantries had been observed, Prince Javed led them through the city. A little rough around the edges, it wasn't all that different to South Parsa. However, the palace left Jaime totally awestruck. It dwarfed anything he'd ever seen, yet every surface looked perfect. Atop the walls, soldiers glittering in their finest armour saluted their arrival, and more still stood to attention at the gate.

Safia herself still displayed no emotion but couldn't keep her eyes off the glistening towers soaring high into the sky. The Royal Mage strode ahead, but the two princes took their time, grinning with pride and exchanging knowing glances.

Approaching the palace, they found the local population lining the streets in welcome, or to glimpse the foreign royal. Suspicious of anyone and everyone, Safia's guards closed in. They needn't have worried, though. As soon as anyone saw the Royal Mage, they shrank back into the obscurity of the crowd.

Once within the palace walls, the crowd change dramatically. The majority of people dressed in much finer clothes, displaying their wealth. A large proportion wore blue robes with gold stars and looked on with respect as much as curiosity.

Jaime searched for Alice, but she was nowhere to be seen. Containing his disappointment, he glanced across at Jordan, who still scoured the crowd. Remembering their previous argument over Alice, his apprehension returned, the monster within waking from its slumber.

Soon they were shown to spacious visitor chambers within the Royal Tower, and with little need for them inside the palace, all but two of Safia's bodyguards were dismissed. Prince Javed offered to show Safia around once she had taken time to freshen up, and everyone else was free to do as they chose until the evening banquet.

The Royal Mage's gaze lingered on Jaime, his small cold eyes piercing in their intensity, before flicking to Safia with curiosity. Jaime's stomach lurched. Could he tell Jaime didn't belong? Before he could get a closer look, Jaime retreated into their allocated chambers.

Hoping he wouldn't have to sit anywhere near the Royal Mage at the banquet, he tried to push the concern to the back of his mind. He attempted to distract himself by admiring a beautiful sandscape decorating the wall, the low sun casting realistic shadows between the slopes. At least the hospitality here was excellent, something that eased his worries for Alice slightly.

A short while later, he set off with Jordan to explore. They knew better than to visit the Mage Tower, so instead they explored the palace grounds. Everything about the palace was far more beautiful and more extravagant compared to South Parsa, but it also felt more fake, as if it existed to distract people from the truth. Also, barred as it was to regular people, it lacked the friendly chaos of South Parsa. Jaime tried to imagine it as it would have appeared if he did not know about the mage caste system and the prisoners being held in the tower, but it was hard to forget with the towers looming above.

"Where do you think Alice might be?" he asked Jordan, bracing himself for another argument.

Surprisingly, Jordan stayed completely calm. "Probably high up in the Royal Tower or with Prince Darien. We could go and search for her before the banquet. It wouldn't give away anything about Eliot's rescue."

"Where would we even start? We can't just go barging into people's rooms," Jaime reasoned, still struck by the sheer size of the palace.

"True, I guess we'll just have to wait for the banquet, then. How far do you suppose the others have got up the Mage Tower?"

Jaime gazed upwards, straining to see anything unusual about the tower. "They might have reached the top by now, if all went well." His anxiety returning, he rolled back his sleeves. "Do you think they might get into trouble?"

Jordan shrugged. "From what I hear, Torvia has been sneaking around the palace for many years without getting caught, and Shirin is a strong illusionist. We've no reason to doubt them." Jordan moved closer, his eyes on Jaime's. "How was Emily when you left her? I can't believe she tried to rescue Eliot all on her own."

"She seemed pretty confident," Jaime replied, puzzled by Jordan's sudden shift in focus. "She'll be alright with Torvia. She's even more talented than she lets on."

"Sounds like you got to know her well." Jordan accompanied his mischievous smile with a wink, completely distracting Jaime from his current train of thought.

He frowned at Jordan's suggestion but decided not to take the bait. "What if we can't get anywhere near Alice during the banquet?" he asked, not for the first time.

"Then you cause a distraction and I'll extract her."

Jaime sighed at Jordan's return to his usual annoying self. "Come on. We'd better get ready. We can't miss the banquet."

CHAPTER 40
North Parsa

Emily stared wide-eyed at the mage slumped over the desk. Without the slightest flicker of doubt, Torvia had strode into the Royal Mage's private library and stunned the mage on duty.

"Torvia, that was a three-star mage!" Shirin shrieked.

Torvia darted behind the desk and placed her hands on the woman's temples. "She'll not remember a thing."

Emily sidled over to Shirin. "What is she doing?"

"A memory spell," Shirin whispered. "When she wakes, she'll never realise we were here." Shirin bit her lip. "Will it take?"

Torvia withdrew her hands. "I think so." She glanced at the door at the top of the steps. "There's only one way to find out."

Shaking her head, Shirin took Emily's hand and led her behind the curtain.

"What do we do if she does remember?" Emily asked.

"We'll have to stun her again." Torvia bounded up the steps to join them. "But if anyone finds her, they'll raise the alarm."

They all huddled together to wait for the mage to regain consciousness, Emily bewildered at how calm Torvia was.

She must have done this before.

A shiver ran down Emily's spine. Torvia was more like the Royal Mage than anyone had guessed. But at least she was helping Emily.

The mage began to stir, and Emily's breath caught in her throat. If she raised the alarm before Torvia could stun her, they'd all be trapped here. With the Mage Tower deserted for Princess Safia's arrival, the blame would be quick to fall on them.

The mage rubbed her eyes and yawned loudly. She pulled a book towards her. Took a drink of water. Turned the page.

Shirin tapped Emily on the shoulder and pointed to the door behind them. It appeared they had got in undetected.

In the next room, Torvia peered out of the window to the courtyard garden below. People were already filtering into the palace, eager to be part of this historic evening. "We should wait until we are sure the Royal Mage has departed. I can't stun him."

Shirin shook her head. "I don't want to be here longer than necessary. He shouldn't be anywhere near the cells." She turned to Emily. "Which way?"

Her heart beating loudly, Emily moved forward. Despite Torvia and Shirin's magic, she was the only one who had been here. The only one who could lead them. But … "What about the three-star mage that serves the Royal Mage?"

Shirin glanced at Torvia. "Torvia had no problem stunning the last three-star mage."

"Quiet," Torvia whispered.

Emily led them through various reception rooms to the main stairs. The cells were near the top, presumably to make it more difficult to escape. She had to hope Eliot was still there. They couldn't search through all the rooms they were passing.

That didn't stop Torvia peering in several doorways, but Emily doubted she was searching for Eliot. If Emily weren't terrified of being discovered, she might be curious too.

On reaching the higher levels, her throat constricted and her breathing shallowed. They were so close now.

At the door to the level that held the cells, Emily's feet came to a stop. The Royal Mage could be on the other side ...

Shirin gently pushed her aside. "Let Torvia go first," she whispered.

Emily nodded, glad for the help. Though if the Royal Mage was inside, it wouldn't matter. He'd catch them seconds later.

She held her breath as Shirin cast some sort of illusion and Torvia slowly opened the door. When the gap was wide enough, Tovia put her head through.

Dizziness washed over Emily. She couldn't take this much longer.

Torvia pushed the door wider and waved them through.

Emily swallowed her fear. Eliot needed her. "This way," she whispered and hurried across the room, trying not to look at the chairs where she'd last been interrogated.

"Slow down," Shirin hissed. "We don't know who's ahead."

Now that the cells were in reach, Emily couldn't stop. But Torvia managed to reach the door ahead of her. "It's clear," she said, darting inside.

Emily caught up with her outside a blue shimmering wall. The only cell that was occupied. "This must be it." She placed her hand on it, but it was as impenetrable as her own had been. "Can you get through it?"

Torvia nodded. "It will take time. Keep watch."

Emily winced as Torvia resorted to blasting the shield. Each thud echoed off the corridor's stone walls, announcing their presence.

"Torvia! That's too loud," Shirin hissed.

"No choice," Torvia replied, unleashing another burst of energy. "Just one more."

Emily stepped back as the barrier shuddered and the air around her reverberated. The Royal Mage must have left for the banquet by now. There was no one to hear.

She clasped her hands together as Torvia blasted again and again. She had to break through.

Finally, the barrier splintered, and white light spread out from the last impact in sharp, jagged fingers. The vivid blue started to dim, then all of a sudden, the entire barrier disappeared completely.

Emily leapt forward, her heart in her throat, only to stop in shock on discovering the person inside. That was not Eliot.

"Elder Thymet!" Torvia exclaimed. "What are you doing here?"

A white-haired senior ambled forward, his shock mirroring Emily's own. "Why, if it isn't young Torvia. How did you find me?"

Torvia rushed forwards to steady the old man. "You're supposed to be enjoying your retirement. How did you end up in a cell?"

"I would tell you, dear, if I knew. Please tell me where I am."

"You're in North Parsa." Torvia guided him towards the open doorway. "How long have you been here?"

"I wish I could tell you." His gaze settled on Emily and Shirin. "Who are your friends?"

The moment his foot crossed the cell threshold, a bright yellow light shot outwards along the walls, heading in all directions. Torvia and Shirin acted as one, streaking colourful spells at the light, but none stopped the yellow flash escaping the corridor.

"We have to leave. Now," Torvia said.

"No!" Emily spun around. "We can't leave without Eliot."

Shirin grabbed Emily's arm. "That spell will alert anyone nearby to our presence. It may even reach the Royal Mage."

"No!" Emily's voice caught in her throat and tears stung her eyes. She couldn't fail again. Eliot had to be nearby. There were other doors off the room she'd been interrogated in …

Her decision made, she tore her arm free and sprinted up the corridor.

"Emily, wait!" Shirin called, but she was too slow to stop her. Emily ran faster than she'd ever run before, her feet pounding on the hard stone. She was almost at the entrance when a figure blocked her path.

The Royal Mage's server!

The server's face twisted in surprise as Emily skidded to a stop. "You? But how—" She flicked her hand to raise a sapphire shield as bright light flashed past Emily. Torvia's spell. Blocked.

Emily dived out of the way as more spells flashed through the corridor in both directions. If any one of them hit her … she had no defence. But as she cowered by the wall, she realised the server was ignoring her. Duelling with two mages was taking up all her concentration.

The server streaked cobalt lightning at Torvia. "Surrender now. The Royal Mage is on his way!"

It was now or never.

Emily shuffled along the wall, past the server, then darted into the next room. All she needed was to find the telltale blue shimmer of a barred room. "Eliot!" she shouted, unable to contain her desperation.

"Emily?" A muffled voice sounded from behind the next door.

"Eliot?" Who else would call her name? But there was no barrier across this door. Emily slammed into hard wood and tugged at the handle, but it wouldn't budge. "Torvia—"

"She's trying a memory spell," Shirin answered, close behind Emily. "Allow me." With the wave of her hand, Shirin blasted the door wide open.

"Eliot!" There he was, standing behind a chair in a room that could have been a comfortable studio. Emily almost couldn't believe it. She'd found him! Though he eyed Shirin with uncertainty. "Come on, Eliot." She held out her hand.

Shirin squeezed Emily's arm. "You've done it. You've rescued someone from right out of the Royal Mage's chambers."

Torvia sprinted over. "We've got to get out of the tower yet."

CHAPTER 41
NORTH PARSA

All too soon, it was time for Jaime and Jordan to join Princess Safia. Since she possessed a relatively small entourage, they would all be eating together, with a few select members of the North Parsan royalty. The remainder of the hall would be filled with important mages, high-ranking officers, and foreign diplomats eager to bear witness to the new Parsan alliance. Just thinking about all the people brought a cold sweat to Jaime's skin and his fingers struggled with the buttons on his tunic.

Jordan raised an eyebrow, pushed Jaime's hands out of the way, and swiftly buttoned it up for him. "We'll find Alice soon enough, then we'll be out of here."

Jaime nodded, his mouth too dry for words.

"Come on, everyone else has already gone." Jordan grabbed his arm and pulled him out into the corridor.

Jaime froze as soon as they were out of their chambers. Right above them, on the twisting stairs, the Royal Mage surveyed them with piercing black eyes.

Had he just teleported, or was he already lurking there?

"Good evening," he stated coldly as he swept towards Jaime. "I've never seen you in South Parsa. How long have you been a royal guard?"

Jaime's stomach twisted as he tried to think of a plausible explanation, but only one popped into his head. "I've only joined Princess Safia's guard recently. I'm from Aveya."

"You must be exceptionally skilled to be included on such an important mission at such a young age." His eyes burned into Jaime's before he glanced him over, making no attempt to hide his close examination.

His skin crawling, Jaime stole Jordan's story. "I was good enough to save her life when her previous guard got injured."

The Royal Mage's face remained impassive, so he had no idea if he believed him. "Is there much magic on Aveya?"

Jaime glanced at Jordan for support, but his friend remained agonisingly silent. "Er, no, nothing compared to what there is on Parsa."

The Royal Mage held out his enclosed hand. "Take it," he ordered. "It's a gift."

Jaime did as instructed and received a small purple crystal. "Thank you," was all he could say. Then he remembered how Torvia had given him a crystal to test whether he had magic. Puzzled, he glanced at Jordan. Why would the Royal Mage care whether Jaime had magic and not any of Safia's other guards? Was this just because he suspected him of being someone else?

Regretting keeping his hair long, he stuffed the crystal in his pocket. At that moment, the door above opened and Safia's voice drifted down the steps.

The Royal Mage greeted her courteously, appearing to lose interest in Jaime. Though from now on Jaime would keep his distance whenever possible. "Princess Safia, you look extraordinary. May I have the pleasure of escorting you to the banquet hall?"

"Yes, of course," Safia said with equal politeness.

He moved close to her, and her protectors shifted uncomfortably. "If I had known you were recruiting new guards, I would have offered some of my most gifted mages to protect the future queen of South Parsa."

"That is not necessary. My guards have all proven themselves highly capable and loyal."

The Royal Mage's eyes darted to Jaime and Jordan as he raised an eyebrow. "No doubt they have, but please do consider the offer open if you ever need magical protection."

With an emphatic wave of the Royal Mage's hand, the entire group found themselves outside the banquet hall, where Prince Javed waited, accompanied by Prince Darien, both looking even more dazzling than they previously had. No doubt imbued with magic, their cloaks shimmered enchantingly, and lions twitched on their tunics.

In fact, most of the people entering the hall had dressed to show off their wealth, making Jaime feel extremely underdressed in his crimson guard uniform.

Both princes bowed to Safia and the Royal Mage, before Javed stepped forwards to kiss Safia's hand. "May I escort you to your seat?"

Safia nodded, a small smile spreading across her lips. Prince Javed must have made quite an impression.

A wrinkle formed on the Royal Mage's brow as he stepped away to talk to a server in a hushed voice.

"What do you think that's about?" Jordan whispered.

"It could be anything," Jaime replied. Though immediately his mind raced to Emily and Torvia. "Maybe he's just giving instructions for the banquet."

The server dipped his head and teleported away, leaving the Royal Mage to take his seat. Jaime tried to decipher his expression, but the man's face remained neutral. No surprise nor anger showed, nor any impatience to leave.

"Torvia can deal with any server," Jordan said. "They must have found Eliot by now."

Jaime nodded, unwilling to voice his fears. If they'd been discovered, a server wouldn't try to apprehend them alone. But there was nothing Jaime and Jordan could do.

Prince Javed guided Safia to her seat next to the Royal Mage, then sat opposite, next to Prince Darien. The other side of the younger prince remained empty.

Jaime's skin tingled. Would Alice sit there?

Despite Jaime's hushed protests, Jordan pulled him along to sit near Safia. The last thing he wanted was to be anywhere near the Royal Mage, but he couldn't do anything now without causing a scene. At least they'd hear the royal conversation.

The hall was full before the king entered, and everyone stood as he walked to his seat at the head of the table. Before he reached them, a beautiful young woman teleported in and joined him, resting her arm lightly on his. Her dress put the whole room to shame, sparkling with tiny jewels, and several men stood gawking as the rest of the room sat.

Taking the chair next to Prince Darien, she didn't look too happy to be there. They exchanged a few words, then she proceeded to ignore him.

Jaime's heart sank. Where was Alice?

"Who do you suppose that is?" Jordan whispered.

Another guard cut in before Jaime could reply. "That must be Princess Yasmin. I heard some of the soldiers talking about her. You don't want to mess around with her, though. She's the niece of the Royal Mage and the second most powerful mage in the kingdom."

Jaime stared in awe, wondering if she had cast a spell on the room. Many of the men in the room still hadn't recovered from her entrance.

He leaned closer to Jordan. "Where do you think Alice is?"

Jordan shrugged. "Maybe she wasn't invited, because it's a diplomatic event."

He slumped back in his chair. He shouldn't have come. This was a perfect opportunity to search the palace, but there was no chance of leaving the hall now.

Perhaps he could sneak out later when all the food had been served. He watched impatiently as extravagant dish after extravagant dish was brought out, but not a single person left the table.

To distract himself, he listened in on the conversations of the royals. Javed and Safia seemed to be getting on very well, but the Royal Mage wore a frown.

"All the worlds that link to South Parsa sound so full of character," Javed said. "I can't wait to see them all."

"You will experience them soon enough. As my husband, it will be important for the people to see you. My brother, who is responsible for trade, will arrange visits for us. He knows all the worlds so well."

"Careful, cousin," Prince Darien said. "Some of these worlds can be very dangerous. South Parsa doesn't have quite the same security that we have in the north."

Jaime focused on the younger prince. His sister still ignored him, so something was amiss. Could it be related to Alice?

"If by security you mean heavily policed portals and high taxes, no, we don't have that," Safia said passionately. "South Parsa flourishes on free trade, but our army is second to none."

Jaime smiled warily at her brave insult, and to his surprise, Darien smiled too. Jaime really didn't know what to think of him.

"It is an impressive army, but a stronger, magical force has invaded the north before, and it is only a matter of time before that army returns or finds a way to the south," the Royal Mage warned. "It is long overdue that we build up our defences across all of Parsa. What do you think, Prince Javed?"

"I agree we should defend all the portals, but Princess Safia knows her kingdom and her people best. It would be a tragedy to take away South Parsa's soul and freedoms in order to protect it. There must be a way we can achieve both."

The Royal Mage looked disappointed in Javed's answer but didn't push it further. Contrarily, Safia beamed at the prince and began to question him on North Parsa, ignoring all others.

Fed up with the talk of trade, Jaime's attention drifted to the doors. Unfortunately, there was no way he could reach them without being noticed. Too anxious to enjoy the food, he barely ate, but Jordan didn't have that problem and devoured enough for the two of them.

Eventually, the evening ended, and they were able to return to their guest chambers. It was much too late to sneak out of the palace to find out about the rescue, so Jaime and Jordan reluctantly returned with the rest of the guards to their shared living area.

Jaime's eyes were soon drawn to the decorative sandscape, now bathed in soft light from three moons. With a frown, he strode to the wall and pulled the picture forward. Examining the back, he expected to see some source of light.

"What are you doing?"

Jaime shrugged. "This depicted a daylight scene earlier this morning. I thought there might be some lights behind it."

"It's obviously magic. I don't know why you're interested. Safia can summon flame, heal wounds and teleport."

Jaime sighed. Jordan was right. Everything was a spell in this world. "Most of the mages here can do that. We should be careful."

Jordan rolled his eyes. "You don't need to tell me that. I can figure some things out for myself."

"You know I don't mean it like that. I'm just tired and stressed. I'm going to get an early night."

With no more argument, Jordan followed him into their twin bedroom.

To their surprise, Torvia sat waiting on Jaime's bed.

"How did it go?" Jaime asked straight away.

"We got him," Torvia answered, grinning. "It took some strong magic, but we found Eliot and broke him out. He's with Emily right now. Why didn't you join us with Alice?"

"She wasn't at the banquet," Jaime said glumly. "We'll have to stay undercover until we can find her."

"Can you take us to Emily and Eliot?" Jordan interrupted, causing Jaime to scowl.

"Of course." Torvia teleported them to an unremarkable building, sparse in decoration and with a boarded-up door, suggesting it could only be accessed through teleportation. Several figures spun around to confront the unexpected intruders.

When they saw Torvia, they relaxed, but continued to stare at the newcomers. Jaime recognised Shirin immediately, but the other mages, distinguished by their robes, he hadn't seen before.

Emily sat in the corner with Eliot, who was huddled against the wall, clearly terrified of the people around him. His eyes darted to

Jaime and Jordan for only a moment before returning to the floor, disappearing behind his scruffy, dark curls.

Before Jaime could say anything, Jordan crossed the room. "Hey if it isn't my little buddy. Do you want to see my new sword?"

Eliot peeped out from his protective huddle, eying Jordan suspiciously.

"I'm a proper swordsman now," he told Eliot. "I'm here to protect you and Emily until we can go back home."

"Really?" Eliot asked, peering closer.

"For sure." Jordan beamed at the young boy. "What do you think of my fancy uniform?"

Emily smiled as Eliot forgot his fear and walked over to inspect Jordan's attire.

"You went into that tower and tried to rescue Eliot from the Royal Mage all by yourself?" Jordan asked Emily.

She nodded.

"Wow, you're even braver than I thought. And you manipulated that poncey prince, too. Then you did it again after getting arrested!"

Jaime stood open-mouthed as he watched their interaction. He'd never realised they got on so well before.

Emily smiled, her cheeks rosy. "I had to. I couldn't just give up on Eliot. Besides, they weren't all bad. I met Shirin, and Torvia was a great help." Her eyes met Jaime's and her face fell. "Where's Alice?"

Another pang of guilt shot through him. "She wasn't at the banquet and we didn't see her all day. We'll have to go back to search the Royal Tower. I think our cover is safe, though the Royal Mage seemed a bit suspicious of me." His stomach churned again as he recalled their encounter, and he was glad he hadn't eaten much.

"Do you think he'll suspect us of rescuing Eliot?" Jordan asked, his attention returning to Jaime.

"He can't. You were both at the banquet the whole time," Torvia pointed out.

Jaime's jaw clenched. Next to Torvia, he felt like a complete failure. But Torvia couldn't share Jaime's annoyance. She wasn't particularly effective at hiding her anger. That was one positive about her.

Before Jaime could speak, Jordan said, "Okay, so we go back and search the tower tomorrow."

"No, you can't go, you have to protect Emily and me," Eliot pleaded.

Jordan exchanged glances with Emily and Jaime. "Maybe I should stay here. You never know who could come looking. You, Torvia and Shirin can search the tower well enough between you. Shirin, do you have any idea where Alice might be?"

Shirin started to pace. "There are numerous guest chambers in the Royal Tower, but she has a close friendship with Princess Yasmin, so she may spend time with her when she's not with Prince Darien." She halted abruptly. "There are rumours there was a big fight between the three of them at the recent royal ball though, so I can't say who she'd be with."

Jaime's heart stopped. A dispute? Was that why Alice was not at the banquet?

Emily caught his expression. "The ball was when Prince Darien was going to steal Alice's memories. Do you think that's why she's disappeared?"

Shirin frowned. "People tend to go missing around the Royal Mage, not the royals, but I wouldn't put it past his nephew to start taking prisoners."

Jaime's eyes widened, and he glanced at Torvia.

"Between the three of us, we should be able to search both Prince Darien and Princess Yasmin's chambers," Torvia said reassuringly.

Shirin nodded. "We should begin with Prince Darien's chambers first thing in the morning. Whenever he's in the palace, he trains with Prince Javed before breakfast. He has rooms near the top and bottom of the tower, so we'll have to split up. One of us should probably keep an eye on the prince too."

Jaime nodded his agreement, though the idea of sneaking around the chambers of mages wasn't exactly appealing.

Torvia agreed too. "Shirin, you will draw the least suspicion, so you should watch the prince. I'll take the chambers at the top of the tower and Jaime can take the rooms at the bottom. Then we can search the guest chambers together, and finally Princess Yasmin's if we still haven't found her."

Shirin ran a hand through her short hair. "Do you think you can stun Princess Yasmin if we need to get away?"

"No, she's much too powerful. We'll have to talk our way out of it or find another way to distract her if we get caught." Torvia turned to Jaime. "We ought to return you to the palace."

Jaime said his farewells to Emily, Jordan and Eliot and they all wished him luck. A moment later, he was back in the twin bedroom, but it felt totally different without Jordan. Even though guards slept in the adjoining rooms, the second empty bed taunted him, reminding him he had been abandoned again, and that he'd failed in his quest.

He flopped miserably into his bed. To his complete surprise, Torvia slid into Jordan's bed. "What are you doing?"

"I'm not going to let a comfortable bed go to waste," she said, as if the answer was obvious.

"What if the other guards find you?"

"They know not to ask questions." With a click of her fingers, all the lights went out.

A little too unsettled to sleep straight away, Jaime stared at the unfamiliar ceiling. He knew they had slept in a cave together, but in the palace of a conservative society, sharing a bedroom felt wrong.

Eventually, he slipped into an unending labyrinth of gilded rooms, where people dressed in shimmering outfits kept disappearing before he could talk to them, all whilst dark empty eyes peered at him from the shadows.

CHAPTER 42

North Parsa

The next day, Jaime was poked awake, and he opened his eyes to a frowning Torvia looming above.

"You sure like to sleep a lot," she whispered.

Blinking the sleep out of his eyes, he hauled himself up and clumsily threw on his uniform. Torvia already wore a blue dress adorned with two stars, identical to those he'd already spotted around the palace. He didn't bother asking how she'd obtained it.

"The prince's entertaining chambers are a few levels below this one. I'll teleport you there, then continue to his private rooms. We should have plenty of time to search if Shirin is right about him training."

Torvia left him facing a door with a shiny lion cub sigil. Still not completely awake, he glanced around the empty corridor before cautiously pushing open the door.

Numerous wardrobes suggested this was a cloakroom, and he contemplated peeking inside to see if the prince owned anything that wasn't overly ostentatious. Then he remembered these chambers were for entertaining, so wouldn't likely contain the prince's own clothes.

He followed steps upwards to a beautiful lounge area, which looked so comfortable he struggled to resist the urge to lie down and rest a bit longer. On the table, a tray of fresh pastries filled the room with a warm, sweet aroma, waking him right up. There was no explanation other than someone would be breakfasting here. His stomach rumbling, he almost reached out to take one of the delicacies, but it would be more prudent to leave quickly before someone discovered him trespassing.

Going against his instinct, he waited to find out if Alice would be eating here, since that was his mission after all. With no decent hiding spots in sight, he investigated a curtain leading to another room.

Little occupied this room, other than a few bookcases holding some old books, a desk, a couple of chairs and another wardrobe. At least he could hide in this room and peer through the curtain to check who came for breakfast, and still have a cupboard to retreat to in case someone came this way.

He didn't have to wait long before soft footsteps sounded in the lounge. He heard no door, so presumed whoever it was had teleported in. Risking a peek through the curtain, he observed Prince Javed helping himself to a pastry. Moments later, he was joined by Prince Darien, a sparkle in his eye. "So, are you ready for married life?"

"I think I'm going to enjoy it."

"I would too if that were my bride," Prince Darien said, taking his own pastry.

"I'm sure you'll find yourself a bride just as beautiful."

Jaime inwardly sighed his disappointment. This didn't sound like the type of conversation Alice would be invited to, and now he was stuck here watching the two men eat, reminding him of how little he had eaten the previous evening.

"And with a sizeable army, too," Prince Darien said with a smirk. Then, more sincerely, he congratulated Prince Javed. "You two really are a good match. Who would have thought a diplomatic marriage could result in two soulmates finding each other?"

"I don't know about soulmates yet, but the way she talks is so inspirational. She makes the south sound so exciting and so full of opportunity." Javed's face lit up as he spoke. Perhaps Jaime should think twice about arranged marriages.

"I'm sure it will be. When will you be off?"

"In a few days. Today I'm going to show her around the city and some of the more impressive worlds. Then the Royal Mage wants to hold a farewell dinner for us."

"And so he should. After all, we won't actually get to celebrate your wedding with you."

No sooner had they spoken his name than the Royal Mage appeared in the room. "Prince Javed, I wanted to catch you before you departed for the day. We have some arrangements to make for your leaving dinner."

Terrified of being caught by the Royal Mage, Jaime crept backwards into the wardrobe. It made it more difficult to hear the conversation, but they were just talking about preparations for another formal dinner. So much of palace life revolved around meals.

When he was sure no one was going to come towards the curtain, he crept out of the closet to hear more clearly.

"I should be getting going. I don't want to be late for my bride," Prince Javed said.

"Have a good time," Prince Darien said, before Javed teleported out of the room.

Jaime expected the other two to leave as well, but the Royal Mage closed in on Prince Darien, almost threateningly.

"Now what are we going to do about this situation?" the Royal Mage asked.

"Situation?" the prince echoed, his body stiffening.

"Timid Prince Javed clearly does not have what it takes to sit on the throne of South Parsa. Princess Safia is already turning him into his puppet and the south will keep failing to protect its people from portal invasion. Eventually, an overwhelmingly large army *will* invade, and if it is not stopped at the portal, it will conquer all of Parsa. I have witnessed technology you couldn't dream of, technology that makes crossing a desert child's play. I've seen armies with dozens of supremely powerful mages that can each render an entire army useless."

"Javed knows the risk. He's dedicated his life to protecting the people of Parsa."

"Do you really think he has the strength to convince that troublesome princess to submit to North Parsan control?"

Jaime gulped. What was the Royal Mage saying?

Darien frowned. "He will, with our help."

"Perhaps. But is that a gamble that you want to take, as the future king of North Parsa?"

Darien took a few steps away from the Royal Mage, his expression thoughtful yet guarded. "What do you propose then, Uncle?"

"Javed evidently is not fit to rule the south, but Princess Safia requires a North Parsan royal who is loyal to the true throne. You would make a better king in the south."

In an instant, Darien's expression twisted with rage. "Blasphemy! *I* am the rightful heir to the North Parsan throne. I will not leave North Parsa or enter into any marriage that lowers my position."

"Are you forgetting that Javed has more right to the North Parsan throne than you? Or who decides who sits on the throne?" The Royal Mage's mouth twisted into a smirk. "Your cousin has served the kingdom well. What have you ever done but indulge your own desires?"

"The king is my father! He will hear about this."

Jaime shifted uncomfortably in the wardrobe. He recalled what Emily had told him about their previous argument and saw this one heading in the same direction. Pity welled within him until he remembered what Darien had done to Alice.

The Royal Mage glanced down at his palm, flexing his fingers as blue sparks danced between them. "Do you not remember what happened the last time you said no to me? Choose your words carefully. The king is my ally and he will see the sense in my suggestion." His tone was calm, almost as if he enjoyed taunting his nephew.

Darien clenched his fists and forced his words out. "If you are going to send me to the south, who will inherit the throne in the north?"

"I'm glad you're coming to your senses, boy. Javed will make an ideal king in the north."

"You mean a puppet you can control."

A wicked smile spread across the man's face. "Of course. That is all the king is. As skilled as I am, I cannot be everywhere at once. Someone has to take care of the mundane ruling in my absence."

Darien scowled. "It will never happen. It is treason to even suggest it."

"I suppose I could marry Princess Safia myself and rule as king in the south and as Royal Mage in the north. Then there would be no need for Prince Javed at all. Though, I can't think of any reason I would prefer you over Prince Javed."

Jaime braced himself against the wardrobe. He could scarcely keep up with this man's scheming.

Darien went still. "I am your own blood! My magic is far stronger than his, and my father sits on the throne!"

"Your petulant whining won't win you the crown. You don't have what it takes to rule the north alone. You can't even recognise a powerful mage when she stumbles into your arms. You're just a stubborn, arrogant child. I will inform your father that you will be taking Javed's place in the south."

Enraged now, Prince Darien erupted, releasing a shock wave that hurled furniture into the walls and juddered the wardrobe around Jaime. "You will not!"

The Royal Mage had obviously expected the outburst, but a blue glimmer protecting him was the only clue he had reacted at all. Jaime braced himself for the worst, desperate now to get Alice away from this tempestuous family.

The Royal Mage laughed at Darien before his inevitable retaliation. "Foolish boy. Do you ever learn?"

Jaime felt the power of the spell as it struck. The air itself reverberated, forcing him backwards into a tangle of clothes. His ears rang with the clattering of the metal serving dishes. With heavy limbs, he could barely right himself to see what had happened to the prince.

Somehow, Prince Darien stood unharmed in the midst of chaos. Jaime was stunned, and he wasn't the only one.

The Royal Mage strode forwards and yanked at a chain around the prince's neck. A dazzling blue crystal fell forwards, and he sharply recoiled, a hiss escaping his lips. "That is not your magic. Where did you get that?"

Darien crossed his arms. "Yasmin enchanted it."

"You went crying to your sister?"

"No. She still thinks you're perfect. Don't worry about that, Uncle."

The Royal Mage shook his head, and scorn edged his voice. "You wouldn't have to rely on her if you took your studies seriously."

"I don't rely on her, but she cares about me enough to want to protect me." Darien turned away and stubbornness entered his voice. "She won't want me to leave."

The Royal Mage's face darkened. "You don't know what I have done to protect you and your kingdom. What I propose is for the safety of us all. You *will* do your duty." He rubbed his jaw. "Perhaps your obstinance can be put to good use as Princess Safia's husband."

Darien glowered. "I won't marry her. She is Javed's bride."

The Royal Mage grasped the crystal, letting his flesh sizzle. "You have more intelligence than I gave you credit for, but don't think you will amount to anything without me. Yasmin serves her kingdom. She expects nothing less of you. If you don't stop this rebellious behaviour, I'll cast you out of both kingdoms and you'll never see your sister again." He pushed Darien away, releasing the crystal.

"Father will never allow that. I am his heir."

"If you force this confrontation, I will ensure Javed and Safia rule over all of Parsa as a single united kingdom. Your father has been working for peace for so long, I'm sure he wouldn't object. And we'll send you off to a world so remote even you won't have heard of it."

Darien paled, his voice dropping to a whisper. "You wouldn't."

"Try me. Parsa has no use for petulant princes."

A victorious expression on his face, the Royal Mage teleported away, and Jaime sank deeper into the wardrobe, exhausted merely from watching the argument. A tension still hung in the air, or perhaps the room had not yet finished resonating from the blast, but it felt like the aftermath of a terrible storm.

Curious what the prince would do after such an ordeal, Jaime resisted rushing off to warn Safia and Torvia, instead pushing the wardrobe open a crack to see better. The prince sat beside the table, deep in thought, absent-mindedly taking bites out of a sticky red pastry.

Soon another guest arrived, and Jaime wondered if he'd be there all day, trapped in an unending stream of palace politics. This visitor didn't teleport in, instead knocking on the door.

Prince Darien sighed before putting on his normal charismatic face, righting the room and waving his hand to open the door.

A man Jaime didn't recognise entered, and despite wearing the uniform of the portal police, he addressed the prince quite informally. "Darien, I—" His eyebrows pinched together. "Is everything alright?"

Jaime strained to see what had alerted the newcomer to Prince Darien's situation, yet nothing appeared amiss.

"Yes, Navid, nothing to concern yourself with. I could do with some good news though."

Darien took a seat, and the visitor joined him, still scrutinising the prince's appearance. "I think I may have found it. The route to Alice's world, that is. One of my men returned with a device similar to the one Alice possessed."

Darien sat up slowly. "That *is* good news."

Jaime's heart skipped a beat. Finally, something worth overhearing.

"I thought you'd be more pleased. We've found a technological world before the mages!"

"I am exceedingly pleased, old friend." Darien placed a hand on Navid's shoulder. "I have just received some rather bad news that may take some digesting."

"Or is it that the lady Alice will be departing?" Navid said tentatively.

His muscles tightening at Alice's name, Jaime leaned forwards to hear better.

When the prince didn't reply, the officer continued. "We don't have to tell her. She could stay here as long as you like, and I'm sure she would come around to your charm."

Jaime frowned. It sounded like Darien was interested in Alice for more than her knowledge.

Darien sighed. "No, I shall tell her. Even though she really does belong here and Yasmin will miss her terribly, it is her choice."

"Sire, may I ask what did happen between you? She seemed so infatuated with you and now even Princess Yasmin will scarcely talk to you." Navid moved closer to the prince, puzzling Jaime at their relationship. They appeared more like close friends than a prince and his subject.

Darien stood and started to pace. "It was a misunderstanding. I was so obsessed with finding her world, I didn't notice her there right in front of me. I should have treated her better." He stopped abruptly. "It doesn't matter now. There are more important things to worry about."

Navid stood too, observing the prince with a tight jaw. "Yes, sire."

"Tell me about the route to her world."

Jaime leaned closer again, keen not to miss anything.

"It's a difficult one, requiring only one portal, but the journey is long. The current is exceptionally strong and must be fought to stay in the portal realm long enough to reach the destination. Numerous portals cluster around the exit to her world, so choosing the right one is challenging. I suspect this is why visitors to her world are so rare. With your permission, I'd like to take a few men and scout out the route myself, so I can be certain of the directions."

"As long as you are careful. I can't afford to lose you to the portal realm, Navid."

"I promise I will return." Navid bowed, exited, and – finally – Prince Darien departed too.

CHAPTER 43

North Parsa

Jaime waited until he was certain no one else was going to appear, then retreated through the door in the study. He had been stuck in the room so long he was unsure where Torvia and Shirin would be, so he headed up the tower, hoping to bump into them as they searched the guest rooms. Shirin evidently wasn't keeping an eye on Prince Darien, so perhaps she had returned to help Torvia.

It took him ages to ascend the tower. He hadn't realised from the outside just how high it was, but eventually, he made it all the way up to Princess Yasmin's chambers without meeting anyone. Torvia must surely be done with Prince Darien's chambers by now, but he couldn't predict where she might be.

He stared at Princess Yasmin's door, as if it might reveal something about the contents. The only door he'd passed with the double-edged golden mage symbol on, it shimmered in welcome, or perhaps in warning.

Empty corridor twisted away from him in each direction, but it might not stay that way forever. Unfortunately, if Torvia teleported straight inside the princess's chambers, he would never see her.

As his frustration turned to anger, he started to pace. He should have suggested a meeting point in case something went wrong.

He could go back to the guard's quarters and wait there, but he didn't want to be that useless.

Putting his ear to the door, he tried to hear if anyone occupied the room. After a few moments, sure there was no sound, he swallowed his nerves and carefully nudged the door open a crack. At least if he got caught, the others would probably be able to rescue him.

Nothing happened, so he pushed it a little further and peered inside. Immediately, his senses were assaulted by the onslaught of rich blue and dazzling gold.

Figures at the edge of the room slid into focus, and he panicked, his breath catching. There was no chance they could not have seen him in the doorway.

But they said nothing.

Adjusting to the dim light, he realised the figures had no faces. They were merely mannequins. He breathed an audible sigh of relief, then mentally scolded himself for making a noise.

He crept inside, his heart beating annoyingly loudly, looking for any sign of Alice. All he found was typical furniture befitting a princess, some books, and the mannequins. Some of the outfits on the mannequins were incomplete – Princess Yasmin must design and make her own dresses.

Grinding his teeth together, he realised he didn't know what to look for. Archery popped into his head, but those memories were of little use here. Why hadn't he paid any attention to anything Alice kept in her room back home?

He racked his brain, but he couldn't imagine what Alice might have acquired in this strange world that would tell him she had been here. Guilt slithered into his mind, twisting his thoughts. Emily had rescued Eliot from the clutches of the Royal Mage, and he hadn't even seen Alice yet. How difficult was it to find a person in a palace?

And then he saw it. A simple dress with an unusual geometric pattern – very unlike the sparkling gown the princess had worn the previous evening – which could only have been inspired by Alice.

She *had* been here!

And surely, she would be again. All he had to do was find an excuse to visit Princess Yasmin, and they'd be reunited. His breathing steadying, he turned to leave.

Without warning, the door began to open.

He dived behind a mannequin with a large skirt, praying that whoever entered would not come this far into the room. He listened intently, but all he could hear was his pounding heart.

"There's no one here," a voice whispered. The door closed quietly, and light footsteps padded across the room.

"Where do you think he might be?" another voice asked, sounding a lot like Shirin.

"He's probably found something and gone to check it out. Don't worry about him. He's quite resourceful for someone without magic."

Jaime almost laughed out loud at the sound of Torvia's voice and stepped out from behind the mannequin. Shirin shrieked, and he didn't dare think about what spell she was about to cast at him before Torvia pushed her back.

"Jaime! Where have you been? We were worried when Shirin couldn't find Prince Darien and you didn't show up."

"That would be because he turned up in his entertaining chambers as I was searching them."

Shirin's face twisted with horror. "What happened?"

"No one knew I was there, but he had some interesting visitors. You must warn Princess Safia that the Royal Mage is plotting to cancel the marriage to Prince Javed. He thinks Prince Javed is too weak for the southern throne and wants to put Prince Darien there instead."

"Those swines," Torvia growled. "Let's go somewhere safer to discuss it."

In the space of a moment, Jaime was removed from the precarious situation and back amongst friends in the house of the resistance. A little disorientated, he had to steady himself against a chair. Magic could do some incredible things, but it just wasn't natural.

At a simple table, Emily, Jordan, and Eliot were tucking into a simple lunch. To his surprise, Jordan and Emily were sitting very close together. Jaime raised his eyebrows, but Jordan responded with a stern look and Jaime knew to say nothing about it.

"Did you find Alice?" Emily asked, oblivious to their exchange.

Jaime shook his head. "Not yet. She wasn't in Darien's chambers, but I'm convinced she's with Princess Yasmin."

"How did you figure that out?" Torvia said.

"It appears she has had quite an impact on the princess's fashion."

"If that's the case, she'll be in the Mage Tower. The princess has rooms there to study and practise magic," Shirin said.

"How do we rescue her from there?" Emily asked.

"We could just send a messenger," Jaime said, causing several doubting faces to turn his way. "It doesn't sound like she's actually a prisoner. I heard Prince Darien saying he was going to choose to let her go home."

Jordan leapt up. "He knows how to get us home?"

Jaime nodded. "Someone may have found a way back, but it sounds difficult, so he's going to make sure before he tells anyone." He tried to remember the officer's words, but there was little point until they knew which portal to go through.

"How do you know all this?" Emily asked.

"I was looking for Alice in the prince's entertaining chambers when Darien unexpectedly teleported in."

Shirin's face twisted with guilt, but there was nothing she could have done.

"He discussed our way home with a portal police officer. But that's not all I heard. He also had a visit from the Royal Mage. It seems the Royal Mage is not pleased with Prince Javed and Princess Safia's relationship and wants a more controlling royal to marry Princess Safia. He suggested Prince Darien, but Darien was not happy about that."

Torvia and Shirin exchanged worried glances.

"Of course he wouldn't be," Shirin said. "The North Parsans look down on the south. He'd never want to give up the North Parsan throne."

"He won't have a choice if that's what the Royal Mage wants," Torvia said resolutely, to which Shirin nodded. "Did they say how they were going to suggest the change?"

"No. I mean, Prince Darien refused."

"What?" said both Torvia and Shirin at the same time.

Shirin stepped forward. "What happened then?"

"Well, the Royal Mage sounded like he was playing with him, but suggested he could marry Princess Safia himself."

Both Torvia and Shirin pulled a disgusted face.

"Princess Safia would never agree to that," Torvia said. Jaime believed her, but what would happen to her if she refused? It was obvious now that this marriage only existed to exert control over the south.

"Then what?"

Jaime grimaced as he continued. "The prince lost his temper and cast a spell at the Royal Mage. The Royal Mage laughed at him and retaliated, but seemed surprised when his spell didn't hurt the prince."

"What?" said both Torvia and Shirin again, amongst a rise of whispers from the others in the room.

"Prince Darien was wearing a protective blue crystal, enchanted by Princess Yasmin. The Royal Mage resorted to threatening to send him to a remote world, but I don't think either thought the king would agree to that." He shrugged. "I don't think the Royal Mage really wants to send him away. He just wants him to obey. He left when Darien seemed worried."

Torvia and Shirin exchanged serious glances before Shirin spoke softly. "No one has ever stood up to the Royal Mage before."

Torvia frowned but looked pensive. "It doesn't matter, the Royal Mage won't let him defy him. The crystal can't protect him from everything."

"If Prince Darien is going to the south, we must find out the route home as soon as possible," Emily said.

Jaime nodded. Even if the prince objected, he might not be in a position to help them much longer.

"Do you remember the name of the officer?" Torvia asked Jaime.

Jaime racked his memory, but there had been so many people, he couldn't recall his name. "No, sorry, there was too much going on."

"Okay, I'll try to find out who he is, but first I have to warn Safia. Shirin can attempt to get a message to Alice in Yasmin's rooms in the Mage Tower."

"Torvia," Emily interrupted. "I've been meaning to ask you something about South Parsa and the Royal Mage."

"Yes?" Torvia frowned at Emily.

"I found out the Royal Mage isn't originally from Parsa, and he first arrived in the south before travelling to the north."

Jaime's brow creased. "When did you find that out?"

"I went back to North Parsa to search the libraries. To help the resistance," Emily murmured, glancing at Shirin and Torvia.

"Are you mad?" Jordan exclaimed, but couldn't help laughing in admiration.

Emily scowled. "I was in disguise, so no one recognised me."

At the mention of a disguise, Jaime glanced at Torvia. She avoided meeting his eye, so she must have been involved, but he decided not to say anything about it. "Go on, Emily," he said instead.

"I couldn't find anything in the palace library, so I went to visit the lower mage library instead. The old librarian there told me some interesting things. He knew Prince Javed should have inherited the throne instead of the current king, and he remembered when the Royal Mage arrived. He said the world the Royal Mage came from had since been destroyed and abandoned, so we won't find any help there, but since Torvia is from the south, I wondered if she might know the world the librarian was talking about."

They all looked expectantly at Torvia. She took a few moments to reply, staring strangely at Emily. "I only know of one world that was invaded and abandoned."

As she paled, Torvia's confessions about her birth-world surfaced in Jaime's mind. "You don't think he could have been from *your* world, do you, Torvia?"

She shook her head. "No, that can't be possible. The people there were simple villagers and nomads. They had no desire to live in palaces and rule over kingdoms. The Royal Mage visited, but he couldn't have been born there. People would know."

"Tell me you're not going back," Jordan said to Emily.

"No, there's nothing more to find. I'll stay here with Eliot until you find Alice."

Jordan nodded and sauntered over. "Well, you'd better take me back to the palace before I'm missed. We'll be back with Alice in no time."

CHAPTER 44

NORTH PARSA

Alice was beginning to get sick of the same four walls, the endless parade of spellbooks and even Yasmin's encouragement. Yasmin had appointed herself Alice's personal tutor and was working her hard.

Annoyingly, before Alice could start on gold one-star spells, she had to master the five silver star levels, usually studied by children. It was immensely tedious, and she couldn't think of a practical application for most of what she was being ordered to study.

However, she was desperate to learn and trying her hardest, which meant after days of concentration she was exhausted. "Can we take a break, please? My eyes are going blurry," she said.

Yasmin frowned. "You need to learn all these basic spells before you can progress to the more interesting enchantments."

"Please, let's go outside for a walk around the garden before it goes dark. We've been inside all day."

Yasmin exhaled and said in a disapproving tone, "I suppose a little break wouldn't hurt."

They used Yasmin's crystal circle shortcut to teleport to the Royal Tower, then straight out into the gardens, where they followed a winding path through leafy palms and yellow buds glistening with dew.

"I wish you would teach me to teleport."

Yasmin frowned. "You're not ready for teleportation yet. Who knows where you would end up if you tried to teleport without learning the basics."

Some of these basics needed for teleportation were more like meditation, requiring a lot of patience, something Alice also struggled with. Becoming a mage was not as exciting as she had first thought.

She brushed her hand along a fern, appreciating the cool leaves against her skin on this unusually hot day.

Yasmin sighed at her expression. "If you don't want to spend all your time in the tower, you should join us at dinner this evening. There will be many interesting people. You don't have to talk to Darien. I don't." Yasmin wrapped her arm around her, flashing her most convincing smile.

The idea of meeting new people was tempting, but Alice's cheeks flushed with the memory of her embarrassment. She wasn't quite ready to banquet with Darien just yet. "I feel so stupid, though. How can I show my face amongst the royalty?"

"No one knows what happened. It's Darien who should feel stupid. You haven't met Princess Safia yet either. I think you'd really like her. I'll ask my uncle if he'll seat us next to her."

Alice contemplated Yasmin's proposal but struggled to imagine Darien feeling stupid or truly sorry.

"I'll give you a complete makeover. You can re-enter society as a mage." Yasmin smiled at the prospect of a new project, and Alice couldn't help mirroring her.

"But I haven't even earned a star yet," Alice protested.

"That doesn't matter. By the time I'm done with you, no one will be counting how many stars you have."

Alice consented with a small sigh, and Yasmin beamed with excitement. Grabbing Alice, she teleported her back to her room to begin the transformation.

Their mood changed when they discovered Darien waiting, his hands clasped together in front of him.

Alice's heart skipped a beat before her irritation returned. More angry with herself at this point, for letting him use her so easily, she cursed his good looks and charm.

"What are you doing here?" Yasmin demanded.

"Yasmin, Alice, I've come to ask for your forgiveness. Please, at least let me explain myself," he began.

"You don't need to explain anything. I saw your thoughts!" Alice burst out. Her rage getting the better of her, flames shot forwards at Darien.

Unflinching, he raised an eyebrow as he absorbed the flames into his hand. Unfortunately, some of the flames went astray and set Yasmin's bed alight.

"Are you going to put that out?" Darien asked calmly as the flames engulfed the frame.

Yasmin tried to quash the inferno, but her spells failed to completely extinguish the blaze, which sparked and reignited after each attempt.

Horrified, Alice stared at the scene, unsure what to do. Her fury at Darien persisted, and it took all her concentration to prevent spreading more flame. Darien wasn't offering any assistance either, so she continued to glare at him.

The fire spread rapidly, faster than any natural blaze. Some of Yasmin's precious outfits displayed on the mannequins ignited, and she shrieked at Alice to do something.

"Can't you put the fire out?" Alice spluttered, confused at Yasmin's ineffectiveness.

"Can't *you*?" Yasmin squealed.

Darien's eyes were on them, his lips slightly curled upwards. With a shield around him, he was immune to the effects of the disaster.

Alice tried to ignore him and focused her attention on aiding Yasmin. "I don't know how!" She rushed towards Yasmin, but the heat stifled, and the fumes stung her eyes.

"Your spell is too strong to negate." Yasmin started coughing now. "Darien, do something!"

"Are you talking to me?" he asked, still calm, despite most of the room being fiercely ablaze.

Alice stifled the impulse to hurl more flames at him.

"Darien!" Yasmin screamed.

With the casual swoop of an arm, Darien drew the fire towards him, making it disappear before it caused him harm. All the smoke whirled towards him too, with a force so strong it knocked both Alice and Yasmin off their feet. Within moments all the fire and smoke had been eliminated.

Alice heaved herself up and surveyed the charred remains that now made up Yasmin's room. "I'm so sorry, Yasmin. I didn't mean to do that," she said, mortified at what she had done.

"It's okay, Alice, I should have taught you better," Yasmin murmured, staring wide-eyed at the state of her room. Yasmin turned to Darien, her eyes narrowing. "Where did you learn how to do that?"

"Not all magic can be learned from those spellbooks of yours," he said with a rather smug expression. "Alice, your magic grows stronger every day," he added, as if trying to compliment her. "Perhaps you both should go to Alice's rooms. I'll have this sorted out before dinner."

Alice took Yasmin's hand and tried to tug her away from the disaster. "Come on, Yasmin, there are plenty of outfits in my room that I need your help with."

Yasmin turned up her nose at her suggestion, but teleported them both there anyway. She sank onto Alice's bed, her face ashen and unblinking.

Alice didn't know what to do, so she started reading one of the spellbooks she kept in her room. Now she had witnessed the consequences of her unchecked power, she vowed to study more diligently. At the back of her mind though, a small voice told her these books were only the beginning if Darien could do something Yasmin could not. Perhaps that was what Yasmin thought about whilst she sat silently on the bed.

Around an hour later, they were interrupted by a knock on the door. In her current state, Alice didn't dare use magic to open it, so she walked over instead. Her body stiffened at Darien's presence.

"May I enter?"

Alice wanted to say no, but her concern for Yasmin outweighed her disdain for Darien, and it was probably best to focus on being calm. Perhaps those meditation lessons were a good idea after all. "Yes, I suppose."

He didn't bother walking in after her, instead teleporting in front of Yasmin. "Yasmin?" he said softly.

Yasmin didn't answer, her eyes still staring off into the distance.

"She's been sitting there the whole time," Alice said. "Do you think she's okay?"

He crouched in front of her. "Yas? Everything's alright now," he said gently. "You can go back upstairs."

She looked blankly at him. "Where do you go all the time?"

"Just palace business. Come on, let me show you to your new room." He offered his hand.

Yasmin stood and offered her other hand out to Alice, and they all teleported up together. The room was perfect again, the decor identical, and the furniture replaced. Fresh mannequins had appeared, but Yasmin's outfits could not be saved or replicated.

However, the wardrobe burst with new material of the finest quality and the princess couldn't resist going over to admire it. "Where did you get all this from?"

"I was going to present it to you as a gift to help you prepare for Princess Safia's arrival banquet, but you stopped talking to me."

"It's beautiful," she exclaimed, stroking the fabric.

"So, will you forgive me now?"

She looked up at him, then across to Alice. "It's not up to me to forgive you."

"Alice," he said, walking over to her, "please tell me how I can make it up to you. Whatever you ask, I will gladly do. I really am sorry I was so obsessed with the technology on your world that I tried to take advantage of you. I didn't know you then. I was a stupid fool, and I value your friendship far more than technology. Please forgive me."

Alice thought about it for a moment. He seemed sincere, but then he always had, so she hesitated. "I need to think about it," she replied, unsure whether her heart raced because of the stress of the fire or because of his presence.

"As you wish. I hope I will see you at dinner." He bowed, then left, leaving Alice feeling very conflicted.

She turned to Yasmin, noticing her colour had fully returned. "Do you think I can trust him?"

Yasmin pursed her lips. "I'm not sure. He's always been kind to everyone, but he spends so much time away from the palace now, I'm not sure I recognise him anymore. He never used to be this manipulative." She returned the fabric to the wardrobe. "I don't know where he learned that spell either. That was far too powerful for him."

Alice bit her lip. "How do you know, if you've hardly seen him practise?"

"No North Parsan can do that. He can't suddenly go from struggling with three-star spells to that."

"Who tells you he struggles?"

Yasmin narrowed her eyes. "Don't start this again. Why do you hate my uncle?"

"I don't hate him. I just don't like what he's doing to you both. He lied to me, too. He knew I had magic and kept it a secret from everyone."

Yasmin pinched the bridge of her nose. "You must be mistaken. Why would he do that?"

Alice shrugged. "To keep me here in the palace where he could question me about my world."

Yasmin held out her arm, to which Alice gave her an inquisitive look.

"We're going to ask him. Then you'll see you're wrong."

Alice frowned, but Yasmin practically dragged her to the crystal circle, before teleporting them to her room in the Mage Tower.

"Yasmin, he's probably busy and he'll deny anything."

Ignoring Alice's protests, Yasmin marched her through the entrance chambers, into the Royal Mage's private rooms, until they found him in his study.

He looked up in surprise. "Yasmin, what is it?"

"Alice thinks you knew she had magic when she first arrived."

His nose wrinkled as he turned his hawk eyes on her. "Why would you think that? If I had known, I would certainly have questioned you about it."

Alice shook Yasmin off. "You saw the crystal glow when I touched it. You gasped."

A crease formed on his brow. "You must be mistaken. I remember no such thing."

Alice turned and pointed to the crystals still on the table. "I was standing right there when I picked them up."

His gaze followed her finger. "Those are not magical crystals. They could not possibly glow. Perhaps one caught the light. You must have been tired and stressed."

Alice strode over to the crystals and scooped up a handful.

None glowed.

Yasmin took her arm. "You see? No one was keeping secrets from you."

Alice scowled. She knew what she had seen. The man was lying, but Yasmin would never believe her. At a loss for words, she exhaled her frustration.

The Royal Mage stood, wearing his best imitation of concern on his face. "I thought I had welcomed you and set your mind at ease when you arrived. No doubt discovering your magic has overwhelmed you and opened the door to confusion."

Yasmin stepped forward. "Alice is grateful for everything you've done. She's just tired. We had an incident with Darien."

"What has that boy done now?" the Royal Mage said. "Do I need to step in?"

Yasmin shook her head. "No, nothing like that. He just performed a powerful, strange spell. Do you know where he might have learned it?"

His eyebrows climbed higher. "I have been giving Darien some private lessons. His skill has been improving, at least when he bothers to turn up."

Yasmin nodded. "Thank you, Uncle. We won't take up any more of your time."

Alice's stomach twisted. There was no way Darien would have lessons with his uncle. The Royal Mage must be lying about that, too. "So, you don't mind Yasmin befriending commoners then, since you thought I had no magic?"

His eye twitched almost imperceptibly. "You have been a good friend to Yasmin."

"And Officer Gul. He is a good friend too."

"He is a portal police officer."

Yasmin glanced at Alice. "He is my friend. You can't stop me talking to him."

"I only want what's best for you, Yasmin. You know that."

"Then you'll make sure he is always welcome at the palace." Her eyes gleaming, she turned on her heel and marched to the door.

Alice tried to follow, but her legs wouldn't move. Her stomach clenched. Yasmin was right behind her ...

The Royal Mage closed in, lowering his voice. "I hope Yasmin isn't ignoring you for this man."

Her throat too dry for words, Alice shook her head.

"I'm glad to hear it. It would be a shame for you not to reach your potential after so recently discovering your magic."

Astonished at the audacity of this man, Alice gulped. "Yasmin is a wonderful teacher."

"Alice?" Yasmin called.

The vice on her legs released, and Alice hurried after Yasmin. She didn't dare think how she was going to pay for this.

Yasmin smiled at her, completely oblivious. "We have to hurry. We've got new dresses to make."

Alice hovered outside Darien's door. Should she knock?

It would be better to talk to him before dinner. Probably. He could warn Officer Gul the Royal Mage was in a foul mood, and look out for him. And he might tell her where he'd really learned that spell – if he wanted her to trust him.

She raised her hand, then stopped as raised voices escaped the room.

"The palace is full of rumours, Father," Darien said. "Few of them are true and even those are heavily exaggerated."

"I'm not interested in rumours. I want the truth from you. Did you burn Yasmin's chambers?"

"Do you think so little of me that I would attack Yasmin, or fail to control a spell?"

"Then who? Don't deny you were involved."

"I stopped the spell. And replaced Yasmin's things. If you want to know who cast it, ask Yasmin."

Alice slumped against the wall. Should she care Darien was in trouble for her error? It *was* partly his fault ... And he could have stopped it sooner.

"I shall. Now what about this other rumour? What did Kavir do to you?"

Alice strained to hear. The Royal Mage had done something to Darien?

"Don't make me summon him."

Darien's voice quietened. "Nothing. He cares only for my spell-casting ability."

The king's voice softened. "Darien, I am well aware of Kavir's shortcomings. If he threatened you, I'll throw him out of the kingdom."

Alice bristled. That was not an argument she wanted to stick around for.

"There's no need for that. I can handle him. Now, if you excuse me, I have some business before dinner."

"No. I want the truth from you. What did Kavir say to you?"

Silence, then the sound of footsteps moving across the room. Had their conversation become too quiet to hear?

"He doubts Javed's ability to rule in the south," Darien said softly. Bitterness crept into his voice. "He thinks I should marry Safia instead."

"That is absurd. You are my heir. The crown prince. His sister's son. Everything Kavir has done is for you to take the throne." Footsteps sounded again. "Unless ... Unless he means to *unite* the north and the south. If you were to marry Safia, our kingdoms would become one. There would be no need for all this posturing."

"That has always been thought impossible. The southerners would consume our kingdom if given the chance," Darien said stubbornly.

"Not with your uncle and your sister keeping order. Perhaps it is time we thought about a true union. As outsiders, the southerners will always be envious of us, but as part of the kingdom, they will ensure its future. Our army can never hope to match theirs, and combined, we may defeat the Iybryrians once and for all."

"They will take all our magic for themselves, then displace our family," Darien said. "Our magic is all that keeps them from conquering our city."

"Nonsense. Royal marriages have strengthened our kingdom for generations. Your own mother was not from this world. Do you think that the kingdom has suffered because of her?"

"She was not ruler of her own kingdom. Princess Safia will always put her own people first."

"Our people would become her people. Her brothers your brothers. And if your teleportation skills become anything like your uncle's, you can maintain a persistent presence in both."

"I can't teleport anywhere near that far!"

"With practice and dedication, your magic will develop. You will become the king of the two richest and most powerful kingdoms. What prince wouldn't want that?"

"Her kingdom needs a king now. I have more training to do."

"I am surprised at you. You have been shirking your training for years. The south will give you the new experiences that you crave."

"What about Javed? Who will he marry?"

"There are plenty of kingdoms with unwed princesses. We will find him a fine match. Do you want to speak with him first?"

"You want me to tell Javed I'm stealing his bride?"

"Nothing has been decided yet, but we can't ignore this idea. Javed understands his position. He will support you. I will speak with Princess Safia. And Kavir. He should have spoken to me first."

As silence prevailed, Alice sagged against the door. Should she speak with Darien? Troubling him with her concerns for Navid didn't seem so important now.

"Is the prince occupied?" a voice behind her said.

Spinning around, Alice stiffened. How long had Ahmad been there?

Ahmad dropped into a bow. "Good evening, Alice."

"Um, good evening, Ahmad." Her eyes darted back to the door. "I thought I heard voices."

"Well, there is only one way to be sure." With perfect confidence, he strode to the door and knocked loudly. A gleam in his eye, he turned to her. "Hear anything interesting?"

Heat rushed to Alice's cheeks, but she didn't have time to respond before Darien opened the door. Again, Ahmad dropped into a low bow before Darien ushered them both inside. The king appeared to have departed.

"Ahmad, Alice … What are you both doing at my door?"

Ahmad strode over to a solid pine cabinet and unstoppered a bottle. "My prince, I suspect we are both here out of concern for you. Isn't that right, Alice?" He sniffed at the bottle, set it aside and selected another.

Darien's dark eyes bored into hers. "Is something wrong with Yasmin?"

"No!" Alice bit her lip. She had to say something now. "Yasmin is back to her usual self and has informed the Royal Mage that she will be spending more time with her friends. Including those without magic."

Darien's eyebrows hitched up. "She said that to him? What did he say?"

"Not a lot."

With a purple drink in hand, Ahmad swooped towards them. "I take it this is about that officer. A terrible shame that he doesn't possess magic, but I see no harm in a friendship. He has an important position after all."

Alice frowned. "Her uncle doesn't think so."

Ahmad sighed. "Kavir has a short temper. He often overreacts, especially when it comes to his niece. Don't worry about that."

"He thinks I should marry Princess Safia."

Ahmad's glass stopped halfway to his mouth. "That cannot be possible. Princess Safia seeks a consort for the south."

Darien flopped into a chair. "My uncle means to send me away. My father thinks I can rule both kingdoms as one."

Ahmad set the glass down and moved closer. "I don't believe it for a moment. Your father and uncle have worked together to ensure the north benefits from your bloodline. To send you to the south is madness."

"It's true. My father has just left to make preparations."

"You can decline." Ahmad crouched down before him, forcing Darien to meet his gaze. "The south is a formidable kingdom, but Princess Safia's magic is no match for yours. It is an offence to combine your blood."

"This is the way it has always been for royalty." Darien jumped to his feet, but desperation tinged his voice. "I can't defy my father and my uncle. It's a sensible proposal."

Ahmad snorted. "Your magic is needed here to defend the city. You don't need to submit to southern fears. Your uncle never has. Let Javed marry their princess and you find a bride who will support your rule." He passed Darien a drink. "I will speak with Kavir."

Darien shook his head. "He won't change his mind about me."

Ahmad placed his hand on Darien's shoulder. "Your uncle has high expectations of you, but that doesn't mean he wants to disown you. He just has a terrible way of communicating his thoughts. And what would Yasmin think if you left to go to the south?" His eyes flicked to Alice, pinning her to the spot. "She wouldn't be pushed into a disadvantageous marriage."

Alice bit her lip. Yasmin hadn't exactly stood up that much to her uncle.

Ahmad lowered his voice. "Have you considered that Kavir may be testing you? The Royal Mage and the king must be able to rely on each other. The king must know his own mind and he must be able to back up his decisions."

"The Royal Mage knows my mind," Darien said through gritted teeth. "But perhaps you are right. I won't back down. And my father ... he will see reason. Though if my father is serious about uniting the kingdoms, there is no reason why I cannot rule from here ..."

"Southerners cannot be trusted," Ahmad said in a low voice. "Let Javed marry their princess and keep her far down the line of succession."

"I shall discuss this properly with my father. Will you be at dinner tonight?"

"I'm afraid I have a prior engagement, but we shall talk again tomorrow. And perhaps you should talk with Yasmin. She would hate to be excluded from important discussions." Ahmad finished his drink then disappeared in a burst of stars.

Darien stared blankly at Alice. "Yasmin wouldn't understand."

"She would. She gave you that crystal. She wants only to protect you." Though she had said she hardly recognised him anymore. But that didn't mean she wanted him to be pressured into marriage and sent away, did it?

Darien set his full glass down and straightened his tunic. "Will you be joining us this evening?"

Alice bobbed her head. "I'd better get back to Yasmin. She's making me a new dress."

CHAPTER 45

North Parsa

Despite the short time available, both Yasmin and Alice donned exquisite new outfits for dinner. Alice hadn't mentioned anything about what she'd overheard, though Yasmin might not believe her anyway. She'd have to find the right way to tell her.

Unusually, Yasmin had designed a sleeveless dress for Alice, creating a criss-crossing golden thread for her to wear down her arms, with blue jewels where the thread intersected. The cobalt dress itself shone with cascading stars, pooling at the hem, then evaporating into the air with a golden shimmer. Yasmin's own dress flickered with a blue flame, making it look like she was on fire.

Alice hovered in front of the mirror, admiring Yasmin's talent. Though she almost wished she'd designed something plainer. Her magic wasn't deserving of something so magnificent. And people were sure to notice her sudden reappearance.

She didn't dare think what rumours had spread about her and Darien. But hiding away would only make them worse. She turned to Yasmin and took her arm.

Arriving early to negotiate the seating arrangements, they managed to be repositioned closer to Princess Safia, with Yasmin sitting right next to her and Alice beside Yasmin. Alice surveyed Safia discreetly, admiring her confident bearing, despite only being in her early twenties. With only her two most senior guards, seated at the opposite end of the table, Princess Safia seemed perfectly at ease.

Set apart in her silky red dress, which also bore no shoulders, Princess Safia didn't quite match the North Parsan extravagance, though she wore gold jewels in her hair and around her neck, and her dress trailed out behind her.

Safia was also joined by a woman called Velia who she claimed to be her closest friend and advisor, but no one seemed to know who she was or how she had arrived at the palace. Her appearance mirrored Safia so much that she could have been her younger sister, though she had black hair rather than fiery red and was more slender than the curvy princess.

Yasmin tried to get Darien moved further away from her and Alice, but Safia insisted he remain beside Javed, to discuss the future of the two nations. It seemed Darien hadn't mentioned the king's proposal to Javed just yet. As Javed took his seat, he nodded to Alice and said, "It's good to see you again."

Alice smiled back, ignoring the knot forming in her stomach. Barely able to keep his eyes off Princess Safia, Javed seemed so happy. Too late, Alice realised she hadn't given Javed the credit he deserved. He had none of Darien's manipulative charm. But both would suffer if the king's plan went ahead.

The king arrived last and took his seat at the head of the table. It seemed that the Royal Mage wasn't attending, but the king showed no signs that there'd been an argument. As cheery as ever, he gestured for the food to be served.

She turned her attention back to Princess Safia, who was already talking about her kingdom. "South Parsa trades with numerous civilisations and has the largest concentration of expert crafts, metalwork and textile producers in all the known worlds."

"Even more than North Parsa?" Alice asked.

Safia nodded, fixing her gaze on Darien. "South Parsa has no equal in any trade."

Not blinking at her challenge, Darien smiled. "South Parsa benefits from a rich undisturbed history of fine craftsmanship, but North Parsa is not without its talented artisans."

"Of course, North Parsa excels in magic, but in everything else, South Parsa is superior."

Alice frowned. Had the king already spoken with Princess Safia? It seemed odd for the princess to be so direct, but then Alice knew nothing about these southerners. Princess Safia could have been angry about a change in the agreement, and was now testing her relationship with Darien, or she could simply be proud of her kingdom.

Velia scowled at the exchange, scrutinising Darien with unguarded suspicion. Occasionally her eyes darted towards Alice, making her uneasy. There was something odd about this silent woman and the way her dark eyes occasionally flashed amber.

Javed grinned. "I will wait until I have seen the south for myself before I make any judgements, but I am sure we can find something here that will take your breath away, my princess."

Safia's eyes flicked to Javed, and her expression softened. "Before we depart, I would appreciate a tour of the Mage Tower." She narrowed her eyes back on Darien. "After all, magic is what is most important here."

A huge crash from the courtyard doors disrupted the conversation, and glass sprayed across the hall, sending diners shrieking and diving under the tables. Many others stared in shock, their faces reflecting Alice's own confusion.

Foreign soldiers dressed in black charged in from the darkness, eliciting more screams. But who would be so bold to attack a palace of mages and how had they got past the city defences?

Several figures materialised near their table, huddled tightly together, answering Alice's question. Ice prickled her skin, and her mind went blank.

Enemy mages had finally come.

Velia reacted first, leaping up onto the table and casting a shield in front of them all. Darien quickly joined her, strengthening the shield to a brilliant blue.

Soldiers and guards poured in from different rooms, shouting instructions to each other and the startled guests. To Alice's horror, Jordan joined them, with Jaime on his heels, both dressed as Safia's guards.

What were they doing here? Now?

There was no time to think. Shaking off her paralysis, she jumped to her feet and pushed the chair aside, intending to run to them. But there simply was no way across the room.

"Yasmin, get Alice out of here," Darien ordered.

"No!" Alice protested, too late, as her chambers appeared around her.

She grabbed hold of Yasmin before the princess teleported away. "Yasmin, don't leave me here, I can help."

"No, you can't. You're not ready yet." She gave Alice a sympathetic look, pushed her away, and disappeared, leaving her alone at the top of the tower.

Her stomach tightened, the disgust of being deposited out of harm's way far more distasteful than the shock of the soldiers' appearance. All her studying and practising was for nothing if she couldn't help her friends.

There was no way she was going to sit up here whilst everyone else was in jeopardy. They didn't even know what they were getting themselves into.

Her thoughts darted to teleportation and the numerous warnings about mages attempting it before they were ready. But there was no time to worry about those. There was no other choice. She had to act.

A clear mind and focus on the destination were key, so she employed a few breathing exercises to calm herself and increase her concentration. Then she visualised the dining hall and focused all her energy on being there. She'd been there so often that the golden columns and long tables surfaced vividly in her mind. And she could almost smell the incense and the fragrant aromas carried in from the courtyard garden.

After several moments, tingling shot through her body and a disorienting lurch dizzied her senses. A nearby crash made her jump. She opened her eyes. She'd done it!

Well, not exactly. She was not in the dining hall, but one of the adjoining rooms. She'd appeared behind an arched glass doorway which mirrored the opposite courtyard wall.

But this was close enough.

Adrenaline rushed through her as she surveyed the scene.

A few dozen invaders surrounded the royal contingent at the head table, ignoring the soldiers and guards pouring in from the courtyard. With their magic, it only took a handful of them to keep the local non-magical forces at bay. Many of the guests had disappeared, but a few still pushed towards the exit, with soldiers and mages guarding their retreat.

Forcing her feet to move, she pushed open the door and scoured the room for her friends. Yasmin had returned to her father's side, protected by the impenetrable shield around them, so strong now it looked as though they were submerged in tropical water.

Flame and cobalt lightning shot from Yasmin's fingers, decimating the invaders one by one. Yasmin's spells mingled with a kaleidoscope of colours. Red, yellow, blue, and white fire hurtled across the room, sizzling against shimmering shields and engulfing the undefended, only to snuff out with a hiss as someone cast a counterspell. Somehow, spells bounced off those attackers who showed no signs of magic, filling the hall with deadly ricocheting fireballs.

Darien and Velia fought side by side. Gold and crimson lightning streaked and crackled with frightening speed, only to halt at the enemy's shield, each impact punching ripples and fractures in the sapphire glass-like surface. Between each strike, white light surged along the cracks, melting the imperfections away.

She could hardly believe her eyes at the speed of spell-casting, and doubt of her own ability crept through her veins like treacle, slowing her movements. What could she really do against these mages, who still managed to retaliate with their own spells, the leaders wielding their own amber lightning?

She jumped as another crash pulled her attention back to the windows, where warriors clashed ferociously. An overturned table provided some defence, but it was no barrier to magic.

There, Jordan dived forward, drawing off an assailant, and Alice's heart leapt into her throat. He fought well but was about to be overrun by more of the enemy surging in through the gaping holes.

As another militant raised his sword above Jordan's head, she instinctively called out to warn him, but there was no way he could hear over the chaos in the hall. She rushed forward, then almost fell, caught by dark tendrils wrapping around her legs.

Despair forced flame from her fingertips towards the dark cloud. It recoiled a little, freeing her feet, but still blocked her path.

Now she understood why no one could reach the high table.

Glancing up, she saw Jaime fighting beside Jordan, doing his best to beat back the warriors, but now the dark tendrils seethed towards them. She couldn't cast fire that far, that accurately. She risked setting her friends alight if she tried.

Helplessness gripped her as she watched her friends in peril, suffering in a world that wasn't theirs. If only she had her bow, the range would be no obstacle to her.

"Safia, you must retreat!" shouted Velia.

Safia scowled as her fireball bounced harmlessly off a soldier. Even their non-magical combatants had magical protection. No wonder the North Parsans feared them. Still furious, Safia ordered her protectors to fall back before she disappeared. Some of them had already fallen, and without magic, they had no chance against the aggressors.

Desperate now, Alice tried to remember her lessons. It was all about focus and serenity. Magic had to be visualised and felt before it became reality. Though how was she supposed to do that in the heat of battle? She had only ever experienced that level of concentration and absorption when shooting.

A jolt of excitement shot through her. Could she shoot magical arrows?

She concentrated hard, remembering the weight of the bow, feeling the smoothness of the wood, the way the string resisted as she stretched her muscles. Next, she visualised the arrow bursting into flames before the familiar sensation of release. Her eyes had closed, but she didn't need to open them to know that a fiery arrow soared through the air. The only problem was she had forgotten to aim. As her mood deflated, the arrow withered from existence and caused no harm to anyone, friend or foe.

But now she had a weapon, she had a chance.

Armed with this new knowledge, she tried again, keeping her eyes open. Focusing on a target, she drew her invisible bow and released the arrow of fire. It soared through the air at near impossible speed, and her target plummeted to the ground. She had never hit a live creature before, let alone a person, but if she hadn't, the soldier would now be attacking her friends.

All doubts eliminated, she concentrated on the next shot. Her unusual fire arrows did not go unnoticed, and most of the room glanced her way, but she appeared to be of little interest to the enemy. More poured in from the window, surrounding Jaime and Jordan, and she wrestled with her concentration and despair, desperate to make every arrow count.

Finally, Velia – observing Jaime and Jordan's predicament – broke off from her current fight and teleported them out of trouble, eliciting a sigh of relief from Alice. However, with Velia's exit, the magical shield protecting everyone weakened, and the attackers, seeing their opportunity, surged towards the diminishing royal contingent.

The enemy leader barked an order through disturbingly crooked lips and all his mages surged towards Darien, attacking the shield with bolts of lightning, an inferno of flame, and blasts of energy that shook the entire hall. The shield splintered, then collapsed, allowing the lightning to break through and pummel Darien, knocking him off the table.

Alice's blood ran cold. She shot an arrow at the leader, but he didn't even flinch as it disintegrated by his side. She could only watch as he closed in on Darien, leaping onto the table without even sparing her a look. As he raised his hand to strike, Javed lunged forward. Fighting with sword and spell, his face betrayed no fear, and slowly he pushed the man back, until they teetered on the edge of the table.

Reappearing beside Javed, Velia cast a blast that toppled most of the attackers and shattered the glass behind Alice. Her ears ringing, Alice breathed a sigh of relief. The invaders had to give up now. Reinforcements had stopped flowing through the doors and their group was split up.

The leader barked a new order, and mages converged on Velia. Yasmin, seeing Velia in distress, rushed to her defence and strengthened the woman's shield, then unleashed a catastrophic explosion, crumbling the entire hoard of assailants.

Shoved back against the wall by the blast, Alice was sure they would fall back then, but an invisible force sent both Yasmin and Velia flying. She looked around for the mage who had cast it, but everyone was preoccupied with other opponents.

Resisting the urge to run towards the defenceless Yasmin, she prepared to shoot anyone that approached. To her relief, the enemy who were able to stand rushed at the king instead of the two girls, but her respite turned to horror as the invaders combined their power together and shot lightning directly at the king. His shield flickered and cracked, until the magic streaked through, punching him squarely in the chest. The smell of charred flesh singed the air, and a wave of nausea surged through her. Deep down, she knew they had intended to kill. The king couldn't have survived.

Unable to resist any longer, she sprinted towards Yasmin. The sickening and unmistakable sound of sword sliding into flesh stopped her midway. She spun towards the source, the other side of the royal table, and cringed when the sound repeated as the sword was withdrawn from Javed's side. His dark eyes met hers as he crumpled to his knees, clutching the wound that already stained his sapphire tunic.

Seemingly in slow motion, she summoned an arrow, but the sword was already on its descent towards the prince. A distant scream escaped her lips, and her eyes squeezed shut even as her arrow unleashed, but it was too late. The arrow would hit its target too late for Javed.

She braced herself for the sound, but instead, crackling accompanied a gold flash so bright she could see it through her closed eyelids. A thud sounded, followed by the repugnant stench of burning flesh.

Her eyes flew open, just in time to see her arrow fizzle into thin air. Darien stared wide-eyed at her for a moment, one hand still outstretched, the other gripping a chair, his knuckles white, before he turned his attention to Javed.

Flame erupted in the centre of the hall, announcing the arrival of a dozen palace mages. Led by the Royal Mage, they quickly cast a defensive shield around the diners. The remaining aggressors teleported away immediately, ending the chaos.

Alice finally ran to join Yasmin, only stopping when she rushed to her father. Not able to bring herself to approach the fallen king, Alice hesitated in the midst of the chaos. A few soldiers in black lay unmoving on the floor, but their wounded seemed to have teleported away. Mages in blue were already spreading out amongst the other injured.

From an internal door, Jaime and Jordan sprinted towards Velia, blood-spattered but unhurt. Relief washed through Alice, and she sped forwards, right into Jaime's arms. Velia eyed her suspiciously, but she didn't care. Words tumbled to her lips, and Jaime was bursting to say something too, but before they could celebrate their reunion, Darien's voice interrupted.

"Yasmin, help!" he yelled.

Yasmin didn't respond, except with sobs so distraught, they shook her shoulders. The Royal Mage swept to her side and knelt over the fallen king. But even he couldn't undo this.

"Yasmin!" Darien repeated. "Javed is seriously injured."

Velia darted towards Javed and assessed his wound. "The sword was enchanted. He will need strong magic to heal him."

"Who are you?" Darien asked, his voice full of suspicion.

"I can help him, but I need some potions," Velia responded, her eyes still on Javed.

"I'll take him to my chambers," Darien said. "I have some supplies there and a healing crystal."

"I'll come with you," Velia said, and a moment later the three of them vanished.

Yasmin's sobs loudened, luring Alice forwards to comfort her.

"There's nothing to be done," the Royal Mage pronounced, his voice betraying no emotion. "The king is dead."

Yasmin buried her head in Alice's shoulder. "Why didn't I protect him?"

Overcome by the princess's grief, Alice gently stroked her hair. "It's not your fault. He could have teleported to safety."

Yasmin shook her head. "They must have blocked him and I was too slow to react."

She couldn't think of anything to console her. The invaders had deliberately converged on the king and ignored almost everyone else. It was as if the attackers had broken into the palace just to kill the king.

CHAPTER 46

North Parsa

His mind still on the battle, Jaime followed Jordan up the Royal Tower. Shouting and the clangs of swords rang in his ears, amongst the screams of the dying. He shuddered. It had been chaos. Fire and lightning everywhere. They had been lucky to survive with no magic.

Jordan pulled him forward. "Hurry up, we need to check on Princess Safia and the others."

Jaime stumbled, distracted by the flashes of light and frightened faces darting through his mind. "We could have waited for Torvia to teleport us." He still couldn't get over her disguise, looking so much like Safia, and without the fiery amber eyes he'd become so accustomed to. Her magic was another thing entirely. He'd known she was a gifted mage by South Parsan standards, but she'd rivalled the North Parsan royals during the battle.

Did she even know how powerful she was?

Jordan didn't slow his pace. "We don't know when she'll be done healing Prince Javed. And did you want to wait in that room with the Royal Mage casting suspicious glances at you?"

A shiver shot down Jaime's spine, and he shook his head. "Alice was there though."

"She's taking care of Princess Yasmin. She'll come and find you now she knows you're here." His voice softened. "Thanks for having my back in there."

"No problem. You would have done the same. I wish I had been there for you in the market square in South Parsa. Then we may never have been separated."

"It wouldn't have made much difference. There was only one open guard position, so only one of us could have gone. Besides, you met Torvia and found your way here before I did."

He nodded. After overhearing Safia's brothers, he knew Safia would never have brought them both and Torvia may never have found him if it weren't for Jordan. Still, it didn't dim his regret.

Jordan grinned his approval. "She's rather more gifted than you let on. I would almost mistake her for a North Parsan mage if I didn't know better."

"Yeah, she's incredibly talented."

"But Alice with those fire arrows! That was awesome. How do you think she shot them?"

"Perhaps she learned some magic during her time here."

"But it takes mage blood to perform magic."

Unable to think of a sensible explanation, Jaime frowned. "We should ask her about it when we see her."

"So, what *is* the deal between you and Torvia?" Jordan asked, without the slightest amount of tact.

Annoyed Jordan couldn't show him the same courtesy he had shown Jordan with Emily, Jaime glowered and strode ahead. "What do you mean?"

Jordan grabbed him by the arm and pulled him back. "You know. She's always helping you out, teleporting you around, then she rescued you in the middle of a battle."

Jaime looked his friend in the eye. "She rescued both of us and we'd probably be dead if she hadn't, so you should be grateful."

"I am grateful, but that doesn't change my question," Jordan said seriously.

Jaime hesitated, unsure how to reply. A long time had passed since that tumultuous day when Torvia had kissed him. Nothing had happened since, but Jordan was right. She was going out of her way to help him.

"What is it with you and girls? She clearly likes you. You should do something about it."

His neck tensed. Why was Jordan so annoying and bold all the time? "There's nothing between me and Torvia," he replied firmly.

"You can say it, but we both know that isn't true, don't we?" With an amused grin, Jordan clapped him on the shoulder.

How could Jordan tell? Was it that plainly written on Jaime's face?

"Or are you scared she'll cast a hex on you if you upset her?"

"Just shut up," he said, exasperated now. He turned away and carried on storming up the stairs before Jordan could say anything else.

Safia waited for them outside their rooms, all her composure gone. Puffy-eyed and wringing her hands together as she paced, her distress was painfully evident. "Thank goodness," she declared as soon as she saw them. "Where's Torvia?"

"She's fine. She's helping Prince Javed," Jordan answered.

"What?" Safia shrieked. "What happened to Prince Javed?"

"He was hurt, but Torvia and Prince Darien are healing him," Jaime said quickly, cursing Jordan's bluntness.

"This is a nightmare." Running her hands through her hair, Safia entered the guard chambers, with Jordan and Jaime following behind.

Two guards had made it up to the room, but one was severely injured. The other was trying to dress his wound, but his blood-soaked clothes gave away the seriousness of his condition.

"Tedric!" Jordan exclaimed. He rushed towards the man expertly twisting a bandage around the torso of the other guard. "Is Kasan going to be alright?"

Tedric exhaled loudly and sat back on his haunches, before his hollow eyes met Jordan's. He shrugged in response. Safia knelt by the injured guard, uttering strange words and moving her hands slowly over the wound.

Jaime glanced at Jordan and his expression told Jaime he shared his thoughts. The healing spell wasn't helping. Safia knew it too, though it took her a while to accept. Eventually, she gave up and rested her head in her hands.

They all sat in silence, holding vigil over the injured man, and reflecting on the horrors of the battle. How many lives had been lost and how many more might die from their wounds?

Hope returned with Torvia.

"Is everyone okay?" she asked, surveying the room. As her gaze reached the fallen guard, she whipped out a green crystal and started another healing spell. Slowly, the guard's shallow, rasping gasps deepened, until he breathed normally again.

Torvia got up stiffly, and Jaime edged closer, worrying he might have to catch her again, as he had when she'd teleported too far. However, she remained steady on her feet, looking more emotionally drained than anything else.

"How is Prince Javed?" Safia asked.

Torvia smiled reassuringly at her. "He should be fine. He's got a lot of resting to do, but the worst of the healing is done."

"Good," Safia replied. Her eyes darted to the green gem in Torvia's hand. "Where did you find that healing crystal?"

"Prince Darien had it." Torvia swiftly pocketed the crystal.

Safia frowned. "I hope you intend to return it to him. We can't go stealing from our allies."

"Of course, but first I should attend to the other wounded." She turned to Jaime and Jordan. "I'm glad to see you two are fine. You fight well." Her eyes met Jaime's, flashing amber for a second.

His cheeks warming, Jaime glanced away. Why did Jordan have to say something?

"You two should get some rest," Safia said to Jaime and Jordan. "It's going to be a long night. And remember, when you're talking to anyone in the palace, Torvia is Velia." From the way she spoke it was clear this extended to Alice, which concerned Jaime. She could be trusted, just as the rest of them could.

His limbs heavy, Jaime retreated to his bedroom and slumped on his bed.

"Er, Jaime?" Jordan frowned at him.

"What?"

"You might want to wash first."

He winced, shrugged off his blood-soaked clothes, and headed into the bath chamber.

The next day, the palace was oddly quiet as Jaime and Jordan made their way down the tower, the usual clanking of swords from the courtyard strikingly absent. Glad Jordan had stayed in the palace overnight, Jaime tried to focus on the positives. They'd found Alice and would soon be leaving, just as soon as Prince Darien revealed the way home.

Avoiding the usual breakfast room dedicated to guards of their rank, they stopped by the kitchen to pick up food and took it outside to eat in the ever-sunny garden courtyard.

Not a trace of the previous evening's events remained. The windows were fully repaired, with pristine blue curtains draped behind. Only the surreal quietness gave away any hint that something unusual had happened.

Torvia soon appeared and provided them with an update, though nothing much had changed. Javed still rested in the tower and would for a number of days. Everyone else who could be healed had been, and everything was returning to normal. She didn't point out the obvious exception.

Torvia had already visited the resistance, so Emily was fully informed and wouldn't worry about Jordan's absence.

Exhausted just hearing what Torvia had been up to, Jaime worried how draining it must have been to perform so many healing spells, even before she spent half the night teleporting around the city. He watched her carefully, noticing the dull colour of her eyes and her sluggish movements.

When she looked like she was about to shoot off again, Jaime spoke up. "Sit with us for a while and have something to eat. There's nothing more to do now."

Out of the corner of his eye, he noticed Jordan smirk, and suppressed a frown.

"Aren't there healers in North Parsa?" Jordan asked.

Torvia contemplated their invitation, then dropped onto the wall with them. "There are, but without a healing crystal, they struggle with the most injured, particularly those wounded by magically enhanced weapons."

"Are the crystals really that rare?" Jaime asked, having seen plenty by now.

Torvia nodded. "Healing crystals are, yes. More so than my own red crystal."

"What about Prince Darien's blue one?" Jaime continued, remembering the Royal Mage's reaction.

Torvia smiled. "Probably more rare than that one, though blue crystals are only as valuable as the spell cast on them, and that depends on the mage that performed the incantation. He's lucky to have a talented and powerful sister who can turn it into such an excellent defensive shield."

"What does your red crystal do?" Jordan asked, but Torvia didn't respond.

Jaime traced her gaze to the blonde-haired vision in blue. "Alice!" Jaime jumped up from the bench. Tingles shot through him at her dazzling smile, just the same as he'd always remembered. Life in the palace seemed to have suited her, and the battle had taken no toll at all.

Suddenly heavy, his arms hung limp at his sides. He couldn't decide whether to hug her or not. They'd never had that sort of friendship.

Before he could figure it out, Jordan stepped in and wrapped his arms around her, angling himself so he could grin at Jaime. Jaime knew Jordan was into Emily now, so he was just teasing him, but he couldn't stop every muscle in his body tensing.

"Hey Velia, do you think you can take me to Emily now?" Jordan asked. "I've got something I really need to tell her," he said, pinning Jaime to the spot with his gaze.

Torvia's eyes burned, but she agreed, whilst Jaime resisted the urge to scowl at Jordan himself. Soon they would be going home and everything would return to normal, giving him plenty of time to figure out what to say to Alice.

"Emily's here, too?" Alice said.

"Yeah, and Eliot. Jaime will catch you up," Jordan said before Torvia teleported him away.

Jaime's stomach knotted as he tried to find the right words, but Alice was far too preoccupied with his journey to detect his awkwardness.

"Tell me everything," she demanded.

He obliged as they walked around the garden. He left some bits out about Torvia, of course, and the resistance, but included the rest of everyone's encounters.

"Emily was here in the palace all that time? I never knew! Are you sure the Royal Mage held Eliot captive though, not some other mage?"

"Definitely. He confessed it to Emily. He's an awful person. And you haven't heard what he did to Prince Darien ..." He told her what he had seen in Darien's chambers when the Royal Mage threatened him, and what Emily had seen when she had been arrested.

Alice gasped. "That must have been when Darien was seriously hurt. But we thought he had been attacked off-world somewhere. Are you *sure* that was when that happened?"

"Pretty sure. It was a couple of weeks before the royal ball, so Emily lost her chance to warn you that Prince Darien intended to steal your memories."

Stunned, Alice slumped onto a nearby bench. "All this time and Emily was here, knowing far more than I did. And the Royal Mage did that to Darien." She shuddered. "I knew there was something wrong with him, but I never would have guessed he'd actually hurt Darien."

Jaime sat beside her. "What did happen though, Alice? Did he steal your memories?"

"He tried, but the spell backfired and I saw his memories instead." Her eyes slid to the palace. "He wanted to know about technology from our world. At least at first. But now—" She twisted around to face him. "You're my best friend, right Jaime, apart from Emily? I can tell you anything?"

"Yes, you can tell me." He slid closer, his eyes meeting hers.

She glanced away, staring at a prickly bush with pink flowers and yellow tips. "Never mind, it's probably nothing. I'm glad you made it here though, all of you."

He put his arm around her and gave her a comforting squeeze. It felt so completely natural that he didn't realise he was going to do it until he already had. "So, what have you been doing with yourself all the time you've been stuck in this palace?"

"Well, there have been a lot of formal meals." They both smiled, then became more serious as they remembered the last one.

"Those arrows you were shooting. Were they magic?"

She nodded. "Normally I'm not very good with magic even though practically all I do now is study, but it sort of just came to me when I needed it."

Alice, studying? Magic?

"Don't you need magic in your blood to cast spells?"

She shrugged. "I guess so. I just happen to have it. Maybe there are people on Earth who have the right gene and don't know because you can't use it there. I didn't know I had it until Darien performed the memory spell. It was as much a surprise to him, too." Her features tightened. "The Royal Mage knew right from the start. He witnessed me touch a crystal and make it glow. Though he lied about it later. But if he could happily attack Darien and lie to Yasmin, who knows what else he's capable of?"

Jaime grimaced. "He tested me too, for some reason. Unfortunately, I am without magic." He sighed his disappointment. It would have been fun to try a spell.

Alice smiled sympathetically at him. "Never mind. You make a good soldier. And magic won't matter when we go back home."

He smiled back at her. "It would be fun to see you do some magic. Can you show me some?"

"There's an archery range in one of the courtyards. We can both shoot!" She leapt up and led him there.

They got as far as the storage sheds before she realised they were locked. "Erm, I guess I could try to magically unlock it." She put her hand over the lock and made it crunch, sounding more like the lock breaking rather than unlocking. "Don't tell anyone that was me," she muttered.

"Who am I going to tell?" Jaime grabbed a bow, and they proceeded to the nearest target. "So, what do you do?"

"I visualise holding a bow, focus, then the arrow appears." She demonstrated, but no arrow appeared. "It's difficult to focus," she said apologetically. She tried again, concentrating hard for a considerable time before an arrow burst into flames right before his eyes. However, it soon fizzled out before Alice could send it anywhere.

After a few more attempts, an arrow shot towards the target, but it was nowhere near as accurate as her regular shooting, hitting the inner circle rather than the centre.

"It's a bit more difficult than a real bow and without a strong reason to concentrate," she reasoned. "Why don't you join in?"

Jaime raised his bow, and soon they were back into their normal shooting rhythm, but it felt totally different. There was no competing with flame arrows summoned by magic, regardless of how many more points he scored with his traditional bow.

Soon Alice began to tire, and he noticed that familiar magical draining effect. "Maybe you should switch to a regular bow?" he proposed.

"Yes, that's enough magic practice for one day." With a bounce in her step, she fetched a bow from the shed. Although much better with the corporeal equipment, she struggled a little with the heavier weight, giving him just the edge he needed to beat her. However, it still didn't feel right. The competitive nature they previously shared just wasn't there, and they engaged in none of their former banter.

Had all the time apart changed them too much or had his feelings ruined their relationship?

Could he do anything about it?

He could only hope that once they returned home everything would go back to normal.

Deciding to call it a day, they wandered back through the garden, stopping short at the sight before them. Safia and Darien walked between the trees, deep in conversation.

Safia glimpsed them and steered Darien over towards them. "Would you both like to join us for an early dinner in the garden this evening before sunset?"

They assented before Safia and Darien excused themselves, bidding Alice and Jaime a good afternoon.

"What was all that about?" Jaime asked, wondering why Safia would be talking with Darien. From Darien's sullen expression, he couldn't imagine the discussion had been his idea.

Alice shrugged. "Beats me. I should check on Yasmin. Meet you back here before dinner?"

Jaime nodded. "Sure."

Left alone in the garden, Jaime spent the rest of the day wandering around aimlessly, a little lost with no one to talk to.

In the garden, ready before anyone else, Jaime found a table fully set, the cutlery and plates glinting in the evening sun. It seemed that even dinner outside was going to be a fairly formal affair.

Loitering by one of the fountains, he dipped his hands in the water, savouring the refreshing caress against his sunbeaten skin.

Without warning, the fountain started to flow in the opposite direction, each tier emptying from the bottom up and arcing high into the sky. He stared in fascination at the violation of gravity, but once the water reached the top of the arc, it had nowhere to go but down.

He dived out of the way just in time to avoid getting completely soaked, but he couldn't avoid getting a little splashed.

"Thanks, Torvia," he said, turning to find her behind him. He tried to sound annoyed but couldn't hide the fact he was very pleased to see her.

She smiled before correcting him. "Velia, remember."

"Right, sorry."

"So, what's this about dinner outside?"

"Safia suggested it. Eating breakfast outside was refreshing, and I suppose no one wants to go back inside yet."

At the mention of her name, Safia appeared. "We're going to enjoy a cosy meal this evening. Just the five of us."

Jaime counted the people in his head. Obviously, Alice and Darien had been invited, so Torvia made five. "Is Jordan not coming?"

"No, he's staying with Emily." Torvia's eyes wandered to the five seats. "Who else is joining us?"

"I invited Prince Darien. Princess Yasmin is too upset to leave her chambers," Safia answered.

Torvia's face immediately screwed up. "Why would you invite *him*?"

Safia sighed. "Because he will either be my ally in the north or my husband in the south. He's actually quite agreeable, once you get to know him."

"What?" Torvia blurted out, frowning at Safia.

"Safia and Darien spent some time together today," Jaime explained.

"I see," Torvia said. "Safia, please tell me you're not falling for his charms. He's an evil mage and a typical royal benefitting from the suffering of others."

"Thank you for your concern, Torvia, but I am no innocent little girl with a crush. I am quite aware of his manipulative nature. You have kept me well informed, and I am grateful for your service. All I mean to say is that he could be extremely useful and is already well versed in diplomacy." She moved towards the table. "You also shouldn't be so hasty to judge all mages as evil, Torvia, or you are no better than the so-called higher mages of North Parsa. And I really hope you don't think all royalty benefits from the suffering of others. We cannot help what we are born into."

Torvia flushed. "I didn't mean you, my princess. I meant the corrupt North Parsan system only."

Their conversation was cut short as Prince Darien and Alice arrived, Alice abruptly letting go of Darien to join Jaime. Jaime smiled at her, but he turned his attention turned back to Darien, keen to figure him out.

Dressed in a flattering black tunic, which Jaime supposed the prince considered simple despite its expensive gold embellishments, Darien bowed to Safia. "Thank you for inviting me to dine outside. It was a wonderful idea." Despite his politeness, he seemed more rigid than normal, as if merely going through the motions.

Safia smiled at him. "It is my pleasure after all that has happened. May I enquire as to the condition of my betrothed?"

"He is still resting, but recovering well. I'm sure he will be on his feet again in a few days." Darien's eyes drifted to Alice and Jaime, a small frown marking his face.

Jaime wished there were more people here, so he wouldn't stand out so much. Why was everyone so interested in him? Fortunately, Darien's attention quickly returned to Safia, his frown growing.

"That is good to hear," Safia declared. "If he requires any further healing, Velia is at your service."

Once all the pleasantries were done, they seated themselves in awkward anticipation, and servers appeared out of nowhere to fill the table with an assortment of sizzling meat and vegetables.

Darien inclined his head to Torvia. "You are extremely talented. Where did you study?"

Torvia opened her mouth, but Safia cut in. "Velia has studied on a number of worlds, all partners with South Parsa. I'd be happy to discuss them with you. And share suggestions on how you might improve your existing relationships."

Jaime sucked in a breath, catching a slight smirk from Torvia. What was Safia planning? Surely dragging Darien out here where he was outnumbered, even in his own palace grounds, was no accident.

Darien raised his eyebrows. "That is most considerate of you. I'm sure you have many wonderful ideas. In return, let me introduce you to our finest magical tutors. They would be thrilled to arrange private lessons for you and your guards." He turned to Torvia. "It would be a shame for such skill not to be refined, and we may soon need all the magic we possess to defend Parsa from hostile forces."

Torvia blushed slightly but kept her features stern. Jaime could almost see her mental effort to rein in her temper, and to refrain from informing him she already had access to North Parsa's teachings.

"We have plenty of abilities in the south," Safia chided.

"Are all these abilities nurtured in South Parsa or have you taken them from the lands you conquer?"

Safia's lips pressed together tightly. "South Parsa nurtures every talent, whether from our long-standing allies or former enemies. We don't hold grudges."

"Not when your brother is so effective at demonstrating what will happen if they stand up to you."

Now Torvia turned on Darien, her face a dark storm, causing Jaime to push himself back in his seat. "Prince Ademir is a noble warrior and an effective peacekeeper who obeys the laws of our people, laws that have been agreed upon by many worlds. He is the one who rescued me and the few survivors when my own world was attacked."

Darien scowled. "It's a shame he didn't get there sooner."

"Darien!" Alice snapped, to everyone's surprise.

She turned pink under everyone's stares, but even more surprisingly, Darien bowed his head. "My apologies. My education of

South Parsan history is a little spotty, but I would be glad to hear more first-hand."

Torvia blinked a couple of times, unable to reply, whilst Jaime turned to stare at Alice in disbelief. She was scolding *princes* now and getting away with it.

Safia cleared her throat, her eyes brightening. "I would be delighted to educate you on any history your tutors may have misunderstood. You will find that South Parsa has a lot to offer."

"I look forward to it, but for now I think I will retire. It has been a long day and I must check on my cousin."

Safia smiled. "Of course. Please pass on my love."

Alice stood with Darien, her brow furrowed. "Will you teleport me to Yasmin?"

Darien bowed his head and held out his arm. Jaime tensed, wanting to object, but he really didn't want to cause a scene with a volatile magical royal. Even if he was inclined to tell Alice what to do, she had magic now and seemed perfectly at ease giving Darien orders, orders which he followed without hesitation. Still, Jaime stood to wish her goodnight.

Alice's eyes widened. "Goodnight, Jaime. I'll see you tomorrow."

He nodded. "Sleep tight."

A second later they were gone, and Jaime slumped back into his seat. He turned just in time to see Safia and Torvia smiling at each other, before Safia herself retired.

"So that's Alice then," Torvia said, reminding Jaime this was the first time they had met. Maybe he should have done a better job of introducing them.

"Yeah. What did you think of her?" he asked.

Torvia hesitated. "Well, she didn't say much, but she's pretty in an odd sort of way."

Jaime blinked. Perhaps it was a bit awkward to be asking Torvia what she thought of Alice, but he had always been straight with Torvia. She didn't seem angry at least, so he continued. "What do you mean, odd?"

She slid out of her seat and stretched her legs. "Well, she has bright yellow hair."

"Oh, I suppose that's unusual here. But what else did you think?" It was much easier to talk to Torvia about Alice, rather than with Jordan, and he valued Torvia's opinion immensely.

"I guess I can understand why you like her. You should tell her, so you can find out how she feels." She strolled around the table to him. "Shall I teleport you back to your room or would you prefer to walk?"

He hesitated, wanting to talk more, but he supposed Torvia was right. He needed to speak to Alice. "I'd appreciate it if you teleported me."

CHAPTER 47
NORTH PARSA

The following morning, Alice sat with Yasmin in silence, debating what she could say to cheer her up. Yasmin blamed herself for her father's death and nothing Alice said could convince her otherwise.

Yasmin wasn't the only person she was worried about. Darien had acted quite peculiarly the previous evening, his charm slipping away. Safia had no doubt provoked him on purpose, but was there any truth to his words? Could the southerners be conquerors?

She'd worried about the northerners conquering their neighbours until Javed had set her mind at rest, but she'd never thought much about the south. They were known for their army, after all. And they weren't concerned about being attacked themselves.

A knock at the door disrupted her thoughts. Yasmin stared absent-mindedly out of the window, so Alice headed over to open the door.

Darien dropped into a flamboyant bow, somewhat over the top for most situations, but Alice smiled, noticing the colour had returned to his skin. The battle must have hit him hard.

Yasmin gently brushed Alice's side as she materialised beside her. "How is Javed?"

"He is recovering well. He'll be on his feet in a day or two."

Yasmin's face contorted with regret. "Were you hurt?"

He shook his head. "Your crystal protected me well. I suffered only a mild headache."

She nodded, and her voice dropped to a whisper. "I'm sorry."

Darien's brow wrinkled. "Why are you sorry?"

"I should have protected you all better."

"We were severely outnumbered, Yasmin, and caught by surprise. You did a fabulous job fighting them off." He crossed his arms. "They should never have reached the palace."

"How did they?"

"It looks like a few arrived ahead undetected and disabled the portal guards before the rest of them came through. Then they teleported inside the palace walls, stunned the guards on duty and let their comrades sneak in."

Yasmin's eyes widened. "Navid!"

"He's fine, Yasmin. He's off-world on a mission."

She sagged into Alice's side, and Alice put her arm around her.

Darien stepped closer. "I'm glad you're both alright." His eyes shifted to Alice. "It was very brave of you to return. But a little reckless. You could have been hurt."

She squared her shoulders. "You could have been killed. That didn't stop you fighting."

"This is my kingdom, my family. We don't flee from our enemies."

"And I don't abandon my friends when they're attacked." Without thinking, she rubbed Yasmin's shoulder.

Yasmin placed her hand over Alice's, holding it in place. "Who were they? They don't fit the Iybryrian description."

"No. But they did target royals. That's what the Iybryrians did last time," Darien said. "Though their magic doesn't fit ..." He rubbed his jaw. "I am still investigating and I have picked up Javed's duties temporarily—"

Yasmin straightened, shifting her weight off Alice. "Then you shouldn't waste time here. Find out who killed Father."

He nodded and swiftly departed.

Alice took Yasmin's hand and led her back to her favourite chair. "What can I do, Yasmin?"

Before she could answer, the Royal Mage appeared before them, concern in his eyes. "Yasmin, how are you coping?"

"It's my fault, Uncle. I was there and I should have protected Father, but I didn't." She inhaled sharply, her shoulders shaking.

The Royal Mage moved closer to Yasmin. "It's not your fault, Yasmin. Those soldiers were clearly after the king and would have stopped at nothing to get to him. I'm just glad you're unhurt."

"But why would they go after the king? What do they gain from his death? I don't even know who they were. They were nothing like the armies that have attacked Parsa in the past."

He shook his head. "It may be someone opposed to the treaty. Prince Javed was seriously hurt too, so it may have been their intention to prevent the marriage and stop the union between the north and the south. There are many worlds that would benefit from a weaker Parsa."

"But they knew exactly when to attack and how to reach the palace undetected!"

"True. Perhaps an insider lurks within the palace. Someone who spends a lot of time off-world and has something to gain by the death of the king." The Royal Mage brushed his hand across the foreign silks of one of Yasmin's designs.

Alice's mind instantly jumped to Darien.

She shook her head, rejecting those thoughts. The Royal Mage might suspect him, but there was no way she could believe Darien would arrange the murder of his father or his cousin, not even for the crown he coveted.

"If there is anything I can do to help you, let me know, Yasmin. You too, Alice. I hear your magic is coming along nicely." Dark eyes burned into hers as he dematerialised, replaced by molten rings.

Alice swallowed nervously. Was he trying to unsettle her? Was this because she'd encouraged Yasmin to stand up for Navid?

She didn't have much time to think about it before Jaime and Velia visited. A welcome relief from the politics and stresses of the palace, Jaime greeted her with a smile. However, Velia didn't seem to like her, and kept sneaking suspicious glances at her.

Wondering if her terrible mage abilities were to blame, she envied Velia's apparent ease with magic. Even without constant studying, Velia rivalled at least Darien's skill and could be no older than Yasmin.

"How's it going?" Jaime asked, plonking down next to Alice.

She shrugged. "The Royal Mage thinks there's an insider in the palace who helped the attackers kill the king and who wants to stop the alliance."

"Huh, that guy gives me the creeps. I wouldn't trust anything he says." Jaime's eyes darted to Yasmin. "Sorry."

Lost in thought, Yasmin ignored him.

Velia leaned back against the wall, one foot crossed over the other. "He does have a point. The soldiers were obviously after the king and Javed was seriously injured. It makes sense to assume they aimed to stop the alliance. The palace is usually better defended. The king should never have been at risk."

"But there must have been an easier way to stop the alliance," Jaime said, frowning at Velia.

Alice was inclined to agree with him. Surely Safia was the easier target, especially when she travelled through the desert with her small escort. However, she didn't feel like voicing that theory with Velia in the room.

Yasmin shook her head. "Father rarely left the palace. It was the only way to get both of them at the same time."

"No one went after Princess Safia," Jaime said quietly.

"Perhaps that was Prince Darien's desperate attempt to secure the North Parsan throne," Velia suggested. "With Prince Javed out of the way, the Royal Mage would have no one else to put on the throne, and Darien wouldn't be pressured into marrying Safia."

Alice frowned at her, but couldn't think of a reasonable counterargument, especially as she had already thought the same thing. As king, he'd probably get more say over who he married, and he'd not be free to accompany Safia south.

But would he kill his father just to get out of a marriage? His uncle could still force him to go through with it.

Yasmin leapt to her feet. "What?! Darien would never do something like that. And what do you mean he wouldn't be pressured into marrying Javed's bride? What's going on?"

Alice glanced at Jaime, but Velia explained first. "Jaime overheard the Royal Mage and Prince Darien plotting. Your uncle doesn't think Javed would make a good ruler in the south and wanted Darien to take his place, but Darien refused."

"That's nonsense." Yasmin pouted, turning to Jaime.

"It's true, Yasmin," Jaime said softly.

Yasmin eyed Jaime with suspicion, so Alice stepped in. "But Darien has been helping Javed."

"If you say so, but he's a terrible healer for someone with an extremely rare healing crystal," Velia argued.

"Darien wouldn't kill all those people," Yasmin said defiantly. "He's friends with a lot of the portal police and the soldiers. He introduced me to Navid!"

"But he knew Navid wasn't there to get hurt," Alice said quietly. She didn't want to believe Darien capable of such a thing, but he seemed to be the one person who stood to gain the most and lose nothing. What if the business he'd been keen to attend to before dinner was to make final arrangements?

"Remember when he was knocked to the ground, and no one attacked him?" Velia said.

"Javed was protecting him," Yasmin countered, but she sounded unsure. She looked at Alice for confirmation.

Unable to think of any other explanation now, Alice hesitated. So much had been going on, she'd not been focusing on Darien alone. "He had the crystal, Yasmin. He shouldn't have been hurt in the first place." If they really had the power to defeat Yasmin's crystal, the fight ought to have been over much quicker. There could be no other explanation, but why had Darien defended Javed at the last moment?

The room fell into silence. It all fitted. Darien's frequent trips off-world, his unyielding desire for the throne, the fact he had been ignored during the attack and had conveniently sent his friend out of harm's way at just the right time.

"I don't believe it," Yasmin said meekly, then started sobbing.

"Should we do something?" Jaime asked. "I mean, he's about to become king."

"What can we do?" Alice asked, looking around the room.

"Someone could tell the Royal Mage," Jaime suggested, glancing at Yasmin.

"What would that achieve? He probably already suspects Darien," Alice said, causing Jaime's face to fall.

Velia took a deep breath. "We could make sure the Royal Mage's plan goes ahead and Darien marries Safia. At least then he wouldn't get the northern throne. Safia will be able to deal with his ambition in South Parsa."

Yasmin frowned. "Then who would the northern throne go to?"

Velia, Alice, and Jaime all replied at once. "Prince Javed."

Yasmin snorted her disapproval. "That's absurd. He could never ascend the throne ahead of Darien."

"Er, Yasmin, the Royal Mage possesses evidence your father stole the throne from Javed, so he is the rightful heir," Jaime said, his voice low.

"Now you're just being silly."

Velia glanced at Jaime. "It doesn't matter anyway. It's what the Royal Mage wants."

Yasmin raised her voice, speaking with the authoritative air of a princess used to getting her way. "I have a stronger right to the throne than Javed, and the Royal Mage won't be disappointed in me. Perhaps I should take the throne."

"Safia rules in the south above her two brothers. Why not have a queen on the throne in the north?" Velia replied with a smile.

Alice contemplated Velia again. Maybe she wasn't that bad after all.

Yasmin beamed at Alice. "You could be my Royal Mage when my uncle retires."

Shocked, Alice opened her mouth to protest, but Jaime replied for her. "Er, Yasmin, we'll all be going home as soon as Officer Gul returns with directions to our world."

Yasmin glared at him. "Not if I order him not to tell you." She turned to Alice, her eyes pleading. "You should stay, Alice. You can live in the palace with me and become an accomplished mage, like you were born to be. If you go back to your world, you won't be able to use any magic at all."

Suppressing the rising guilt, Alice smiled sympathetically back, almost tempted despite the danger.

They carried on debating the dilemma for some time, but no one came up with a different viewpoint. They merely sifted through the same information again until they became convinced it made sense.

Who else had more to gain than Darien? And who could be more desperate?

"I shall inform Safia of the situation and our suggestion," Velia said finally.

When Alice and Yasmin arrived in the Grand Hall for dinner, only the Royal Mage and Darien occupied the vast space, conversing quietly with guarded expressions. At the girls' entrance, they split apart, taking their seats, the Royal Mage nodding to Yasmin as he whipped his plain golden cloak behind him.

Completely in black, aside from a small golden lion on his tunic, Darien took his seat more slowly, staring off into the distance with a pained expression. Alice's heart lurched. The outfit reminded her of the first time she had seen him wear black, and the memory of his confused face after they had kissed rose to the surface.

How could this man have anything to do with his father's murder? He was just a young man struggling with the loss of his father and almost his cousin.

Deciding it wouldn't hurt to show a little kindness, she sat next to Darien, eliciting a look of surprise from Yasmin.

Darien's eyes flicked to her, his expression unreadable, before he resumed staring ahead absent-mindedly. Only Safia's entrance drew his attention. There was something unsettling about the way he stared at the South Parsan princess, almost as if he feared her.

Was this unusual attitude due to his mourning, the half-finished plot or just his reluctance to marry her?

Alice took a deep breath, the lingering incense failing to calm her, nor Jaime and Jordan's presence at the end of the table. At least they had each other to draw strength from. Who did Yasmin and Darien have if they couldn't get along?

People filtered in to occupy the other tables, haphazard in their attire. Some wore plain clothes, but others again wore their finest. The room felt torn in half, lost and leaderless.

In deep blue, Ahmad joined the table, nodding his respect to Darien before taking a seat on his other side. At least that was one person who showed Darien some support.

Insisting Safia sit with him, the Royal Mage seemed unfazed, and ignoring his nephew's peculiar behaviour, he began to discuss politics before the food was served. "Princess Safia, the recent events have been a tragedy, but it is my strongest desire to uphold the treaty the king worked so hard for. However, I am concerned Prince Javed will take a long time to heal and won't be able to join you in the south for a considerable time. Perhaps we should consider an alternative."

Alice shifted nervously in her seat, and she wasn't the only one. Velia fixed her eyes on Darien, barely blinking.

"I am happy to wait for my prince to recover," Safia declared, before taking a sip of her wine.

Darien's eyes twitched, then moved to his uncle.

The Royal Mage pursed his lips. "That is extremely kind of you, but South Parsa needs a leader, and you have been absent so long already. I also fear Prince Javed may not be up to the dangers of South Parsa and will not be able to protect you."

"My brothers and the council of elders are capable of keeping order without me for however long is required, and I have numerous guards to protect me."

Alice admired her tenacity, but there was no way Safia could risk defying the Royal Mage, not with his power to intervene.

"That is very trusting of you," the Royal Mage replied with a hint of annoyance. "Perhaps you would be more enthusiastic if I were to provide assurance that you have my deepest respect, by offering an even more advantageous suitor?"

Darien tensed, clenching his fists under the table.

Alice glanced around at the frozen faces of their companions. Everyone knew exactly what was coming, and the air was thick with anticipation. She clearly wasn't the only one expecting an explosive outburst.

"More advantageous than the cousin of the heir to the North Parsan throne?" Safia asked innocently, not looking at Darien once.

"Yes, someone with stronger magic in their blood, my own blood. Prince Darien."

Silence filled the room. Despite knowing about the plot for some time, the words still sounded wrong. No one spoke, perhaps waiting for someone to yell treason and stop the nonsense. But everyone knew that was not going to happen.

Eventually, Safia broke the silence, first taking a sip from her glass. "That would indeed be a more advantageous marriage, but what about the throne of the north?"

"After a period of mourning, we may consider Prince Javed for the role. He is the most suitable candidate after Prince Darien. Consider it an affirmation that we view the south as equal to the north."

Alice bristled. That wasn't what the king had decided. He'd wanted Darien to rule both kingdoms. Had he not discussed it with the Royal Mage? Or had the Royal Mage disagreed and decided to get rid of the king? It would certainly suit his plans for control of both kingdoms.

Darien ground his teeth, but still said nothing.

"Then you accept my proposal?" the Royal Mage asked, failing to mask his surprise at Safia's sudden acceptance of Prince Darien.

"I do."

He hesitated for a moment. "You have no further concerns?"

"Should I?" Safia looked straight at him, seemingly enjoying confusing the Royal Mage.

"I expected you might have some, particularly concerning his young age, but I see you are more open-minded than I anticipated."

Alice frowned, confused. His tone almost sounded disappointed. Did he not want Darien to marry Safia after all?

"Darien is old enough for marriage in the south. He will be given duties appropriate for his age."

Clearly uncomfortable, Ahmad coughed. "Our rules dictate that a ruler cannot be crowned until he turns twenty-one. Prince Darien is only eighteen."

Safia turned her warm smile on him. "Your rules allow an underage prince to be crowned with a regent. He will have plenty of advice in the south."

All eyes turned to Darien. It was extremely unusual for him so be so quiet, and given what people had told her about his outbursts when enraged, Alice expected something to happen.

"Prince Darien, do you consent to the new arrangement?" the Royal Mage asked in a tone he might have used when discussing place settings for dinner, rather than whether Darien would give up his throne, his future, marry an almost complete stranger and move halfway across the world.

The tension palpable, it felt like hours passed before Darien answered, but he calmly replied. "It is my duty to serve all of Parsa, and I strongly support the alliance my father worked so hard for. If I must take my cousin's place to uphold it, then I will do so."

"I can't believe Darien agreed to give up the throne," Yasmin exclaimed, once they returned to her chambers.

Alice nodded her agreement. "He didn't have much choice though, did he?" If he'd disagreed with the Royal Mage so openly, he'd have wound up king of nothing.

"I can't believe my uncle would give the throne to Javed, either. Why does this alliance need a marriage, anyway?" Yasmin waved a hand, knocking the mannequins aside.

Alice raised an eyebrow. Was Yasmin angry at her uncle's decision? "I guess that makes it harder to break. Do you think we should check on Javed?"

"You don't think Darien would harm him, do you?"

Alice bit her lip, before Yasmin grabbed her arm and teleported them outside Javed's chambers.

Shouting reached them even from the corridor, and Alice and Yasmin froze.

"You can't marry Safia. She is my bride!" Javed shouted.

"I don't want to marry her. I'm being forced to!"

"You don't even care about her, you only care about power, the throne and magic."

Alice raised her eyebrows at this assessment from his own cousin.

"I'm not trying to steal her away from you. I'm being ordered to uphold the alliance. I'm going to lose my throne, everything I've ever worked for and everyone I care about."

"We've worked for the same things." Distress replaced the anger in Javed's voice. "The south was *my* opportunity to rule. A kingdom of *my* own. And Princess Safia was keen to implement my ideas. I've already made promises."

"You're going to be the king of North Parsa, Javed!"

"I don't want to be king here. I want to marry the woman I am promised to. I am going to the Royal Mage straight away to sort this out."

"No, you can't! This is what the Royal Mage wants. Do you think I would ever agree to this if he hadn't threatened to destroy me?"

Yasmin tensed, her whole body alert. Fire roared from the torches, turning the walls more orange than blue.

"What do you mean?" Javed asked, more calmly now.

"He gets what he wants by threatening people, and those who don't do what he wants disappear. Or have their memories altered. He won't stop until he's removed all opposition and extended North Parsan rule over the south. That is what he wants me to do. To force our laws upon Princess Safia and seize control of their portals."

"You can't! Princess Safia trusts us."

"I won't have much choice."

Yasmin crossed her arms, frowning her disagreement, as the flames leapt higher. Alice winced at the heat, sweat already clinging to her, but Yasmin had to hear.

"That's absurd. You're his nephew. He wouldn't do anything to you."

"He would if I challenged his will. And he will do the same to you if you don't do as he says."

As Darien's anger subsided, his tone became more pleading. "Javed, *please* listen to me. You must not challenge him. He only needs one of us. If something were to happen to one of us, the other would sit on the northern throne and he would marry Safia himself."

"That's ridiculous!"

Darien's tone turned cold. "Safia must know it too, or she never would have accepted me so readily."

Suddenly, all the torches went out, plunging the corridor into darkness.

"Then all you need to do to get your throne is kill me," Javed deduced.

"Now you put it that way, it sounds simple."

Alice's skin bristled. Darien talked so calmly about murder, but he couldn't be serious. Javed certainly didn't sound worried.

"Simple? You couldn't beat me in a sword fight if I had one leg!"

"It's a good thing I have magic to fall back on then."

"Seriously though, I'm not giving up Safia. We must find a way around this," Javed declared, in a tone that invited no objections.

"There isn't one."

The room fell silent, and Alice looked back at Yasmin, illuminated only by starlight. Leaning against the wall, her head was bowed and her lips tightly drawn.

"Yasmin?"

Yasmin looked up at her, her lashes heavy. "My uncle attacked my brother, didn't he? That's why he needed the protective crystal."

And neither of them told you, Alice wanted to say. They might be protecting her, but how could she protect herself if she didn't even know what was going on in her own palace?

Not that Alice was much better. She hadn't even told Yasmin her uncle had been holding Eliot in the tower. But they'd surely both make excuses for that. Resisting a shudder, she nodded and put her arm around the princess. "I'm sorry, Yasmin."

"No wonder he wants to send Darien away." Yasmin looked extremely conflicted as she sank into her. "I can't imagine what Darien could have done to upset him so much."

Alice winced. Was it so difficult for her to believe her beloved uncle was in the wrong? Or was Alice wrong about Darien? After all, Yasmin knew them best.

CHAPTER 48
NORTH PARSA

Jordan winced at Kasan's scar. "Shouldn't magic have healed that?"

Kasan dropped his tunic. "The sword was imbued with strong magic. It will take time to heal completely."

"Torvia has a healing crystal. She could look at it again—"

Kasan turned away and slipped on his boots. "Torvia has done enough. Healing everyone must have exhausted her."

"She's doing fine. It will be little effort for her."

Unusually serious, Tedric fetched Kasan's sword. "Torvia needs to conserve her strength to protect Safia. There are few of us left, now."

"There's not a lot we can do against mages like that," Kasan said. The strongest mage of Safia's guards, aside from Torvia, Kasan had fought valiantly, but almost been killed. How could they all rely solely on Torvia in a place like this?

Tedric released a sigh. "We shouldn't need to do anything. Safia is a skilled negotiator. With Darien as a husband, she'll be much better protected."

Jordan grimaced. "I don't trust that *prince*. And he can't even stand up to his own uncle."

Kasan strapped his sword to his side. "His power will grow and one day he might be able to challenge him. With Safia's guidance, he could be a decent king."

Jordan snorted. "Safia can do better."

"No, she can't. No one, on any world, matches his bloodline."

Jordan couldn't stop disgust twisting his features. "Safia doesn't care about blood."

"She cares about protecting her people, and the magic in his blood can topple an army."

"Yasmin's is stronger."

Tedric laughed. "The Royal Mage would never agree to that union. He barely lets her out of the palace."

"But you think he'll let his nephew rule half a world away?"

"That's an interesting question," Safia said.

Jordan whirled as Tedric and Kasan bowed to their princess. Safia inclined her head in return. "Are you feeling well again, Kasan?"

Kasan gripped his sword. "I am ready to return to my duties."

Safia smiled. "Good. Take Tedric for some exercise. I want to talk to Jordan."

Jordan straightened. "How may I be of service?"

Safia held out her arm. "Join me for a walk."

A moment later they ambled through pink and yellow blossoms, the delicate violet and peony fragrances reminding him of his mother's expensive perfumes. His heart clenched at the memory, but it was pleasant nonetheless. She'd be proud to see him now, escorting a princess in a foreign kingdom.

Rounding a prickly bush with purple needles, they spotted Jaime and Torvia, too absorbed in knife throwing to notice their approach.

Safia cleared her throat. "I hope you have permission to throw those here."

Torvia shrugged. "There are so many trees here and so few people, they'll never notice."

Jordan ambled closer to Jaime. "Learning anything useful?"

Jaime shook his head. "Knife throwing is nothing like archery or fencing. I just don't have the talent for it."

Torvia handed him a knife. "You just need more practice."

"I'll have a go," Jordan said eagerly, taking a knife from Torvia. He threw it at the tree Torvia had been aiming at, and it clattered off harmlessly.

"Not so easy, is it?" Jaime said with a grin.

Jordan shoved him away. "I bet it wouldn't take me long to learn."

Safia smiled. "Torvia has spent years refining her talents, and she has magic to help aim."

A frown formed on Torvia's face. "I don't use magic to aim. Knives and daggers are for worlds without magic."

Safia laughed. "Don't ever insult Torvia's abilities." She turned to Jordan, her face becoming more serious. "Jordan raised a good question."

Jordan's mind went blank. "What did I say?"

"You asked whether the Royal Mage would let his nephew rule half a world away. He did seem surprised at my agreement yesterday, so perhaps he will not go through with the arrangement."

Jordan scowled. Dishonourable northerners. "But they both agreed."

Safia glanced around, then beckoned them to follow her through the garden. "The North Parsans have always been against marrying a direct heir to a South Parsan. They don't want us to have a strong claim on the northern throne. I suspect the Royal Mage thought I would refuse Darien after declaring that Javed would inherit the northern throne and now he needs another excuse to call off the betrothal. Darien isn't *quite* as committed to the Royal Mage's plans as he needs him to be. But I don't need Darien to be obedient. With some gentle guidance, he will make a fine king."

"But he bullied Darien into it! Jaime heard him."

Safia nodded. "Darien is very resistant to the idea. There is probably little else the Royal Mage can threaten him with. At least that was the case when his father was alive. Now the Royal Mage's rule over the north is absolute. Whilst Darien remains here, he has little choice but to obey him."

Jordan grinned. "Then you probably won't have to marry Darien after all."

Safia turned to him with an expression he couldn't read. "Darien is promised to me, and I shan't leave without him."

"But, he's— he doesn't want to marry."

"He has agreed. And I shall talk him around. There is no rush."

"What about Javed? You liked him."

"I do." She sighed. "But this is a more advantageous arrangement. For both of us."

Jordan grimaced. "But—"

Jaime grabbed his arm. "Would you rather Safia marry the Royal Mage?"

Jordan shook his head vigorously. "Javed will heal."

Safia smiled. "Your concern is touching, Jordan. But I must put my people first. A powerful mage for a husband will ensure the future of my family and my people."

Jordan's hands flew to his head. He couldn't believe what he was hearing. He turned to Torvia. "You don't think Darien is trustworthy."

"Certainly not, but it is Safia's choice. Even if he is a poor husband, depriving the north of his power is a victory for the south."

Safia raised an eyebrow. "He will not be a poor husband. And we will not be depriving the north of anything."

Torvia's eyes widened. "You can't let him stay here."

"We will both go where our people need us." She turned to Jaime. "Now, Jaime, will you invite Alice to talk with us?"

"Alice?"

Safia smiled. "No doubt you've noticed her friendship with Darien. If there is anything romantic there, then I might have to call off this betrothal."

Jaime paled. "There's nothing romantic going on between them."

"I'm sure there isn't, but I would like to rule that out as a cause for Darien's resistance."

Jaime gulped, his devastation written all over his face.

Jordan put his arm around Jaime's shoulders. "We'll ask her right away, if Torvia will teleport us."

Torvia nodded, watching Jaime closely.

"She'll be with Yasmin," Jaime said quietly.

Torvia grabbed both their arms and teleported them directly to Yasmin's chambers.

"Wait," Jordan said, before Torvia knocked on the door. He glanced at Jaime. "It might be better if I ask."

Jaime frowned. "She's my friend. I'll ask her. Wait with Torvia."

Jordan shrugged as Jaime went inside, then turned to Torvia. "Sorry about him. He can be a bit clueless."

Torvia leaned back against the wall, propping one leg up. "You think there *is* something romantic between Darien and Alice?"

"Er, I don't know about that. But Jaime is the last person to know when a girl likes him. If he's disappointed you, I'm sorry."

A smirk tugged at Torvia's lips. "Jaime is one of the few people who hasn't let me down. Why would you think he had?"

Jordan's cheeks warmed. "I, er … thought you might be interested in him."

Torvia smiled. "He is interesting. But I don't have much time for romance in my line of work."

"Right, sorry. Thanks, er, for rescuing us during the battle."

She nodded. "You're welcome."

Jaime emerged from Yasmin's chambers, Alice beside him. She turned curious eyes to Torvia. "Jaime said Princess Safia wanted to talk with me?"

Torvia pushed herself away from the wall. "I can teleport you to her."

Jordan shoved forward. "Us too."

Torvia raised an eyebrow. "Alright. Hold on to my arm."

Safia was sitting beside a fountain when they reappeared, the water gently tinkling against ochre stone as it wound its way around a crystal-eyed lion. She smiled and dipped her head to Alice. "Thank you for joining me, Alice."

"It sounded important." She turned to Torvia. "Will you teleport me to Emily afterwards?"

Torvia stiffened, her expression becoming guarded. "I'm sorry. Emily is in a safe house. I can't take you there."

Jaime made to intervene, so Jordan pulled him back. "I'll pass on any message."

Alice shook her head. "It's not important. I just wanted to see her."

Torvia's features softened. "I'll see if she will visit the palace."

"It's not safe for her here," Jordan said, his voice full of alarm.

Jaime frowned at him. "Velia won't put her in danger."

Jordan shook his head in disbelief. Torvia had brought her back to the palace before, and let her roam through the city alone, despite the threat of exile if she'd been discovered. That sentence still hadn't been overturned, and he wasn't going to count on Princess Yasmin to step in if Emily got caught again.

Safia gestured for Alice to join her. "I won't take much of your time, but we haven't had a chance to talk."

Keen to hear the conversation, Jordan quietened his anger, but this was probably something Jaime didn't want to hear. He turned to his friend, speaking up. "Are you sure you don't want to carry on practising knife throwing?"

Luckily, Torvia caught his meaning, and ignoring his scowl, escorted Jaime back into the trees.

Alice frowned after him. "Is Jaime okay? He doesn't really like knife throwing."

Jordan shook his head. How did Alice know that? And not know how he felt?

"Alice," Safia said. "I asked you here because I need to talk to you about Darien."

Alice stiffened. "What about him?"

"You were there yesterday. Darien wasn't keen on the marriage arrangement. If he is to be my husband, I need to understand why." She took Alice's hand. "If there is anything romantic between you, now is the time to say."

Alice withdrew her hand sharply, and pink spread across her cheeks. "He's a North Parsan prince. He's not allowed to have romances."

Safia smiled warmly. "He is also a young man and you are a beautiful girl. Feelings can't be stopped by palace protocol."

Alice shook her head. "He is perfectly well behaved. At least in that regard."

"I am pleased to hear it. Do you know, then, what might be holding him back?"

Alice twisted her hands together in her lap. "He's so young—"

"That doesn't stop him venturing off on his own regularly."

"Only for a day or two at a time. He always returns." She bit her lip. "He probably just doesn't want to be forced from his home. He has a strong bond with Yasmin as well."

Safia nodded. "Thank you, Alice. The happiness of my future husband concerns me greatly. I will do my best to make the transition easier for him."

"Is there anything else you want to know?"

"That is plenty." Safia offered her arm. "I will return you to Yasmin, if that is what you wish."

Alice shook her head, glancing into the trees. "I'll stay and catch up with Jaime." With an awkward dip of the head, she swiftly disappeared.

Jordan sighed his relief. "Jaime will be happy."

Safia raised an eyebrow. "She was hiding something. She feels deeply for him, even if there is nothing romantic going on."

Jordan grimaced. "What will you do?"

"I now know what is holding Darien back. Alice has given me a great gift. It is up to me to make the most of it."

Full of admiration for Safia, Jordan caught up with Jaime, Alice and Torvia.

Alice hurled a knife into the trunk with a deep thud as he approached.

Torvia grinned appreciatively. "You're a natural, Alice."

"I've had some practice." Alice lowered her hand. "Velia, do you know anything about the soldiers who attacked?"

A shadow of fear swept across her face. "They're not from Parsa, but they are familiar."

Jaime edged closer to her, concern in his voice. "You've seen them before?"

Jordan rolled his eyes. How did no one else see his affection for her?

Torvia nodded. "They reminded me of the soldiers who attacked my birth-world. It was a long time ago, but their magic is familiar, and their tactics."

"You can tell mages apart by their magic?" Jordan asked.

"Usually. North Parsans favour blue in their spells. South Parsans naturally cast red lightning, if they are skilled enough to cast it. Shields are always sapphire if cast using our magic. But I've seen emerald when the Iybryrian assassins came for our royals."

Alice leaned closer, her voice a whisper. "Their shields were blue. They can't be Iybryrians."

"It is unlikely."

Jordan shook his head. "Darien's lightning was gold." He remembered that clearly.

"Darien is odd." Torvia shrugged. "He embraces magic from other worlds." She twirled a knife in her hand. "Many mages can change the colour of their spells, but some of them wouldn't be so skilled. But fire, lightning, concussive blasts ... that's standard North Parsan magic."

Alice paled. "It *was* an inside job?"

"Not necessarily. Over the centuries, mages have left and taken their magic with them."

"Tell us more about the soldiers who attacked your world, Velia," Jaime said softly. "Could they be linked to North Parsa?"

Torvia shook her head. "I can't see how. The Royal Mage fought them. Safia said he went there looking for someone, but we never found out who. If he knew who the soldiers were, he would have punished them. He doesn't forgive easily."

Jordan frowned. "So we have no idea who they were or if they might come back?"

"They took heavy casualties. They probably won't be coming back soon."

Jordan nodded. "I hope Darien hurries up and tells us how to go home, or I'm going to be paying him a visit."

Jaime shook his head. "You wouldn't get anywhere near him."

"You were sneaking through his rooms!"

"And I almost wish I hadn't. If the Royal Mage had caught me—" Jordan shuddered. "Good point."

Alice sighed. "I'll ask him if he doesn't tell us soon. But he does have a lot on his mind."

Jordan raised an eyebrow. Safia might have been right about Alice having feelings for Darien.

CHAPTER 49

NORTH PARSA

The following morning, a beautiful blue flower with silver tips appeared in Alice's room, one she recognised from a tree in the garden.

An invitation?

It could only be from Darien, but she couldn't decide what she thought of him at the moment. On the one hand, he had been nothing but nice to her except for that one mistake, and now she had seen an invading magical force for herself, she understood why he would be so determined to find technology to defend Parsa. On the other hand, he might have been responsible for the attack to advance his own interests.

It had made so much sense when she had discussed it with the others, but when alone, she just couldn't believe it. She'd seen him with Javed – there was no way he'd arrange to have him killed, no matter how his uncle pressured him.

Meeting Darien in the garden would also mean a long climb down the tower. Still, it would be a welcome break from Yasmin's grief, and she could use it as an opportunity to ask for news about the portal home. When Jaime had mentioned it, she hadn't thought it right to bring up with Darien, but she didn't want them to be in danger any longer than necessary.

After taking her time, she eventually reached the garden and meandered around to the unusual blue tree, its silver tips glistening in the morning sun. No one lingered there, but when she approached, she felt Darien's familiar presence behind her. She plucked another flower from the tree before slowly turning to greet him.

Still wearing a black tunic and a solemn expression, he forced a smile and dropped into a flamboyant bow.

"Is there a special reason you wanted to meet in the garden?" she asked.

"I thought it might get you away from Yasmin. I have some news she won't like. I also have a favour to ask."

Alice's mouth dropped open. "You want a favour from me?"

"More a favour for yourself."

Not bothering to hide her annoyance, she frowned. "What do you want?"

"I want you to stay, Alice. You owe it to yourself. You were born to be here. You fit in perfectly. With your golden hair and blue eyes, you embody our royal colours. Stay here and become my queen."

Alice's heart stopped. "What?!" Nothing could have prepared her for that. "But you're already promised to Princess Safia."

"That can change if you want it to. What are you going back to that is better than becoming queen of a magical kingdom and truly becoming a sister to Yasmin? You'd have every resource at your disposal to discover the limits of your power."

Her mind racing, she tried to think of a response. How could he ask her to forget her home, her family, her friends? Disappear without a word and become trapped here instead?

Fixing her with his gaze, he took her hands. "Think about what you really want, Alice. You could have anything here. All you have to do is agree to become my queen."

Trapped in those depths of liquid cocoa, her heart pounded and old feelings started to return. "No, this is ridiculous, I'm not becoming your queen." She pulled away. Even if she were certain of his intentions, there was no way she would consider marriage at this time in her life.

"What if it weren't me?" he said quietly. "What if you married Javed and you both stayed in the north?"

Alice frowned. She couldn't imagine how he would benefit from that arrangement. "I'm not marrying anyone," she declared, rather louder than she intended. Darien let out a slow breath, but she wasn't done. "Is this just to get out of marrying Safia? No one will accept it."

He tensed and straightened his tunic. "Can you blame me for not wanting to marry a stranger?" He moved closer, taking her hand. "I like you, Alice. You'd make a great queen. You've made—" His cheeks flushed, and he lowered his voice. "You've awoken something inside me, Alice. I've always been a dreamer, seeking adventure and mystery on foreign worlds, but for the first time, I see what Parsa could become. Even my magic is stronger."

She pulled away, her heart fluttering. But how could she trust his words? He charmed people to get what he wanted. "I'm sorry, Darien, but if you don't want to marry Safia, you need to talk to your uncle."

He dropped his hands to his side. "I understand. Will you do me one favour? Will you take Javed back with you to your world?"

Her breath caught in her throat. "What? Why?"

"He's not safe here, and will heal better on your world where magic has no influence. He also thinks he can reach South Parsa from your world, the way your friends did." Doubt crept into his voice. "Then he can be with Safia."

Alice crossed her arms. "That would make you king."

Darien sighed. "Not if my uncle doesn't wish it. I swear I am only thinking of Javed's safety. Will you take him?"

She bit her lip. What did it matter who became king when she left? "If Javed wants to come with us, we will take him."

"Be ready first thing tomorrow. Officer Gul will be waiting, and we don't want to attract unnecessary attention."

Alice nodded, her muscles already tense.

Again, Darien stepped closer, brushing her hair out of her eyes. "I really am sorry for hurting you. I was a thoughtless fool. I hope it hasn't ruined your opinion of Parsa."

Her breathing shallowing, she felt lightheaded all of a sudden. His kiss had been true, hadn't it? All his charm couldn't fake that.

"Hey!" Jaime called, butting in and pulling her away from Darien. "Is everything okay?" he asked Alice pointedly.

She blinked a few times, remembering where she was. "Yes, everything is fine. Darien was just telling me we can go home tomorrow."

Jaime eyed Darien with suspicion. "He was?"

"Yes. Be ready first thing tomorrow morning," Darien said abruptly, before bowing, kissing Alice's hand, and disappearing.

Jaime edged closer. "Are you really okay? He looked like he was getting a bit too close."

"Yes, I'm fine," Alice answered, her thoughts elsewhere.

Jaime frowned. "Are you sure? You seem a little out of it."

"Oh, perhaps he cast a spell on me," she joked. Should she tell Jaime about Darien's proposal? He seemed rather worried, so it probably wasn't a good idea.

"Maybe you shouldn't be alone with him. Who knows what he might do." When she didn't respond, Jaime continued. "Let me walk you back up to your rooms." He held out an arm, and Alice took it, her mind a daze. When had Jaime become the overprotective type?

They ascended in awkward silence, Alice losing herself in her thoughts. What would have happened if Jaime hadn't butted in? Was there still something between her and Darien?

She pushed those thoughts away. He was just playing on her sympathies to escape an arranged marriage. Jaime had probably saved her from doing something stupid. She glanced sideways at him as they climbed. Why *had* Jaime been there? He never usually stopped her from doing silly things.

When they reached her chambers, Jaime hesitated in front of the door. "Alice? I wanted to say something."

She waited for him to continue, but he didn't. "What is it?" she asked.

Shifting from side to side, he couldn't stand still. She didn't blame him for feeling uncomfortable here, without any magic.

"Erm, I'm really happy that we're going home together. I mean, all of us. I mean, I'm glad I found you." His hand moved to his sleeve, fidgeting with the crimson fabric.

She couldn't recall ever seeing him so nervous. This entire experience must have been extremely trying for him. He had never wanted any adventure. Soon they'd be home though, and he could relax. "I am too. I should go say goodbye to Yasmin though."

He nodded. "That's a good idea. I'll see if I can find Velia and warn the others." He hesitated before returning down the stairwell.

After a few steps, Alice called out to him. "Jaime, do you think Darien *was* involved in the attack?"

Jaime shrugged. "Perhaps. Or it could have been the Royal Mage."

"Did the Royal Mage have reason to? It seems he always gets his way."

Jaime scratched his jaw. "The king would not have permitted him to send Darien away. And there's something seriously wrong with his relationship with Darien. The king probably got in the way of that."

Alice's stomach tightened. "Navid told me he might be afraid of Darien and Yasmin uniting against him. Do you think he intended to kill Darien instead of Javed?"

Jaime shook his head. "With Darien's trips off-world, he'd be easy to get rid of without suspicion. He wants to control him, and with the king out of the way, he can do so much more easily." His face flashed with concern.

"What is it, Jaime?"

"Darien has too much power. Everyone wants to control him. Even Safia. She could start a war with him and conquer the north."

Alice laughed. "Darien wouldn't do that. He loves his sister." Though Safia might not know that ...

Except Alice had told Safia. Dragonflies erupted in her stomach. Had she betrayed Darien or made things easier for him? Safia did at least seem to care about his happiness, more so than anyone here.

Guilt twisted her insides. Yasmin cared. She was just brainwashed.

"Maybe." Jaime shuffled closer. "But we don't have to worry about them anymore. We're going home."

Alice nodded. They didn't have to worry, but she should warn Yasmin.

A dark cloud descended over Yasmin's face when Alice shared her news. "Why would you want to leave at a time like this?" she asked.

"We should go home while we can," Alice said. "Who knows how long the portal will last?"

The princess scowled at her. "But you can't abandon me right after my father's death. Not whilst my brother and uncle are fighting."

Remorse twisted Alice's stomach, but there was nothing she could do about the timing. "I'm sorry. Javed will be here, and you've got Navid," she said, not wanting to ruin Javed's escape.

Yasmin pulled a face at Javed's name, but she couldn't argue about Navid.

"You could come with me to my world."

Yasmin raised her eyebrows. "Where there's no magic? What would I do there?"

Alice tried to sound enthusiastic, even though she knew Yasmin would never leave magic behind. "You could still design dresses."

Yasmin pulled a disgusted face. "You mean I'd have to sew like a commoner. Life is better with magic, Alice."

Alice sighed, then hugged Yasmin goodbye.

Yasmin pouted. "I thought you liked it here. I thought you wanted to learn magic. I thought you enjoyed spending time with me."

She squeezed Yasmin's hand. "I did, and I will really miss you, but I don't belong here."

"You do. We *need* you. Who will convince me to leave the palace when you're gone?" She smiled, but her eyes remained sad.

"You don't need me for that. You're the second most powerful mage in the world!"

Her mouth twitched. "In all the worlds. But it's no fun on my own."

"You've got Navid and Darien."

She scowled. "They're not you. You've filled a hole I never knew existed."

Alice winced. Yasmin's feelings were so close to her own, but she had her own sister to get back to. "You don't need me, Yasmin. You have everything you need in your people."

Yasmin scrunched up her nose. "I hope you don't mean the arrogant mages."

Alice repressed a smile. Yasmin wouldn't struggle to fit in with them. "Navid, your brother. You could be closer to them. And Darien needs you."

Yasmin sighed. "He's more amenable with you around. If you're leaving because of what he did—"

"I'm not. But he really doesn't want to leave the north. If you talked your uncle around, he'd be eternally grateful."

Yasmin crossed her arms, and her lips formed a practised pout. "You're leaving and your last thoughts are of him?"

"Of both of you. You're stronger together. Do you think he should be forced to marry Safia?"

Yasmin turned away. "He has responsibilities. He's just young."

"Too young to marry. He still needs your protection."

Yasmin sank into a chair. "If it means that much to you, I will talk to them. Perhaps the marriage can be postponed."

Alice grinned. "Thank you, Yasmin. Darien will appreciate it."

Unable to get Darien's predicament out of her mind, she decided to visit him late that evening. She needed answers, and perhaps – since she was leaving tomorrow – Darien would be more open with her.

Her heart racing, she knocked on his door, then pushed it open. Darkness greeted her, but a shadow shifted by the table. "Darien?"

The shadow jumped and dropped a glass, which smashed across the tabletop. Fire leapt into life, revealing a surprised server, who abruptly managed a bow.

Her cheeks warming, Alice spoke as authoritatively as possible. "Do you know where I can find the prince?"

The server frowned. "He's in the king's favourite study. You ought not disturb him."

Alice thanked her, then exited through the door, contemplating how long it would take to reach the study behind the Grand Hall.

If only she could teleport ...

She had managed it once, so perhaps she could do it again. After all, she would only be able to do it for one more day.

Taking several deep breaths, she closed her eyes. She'd never been in that study, but she could try visualising the Grand Hall. Those beautiful tapestries. The rich golden columns. The long tables she'd never eat at again.

Her skin tingled and her stomach lurched. Not so much as before, but when she opened her eyes, she found herself outside the Grand Hall, in exactly the same spot as her last teleport. Her aim was a little off, but she'd spared herself considerable effort. If she'd had more time, she might have become quite proficient at teleportation.

But not just that. She'd exceeded her wildest dreams in many aspects here. Learning magic, exploring new worlds, finding a friend in Princess Yasmin ... and perhaps even Darien too.

On the short distance to the study she debated what she would say to Darien. What was he doing in there this late in the evening, anyway?

Without knocking, she pushed open the door, attempting to catch him off guard.

From behind the large desk, he looked up in surprise, blinking away tiredness. Papers were spread out in front of him, but the light was too dim for reading.

Alice frowned, her words abandoning her.

He stood, and with the wave of his hand, fire leapt from the torches on the wall, casting him in a golden glow, highlighting his strong jaw and masculine features. The effect was quite dramatic, and Alice's heart raced once again.

However, with a step to the side, the dark circles under his eyes flickered into view. Pity surged through her.

She squashed those feelings immediately. She wasn't here to give him sympathy.

"Is everything alright, Alice?" he asked with a frown.

She nodded. "I need to ask you something and I need you to be honest."

He walked towards her, fixing her with his gaze. "I promise."

She took a deep breath. How did someone ask if a person arranged the death of their father?

She looked deep into his soft brown eyes. "Do you know anything about the attackers who killed the king?"

He shook his head, his eyes moving to the desk. "They came from nowhere and returned there swiftly as soon as their ... *business* was concluded. No one seems to know anything about them."

Alice shifted uncomfortably as his voice caught on the word *business*, but she couldn't tell if it was an act. "Do you think they intended to stop the alliance?"

Darien sighed. "It seems likely. I've been trying to figure out who could be behind it, but the answer isn't here." He scattered pages of parchment across the desk, many with colourful sigils.

"Weren't there any prisoners?"

Darien shook his head. "They only left their dead behind. All others escaped."

A room full of bodies pushed its way into Alice's mind. They couldn't all have died. There must have been some unconscious. "How is that possible?"

"They must have teleported the unconscious to safety."

"But there were so many! They couldn't have reached them all." She paused, remembering not everyone needed to touch to teleport. "Can many mages teleport that many people, the way your uncle can?" Alice moved forward. "Can you?"

Darien's jaw twitched. "It's a rare gift. I've not heard of anyone else with it, but I've never heard of these mages. They were extremely powerful, so it's entirely possible. If they can't be tracked down, we may never know."

Alice's eyes moved to the desk. She never thought he would resort to looking through papers. "Do you still intend to carry out your father's wishes?"

Failing to hide his despair, he slumped back against the desk. "I will uphold the treaty. I won't be responsible for further bloodshed."

"But you don't want to marry Safia?"

Darien scowled. "No. I don't want to leave my home and my sister and marry a stranger. But I will if I have to."

"*If* you have to?"

Darien took a deep breath. "My uncle … may change his mind, or he may not. Either way, my only choice is to obey."

Alice frowned. She was so sure the reason Darien wanted her to take Javed away was to ensure his uncle had no option but to allow Darien to stay. She waited for him to say more, but he turned away and wandered across the room.

"Safia could help you," she said. "Her people are behind her. Together, you could stand up to your uncle and make Parsa a better place. A place where commoners are valued. You wouldn't have to do what he says when you're in the south."

Darien scoffed. "Don't be so naïve. Safia has her own agenda. My uncle is right to be worried about her."

Alice's eyes widened. "You can't possibly mean that." Her skin crawled with every footstep he retreated, and she realised everyone's fears about him were already coming true. Now the façade had dropped, and he was no longer trying to charm Alice, his true thoughts were shining through. He could turn into his uncle.

To her surprise, she was more angry at everyone else for not trying to do something. They were abandoning Darien to his fate.

Even worse, Safia was pushing Darien towards his uncle.

She opened her mouth to object, but what could she say when she wasn't even bothering to stick around?

Instead, she risked pushing a little further. "Do you think your uncle may have had something to do with the attack?"

Darien's mouth twisted into a smile, then he laughed. "My uncle doesn't need to resort to murder. He runs the kingdom." His face turned dark and his eyes smouldered.

Alice glanced away, biting her lip. She wanted to tell him what she knew, tell him she understood his anguish, but she didn't know how. He might even be angry with her if he found out she knew he was a victim of the Royal Mage himself.

He sighed, his eyes darting back to the desk. "Princess Safia may get more than she bargained for," he muttered.

"What do you mean?"

He smiled and shook his head, returning to his seat. "Nothing. Nothing at all. It's just a little odd that a powerful mage turned up at the right moment to defend Safia, don't you think?"

Alice frowned at the insinuation. It was quite clever to blame Safia, but she wouldn't be fooled that easily. However, the resentment in his eyes had her hesitating. "You don't really suspect Safia, do you? She had little to gain."

Darien's eyes pinned her to the spot, almost as dark as his uncle's. "Safia has gained a far more advantageous marriage. She will have a strong claim to the North Parsan throne."

A shiver shot down Alice's spine. Is that why Safia was so interested in Darien? She'd been foolish to think Safia cared about Darien's happiness.

"What is it, Alice?"

Her mouth went dry. She couldn't tell him she'd spoken to Safia. "You might be right about Safia wanting your hand, but I don't think she had anything to do with your father's death. She lost guards. And her mages aren't that skilled. Except Velia, who fought by your side."

Darien collapsed back in his chair. "Velia was very helpful. Perhaps you're right."

"It was your uncle." She took a deep breath. "He wants to control you. After Yasmin gave you that crystal, he started to fear you."

Darien stared at her for a moment, then laughed. "He fears no one, least of all me."

"He does. Your powers will grow, and with Yasmin as your ally, you could overthrow him and cast him out."

Darien shook his head. "That is absurd. Yasmin adores him. And he was stronger with father on the throne."

"No. *You* were stronger with your father around. Now you have no choice but to obey him. You said it yourself. Your father would never have agreed to send you to the south. But the Royal Mage is obsessed with controlling the portals there."

Darien sagged backwards. He was quiet for some time, his expression turning from confused, to concerned, to horrified. "But then ... He couldn't—" He raised his hands to his face. "He ... He killed Father because I challenged him?"

Alice's blood ran cold. They'd all challenged the Royal Mage, even Yasmin about Navid. "He killed the king because he wanted more control. It's not your fault."

Darien slumped forward, still clutching his face, his fists balled.

"Darien?" She tentatively rounded the desk and her voice dropped to a whisper. "Darien?"

He dropped his hands, his face pale. "There's no proof of this. You could be wrong."

She nodded. "I could be, but it makes the most sense."

"Alice—" He looked up at her with desperate eyes. "Are you *sure* you have to leave? You see things that others don't. I could use your help. Yasmin too."

Alice sighed. She'd known that for a long time. "Yasmin knows you are too young to marry. She'll protect you from him."

Darien's eyes widened. "You told this to Yasmin?"

"No. She'd never accept it. But she can still help you."

"She can't. No one can. If what you say is true, nothing has changed. I can't disobey him."

"Darien—"

He rose, his face calm. "You care about us, Alice. Ask Yasmin to make you her official confidante. Then you could do almost anything you wanted. And you can keep helping us."

Alice shook her head. "I have a home to get back to. My own sister I haven't seen in months."

He moved forward. "They will miss you, but here you could influence a whole kingdom. And all the worlds that depend on us." He took her hands. "Must I beg? I would do it for my people."

Alice blushed, her cheeks on fire. Her voice a whisper, she forced her words out. "I can't trust you, Darien. You're all charm. You manipulate people."

He recoiled as if he'd been slapped. "At least give me a chance to prove myself. Stay a little longer."

She shook her head. "Tomorrow, we leave. It's best for everyone."

CHAPTER 50
NORTH PARSA

The next morning arrived quickly, and Alice was sat ready and waiting in her chambers when Darien came for her. He didn't bother knocking, but teleported straight into her room.

"It's not too late to change your mind," he said softly.

Shaking her head, she repeated the words that she had told herself so many times. "I'm doing the right thing." She'd done all she could for him and Yasmin. They knew all she knew. It was up to them now. What else could she possibly do in a world such as this?

He nodded. "We need to collect Javed before we meet your friends."

Alice frowned. "Can't he teleport himself?"

"Not in his current state."

Confused, Alice took Darien's outstretched arm. A moment later, they appeared in Javed's chambers, and Alice saw what Darien meant. His skin grey and clammy, Javed could barely keep his eyes open.

Safia sat next to him, her features contorted in concern. She leaned down and whispered something in his ear before curtsying to Darien. He stiffly bowed in return.

"Good luck," Safia whispered before disappearing.

"What happened?" Alice asked. Javed looked just as Darien had after his disagreement with the Royal Mage. Her throat went dry. Javed had been insistent in his desire to marry Safia, against the Royal Mage's wishes. Had the Royal Mage done it again?

She smiled sympathetically at Javed. Everything was a mess, but there was no more time.

"He's taken a turn for the worse. That's why we need to get him out of here." Darien heaved Javed up, then teleported them all to Jaime's room.

Rather crowded, the twin room contained Jaime, Jordan, Emily, Eliot and Velia, all waiting for them.

"Jane?" Darien exclaimed as his eyes rested on Emily.

"Hello, Prince Darien," Emily replied with a smile.

Darien grinned back. "Why didn't you tell me you were Alice's friend?"

"I didn't want to get locked up and interrogated. Finding my brother was my priority."

Velia raised her eyebrows at the conversation, strode forward, and placed her hand on Javed's chest, muttering a few words. He straightened instantly and nodded his thanks.

"Are all the people on your world as surprising as you two?" Darien asked Emily. A pang of disappointment shot through Alice that Darien didn't think of only her as special.

She shuddered. What was wrong with her?

"Shall we go?" Velia interrupted, hands on her hips.

They all linked arms, and Darien and Velia teleported them to the portal.

Away from the denser clusters, Officer Gul waited for them with a small contingent of portal police. "Prince Darien," he said, bowing.

"Lady Alice, it is sad to see you go, but I wish you and your friends well."

Alice smiled at him. "Look after Yasmin."

"I will. Now, you must follow my instructions exactly. When you step into the portal, you must push into the strongest part of the current and count for thirty-two of your seconds. You will see a number of portals in front of you. When you see a portal filled with blue, move towards it, but don't go through. You should then find yourself in a weaker current with more time to find your own portal. You're looking for snowy mountains, which may be difficult to discern against the white background of the portal realm, so stay focused."

He repeated the instructions until they were all sure of the route.

Glancing at each other in anticipation, no one spoke for several moments.

"I'll go first," Jordan announced. "Eliot can hold my hand and Emily's. And Javed can lean—"

Javed raised his hands. "I am well enough to fall through a portal or two."

They all nodded their agreement, and Emily and Jordan moved towards the portal together, Eliot between them. A few seconds passed as they paused in front of it, but then they were gone.

Tingles rushed through Alice's body. If something went wrong, there was no returning.

Darien approached Javed, his face full of worry. "Good luck."

Javed pulled him into a hug. "Be careful. I expect you to be king when next I return."

Darien nodded, then stepped back to let his cousin and sparring partner limp through the portal.

"Our turn," Jaime said, holding out his hand to Alice.

Alice froze, her world dizzying as her legs turned to lead. Yasmin's distraught face surfaced vividly in her mind, far more compelling than any of her memories from her old life.

All she'd ever wanted was a little control over her own destiny, to feel that she belonged somewhere, and that she could make a difference to her friends. Both Yasmin and Darien had practically begged her to stay. They needed her far more than her own family. They'd become family to her. She couldn't abandon them.

Her heart pounding, panic washed over her.

"It's okay, Alice. We'll go through together. I'm not going without you." Jaime took her hand and led her to the portal.

As she shuffled forward, her limbs turned to jelly, and the sight of the flickering disc raised fresh waves of nausea. Here she had been offered everything she could ever want by three separate, powerful people. There was so much more to discover, so much more to do, and all she had to do was stay.

She glanced back at Darien, who watched them with a blank expression. Her heart beat as loudly as the voices screaming in her head. There was no way she could go through the portal. She had to stay.

But how could she explain it to Jaime? To ask him to leave her behind?

Far too late, she registered the way he looked at her, the way he had suddenly become uncomfortable around her, the way he stumbled over his words. He really wasn't going to leave without her, but he didn't belong here.

She couldn't let him get stuck here, because of her. As Jaime reached the threshold, she planted her feet firmly in the ground.

"What's wrong?" Jaime asked. He was looking at her like that again, his eyes so full of expectation and hope. Deep down, she knew there was nothing she could say to make him leave her, but she had to protect him from this place.

Slowly, she leaned forward, closed her eyes against what she was about to do, and brushed her lips against his. As he let go of her hand, she placed her hands on his chest. Then she pushed him. Hard. Straight into the portal.

EPILOGUE
North Parsa

A lice tried to tug her hand free, but Yasmin's grasp was firm. "Yasmin, do you have to drag me along?"

Yasmin turned, her face puzzled. "Of course I do. You're my confidante now. You have to stay by my side." She closed her eyes, focusing hard. "They're in Darien's chambers!"

Yasmin's balcony blurred from view, replaced by the familiar blue and gold of Darien's private chambers. Both the Royal Mage and Darien turned to Yasmin in shock.

"Uncle, wait! I need to say something."

The Royal Mage's brow creased. "What is it, Yasmin?"

Yasmin glanced at Darien, who stared at them with a bemused expression. "Darien is too young to marry Safia. I insist you reconsider. At least don't let him leave until he comes of age."

The Royal Mage scratched his jaw as he appraised Darien. "You may be right, Yasmin. He is immature and inadequately trained."

A slight scowl flickered across Darien's face. "Father trained me well. I am prepared to become king of South Parsa."

"Are you? You have not endeared yourself to Princess Safia. I am quite disappointed."

Yasmin swept forward, to stand beside Darien. "He should be king of North Parsa, not Princess Safia's consort."

The Royal Mage raised an eyebrow. "What has got into you, Yasmin?"

"It's what Father would have wanted." She glanced out the window, her gaze resting on the funeral pyre being assembled below. "Who will you name as successor?"

The Royal Mage turned his gaze on Darien. "We were just discussing that, and I thank you for your contribution, Yasmin. Darien is too young to become Safia's husband, and too young to be crowned king in either kingdom."

Darien clenched his jaw, and Alice sent him a sympathetic smile.

"So, you won't send him away?"

"That depends on Darien. He has agreed to the marriage, so I cannot stop it, but if he wishes to postpone his departure to undertake more training, under my direct tutelage, I shall speak with Safia."

Everyone turned to Darien, and to Alice's surprise, he smiled. "It will be an honour to learn at your side."

The Royal Mage's eyebrows ascended sharply.

Yasmin grinned. "And I shall help you with your magic. And Safia too. If she is to stay here."

The Royal Mage nodded. "I shall inform her of your desire to remain in the north a little longer. Then we will get started."

Darien dropped into a bow, the perfect, obliging subject. "You have my sincerest gratitude." As he stood, he half turned and winked at Alice.

Alice stiffened. What was he up to? Grinning herself, she shook her head. At least life here would never be boring. And she had plenty of time to discover who was really behind the king's murder.

Not ready to leave the world of Parsa? Find bonus scenes and more on the website: https://ljevias.com/bonus-material/

If you have enjoyed the story, please let others know by leaving a review. Your words can make a significant difference helping others discover this book and supporting the author. Thank you!

KEEP EXPLORING

To find out more about the world of The Intrigue of Magic, please visit ljevias.com.

ACKNOWLEDGEMENTS

Many thanks to everyone who generously contributed feedback, shaping both this book and my writing journey. Your thoughtful insights have left an indelible mark on the story, and it truly wouldn't be the same without your invaluable contributions. A special appreciation to the many beta readers, including Emily Marquart, Jodi Clark, Lisa Wong, Tali Jayne, Samantha G @Ravenwingedits and Juliette T @jtownsend1211 who helped make *The Discovery of Magic* the story it is today.

I would be remiss not to acknowledge the exceptional writing communities fostered by Autocrit and Daniel David Wallace. The wealth of craft talks, lessons, and resources within these communities not only played a pivotal role in shaping the book but also served as a wellspring of inspiration. The techniques, styles, and tools discussed have enriched my writing in ways beyond measure. Thank you for being an integral part of my creative journey.

9 781917 107020